ROSEMARY WOLFE, M.D. (MONSTER DOCTOR)

LOVING MONSTERS, BOOK I

REXANNA IPOCK-BROWN

Printed in the United States of America

Copyright © by Brown Squared

ISBN-13: 978-0-9997004-0-2

ISBN-10: 0999700405

This is a work of fiction. Names, characters, places, and incidents either are the products of the author's imagination or are used fictitiously. Any resemblance to actual persons, living or dead, businesses, companies, events, or locales is entirely coincidental.

Cover art by Angela Fristoe of Covered Creatively (www.coveredcreatively.com)

Edited by Frankie Sutton of Frankie's Free Lance Editing (frankiesfreelanceediting.blogspot.com)

Formatted by Holly Atkinson of Evil Eye Editing (www.evileyeediting.com)

For everyone who has felt unworthy of love

CHAPTER 1

I love kids. I really do. Dr. Rosemary Wolfe used her head to knock on the door of the exam room in her small medical office.

A young female's bellow answered, "It's open."

Two steps into the room challenged that love.

"Let me have those!" Snatching the scissors from the shaking hand of the teenage patient, Rosemary tossed them in a drawer. A loud clatter rang out when they hit the other instruments.

One more thing to sterilize.

"Why'd you do that? I'm better off dead," Marcie wailed, thrashing her arms as Rosemary tried to restrain and comfort her all in the same grip. The girl lunged towards the door, using the magazine rack hanging on the wall as leverage.

"Oh no, you don't!" Rosemary caught her with ease, but not before magazines swan dived in a race across the floor, landing atop a heap of shattered plastic and bent aluminum.

"Really, Marcie?" The physician wrangled the female to a chair in the exam room and sat, still holding her hands. "What makes you think you'd be better off dead?" Teenagers of any species made Rosemary crazy, and this one was certainly testing her limits. Her specialty as a physician and veterinarian included all Genetically Diverse

Beings of all ages and forms. Vampires, shifters of all varieties, and of course, witch werewolf hybrids. *I will remain calm. Remain calm. Remain...Oh crap.*

Marcie didn't reply. Thick, dark hair spilled over her moon-round face as she studied her scuffed shoes instead.

"Don't you think your friends would miss you?"

Marcie's head shook, splattering tears down her face and onto the floor. "No, they call me names." Her head bowed even lower.

"Like what?"

"Big, fat, hairy whore," she sobbed.

The doctor gave Marcie's hands a squeeze. "That doesn't sound friendly, but cutting your wrists with scissors won't make it better. Would it help to put you in the hospital for a suicide watch?"

Marcie turned away, her mouth in a pucker. Silence filled the room.

Let her pout.

Marcie's head shot around, ice blue werewolf eyes flashing.

That didn't take long. The older witch/wolf jumped to attention, strengthening her grasp. Bones snapped as the girl's body tried to go into a shift.

Oh, crap! Is it too late to become a coroner?

"Nothin' is gonna help." The young witch/wolf's lips curled in a snarl. Thick, wiry hair sprouted from her knuckles. She shoved her hands towards Rosemary. "Look! I'm growing hair all over my body. What do you think happens when I want to hook up with every boy around, which isn't happening because, oh yeah, I'm fat?" She started bawling as only a mixed-species teenage girl could.

I can relate. A blinding flash of white light interrupted Rosemary's vision as her own witch/wolf body tried to change. *Damn it! I forgot my werewort tincture this morning.* The last thing she needed was to shift while trying to help Marcie gain control. With a deep breath, Rosemary shoved the threatening change down and pulled Marcie towards her.

"Do me a favor. Take a deep breath and listen a moment." Rosemary thanked the gods her vision cleared, her head ceased pounding, and most importantly, for her werewolf strength.

Marcie stilled and sniffed up the snot running from her nose. Rosemary handed her a tissue and said, "When I was your age a group of girls called me the same thing. Guess what I did?"

Her bones stopped rearranging. "You were never like me."

The doctor nodded. "Yes, I was, but I started reading about genetics which led me to becoming a physician and a veterinarian."

"You think I'm smart? You might as well put me out of my misery." A bone popped in the witch/werewolf's arm as the shift continued.

Rosemary caught her hands again, avoiding the claws. "Your mom told me you were an A student until this year."

"Yeah, well, I got stupid." Marcie's body calmed, her hair and claws receding.

Rosemary gently rubbed her young patient's hands. "How did that happen?"

With a stare that would have intimidated her, if she hadn't been an older version of Marcie, the young female said, "My wolf and witch powers came in at the same time."

"That's wonderful! You're lucky to be blessed with those abilities." The smile she plastered on her face hurt. She had never planned on treating children, let alone having them, but they came with the territory.

Marcie looked at her as if she had grown another head. "What?"

"You possess super senses from your wolf side, which can come in handy. Think of the magic you can do with your witch powers." Rosemary fought to keep her smile from wavering.

She readjusted her body to face Rosemary head-on and asked, "If I change into a wolf, you know what to do?"

"You bet." *Finally.* Her face relaxed.

Marcie leaned forward. "Can you do something about the hair?"

"I can help you control the growth and the changing to a werewolf with an herb tincture containing werewort. I developed it in med school to help me control my shifts.

Just a couple of drops a day in water is all it takes." Rosemary paused, giving Marcie time to process.

"Okay, got any bully-bashing ideas?"

Poor kid. The genetic combo of half witch and half werewolf is hard enough, without being bullied. She had learned that the hard way. On a warm day smelling of fallen leaves, she sat on the ragged seat in the fading yellow school bus across from the part demon, part mean girl. Jeselda leveled a wicked gaze her way and called out.

"What are you staring at, twit? Are you lookin' at my boobs?" A cackle at Rosemary's hot flushed face dismissed her. Turning back to hold court with the boys drooling at her feet in hopes of catching a peek at her panties de jour, she wriggled her dress higher on her thighs.

That moment motivated Rosemary to find out why she was so different, and what she could do about it. Now, she could help Marcie.

"A friend of mine runs a group focused on helping young ladies with self-confidence and selecting better friends. Would you give that a try if I help you with the physical changes?" Her grip loosened on hands that were human once more.

"Yeah." Marcie raised hopeful eyes, a little sob escaping into a hiccup. "Can you make me skinny too?"

"Let me give you a diet and exercise plan that has helped many a maturing witch and werewolf."

"Can't I take a pill for that?"

"Sorry, no."

"That's okay." Marcie stared into space for a moment. "Can you help me with my powers?"

This kid is pushing every limit. Rosemary chuckled to herself. "That's more for your mom and dad to do."

"Ah, come on, they won't let me do anything. I wanted to change my little brother into a muskrat and they had a fit." She smiled, her eyes shining with mischief.

Rosemary lifted an eyebrow. "Can I let go of your hands?"

"I wasn't really going to cut my wrists with your scissors. They're kind of dull. Can I use one of your scalpels?" Marcie gazed over Rosemary's shoulder in search of her instruments.

Shaking her head, she squeezed Marcie's hands. "Let's work on a safety plan in case your angry feelings return. You're a smart girl who I want to succeed. With that in mind, is it okay for me to ask your mom to join us while we set up your positive changes?"

"Okay." Marcie grinned as Rosemary picked up the magazines, put the vampire blood supplies back in place, tucked the supply of prenatal shifter supplements back in the cabinet and headed to retrieve Marcie's mom.

Thirty minutes later, Rosemary handed Marcie and her mom the proper medicines with instructions and sent them on their way. As the door closed behind them, she sighed. Maybe kids weren't all that bad. The younger ones often kidnapped her heart. The danger of letting herself think about children frightened her. Passing on her messed up genetics wouldn't be fair. Besides, at thirty-two, with her lifestyle, she couldn't imagine trying to raise a child alone.

She shook off the thought. Her hand reached up to turn the lock, stopping when a man with white blond hair sauntered in. He took off his designer sunglasses and regarded Rosemary with laughing blue eyes.

Her lips tipped in a grin. "Jonathan Russell, what're you doing out of your coffin this early?"

"Smart-ass, you're well aware I sleep in a California king-sized bed." Jonathan hugged her. "I'm checking on your plans to attend our Come-as-Your-Own-Madness party tomorrow night."

She stepped back. "Ah...I don't believe I can make it. I can't come up with a madness, let alone a costume yet."

Lowering his bright eyes, he gave her an I-know-best-look. "Your goal of getting your practice up and running is admirable, but you need to get out more. How else are you ever going to meet someone magnificent and fall in love?"

With a wave of her hand, she walked into her office. "You're one to talk. If you're not at your restaurants, you're home decorating something."

Jonathan followed. "Yes, but my love, Edward, is at home for me to decorate."

"There's no time for a relationship in my life." Rosemary slid files into a drawer as she talked.

"I could introduce to you an agreeable vampire or two." He lifted his eyebrows.

"No vampires! One date and they think they own you. No offense, they're great as friends." She came up behind him and hugged his waist.

"Some offense taken! We're all not that bad," he said, turning to face her. "I believe you're afraid to fall in love."

For a second, the longing for a soul mate drowned her in sadness. Hollow words slipped from her. "I gave up on love a long time ago." With more conviction, she said, "I like my friends-with-benefits lifestyle. No one tells me what to do, where to go, or who to be."

"No one tells you how much they love you either." Jonathan tilted his head.

The mood broken, she recovered her sarcastic tongue. "Did you come here to harass me or was there something you wanted?"

"Yes. Come join me for a drink at Nip and Sip before I head to work at my restaurant this evening. Edward's out with a client, and I'd like to catch up with you, I think." He laughed at the face she made.

"Give me a minute to lock up." She turned the key in her office door. "A drink would do me good, and I can't wait to tell you about my crazy day."

~

The diner clattered with the noise of life. Early rising vampires sat in the shadows while shifters crowded their families around tables. The chair squeaked across the floor as Jonathan pulled it out for Rosemary. A smile dashed across her face. Jonathan would never have a squeaky chair in one of his restaurants, but he loved the casual atmosphere here. She dropped into the seat with a grateful nod of thanks. This table was a favorite of theirs. Shaded by screens painted by local artists, the pictures depicted various aspects of the lives of the patrons.

Rosemary picked up the Nip and Sip menu. "Is there time for me to eat a burger with my beer?"

"Plenty of time. Did you take your drops today?" His eyes peered over his menu, observing the stiff, dark hair sprouting from her knuckles.

Fear slammed inside her as she imagined everyone in the room could sense her shift.

"No. Thanks for reminding me. In a couple of minutes, I would've needed to go the little girl's room and shave." Out came a dropper bottle she used to measure a dose into her mouth and grimaced as she swallowed. *Nasty.*

"Better, but aren't you supposed to put it in the water?" He beetled his eyebrows.

"Water improves the taste, but since I almost shifted this afternoon while grappling with a teenage witch/wolf, faster is better."

"Talk about karma," He said, grinning. Rosemary stuck out her tongue at him. "At least there's no hair on your tongue, yet."

"My tongue does not get hairy, thank you." She lifted her head to lock eyes with the waiter. His storm cloud gray eyes flashed his inner wolf. Her insides went on red alert. He moved with a predator's grace, flipping his obsidian hair to the side. *Just my luck.* Roger, a member of the family that owned Nip and Sip was on duty.

"Hey, Jonathan, good to see you. Are you ready to order? By the way, we got in some of that new Bloody Good Beer with a tangerine twist."

"Give me one. You must know someone at the distributing company. I don't get a shipment for my restaurants for another couple of days." Jonathan handed him the menu.

Roger turned his attention to Rosemary. "Hey, Rosemary, I've missed you. What's kept you so busy?"

"Between finishing school and setting up my healthcare practice, nothing much." She unfolded her napkin and laid it in her lap.

"When you feel like socializing again, call me." Roger winked. "What would you like this evening?"

"A Werey Wolf beer and the Werewolf burger special with fries."

"Umm! I love a woman with wild hungers." With a nod to Jonathan, he headed back to the kitchen.

A deep breath helped her will the rising awareness to a safe level. Roger was a habit she needed to quit.

Distracted by another patron, Jonathan said, "Excuse me for a moment, Rosemary, I see an old friend. I'll be right back."

He greeted a man sitting in the shaded vampire section with a hug. As Jonathan's friend slid back into his booth, Rosemary nodded in appreciation at the way his biceps stretched the sleeves on his black tee shirt. *Nice.* Her sensitive ears strained to pick up the conversation, but no luck. She settled on admiring the view.

Umm, I bet he's good in bed. Those strong hands and wide shoulders could tantalize her body with pleasure. She glanced lower to gauge what kind of pleasures his package could provide. *Stop it! He's in the vampire section. That's the last thing you need.* Still, she continued to ogle the man until Jonathan headed back to their table.

"Who's your good-looking friend?" Rosemary put a finger on her chin.

"A vampire that would love to meet you," Jonathan said.

Her head shook. "Never mind."

"Okay. You and Roger Rougarou, hmm?"

Her eyes followed Roger as he worked. A wistful sigh escaped her lips. "Roger is a friend who I enjoyed, uh, getting to know once or twice." She took in his powerful frame and tight ass made firm from playing rugby, remembering the feel of him inside her. Sex with him had been crazy-good, but she couldn't take the chance of shifting and then blacking out. Who knows what she did when in that state? Why with him? She sure didn't remember.

"If by *getting to know him* means you slept with him, why don't you ask him to the party?"

Rosemary's eyes flashed a warning to Jonathan, as Roger set a beer and a burger the size of a dinner plate down in front of her.

He placed Jonathan's drink in front of him and turned to place catsup and mustard down near Rosemary's plate. "Anything else?" he asked, stroking her back with his large calloused hand.

Lust shot through her, but she managed to smile. "No thanks."

"All right, but if you need anything, anything…" His bedroom eyes invited her to play. "Just call." He squeezed her shoulder and left.

Rosemary took a long drink of her beer. "I never slept with him. I had lots of sex with him. Roger is an animal in bed, but he wants more than I can give."

"Jeesh, it's just a party. You're not asking him to marry you."

"In Roger's mind, it would be. Most werewolves don't mind hooking up, but Roger wants to make me a permanent part of his life."

He stared at her for a moment. "You don't like Roger?"

Tension pulled her head back. "I don't want to belong to anyone."

"Especially not someone like Dear Daddy." Jonathan patted her knee.

At his touch, her tight muscles relaxed. "I asked my mom once about Dear Daddy. Her eyes glazed over, and she said he was a handsome dawg and a helluva man. Then she wouldn't say anymore."

"I can guess where you got your unruly red hair." Jonathan watched as she bit into her burger.

She rolled her eyes and moaned. "The red is from Mom. The unruly curls are rumored to be from Dad." She sunk her teeth into the burger again.

"When is the last time you ate?"

"This morning, no time for lunch. I need to hire a nurse." She took another drink of beer. "Who's coming to your party?"

"Shifters, vampires, humans, mages, witches, the usual. This party has become a legend since we started throwing it years ago." He paused.

"I love meeting the different folks. Attending last year netted me several new patients."

"Always happy to help your business, but seriously, you need to have some fun. I could introduce you to my friend who's new to the area. I think you would like him."

She raised her eyebrows and tilted her head. "Vampire?"

"Well, yes but…"

"No."

Jonathan leaned forward. "He's different."

"Vamps, particularly old vamps, as a rule are extremely possessive and territorial." She patted his manicured hand. "What do you think will happen the first time I decide to go home with someone else?"

He placed his hand over hers. "I'm sorry we introduced Leon to you. Edward and I have taken so many guilt trips over that mistake we have frequent flyer miles, but not all vampires are overly conservative or crazy. I realize he hurt you, but it's been a few years since you've dated anyone serious."

"Is your friend over a hundred?"

He sighed. "Yes."

She leaned forward. "I repeat, what do you think will happen the first time I decide to go home with someone else?"

He pulled away and picked up his glass. "Point made. However, I seriously doubt we'd ever need to stop him from trying to kill another male in a jealous rage." Jonathan finished his blood. When he set his glass down Roger appeared to clear the table.

"Anything else for you, Good Lookin'?" Roger twirled one of Rosemary's wild curls around his finger. His touch was lightning that traveled down her neck, sparking her breasts into diamonds and ending deep inside her center.

"Just the check. How's your mom?" Rosemary choked out, playfully squeezing his finger. She couldn't help noticing the gleam of interest in his eyes.

"Coming right up. She's great. I'll tell her you asked." Roger brought her hand to his mouth for a kiss.

Hand snatched back to her chest, she gave him a tight smile, as he walked away. *Maybe I should give him a chance.* The swagger of his ass held her attention all the way to the register.

"You should ask him to the party when he comes back." Jonathan lowered his chin and stared at her with his dark-ringed, blue eyes.

"Not a chance. His mama wants me to marry him almost as much as he does. I'm not interested in being in the Nip and Sip family restaurant business. Besides, you and Edward will keep me entertained."

"True, but I would like for you to enjoy yourself in a more carnal way. If you're not interested in Roger, how about that woman you go drinking with sometimes. What's her name?"

"You mean Pauline?"

"Yeah, Pauline. She isn't interested in anything long-term, and she's a hoot in a pushy-bitch sort of way."

Rosemary sighed in resignation. "If it's that important, I'll ask if she's up for a party."

"If I remember right, she's always up for a party." Jonathan grinned while holding the door of the restaurant open for her.

Rosemary raised both eyebrows and walked out the door. "Therein lies the problem."

Bryce's tongue ran over his fangs as his friend, Jonathan, walked out of Nip and Sip with the woman. Something about her made him go against his rule to never seriously date again.

Too dangerous. But, he was not sure he could stay away. He hadn't seen her face clearly, but a beacon from her aura called to him, like no one had in over forty years. Maybe just a fling. *No.* He needed to stay away, but his heart told him to find her.

CHAPTER 2

Pauline wrinkled her button nose. "Do you think the rumor about Jonathan and Edward is true?"

"What? That they're gay or vampires?" Rosemary turned to Pauline as they walked in a fast clip up a long driveway, the chains connecting their wrists clanking with each step.

She waved her free hand in dismissal. "No, everyone knows that." Pauline's eyes widened. "I'm thinking of the one where they keep young boys in the basement to fulfill their *needs*, if you know what I mean?"

"Good grief, Pauline, of course, that's not true. I've been in their basement, and the only thing that gets out of line is the occasional magazine on the coffee table."

Rosemary sensed the rainstorm moving their way, motivating her to pick up the pace. Her strong body filled out the black-as-night slacks and matching blouse. The midnight blue cape swirled around her head, messing up any semblance of a hairdo she had coaxed her red curls into earlier.

"Sorry, I know this is a 'Come-as-Your-Own-Madness' party, but I was curious if there would be whips to go with our chains?" Pauline struggled to keep up with Rosemary's long strides. Her short legs peeked out from her dark skirt when the wind lifted it and her blue cape high into the air.

"No whips, no chains, just costumes." The first drop of rain plopped on her face. She raised her eyes to a downpour catching them right before they reached the wrap-around front porch of the modern Victorian home.

Pauline shook herself like a wet dog, setting her melon-sized breasts to swaying.

Rosemary backed off and held up her hands against the spatter.

"Really, you didn't think I got soaked enough?" *Why had she let Jonathan talk her into inviting Pauline to come to this party? Her friend came from a long line of witches and werebats. Talk about unpredictable.* She also made no secret of the fact she liked to play on the dark side. Rumor had it that, if she didn't like you, it was possible you'd wake up far, far from home. If you crossed her, you might not wake up at all.

Rosemary stepped up to the double glass doors to ring the bell and listened as the theme song from Jeopardy played. She grinned. "I wonder what the boys do in all those secret hidey holes in those towers." She couldn't help taunting her friend.

"This ocean blue is one of my favorite colors." Pauline touched the side of the house with a stubby finger, showing no reaction to the taunt.

"And the white trim sets off the blue." Rosemary ran her free hand through her hair in a futile attempt to tame it.

The sounds of "Monster Mash" poured out to greet them, as Jonathan swung the double doors wide to reveal dark walnut floors. Inside, two curved staircases rose to meet at a polished marble landing, lit by thousands of twinkling crystals in the chandelier holding court in the center of the entryway. "Ladies! Come in."

Rosemary assessed the vision Jonathan created in a pink dress with a white frilly apron, completed with a big-hair blonde wig. "Your madness is being a woman?"

He pushed his pink rhinestone glasses up before replying, "Not just any woman, Sweetheart, a soccer mom." He emphasized his madness by tossing and catching a soccer ball.

"Oh-h, you're scaring me." She gave him a big hug, breathing in the scent of patchouli. The couple was careful only to drink the freshest and finest blood, which helped diminish the vampire scent. Except for their love of patchouli, their scent was almost human. Rosemary glanced down and saw Jonathan's pink stiletto heels.

"How'd you learn to walk in those come-fuck-me pumps?"

"Centuries of practice, Sweetheart, centuries!" Jonathan was joined by Edward, whose imposing height and size made Jonathan look petite at six three.

Rosemary admired the striking pair. Jonathan's alabaster skin complemented the deep obsidian of Edward's. "In that white suit, you're the epitome of a drop-dead gorgeous Colonel Sanders in ebony. Where's the madness?"

"It's madness to dine on southern folk. All those fried foods make their blood thicker than cold molasses, but um um good." Edward picked her up in a hug, jingling the chain connecting her to Pauline.

"What's this?" Jonathan rubbed the chain between his fingers.

"We're a witch with a split personality," Pauline said. "She's the good one, I'm the bad one." With a jerk, the chain flew out of his hand.

Rosemary glanced at her friend, gauging whether her cackle would stir up a dark cloud of her qualities or not. Rumors flooded the community about Pauline's maternal grandmother transforming into an oversized black bat on occasion. When she wasn't flying into people's faces, she was putting spells on those who had crossed her.

Rosemary considered Pauline an entertaining distraction, even if she was a chip off the old bat.

When Edward put Rosemary on her feet, she put her arm around Pauline and turned to the men. "Gentlemen, you throw the best parties! Thank you for inviting us."

A sudden peal of laughter had them all turning to the sound.

Rosemary glanced back to the men. "Who's that?"

"Twylene Turner. Don't you love her madness? She's the embodiment of OCD. Everything clean, tidy, and in place." Edward pointed toward a lanky blonde dressed in a pristine white satin gown accented by a pearl necklace.

"I could use some of that." Rosemary nodded. "Is she kin to Jack and Sandra?"

"The shape shifter family? She's their daughter," Jonathan said.

"She's cute." Pauline's eyes traveled from Twylene's slim ankles in pearly stilettoes up to her prominent collarbones and grinned. "Does she prefer girls or boys?"

"Last I heard she had a thing going with a guy at the hospital. One of those affairs no one is supposed to know about." Jonathan's voice came out in a whisper.

With a cocked eyebrow, Rosemary settled her dark blue eyes on him. "How do you collect everyone's secrets in this town?"

"You'd be surprised at what my wait staff hears at my restaurants, and they're always kind enough to share their confessions with Father J." His hands were together in prayer as he bowed his head. With a quick glance up, he winked at Rosemary.

She patted Edward's arm. "You better be glad he's in love with you."

"His countless talents are many, aren't they, honey?" Edward draped his long arm around Jonathan's shoulders and drew him to his side.

"You would know." Jonathan reached up and pecked Edward on the cheek. "Now let's get these girls a plate of food! You must try the fabulous blood sausage with caviar guaranteed to put an extra beat in your little werewolf heart." He lifted up a glass. "And there's fresh southern blood. Smooth and thick, the texture adds to the experience. The plasma chaser is the perfect finish." Jonathan kissed the fingers of his right hand in a dramatic gesture.

"I think I'll stick to the red wine, but I'll sample the blood sausage. Come on, Pauline, stop ogling Ms. Turner and let's eat." Leaving the men to greet a new round of guests, Rosemary led Pauline with filled plates of the exotic food. They wandered deeper into the crowd scattered in the living room. A friend of Pauline's engaged her in conversation, leaving Rosemary to take a taste of the sausage. Blood could be a conundrum for her. When she was a child, the nighttime brought on what she thought were dreams, but instead, it turned out they were her shifting.

Instead of dreaming about a boyfriend or a career, her nose elongated, and the soft thud of her paws running through a darkened forest alerted her to her transformation.

The musky odor of damp, decaying wood mingled with the crisp aroma of evergreens would fade way to the scent of a deer. Body slipping through the underbrush protected by the heavy fur with an unerring leap, she would lock her jaws onto the deer's throat.

On tasting the blood and feeling the life drain from the animal, she would wake. In full werewolf form, she somehow would find her way back to her bed. There she would shift back into her witch form in tears at what she had done. Her mom would be there to clean up the blood and hold her.

The bite of blood sausage with the sharp cheese brought her back to the party. She stood, eyes closed. Jonathan was a master chef. This helped erase the bad recollections.

A deep voice, resonating with compassion asked, "Hey, are you okay?"

Rosemary shook her head to clear the memories. "Long day." She lifted her eyes to the strong face of a golden-eyed god of a man stepping out of the shadows. With a come-hither grin, he opened his black leather trench coat and flashed a set of abs that spoke of hours in the gym and legs that promised long nights of lovemaking. Silver Speedos hugged his powerful torso. Out of the tight briefs, popped a plastic hand posed in a classic middle-finger-extended position. Where had this cutie been hiding?

Rosemary giggled. "I'm much better now." The tension she was nursing shattered as she snorted, almost spilling her plate of food. He had her at the first flash. Rosemary connected with this man's soft golden gaze, and a psychic thrill vibrated through her. His body made her drool, but something about his voice, his concern for her, was an arrow to her heart.

Mischief and the need to flirt aimed her attention his way. Pauline, on the other hand, rolled her big green eyes and put on her best bored expression, scanning the guests in the living room.

"Hum, your madness is flashing people?" *Why this man was on her psychic radar?* Something about his scent, maybe nutmeg, called to her soul, but she couldn't place it.

His slow advance towards her should have alerted her to his intentions, but she was mesmerized by his eyes. His lips were kissing her hand before she realized he had moved closer to her.

"Only beautiful women." His voice soothed her nerves with a velvet touch.

Damn! What a night to have wet hair and to be chained to crazy Pauline.

Pauline chose that moment to tug on the chain connecting them. Rosemary frowned, and Pauline stopped, but raised her auburn eyebrows. She grabbed a glass of wine from someone passing by and molded her face into a sulk.

Whirling back to the hunky god, Rosemary licked her lips. "Tell me; is that the flasher talking or you, Mister...?"

"Bryce Gold. And, you are?" He moved closer, allowing his coat to close around the dark hair on his chest. His intoxicating scent of oakmoss and nutmeg enveloped her.

"All yours."

"Interesting name." He paused, staring into her eyes. "Want to come back to my den?"

Eyes focused on him, she considered her answer. She was insanely attracted to him, but not crazy. Could he be Jonathan's vampire friend? Not sure, she held her ground. "You don't waste time, do you?"

He picked up a slice of blood sausage and took a slow sensual bite.

Fascinated at way the muscles in his strong jaws moved, her eyes followed his face. When his tongue ran over the side of his mouth, a warmth exploded in her sex.

Then he swallowed. "When I see something that I like, I go for it."

I need to get laid. Catching herself staring, she asked, "I don't remember seeing you around before now?"

"I relocated from Boston to take a new position."

Amused by the smiling smirk spreading across his face, she leaned forward showing off her ample breasts. "Okay, I'll bite. What's your new position, Mr. Gold?"

His eyebrows drew together. A flash of wariness flitted across his face. Just as quickly, he recovered, answering in a voice reminiscent of a smoky bourbon. "What position are you looking for?"

"Well, I'm all tied up this evening." She held up her chained wrist. Pauline tilted her head in question.

"Maybe another time," Bryce said with the promise of sex in his voice. "I'm the new director for the Community Blood Bank."

"Are you the caterer this evening?" Her eyelashes batting while she crooked up her mouth in a flirtatious grin.

"Do you always ask so many nosy questions of people when you first meet them?"

"Only the interesting ones." She scowled as Pauline tugged on her chained arm again.

Pauline jerked her head toward a drunk mortal busying himself by trying to give her cleavage a tongue bath. "Come on, let's go."

Rosemary attempted to pull her away from the guy. No need for her psychic abilities to realize Pauline had high hopes of licking her breasts later that night. "We just got here, so tell him to get lost."

"He's drunk and hasn't gotten the message." Pauline was making a scene Rosemary didn't want to deal with.

The clueless man tried to locate a nipple like a hungry puppy. Rosemary raised a hand to intercede, when Bryce placed an arm around him and pulled him off Pauline.

Sometimes, party crashers got more than they bargained for when coming to one of the Genetically Diverse Beings' parties. Rarely, humans ended up on the invitation list, and only those that accepted all that the GDB world entailed. They made her nervous.

"Have I got a girl for you." Bryce directed him to a beautiful vampire across the room.

Rosemary smirked. Lacy had an obsession for drunken mortal men. She wouldn't kill him, but he'd be a quart low in the morning and not remember a thing.

A bleached blonde shifter grabbed Bryce on his return. Her boobs were missiles ready to launch through her slut-red dress. Rosemary cringed as the blonde made sure he noticed her impressive weapons by rubbing them against him every so often. *"C'est la vie"* With a sigh, she directed Pauline toward the living room.

~

"Hey, girls, how's it going tonight?" A demon who filled out his blue-striped mechanic's uniform with biceps begging to be touched, smiled down at Pauline.

"Now that the man who can't hold his licker is gone, great." Pauline snorted at her pun. Her hands meandered up his well-muscled chest. "What are you dressed as, Cy?"

"A Satanic mechanic, of course. Don't the horns give it away?" He tipped his head and wiggled eyebrows that framed his sexy green eyes.

"Horns? Really? I guess I need to plaster a wart on my nose!" Pauline played along.

"Ah, you know I'm having fun with all those humans that think demons aren't complete without horns and pitchforks, don't you?" Cy held her hands against his chest.

She smiled. "It's obvious to me you are one hot demon."

Demons are always handsome. That's what they project for the humans and GDBs to see, anyway. "How many times have you seen the Rocky Horror movie?" Rosemary wouldn't mind a one-night stand with this demon. *He's hot!*

"Thirty or forty, I guess." Cy gave Rosemary an appreciative glance, before returning his attention to Pauline.

Pauline rubbed against him. "Wow, I've watched that movie several times myself, but you're better looking than that handsome satanic mechanic. Too bad, I'm not into boys, because you're an adorable mechanic in real life. Play your cards right, and I might let you check out my engine."

"Anytime." Cy rubbed his hands up and down her arms.

Cy was attracted to Pauline. He was probably one of the few GDBs that could handle her. Rosemary wished Pauline would expand her desires to men. She'd really like a night with both of them.

"Staying busy at the garage?" Pauline smiled, pulling back.

"Busy enough, but come cooler weather and the first ice, everyone will be sliding into each other." A glint in his eye, he bumped Pauline with hips meant for making love.

"Hey, did you hear about Cecil? He's been seen at the bar with..." Pauline and Cy compared notes of who had done what to whom while Rosemary's interest zeroed in on the blonde with the missile boobs who still had her tiger claws wrapped around Bryce.

He chose that moment to turn and wink at Rosemary. Despite herself, her heart went pitter-pat. She smiled back and took a gulp of wine while cursing Pauline for "losing" the key to the lock on the chains. Rosemary's curiosity concerning Bryce churned in her thoughts, leaving her grateful when Pauline tired of flirting with Cy.

The two of them mingled and drank until she managed to kick Bryce out of her mind. As the evening wound down, she caught sight of Twylene.

"Hi, I'm Rosemary Wolfe and I just wanted to meet you. This is my friend, Pauline."

"Hiiii! Good to meet you," Pauline reached for Twylene's hand and missed.

Rosemary steadied her by pulling on the chain connecting them. Pauline had made sure to try every type of alcohol Jonathan and Edward offered.

"I've met your parents, but I always missed meeting you." Rosemary held out her unchained hand.

"Hey, I've heard about you too." Twylene shook her hand. "You're something else being a physician and a vet. Good to meet you both."

"I'm ready for human, animal, and anything in between." Rosemary's mouth lifted in a grin.

"With your background, why did you stay in the Midwest?"

"I had offers on both coasts, but I love the Midwest, and my family's here."

"I'm sure glad you're here. Even though I work at the hospital, there aren't many healthcare professionals I trust with my special needs." Twylene lifted her eyebrows over whiskey brown eyes.

"I understand. If you ever need a healthcare provider, call me." Rosemary shook off her exhaustion. "Speaking of needs, sleep is high on my list. The day's been long and the patients many. Nice meeting you. I hope to see you around."

"Since we both work in GDB healthcare, it's likely." Twylene wiggled her fingers in a parting wave.

Rosemary and Pauline left in search of their hosts. The guys were doing shots of synthetic blood with plasma and lime chasers. Rosemary touched Jonathan's arm to get his attention.

The shot glass in his hand paused. "Hey, Sweetheart, you leaving?"

"My day started in the early hours of the morning and I'm ready for bed. I'm not the night owl you and Edward are." Rosemary kissed his cheek.

"Vampires love the nightlife." Jonathan kissed her back. "Hey, did Roger find you?"

"No, he didn't, so if you see him, tell him I left, please!"

"That wolf has it bad for you." Jonathan returned to his drink.

Rosemary led Pauline to the door and headed out into the rainy night. As they walked down the driveway taking slow, uneven steps, Rosemary stopped and shivered as if someone had poured a shovel of ice pellets down her back, even though it was a warm summer night.

"What is it?"

"Do you feel that? It's like someone's walking over my grave." Rosemary turned and squinted her eyes. In the second story tower window, she could just make out the outline of an imposing figure. Her psychic senses flashed a warning, but no specifics. "Who is that guy?"

"I saw him from a distance talking with a few of the vamps at the party, but I didn't get a name. Even though he's as handsome as sin, his eyes creep me out." She drew her cape a little closer around her shoulders.

"What about his eyes?"

"They're a strange greenish yellow, like a feral cat. I couldn't get a read on him." Pauline sobered for the moment.

"Now that you mention it, he seems to slip around my radar." She turned to Pauline. "I hope Jonathan and Edward aren't in danger. Sometimes, they end up with crazies at their parties."

"There were enough of their good friends around to take care of any trouble makers. Let's go end the evening right!" The alcohol in Pauline's system reasserted itself.

Nodding, Rosemary let herself be dragged along.

~

A ten-minute taxi ride brought them to Pauline's apartment. It took another five minutes for Rosemary to walk a very drunk Pauline up the sidewalk to her front door. Not only did she have to deal with being chained to her friend, she had a wine cooler in her other hand.

"Shh!" Pauline giggled as she tried to unlock the door to the apartment she shared with a couple who were snake shape shifters.

"Ha, you can't find the hole." Rosemary giggled. Pauline laughed out loud.

"See what you did? If you wake up the women I live with, they will throw me out!" Pauline tried to frown but ended up snorting.

"Those two lezzies need to get a life. They're crazy and not in a good way. They're constantly making asps of themselves." Rosemary finished off her drink, leaving the bottle on the step.

"I will never get in the door if you keep that up." They both broke into uncontrollable laughter. When Pauline finally got the key in the lock and the door open, they both tiptoed into the room and tripped over the rug before catching themselves. Pauline grabbed the chain to stop it from clanging into a chair. They held each other to stop the laughs threatening to erupt. When no irate snake women appeared, Rosemary's attention went to Pauline's soft body pressed against hers.

"Want to stay the night?"

Rosemary considered her options. Not as drunk as Pauline, she still needed to sober up before trying to drive. "Since we're chained together, sounds like a good plan."

They made their way to the darkened bedroom where Pauline turned and embraced Rosemary. "I've wanted to do this all night." Her lips brushed over Rosemary's mouth.

Caught in the moment and tipsy from the wine, Rosemary returned the kiss.

Pauline's tongue tasting of cinnamon Schnapps slipped into her mouth, awakening a need in Rosemary. Lust rose from her core as Pauline feathered hot kisses down Rosemary's throat. Soon, Pauline's warm hand slipped under the satin of her bra, finding a nipple hardened to a point.

Rosemary's gaze slid down to see Pauline uncover the nipple. Her eyes closed. She tilted her back and tried to banish Bryce from her consciousness. Something about him fascinated and frightened her all at one time. Pauline lowered her head. *Oh Goddess, I need this.* Pauline took the peak between her full lips.

Images of Bryce still invaded her mind, but he wasn't here nibbling her tits at the moment. Still, Rosemary wondered how it would feel to have him tasting her like a decadent dessert. Psychic senses going crazy, a vision flashed across her mind of Bryce about to kiss her when Pauline's hand moved down Rosemary's body until her fingers strummed the bundle of nerves between her thighs triggering her core to warm with wetness.

Pauline's touch drove Bryce to the back burner of her mind and filled Rosemary with a burning need to fondle Pauline's breasts and taste her essence. Urgent hands pushed the low-cut neckline down to reveal a black cutout bra barely containing her nipples that strained to be stroked. She pinched the nearest one, delighting in Pauline's jerk forward. Rosemary smirked at her reaction. Sucking the red berry into her mouth, she felt Pauline buck against her. The heat between them blazed and clothes went flying, until only the two black shirts were left, hanging on the chains that connected them.

"We can do this," Pauline backed her onto the bed. Rosemary

panted as Pauline kissed her warm, wet center, while her fingers sought entrance deep inside.

"Oh, your tongue is amazing." she arched her back in response to Pauline licking her folds with fast, sharp strokes.

Wanting to taste Pauline at the same time, Rosemary adjusted positioning her tongue to twirl around Pauline's nub, while her fingers explored the secrets of her body.

"Oh yes! Right there, more, more," Pauline screeched, her werebat close to the surface, as her climax vibrated her body.

Her orgasm jettisoned Rosemary into her own climax marked by a howl.

The women in the next room pounded on the wall which caused Pauline and Rosemary to laugh.

"Who needs a key?" Pauline lifted her sex-slickened hand, allowing the chain to slip off.

As Rosemary settled in beside Pauline, her mind returned to Bryce. She kept seeing the blond shape shifter launching her boobs at him and wondered if Bryce was having a sleep over with her. *None of my business.* She told herself, drifting off to sleep.

~

The next morning driving home, Rosemary realized her night with Pauline had left a dark hole in her heart. Her maternal Grandma Rosie's words haunted her. "Like attracts like, good or bad."

Sex with Pauline was fun, but afterwards there was no connection. No "I love you" or the sense of belonging. It was as if a part of Pauline's negativity wormed its way into her being, leaving her drained and depressed.

On the other hand, she had confusing feelings for Bryce hanging out of the chest of drawers of her heart. She thought they were neatly tucked away. Was it physical attraction or had she run into her soul mate? She had accepted life alone, with the occasional lover to satisfy her physical needs, hadn't she? Her practice was her passion, but

Bryce had marched into her head and clanged her psychic bells. *Grandma Rosie, where are you when I need you?*

When she got home, she checked her messages. The usual. Werewolves with shedding problems and vampires with sleep issues. No emergencies, thank goodness. As she listened to the last call, she heard Roger's sexy growl telling her how much he enjoyed seeing her at the diner and asking her to call to catch up. His voice stirred something in the depths of her body making her want him.

However, Bryce had awakened something inside she couldn't ignore. *What am I thinking?* She'd probably never see him again. She stared at the phone, wondering if maybe she should consider celibacy. *Nah.* She wrote Roger's number on the list of calls to make on Monday morning and headed for the shower.

CHAPTER 3

Good God! This woman's trouble, Bryce escaped from Marie's claws and searched for his hosts, determined to find out about the mysterious stranger. He learned her name was Rosemary. She had to be Jonathan's friend from the restaurant. The draw to her had hit him even stronger tonight. Hopefully, he could take her on a date or two and the fascination would wane.

Spotting Edward, he asked, "There was a bewitching woman here earlier chained to a batty babe. Do you know where they might be?"

"Bryce, you old rounder! It's been centuries since you've bedded two women at once. Boston changed you!"

Bryce's eyebrows shot up at Edward's comment.

"Rounder? You need to update your slang! I believe you meant to call me a player, which I'm not. The last time I had two women in my bed was in 1756. I'll never forget the shock plastered on the man's face when he discovered his wife, her sister, and me enjoying the comforts of their featherbed. I learned my lesson that night when he tossed me out of the second story window. Right now, though, I'm interested in a woman named Rosemary. At least that's what her friend called her. I missed my chance to get her number or address. Would you happen to have it?"

Edward's face grew still, and with a smile that didn't reach his eyes he said, "Rosemary's a dear friend. She's not your type, Bryce."

"Edward, are you okay?" Bryce caught the warning look Jonathan tossed his way as he approached.

I just want to ask her out. There was something about her, but he had no business taking it any further than sex. He would not be responsible for any more women being killed. He was certain Jonathan and Edward didn't know of his stalker. Besides, the creep didn't hurt anyone he wasn't serious about. Surely, in forty years, he had moved on.

"Bryce wants Rosemary's phone number and address. I'm trying to explain to him why she's not his type."

Bryce felt Edward's dark eyes on him.

"Oh, I see," said Jonathan.

"Well, I don't," Bryce said. "She's one of the most fascinating women I've had the pleasure of meeting in a long time, and I simply want to ask her out on a date to find out more about her."

"What my love is trying to tell you is that Rosemary doesn't date vampires. While she understands our need for an extremely loyal partner, she isn't convinced that lifestyle fits her. In fact, it has been our observation she isn't interested in any close romantic relation-ships." Jonathan stopped for a moment.

"Gentlemen, we've been friends for centuries. Come on, I'm not looking to hurt her. We connected tonight when we talked. I want to get to know her better."

"That's the problem. She's already been hurt by another vampire." Edward lowered his gaze to Jonathan.

Jonathan and Edward stared at each other, sighed, and turned back to face him.

"How about this, we give you her information and you tell her you're a vampire before she gets too involved?" Jonathan said looking Bryce in the eye.

"Absolutely. I'll be completely honest with her, and I'll back off anytime she asks. What happened with the other vampire?"

"That's Rosemary's story to tell. I will only say it devastated her."

Jonathan plucked a calling card from his pocket, unsheathed a heavy gold and white marble fountain pen and with perfect Palmer penmanship, wrote down Rosemary's information.

Bryce took the card and studied it intently for a moment. "One more question, what's her favorite flower?"

"Orchids, the redder the better," Jonathan said giving Edward a look. Edward crossed his arms and sighed but remained silent.

Bryce's eyes lit up. "Red orchids for a passionate and powerful woman."

"Remember, she is special to us." Edward's eyes glowed with intensity.

~

Eyes wild with excitement took in the exchange of information between Bryce and Jonathan. With his enhanced hearing, he noted every word. His face pulled into a grim smile showing his fangs. He slipped out of the shadows and into the crowd filling the next room. He had work to do. Bryce hadn't learned his lesson.

~

Rosemary stood under the hot spray of water letting it rinse the shampoo out of her hair. Water ran over her nipples, inspiring her to imagine Bryce's hands teasing them into ruby red points. She cupped them, water dancing in all different directions and held them up to intensify the sting. Releasing them, her hands wandered between her legs and explored the sensitive places there. In her mind, Bryce filled her as she came with a moan.

She stood for a moment letting the shower spray caress her back. Indecision fought with her need. *Do I call Jonathan and Edward, or not? Bryce was good looking, but I suspect he's a vamp. I couldn't tell with all the other vamps scents there. Maybe I could persuade him for just a hookup.* "Oh-h-h-h, what is it about this guy?" Rosemary shut the water off and decided to call Edward and Jonathan that evening.

Why couldn't she stop all this flip-flopping? Jonathan and Edward's relationship spoke of how loving and loyal vamps were. That damn Leon Villenevue broke her heart by trying to chain it to his fancy vampire sleeve. He hid his insanity well until their engagement party. Too late, she realized his old-fashioned values covered his abusive actions and cheating ways. A friend from medical school had hugged her to congratulate her, when Leon attacked him, knocking him down. He would have killed him if Jonathan and Edward hadn't intervened. Leon had been escorted out the door. For weeks, flowers, letters, and phone calls arrived daily. Perhaps he had been sorry, but she had no desire to take a chance the same thing could happen, again. *No vampires.*

As she stepped out of the shower, the doorbell rang. She ignored it. In no mood for company, she kept moving the towel over her body. The bell rang again. *Could be an emergency.* Tucking the towel over the rack, she hopped into a pair of jeans and pulled a tee shirt on as she rushed to open the door. What greeted her was a large pot of blood red orchids with a card held by a man with honey blond hair and wide shoulders.

"Rosemary Wolfe?" He flashed her a crooked smile.

"Yes?" she answered.

"I'm Mitchell. Bryce Gold send me to deliver these." He handed her the orchids.

"Thank you and thank Mr. Gold for me." She took the fiery orchids, set them down on the table, and with her hand on the door, started to close it.

Mitchell held up an envelope. "And, this invitation. I'm to wait for your answer."

She plucked up the envelope. Her hands were shaking as she pulled out the card. It read:

Rosemary,

I'm sending you these orchids because they remind me of how red hot you are. I enjoyed talking with you last night, and I would love to continue talking with you over dinner tonight. If it's okay, I'll pick you up around eight p.m. or you can meet me at the restaurant. Jonnie's down by the river is my favorite, but if you prefer another restaurant, tell Mitchell.

Bryce Gold

Like an asthmatic goldfish, she stood with dripping hair, gasping. Maybe he wasn't a vampire. His letter was nothing like the stuffy sounding missives she received from Leon. After Mitchell raised his eyebrows and spread his hands in hopes of her answering, she said, "Dinner with Mr. Gold at Jonnie's would be lovely. Please ask him to pick me up at eight here at my apartment."

He smiled and said, "I'll tell Bryce the good news."

Her eyes followed him as he disappeared down the street in a white delivery van with the Community Blood logo. She stood staring at nothing, wondering why she agreed to dinner. How did he get her address? Surely, Jonathan and Edward wouldn't hand out her info without asking her first. She turned to close the door, but her eyes caught a quick movement at the end of her driveway. Strange. Psychic senses on alert, she scanned the area. Whatever, or whoever it was had disappeared. Shaking her head, she locked the door and went to pick out a dress for tonight.

Bryce polished the stone sculpture of a gray wolf with an intense sweep of the cloth in his hand, wondering if Rosemary had accepted his invitation. Cleaning calmed him and the wolf helped him to tune into his primal power. The minute Mitchell entered his office Bryce glanced up and asked, "What did Miss Rosemary say? Thanks, but no thanks?" Bryce scanned Mitchell's solemn expression which lasted all of five seconds before he broke into a wide grin.

"Stop jerking me around like a bat on a rope and talk, you sadistic wizard!" Bryce put the wolf back on the shelf.

Mitchell rolled his eyes. "Are you for real? Over the centuries, any woman you pursued became yours. Unlike me, you didn't even use magic. Surprise, she said yes."

Joy blossomed on Bryce's face. "Thanks for doing this for me." Bryce clapped him on the back.

"It was my pleasure. When I arrived, she'd just showered and dressed in a tee shirt and jeans. Since she didn't take time to put on a bra, her nipples were standing up and waving howdy. Call me if it doesn't work out, I'll be waiting in line. I could fall for her in a heartbeat."

Bryce threw him a territorial glare.

Mitchell laughed.

By six o'clock, Rosemary sashayed to her couch, her dress and flowing black wrap swinging in time with her dangly earrings. Hair shining with auburn sparkles and her deep blue eyes exuding excitement, she settled, and then dialed Jonathan and Edward. Jonathan answered on the first ring.

"Were you sitting on the phone?" she asked.

Jonathan breathed in deeply. "No, but I had a feeling you might call. I may have stepped out of line."

The skirt of her dress provided a plaything for her nervous fingers. "If you mean giving Bryce my address, possibly."

"The guy is trustworthy." Jonathan's voice wavered.

She picked harder at her dress. "Tell me more about him and I'll tell you if you did."

"Actually, I've known him for years through a circle of close friends, if you catch my meaning?"

She paused. "Are you saying what I think you're saying?"

"If you mean that he is one of us, yes."

"He's gay! Oh. I should have known."

Jonathan laughed. "No. He's a vampire."

Rosemary's head hurt as visions of Leon hammered at her heart.

She heard his laugh cut into her again, sharp as it had years ago, at her simple ways. An old vampire, he thought she should behave as he decreed. To him, shifters were nothing more than animals. Thanks to her werewort and her ability as a witch to block any suggestions from vampires, he had no idea that she was part werewolf. *Damn.*

Jonathan's concerned voice brought her back. "Rosemary, are you still there? Are you okay?"

She stood up, pacing as she talked. "I will be. I should be mad at you, but I'm not. Leon frightened me. He still frightens me. He was kind and generous until I didn't agree with him. I cannot go through being humiliated and abused like that again. Even though there's something about Bryce that stirs my soul, he's still a vampire. I've spent too many years being my own woman. As you're aware, vampires are touchy about that sort of thing. I hid my werewolf half from Leon. I won't ever do that again."

She heard the panic in his voice. "Rosemary, darling, don't go. I'll call him and explain. I'm sorry I gave him your information, but he was taken with you. He's different from Leon. Raised in much different circumstances, Bryce is compassionate. He is very accepting of all the GDBs. I am positive he would never knowingly hurt you or try to control you like Leon."

"Are you sure?" Her voice a whisper. She desperately wanted to find someone who was hers only, but vampires scared her.

Jonathan's voice soothed her. "I am. I wouldn't have given him your information otherwise. The whole experience with Leon made you afraid you're not enough, too different to be loved. As your friend, I'm telling you that simply is not true. However, it's obvious I stepped out of line. I'll call him right now and tell him not to come."

She stopped in front of her living room window to stare out. "No. I owe him the courtesy to show up and listen. You're right. I'm confident when it comes to my career, but timid when it comes to relationships. I'll go out with Bryce and take a chance. We're going to your restaurant down by the river at eight o'clock. I'll call when I get home."

"Please do, even if it is tomorrow morning. I won't sleep until I hear from you. And if he gets out of line with you, he'll answer to Edward and me."

"You know, Jonathan, the real kicker is that I'm attracted to him. I may end up rethinking my whole no-dating-vampires rule. We'll talk later." She didn't miss the smile in Jonathan's voice as they said their goodbyes.

CHAPTER 4

Hi, I love you; let me bite your neck. Too forward, Bryce decided as he rehearsed what he wanted to say on the drive to pick up Rosemary. He gripped the steering wheel tighter. He hadn't fallen for a woman so fast and so hard in forty years. The feeling overwhelmed him.

"I'm practical and disciplined. I'm not a newly turned vampire simply following animal instincts." *Well, that wasn't convincing.* How could he keep this casual? For Rosemary's safety, he had to keep it low key, at least, until he caught his stalker.

In his younger days, women hung all over him, eager to satisfy his any whim. However, the lies that sprouted from that lifestyle led to chaos. Often, he found himself juggling four or five women. When he did business with some of their husbands, he didn't always keep his little white lies straight. After a couple of hundred years, he discovered there were ways of getting blood and sex without all the trouble.

Yet, he couldn't remember wanting any woman as much as Rosemary. Thinking of her sexy smile, he missed a stop sign. Brakes squealed, and Bryce managed to stop the car halfway into the intersection. The offended driver laid on her horn and gave him a dirty look as she went through the stop sign. Bryce sighed and tried to concentrate on driving.

When he pulled into Rosemary's driveway at eight, he saw her peering at him from behind a curtain. He climbed out of his Lexus SUV and pulled on his favorite black leather jacket. Bent, straightening a cuff on his black trousers, he lifted his gaze up in time to see her intently staring. *She's looking at my ass.* He grinned up at her, and she whipped the curtain closed.

He walked to the front door and rang the bell. Rosemary was more gorgeous than he remembered. Her pale skin, highlighted by pink cheeks, tempted him to stroke his hand over her face to determine if it was as soft as he imagined.

"Good evening. Like the view out your window?" He stood in the doorway, gauging her mood.

With a good-natured chuff, she invited him in. "It had its moments."

He stepped in and met her eyes. "Good to know."

A quick wave of her hand directed his attention across the living room splashed in bright reds, yellows, and blues to a table.

Her voice crept up to a higher note. "Thank you for the orchids. They're a beautiful shade of red."

"I'm glad you liked them." He motioned to the door with his right hand. "Are you ready?"

She grabbed her purse and nodded. "I am."

He held the door for her and made sure it was locked before they strolled down the sidewalk to his car. "Sorry I didn't get back to you last night. Marie, the woman I was talking with, works with one of the hospitals in the area. She had questions about the blood bank."

"You don't say." After she passed in front of him to the SUV, she whispered under her breath, "I bet."

His lips quirked. "No, really." She whirled around with her eyes wide. He shrugged his shoulders and said, "Sensitive ears." He reached over, opened the car door for her, and gently touched her elbow to guide her inside.

She glanced at him through her long lashes. "Uh, I mean, I'm sure she's interested in your business."

He couldn't help the laugh that bubbled up. *She's jealous.*

She stopped and frowned at him. "What's so funny?"

"I'm sure she's interested in my business. Doesn't matter. You're the one I can't stop thinking about." He shut the door after making sure she was tucked in and made his way to the driver's side hardly containing his excitement. *For someone who doesn't date vampires, she seems interested.* He slid into the driver's seat and caught her studying him.

Her lips twitched. "I admit thinking about you, too."

Those smoke and mirror eyes held his.

She nodded. "Tell me about yourself."

His excitement threatened to burst out, but instead, he reined in his enthusiasm and found his calm voice. "You're aware of my new job, but are you aware I'm intrigued by your choice of profession? Not all healers can take on such a variety of clients."

"That's what this is all about. You want to play doctor?" A gleam sailed from her eyes.

"Would you mind?" He winked.

She did a quick bounce of her brows. "We'll see."

He loved the blush spreading across her face. "Jonathan and Edward also mentioned you're more than just a physician."

She took her time exhaling. "That's right. My majors in chemistry and biology helped when I applied to med school. After I graduated, I enrolled in an accredited veterinary program. Completed it last year, as a matter of fact."

"I suspected that smart mouth had a smart brain behind it." Bryce started the car and maneuvered out onto the street.

Rosemary shifted in her seat, contemplating him for a second. "How does one become an Executive Director of a blood center?"

He concentrated on his driving, taking a corner with smooth precision. "They start with an extensive background in medical administration and add complementary degrees. With my particular skills and interests, I'm a natural for the position."

"And, those skills and interests are?"

He paused. The promise to be honest with her was happening

sooner than he planned. "You checked with Jonathan and Edward, didn't you?"

She nodded.

So much for wooing her before revealing all. "In the interest of starting this relationship with as much honesty as possible, I'm a vampire."

"I appreciate your honesty." She swallowed hard. "In the same vein, I don't date vampires."

Shaking his head at the old pun that sounded charming coming from her, he stopped at a light, turning his eyes to search her face. "They mentioned that."

"Oh." She held his gaze.

At the memory of his friends' words, his throat clenched for a moment. "There were indications I would take a one-way trip to a sunny beach without clothes, if anything happened to you." The light changed, and he pulled forward.

Her face had paled.

Damnit! His attempt at humor had scared her. "You've nothing to fear from me, but I hope to change your mind about vampires."

Her voice came out in a thin whisper. "I'm not sure I can be a one-vampire-woman."

Gods! This wasn't a conversation he wanted to have while driving. He pulled into an empty parking lot. "Would you be willing to try? I've never met anyone as unique as you are in my life."

In the silence, her face reflected a myriad of emotions. "Speaking of that, how old are you?"

She wasn't wasting any time. His eyes went wide. "You go for the jugular, don't you?"

The sharp move of her head trained her eyes on him. "They told you I'm part werewolf, didn't they?"

"Yes." His eyes lit up as he bounced his knee. "Actually, that's part of your appeal."

Her jaw set, she shook her head. "Quit stalling, how old are you?"

He shrugged. Would he lose her over his age? "I will be four hundred and three come October 30th."

"Wow." She sat in silence, hands clutched tightly in her lap.

He'd bet she was considering the age difference. He lifted one of her cold hands into his. "I'm familiar with that look. However, I'm just a guy who's been around a little longer than most. My body will always appear to be forty, and I practice more nocturnal habits than most."

She glanced at her hand in his but allowed it to stay. "Uh…can you elaborate on those habits?"

He nodded. "I do tend to sleep in the daylight hours and be more active at night."

Slipping her hand back, she crossed her arms. "I'm more concerned about the blood part. I assumed you were a day sleeper."

His hand ran through his hair. "I don't go out seeking fresh blood. As a founding member of VIEW, I try to abide by their rule of bagged blood, when possible. One perk of being a director of a blood bank. I imagine you come across vamps with a variety of abilities in your practice."

She bobbed her head. "You're right. You're telling me you helped found Vampires and Immortals Enclave of the World?"

His hands rested on the steering wheel. "I am. The other members and I all wanted to help guide the civilizing of our kind as we evolved."

"VIEW has a sterling reputation among the vampires I deal with. I'm impressed. Can you eat food?"

He was encouraged she was asking these sorts of questions. "As long as it contains blood. To stay alive, I must drink real blood at least once a day."

She shifted in her seat, looking out the car window to her side. "Do you miss live feeding?"

In other words, is she tonight's dessert? "Not much." With a gentle touch of his hand, he turned her face to him. "Why don't you ask what you really want to know?"

She leaned back. "Are you going to bite me tonight?"

"No." He stroked her cheek. "There may come a time when and if we become lovers, I might want to bite you during sex, but only if you give me permission."

"Promise?" Wide blue eyes rose to meet his.

"What? That we'll become lovers, or I'll bite you?" He teased her to see the fire shoot from her eyes.

She playfully swatted him. "You know what I meant."

He grabbed her hand and placed a kiss on her palm. "I will never knowingly hurt you. As I was saying, after four hundred and two years, I've figured out that the people who are in your life are what keep you sane. I'm not always happy about what I am, but I'm happy about who I am." He gave her hand a final squeeze and drove out of the parking lot, aimed towards the restaurant.

After a comfortable silence, in which he discovered a sense of confidence in this almost-date, her phone made a knocking sound.

"Sorry, I have to check this in case it's a patient." Bent over her phone, she made quick work of texting a reply.

He glanced over as she finished. "Do I need to take you to your office?"

A genuine smile greeted him. "No, I'll take care of it tomorrow. Thanks for offering. I appreciate your concern."

"Not a problem. I get plenty of after-hours texts and calls myself." His attention returned to the road.

She took a deep breath and adjusted her smile. "In my experience, older vamps are often challenged in adjusting to modern times. How do you cope?"

Silence filled the car as he stared into the night. Fear twisting deep in his gut, he struggled to say the right words. He gathered the vampire that had hurt her had been stuck in the past. The wrong answer could scare her. The motion of flexing his fingers around the leather steering wheel calmed him.

"I've invested well financially over the years and have the right connections to keep my identity and person safe." He paused. "I cope by keeping up with whatever the current culture dictates. Most importantly, I adjust by cultivating good friends and loyal lovers."

Her low voice cut the silence. "You own a cell phone?"

He laughed. "Yes, and I know how to use it."

She held up her phone. "Can you show me? I'm still puzzled with an app or two."

"Anytime." The car pulled into the parking space and Bryce turned off the motor. Turning to her, he cupped one of her hands in his.

"When I met you last night, something happened. I admit, I'm not looking for a serious relationship, but there's something about you. All I'm asking is for you to give us a chance to get to know each other."

She paused, searching his face. "Let's see how dinner goes, okay?"

"Fair enough."

Her delicate hand rubbed his. "My first inclination was to cancel this date after finding out you were a vampire. However, when I'm with you, something makes my intuition go on full alert. It may not go anywhere or it may go all the way. I don't know."

His eyes crinkled at the corners. "All the way, huh?"

Hand drawing from his clasp, she pointed a teasing finger at him. "You have a dirty mind."

"Hey, it's been a few years." He gave her his most pitiful look, complete with his best puppy-dog eyes.

"A good-looking guy like you?"

He couldn't help regarding her with a quizzical glint. "You think I'm good looking?"

She rolled her eyes. "Bryce."

A new warmth surged through him. "There's been no one who's sparked my interest enough to take a chance on a long-term relationship for the last forty years."

Her eyes lowered to stare at his crotch. "I guess you had to take matters into your own hands, huh?"

"Who has the dirty mind now?" Her warm lips sent a thrill through him as he brushed them with a kiss, and then he climbed out of the car to come around and open her door.

They walked into the restaurant, and the maître d` escorted them to a private room, showing them to a rough-planked table with heavy wooden chairs, elegant cloth napkins, and fine china. A smiling waiter came and took their order.

"I'd like one of your special Bloody Marys," Bryce told the waiter.

"A glass of your house red wine." When the waiter went to fill their orders, Rosemary asked, "What's a special Bloody Mary?"

Bryce gave her a sly wink. "It's a glass of chilled blood with a celery stick."

"Remind me to be specific if I ever order a Bloody Mary here." Her big blue eyes traveled around the room. "I love all the scented candles."

"I requested them for this evening. Don't you think the semi-dark atmosphere highlights the view of the river?"

Attention turned to the flowing water outside, she paused. "Among other things." They sat, watching the river flow by, a comfortable silence settling between them.

Soon, the waiter returned with their meals. As Bryce dined on his usual rare steak, he watched, fascinated while Rosemary ate her steak and vegetables with great joy.

She was adorable. Now, to make her his. He had his work cut out for him. *Damn the vampire that hurt her.* If he ever found out who he was, he'd make sure it wouldn't happen again. And, damn the vampire stalking the women he loved. Maybe he should just back off and hide in his solitude. Her blue eyes caught his amber ones, and his heart clinched.

Deep within his being, Bryce sensed Rosemary felt their connection too. *Mine. She is mine.* Eyes glowing, he gazed at Rosemary finishing her last bite of steak and sighing with contentment.

"Did you enjoy your steak?" Bryce's mouth lifted into a grin.

"I did and the veggies too." Rosemary sat back to allow the waiter to clear the table.

Bryce offered his hand. "Care to join me on the sofa?" He escorted her across the room to sit down side-by-side. He hoped the view of the river bathed in the soft orange light of a half-full moon from the floor-to-ceiling windows, would provide a romantic setting for Rosemary. He handed her the frozen mango margarita she ordered and squeezed the lime wedge into his glass of plasma.

She took a sip and set the glass down. "Dinner was delicious and this is delightfully romantic."

Bryce put his arm around her, pulling her to his side. "Glad you like it. Am I earning any points as potential dating material?"

Her laugh gave him intense pleasure.

She paused, her face relaxed. "Maybe."

That answer wove a strong current of pleasure through his body. He inhaled her sexy scent of cinnamon, honeysuckle, and witchy woman. His tongue touched his fangs, extending out of their sockets. *Good grief! He had stared down armies of vampires that had him less frazzled.* This redheaded ball of fire had him acting like a teenage boy. How was he going to slow this down? He had to convince her it was safe to be with him, safe to love him, and, there was that business with his stalker. *Time for that to end.*

"What are they doing now?" Edward whispered to Jonathan who waved at him to be quiet. With Bryce's keen hearing, Jonathan had no doubt he was aware they had skulked to a conveniently open window to spy on him and Rosemary.

He sighed with relief. It appeared Rosemary was warming up to their friend, a vampire. He had to make it right after the horrible fiasco with Leon. "Sitting and enjoying the view. He's being a complete gentleman."

"Good!" A soft growl slipped from Edward.

Jonathan came back to where Edward stood and put his arm around his shoulders and kissed his cheek. "We will protect Rosemary, this time, but Bryce is an honorable friend whom we've known for centuries. I hope they can work things out."

Edward wound his arm around Jonathan, as they strolled to Jonathan's office to check on the evening's receipts. "I do too. Rosemary deserves to be happy."

His super-sensitive hearing picked up the hushed exchange. Bryce smiled at the thought of his old friends sneaking around to protect Rosemary. He had no problem with them checking on how things were going. Later, might be too much, but right now, he was taking it slow. He needed to figure out how to slow it down further until he found out who was stalking the women he loved. His arm gathered Rosemary toward him, and stroking her face, he asked, "Would you like to take a walk?"

Her eyes rose to his face. "A walk would be perfect."

Bryce slid his hand into hers and they headed outside to wander along the boardwalk. The slight stroke of her fingers along his brought certain parts of his anatomy to attention. To distract himself from picking her up and making love to her on the boardwalk he asked, "Do you have any brothers or sisters?"

She paused to sniff a planter of dark purple petunias. Her face reflected the pleasure the scent had brought her. Finally, she answered. "A half-sister. She's my mom and stepdad's child. Greta's an attorney. How about you?"

He couldn't help himself. Face buried in the blossoms, he took a deep breath. On releasing it, he answered, "I had two brothers and a sister. I outlived two of them."

He loved the way she took time to experience life.

She digested his answer then asked, "Were any of them vampires?"

He understood he needed to share this information, but his stomach knotted up. The deep breath flowed from him. "My younger brother and sister weren't. My older brother and I were turned at the same time. We were working out in the fields on a cold February day, when we were attacked by a group of rogue vamps. They left us for dead. However, they were sloppy and Rhys ingested enough blood to turn. He fed me some of his, hoping to save my life. It worked."

Her voice was soft, calm. "Where was this?"

Pleased in her interest, Bryce nodded his thanks to the gods. "Scotland. We lived in a cave and drank the blood of rabbits and deer until we could make it back to the house."

She beetled her brow. "How did your family react?"

They stopped by a railed overhang to take in the view of the landscape and river. He let the rhythm of the river calm him. Rosemary seemed to be warming up to him. Honesty was always best, but would she dismiss him if she found out all his secrets?

His courage renewed, he said, "Our parents were dead and Rhys' wife had died in childbirth while we were gone. All the family left was Helen, my wife, and our two boys. Helen sensed something was off, and when I told her, she insisted on being turned. I did. I'm not sure if it was for the best, but we got to be together for many years after."

"What happened to Helen?" Rosemary's head dropped as she waited for his answer.

He stared off into space, gauging how much to tell her. Helen had been beheaded by a vampire intent on hurting him. Not the same one as the current menace, but still a bad example to confess to a woman he desperately wanted to at least date. He filled his lungs, releasing the air in a long slow sigh. "Not knowing the ways of other vampires, we ended up in a clan's territory in Glasgow." Fighting back the memories and tears, he took a deep breath.

Rosemary raised eyes full of concern to his. She started to speak, but he held up his hand.

"I want you to know." He swallowed and continued. "Instead of backing away, I attacked the leader, thinking I could take him. His clan caught and held me while he beheaded Helen." The tears flowed down his cheeks.

"I'm... I don't know what to say. Sorry doesn't even begin to express my feelings." She stood in the moonlight, studying his face.

He dropped his gaze to hers. "There's nothing to say. They let me go after beating me to the point of losing most of my blood, and told me if I lived, it would be a lesson I'd never forget." He sighed. "They were right."

Way to kill the mood. The two continued their walk. Bryce, desperate to return to the playful aura of before, asked, "Too much information?"

She grimaced and shook her head. "No. I'm sorry you lost her."

He nodded. "Me too."

She curled her arm around his elbow, leaning in to him. "Rhys is a vampire too. Where is he these days?"

Bryce's eyes cleared. She was snuggling close to him. He prayed it was because she was interested and not cold. "He lives in Boston now."

"Isn't that where you moved from?"

"Yes. It was good to be close to him again. Like your sister, he's an attorney. He's graduated from Harvard Law School a few times now."

She chuckled. "A few times, huh?"

His eyes flicked her way. "Yes. His insight into vampires' way of life is invaluable when it comes to keeping my assets and legal matters secure."

They were headed to the back to the parking lot and possibly her decision on whether to date him or not. He made sure to go at a slow pace to give her more time.

The corners of her lips rose. "That would get complicated. Is he married?"

Relieved, he watched her face release the tension and crack into a smile. "Not currently. He's become wrapped up in his work. When I lived in Boston, I'd make sure we'd go out for a drink every couple of weeks to keep him from turning into a complete hermit."

"You're a good brother." She leaned her head on his shoulder and squeezed his hand.

The night air filled his lungs, bringing the rush of power he craved. He wished Rhys lived closer. "Rhys' life has been rough. He's a good man but tends to have one-night stands compared to long-term relationships. Sometimes it takes a sibling to understand what you've gone through."

She raised her head to study him. "I'm getting the impression you possess a real nurturing streak. Earlier, you mentioned you had children. Did you turn them?"

Their footsteps echoed on the wooden walk. He was happy she asked questions, but remembering his past filled him with sadness. "No. We told them what we had become and left the farm to them. We'd check in on them from our travels on occasion, but not aging brought up questions and accusations we didn't want to face. They lived to ripe old ages and gave us grandkids we only knew from afar."

"Have you ever wanted a child since that time?"

His old friend, regret, hit him. He'd wanted children. "Yes, sometimes, with some of my wives, we'd adopt. The emotional price in outliving them and not being able to become involved in the grandchildren's lives in any direct way discouraged me from repeating the process. Recently, there are rumors that VIEW scientists are working on ways to help vampires become pregnant."

Her face lit up with wonder. "That would make many of my patients happy. Wow, what a life you've lived. How many wives have you had?"

"Uh, well..." Bryce hesitated. How was he going to spin his many marriages?

She stopped and directed her gaze his way, eyebrows reaching for her hairline. "You promised to be honest."

"I did, didn't I? Here goes, I've been married to seven women." Bryce looked at her, fearing her reaction.

Her cheek twitched on an otherwise calm face. "Hm. Practice makes perfect. How did you handle being married that many times?"

Okay, that went better than I hoped. The car was in sight. He had better make this good. "For years at a time, I would give in to my wild side, but I missed the deep love I found in true relationships. Marriage satisfied that need."

She gave him a smile and they walked toward the car. He held the door and helped her into the seat. He circled around the back of the SUV, shaking his head. *I've got to slow down before I scare her away.*

Seven wives. Seven. What am I thinking? The car pulled up to Rosemary's apartment, and Bryce appeared at the passenger side offering to help her out. *There he goes with opening doors. It's nice, but what other old-fashioned ideas like Leon does he have?* They walked hand-in-hand to her apartment's front entrance. She shivered when Bryce closed his long fingers over her hand taking her key. The lock clicked, and he moved back to allow her to enter. Her attention glued to him, she bumped an entryway table sending a lamp careening to the floor. Spinning around too late, she tightened. In a blur of action, Bryce caught it.

With shaking hands, Rosemary took a moment to position the lamp back on the table. "Thanks, it belonged to my grandma on my mom's side."

"No problem. What's the use of having vampire reflexes if you don't use them?"

His smoky voice set fire to her lady parts. Her imagination concocted a slew of uses for his talents.

She was lost. He saved her Grandma Rosie's lamp. She was shocked to discover she wanted to give him a chance. "So true." *How to say this?*

"Okay, then." He suddenly appeared vulnerable.

"Thanks for a great night. I enjoyed myself." She edged closer until his warmth flowed over her.

His voice came out almost in a whisper. "Did you enjoy yourself enough to consider going on another date with me?"

She edged closer and tilted her head. She shook with the need to kiss him. She stroked his cheek with her hand. "Yes, I would like that."

He grabbed her hand, giving it a firm shake, and then he headed for the door. "Great, I'll call you. Good night."

What the hell? Her mouth flew open as she stood there in shock. "Good... goodnight."

Before she could say more, he turned around and his strong arms wrapped around her, holding her close, her breasts flattened to his broad, powerful chest. He lifted her chin and gazed into her eyes. A psychic tingle passed between them leaving no doubt in her mind he wanted her.

"You didn't think I'd leave without kissing you, did you?" And, then he smiled. Rosemary started to speak, but before the smart-ass answer shot out, he possessed her mouth.

Her pulse banged in a primal rhythm of need. All thoughts abandoned her mind. He slipped his tongue slowly between her lips. As she kissed him back with a passion she could barely control, tendrils of fear slipped into her thoughts. Her tongue felt the fullness of his fangs pushing at the corners of his mouth. *Am I nuts? He's a vampire. A big, strong, sexy vampire.*

Her body arched as his large hands caressed her back, dropping lower and lower until with a palm on each of her butt cheeks, he pulled her into him. She glanced for a second at his eyes that glowed. The pulse of his throbbing manhood beat a tune of need across her belly. She moaned as his leg slipped between her thighs. She welcomed his fingers searching for her breasts as he deepened the kiss. When he found them, he pinched her nipples, releasing a flood of need between her legs.

Eyes flying open, she realized his fangs had extended to their full length. The knowledge they were approaching the point of no return, froze her. For a moment, they stared at each other. With obvious effort, she pulled back. He growled but allowed her to step away.

Afraid of what she had almost done, she swallowed, trying to control her lust. "Bryce, I'm sorry. I need more time."

Bryce shuddered. "I have to go, before I can't." Trembling, he kissed her gently in the center of her forehead and left.

CHAPTER 5

Rosemary closed the door and locked it. She watched Bryce drive away and let out the breath she had unconsciously been holding. Sleep wouldn't be possible for a while since her body was revved up with desire. She put on an oversized tee shirt with wolves on the front, fixed a cup of herbal tea, and called Jonathan.

"Rosemary, darling! How was your date? What happened? How'd he take you breaking it off?"

She heard the anxiety in Jonathan's rapid-fire questions.

Cup placed on the nightstand, she leaned back on plush pillows. "It was lovely. I agreed to see him, and he took it quite well."

"What happened to your no vampire rule?" Jonathan's voice slowed.

Rosemary paused. "Bryce is different than any vampire I've met before."

"Really? Explain." He sounded amused.

She picked up a file and worked on a rough nail. Was there any explanation that didn't make her sound foolish? "I wish I could. Maybe it's because he's considerate, or maybe because he makes me tingle in my special places."

"Did he use his fangs to tear through the lacy little thong you wore tonight?"

His suggestive chuckle brought heat to her face. "I don't kiss and tell!"

His voice boomed over the phone. "Oh, yes you do! At least to me!"

"Okay, fine." The file swished across her nail, helping her gather courage. Her nipples still ached from his touch, not that Jonathan needed to know that! "We had a hot goodnight kiss, but that's where it stopped."

"What? You didn't have your way with him?" Silence filled the phone lines. "Are you okay?"

Genuine concern sounded in his last question. Was she okay? No sex on the first date and agreeing to date a vampire were not her usual behaviors.

"Do you want to hear something strange?"

A tentative noise came from her friend. "Sure."

"I want to know him better. Vampires can be very possessive."

The sigh from the other end of the phone let her know he understood. "But we're very loyal."

"You are." She took a sip of tea. "Thanks for giving Bryce my information. I'm not sure if I'll ever see him again after I asked him to stop tonight, but I definitely want to."

"You'll see him. Time for me to confess. He called a few minutes ago, asking what your favorite stone is. Sapphires, right?"

Rosemary paused a moment, "I love sapphires, but this is too fast." Panic crawled up her back, making her scrunch her shoulders.

"I suggested he might want to slow down. He agreed, but he's not been this interested in anyone for years," Jonathan said.

The tension in her shoulders took over her whole body. "It's too soon for either of us to be too serious! We've only known each other for a day. Besides, he's been married seven times." The deep breath she forced into her lungs and released eased away some of the worry.

"Ah, seven times in four hundred and two years, that averages out to be only every fifty-seven years. That isn't bad."

He could use humor all he wanted, but it wouldn't work tonight.

"Jonathan, don't tease!" Rosemary blew a sigh into the phone.

Jonathan hesitated. "Do you think you're serious about him?"

"I don't have a clue. You know my history. That's why I keep my relationships open and casual. The problem is Bryce is different."

Jonathan's low voice hit her with the truth. "He's serious about you."

"That scares me shitless. I don't know if I can settle down, but if I was going to," she sighed, "he would certainly be in the running." Fear battled with her attraction to Bryce.

"In my opinion, he'd be worth it."

Jonathan had always protected her. Her belief in him now gave her courage.

"I'll think about it."

"Good luck. Let me know what I can do. Kisses."

"Kisses to you, too. Thanks for listening."

Covers cocooned around her, Rosemary fell into a troubled sleep.

Standing on a rocky knoll, the wolf lifted her nose in the air and read the news that circulated in the atmosphere. A whine split the air as Bryce came towards her. Confusion clouded her mind as he changed into Leon. A second later, he grabbed her throat in a jealous rage. Anger exploding in her, Rosemary woke up in her wolf form fighting an unseen foe.

After a night of disturbing dreams, Rosemary woke up early Sunday and decided to clean the floors, reasoning that a mindless task would let her focus on what really mattered. She was giving the kitchen floor a particularly thorough scrubbing when the phone rang.

"What are you wearing, darling?" Bryce's silky voice greeted her. l

"A dirty tee shirt and jeans. I'm cleaning the kitchen floor. What're you wearing?"

"Nothing." The way he said it, made her mouth go dry and her heart speed up. She imagined how he looked standing nude in his bedroom. All muscles and golden skin framing his magnificent manhood.

"I was just getting ready for bed and had to hear your voice. Sorry if I rushed you last night. Forgive me?" Bryce asked in a low sexy tone that led her to suspect he still had some naughty thoughts.

Get ahold of yourself! She took a deep breath. "There's nothing to forgive. I was enjoying myself, how about you?"

"Definitely! I can't stop thinking about you." Bryce sighed heavily into the phone.

"Look, Bryce, I don't mean to be a fang tease, but you know I'm attracted to you. I've been surprised by the serious feelings I have for you. They go beyond jumping in bed with you."

"Rosemary, I admit in the beginning all I wanted was a casual fling. Something happened to change that last night. It's probably crazy, but I want to end up with you. Because of that, I promise to let you set the pace."

She put her hand to her forehead and paused. "It does sound crazy, but you know what?"

"What?"

"I'm willing to try."

"I've got a question, though."

"Yes?" Caution poured through her veins.

"Are you a dirty girl under zat dirty tee shirt?" Bryce used a horrible French accent.

Laughing with relief, she played along. "You're a dirty old man."

Bryce laughed, but then returned to a more serious tone. "Because of my age, I know what I want. However, I've got time to wait for you to realize how smart I am!"

"Thanks, I think. You sleep in the nude? Don't you get chilly?"

"Oh, my little Wolfie, thinking of you keeps me warm." Bryce teased her with his French, again. She wondered if he knew just how unsettled her wolf had been last night.

Reverting to his sexy almost-Scottish accent, he asked, "Can we grab supper some night this week for our second date?"

Relieved to back away from thoughts of her wolf, she let excitement trickle into her thoughts. "Sure."

"How about I pick you up around six on Tuesday and we go somewhere casual?" His warm tone touched something deep in her, releasing a flash of lust to bloom throughout her body.

"I'd like that. Bryce?"

"Yes?" Her lust ratcheted up a notch.

Slowly releasing her pent-up breath, she said, "Thanks for understanding that I need to take this slow."

"You're worth it."

Rosemary stared down at the mop in her hand and picked up the bucket of water. Pouring it out, she heard the doorbell rang. Wiping her hands on a rag, she headed to open the door.

"What are you doing cleaning house on such a lovely day?" Roger's broad shoulders filled up the doorway.

"Uh, hi Roger. What's up with you this morning?"

"Can I come in?" He tilted his head and raised an eyebrow.

"Sure. I was trying to catch up on housework, so ignore the mess." Rosemary led the way to the living room and sat in an armless chair while holding out a hand, indicating for Roger to sit on the sofa.

"Thanks." Roger sat with careful maneuvers to avoid hitting his knees on the coffee table.

"I have a rugby game this afternoon. Would you like to come and cheer my team on, and then I'll take you out for a burger at Nip and Sip. And if you are up for it, there's a double feature showing at that old-fashioned drive-in movie theater over in Holden." He observed her face go from perplexed to thoughtful, and finally she nodded her head.

"Let's do it. I'm going take a quick shower and I'll be ready." Rosemary got up and started down the hall.

"I'll come help you take that shower." Roger gave her what he hoped was a sexy wolfish grin.

"We'll never make it to your game." She winked and disappeared into the bedroom.

Roger sat back on the sofa, wondering how to convince Rosemary to become his permanent cheerleader and dinner date.

$$\sim$$

Rosemary jumped up, fist pumping the air, as she shouted out Roger's name. He turned to her and smiled, showing his big, white, canine teeth. *What am I doing?* He sidestepped another player, twisting his long, lean body into place. Then he passed the ball to a teammate for a try.

She cheered, but Bryce flashed across her mind. We're not going steady. Her thoughts rebelled against her feelings. Her body betrayed her as a heat began to stir in her center. Good thing Bryce couldn't sense her thoughts right now. Fear of being in a stifling relationship had her running crazy.

The game ended and she worked her way through the crowd to meet Roger.

"I could get used to you being my cheerleader," he said throwing an arm of steel around her and drawing her close. He gave her a quick peck. "Are you ready to eat?"

"I'm ravenous. You'd think I was the one playing rugby." She curled her arm around his waist, enjoying the comfortable comradery. They jumped into his Subaru SUV and headed to Nip and Sip. She couldn't take her eyes off his chiseled forearms guiding them through traffic. Once there, Roger guided her to the booth his family used and soon they were sipping beer and biting into burgers as they talked.

"So, you want to go to the drive-in tonight?" Roger's gaze searched her face.

"You've bought me dinner and given me quite the show on the field today, why don't we go back to my house and watch a movie?" Rosemary suspected being alone with Roger could lead to complications, but at the moment, she wanted the coziness of Roger wrapped around her on the couch.

"Sounds great to me. Will there be popcorn?"

"Of course." She smiled as they headed out of the restaurant. On the drive back to her apartment, she snuck a peek at Roger as he handled his SUV with ease through the streets. She relaxed into the seat and tried not to think of Bryce.

On entering her apartment, she threw her purse on the entry table and handed Roger the television remote.

"You find a movie on the service, and I'll make popcorn," Rosemary headed to the kitchen, while Roger clicked through the movie selections. Soon, she returned with a tray with popcorn and beer. Handing him a drink, she sat down beside him.

"What did you choose?"

"Vampires Beurre'," he said, watching for her reaction.

"Isn't that the French movie where the vamps all royally get plastered from drinking bad blood and go on a killing spree?"

"Oh yeah," he smiled. "And the *weres* all come to the rescue."

"I thought you liked vampires?"

"Some of them are okay." He leaned back, putting an arm around her shoulders and tucking her next to him. She wriggled closer to him and grabbed a handful of popcorn. As she watched the movie, the hot and heavy romance between the male and female werewolf awakened her desires. Roger's warmth and the smell of the sandalwood soap he used gave her several naughty ideas. *I only promised Bryce to give him a chance. Not to be exclusive.* Her small hand found a place to rest on Roger's solid chest. He picked it up with his strong, tanned hand and kissed her pale freckled fingers. When she didn't pull back, he began to lick her palm gently.

"Umm, buttery popcorn, my favorite flavor of witch," he said. Leisurely, he worked his way up her arm with a stop to kiss or nip ending at her lips. He paused, looking into her eyes with a heat that warmed her to her toes.

"It's been awhile. Do you want this?"

She closed her eyes to block out the voice in her head screaming Bryce's name and nodded. She knew Roger. Feeling free, she drew his mouth down to hers and kissed him lightly at first, and then she lost herself in his scent and fire. Her tongue plunged into his lips, igniting his barely controlled passion. When his strong arms lifted her onto his lap, she felt safe. Her body settled to face him, aware of his hard need jumping to life. Long, dark hair glided over her hands while he unbuttoned her top to reveal a black cutout bra straining to hold her breasts. With a primitive growl, he lowered his face to capture a stiff nipple encased in the lace and blew warm, wet air until she screamed in ecstasy. The bra became a blur, as he ripped it off and fondled her sizzling globes in his hands. She tugged at his shirt, rewarding herself with his bare chest. Nails scraped across his nipples resulted in a howl. His erection throbbed against her sensitive center.

"Did you like that?" Her eyes sizzled with sin.

"Yes," he panted. "Do you like this?" His hand slid down her pants and circled her nub of nerves.

Her face answered the question, as she threw back her head and moaned. A flash of light warned her of the change coming. She realized the bottle of werewort sat untaken on her bathroom vanity. The wolf within her threw herself against the cage Rosemary created and started the conversion.

She. Didn't. Care.

Realization dawned on Roger's face. He stood bringing her with him and removed the rest of her clothes, before she ripped through them. Naked and seething with sexual heat, she reached for him. He stripped and gathered her into his arms. She licked his lips, before nipping the bottom one. His eyes flashed at the blaze of pain. Then he nuzzled her neck, distributing tiny bites down to her breasts. Between her legs, honey flowed, drawing him there to taste her essence. Each stroke of his rough tongue drove her deeper into animal lust until she pushed him on his back and started for his erection. Before she could manage a taste, he grabbed her and turned her, pushing her onto all fours to take his pulsing penis. He roared, shoving into her ready passageway. She snarled, meeting his fury with desperate thrusts of her own.

"Yes. Yes!" she shouted, close to the release she needed. He grunted and then strummed her clit, sending them both over the edge.

"Yes, yes, yes! No...no!" she cried. Bones cracked and claws erupted as she shifted, sending her into a world of darkness.

CHAPTER 6

The next morning, Rosemary started awake to the scent of sex and wolf. She shut her eyes in a grimace as a small shudder passed through her. Eyes flying open, she glanced down at her arm in a panic. *No fur. That's good.* Raising up, she breathed a sigh of relief, realizing she was alone. She slapped her forehead as memories awakened. Wrong thing to do. The unexpected shifting from last night made her head pound in pain this morning. She folded back the covers with slow precision and discovered a note on top of the books piled on her nightstand that said:

Gone to work. Loved the evening, my sexy little wolf.

Love ya,

Roger

Her head turned up the rhythm of the pounding. At least he was gone. She breathed out her relief. *Oh, my Goddess! What was she going to say to him? More importantly, what was she going to say to Bryce?* She searched her memories. Fear ate at her thoughts. She couldn't remember what she did after she changed. With luck, it would come later, but now there was an office of patients to heal. She rushed through her shower, dressing while drinking a green smoothie laced with aspirin to ease her headache. Throwing a glance around her living room, she picked her way through the debris. The beige sofa gaped open from what she guessed was a tear from claws. Probably hers. A cold chill made her shiver. Often when she shifted, she would black out the events while she was a wolf. She couldn't afford for this to happen again. She was headed out the door when she grabbed the bottle of werewort and squirted a dropper full into her mouth.

"Yuk, that's nasty," she said, *but necessary after last night.* The door locked, she headed to the office.

⁓

Rosemary unlocked the front door to allow Roberta, a pregnant werewolf, to waddle into the waiting room, followed by Fred, a vampire who almost rear-ended her before he opened his eyes.

"Good morning, I'll be right with both of you." Rosemary's schedule popped up on the computer as she set an appointment for the werecat on the phone. This Monday morning was crazier than usual. The ache in her head went up a notch. *Oh God! She did the dirty with Roger.* Memories started to unfold in her mind. Ignoring them for the moment, she headed to her patients.

"Okay, Roberta, let's get you started in exam room one." Rosemary handed Roberta a gown to change into, making sure she was settled. In record time, she made it back to the waiting room to guide a droopy-eyed vampire to room two.

"Hi, Fred. You're either up very late or very early, which is it?"

"I can't seem to go to sleep! Some vampires sack out at the first hint of light, but I'm not one of them. Can you prescribe something to help me?"

"Let me check your blood first to make sure there's nothing unusual. Take a seat while I grab my supplies and check on the patient in room one. I'm finding new uses every day for that ultrasound you provided. Thanks again for your generosity."

"Glad to help. The community needs you," Fred said with a toothy grin.

"I'm going to dim the lights, and I'll be right back to take a sample of your blood." Rosemary smiled and hurried to check on her first scheduled patient. Halfway down the hall, the thought plowed into her. Would *Roger keep his mouth shut?* She didn't see that happening. *Oh, crap!* She turned the knob to exam room two and walked in.

"How's it going this morning, Roberta? Those pups kicking and moving like they were last time?"

"You betcha! They're keeping me up nights now. I think they take after their father."

"Let's take a peek then. Why don't you head to the bathroom and give me a urine sample, then meet me in the room across the hall?" She escorted Roberta to the bathroom. "I'm going to get a blood sample from another patient and then be right back."

"I'll be here."

"Do you know any good nurses who would be interested in working here? I'm meeting myself coming and going!"

"Not off the top of my head, but I'll think about it."

"Thanks. I'll be right back." *How do I get Roger to keep his mouth shut?* With no time to ponder, Rosemary scooted into exam room two. "Hi, Fred, let me slip my headlamp on and turn the overhead light off."

"You would think bright lights would make me sleepy, wouldn't you?" He laughed.

"One would think." Rosemary's lips curved into a grin as she prepared to take his blood. "Is there a good vein anywhere in this arm?"

"Vamps always know where their good veins are," he laughed as he pointed to a prominent one.

Rosemary slipped the needle in and out, drawing Fred's blood. Placing the blood in a holder, she sat down across from him. "I want to check out your eyes to make sure everything is okay with them."

He nodded, flinching when the bright light illuminated his eye.

"Sorry, bright lights are the only way I can tell if your inner eyelids are functioning." She wiped a clear tear before it could run down his cheek. She chuckled to herself at the misconceptions about vampires. They didn't cry blood. Their bodies did have some differences, but they resembled humans more than not. She finished and handed him a box of tissues.

"Your eyes look fine. I'll run your bloodwork and see what pops up." She headed out of the room and dropped it off in the lab to start the processing. On the return to Roberta, a vision popped into Rosemary's head. She was in her wolf form howling with pleasure as a shifted Roger took her from behind on the front lawn while her neighbors watched in fascinated horror. A blush crept over her face as she shook her head. Thankful they wouldn't recognize her as a wolf, she pulled herself together and knocked on the door to alert Roberta.

"I'm ready."

Rosemary opened the door to see Roberta's face beam in anticipation. "Okay, here comes the cold gel. This one smells like lavender." Rosemary squirted a dab on Roberta's abdomen and started running the scanner across Roberta's wide expanse of tummy.

"Look, Roberta, you can see their little hearts beating."

"Are they normal? Are they okay?"

Rosemary analyzed the screen with a sharp glance. She dreaded telling new moms their child was not healthy. "They're just fine. They're healthy and well positioned for twins. I want you to be extremely careful this next week with the full moon. Let Lester be the big bad hunter for you this month."

"Aw, he's such an excited daddy. He's planning big things for those little pups."

"He'll have them soon enough. You're due in a couple of months. Are you ready?"

"The nursery is set up with fresh supplies for human and wolf babies. No matter whether I'm in human or wolf form, we'll be ready."

Rosemary finished the exam and handed her a small brown bottle.

"Take two droppers a day with your meals of this Birth Drops tincture. The herbs, Blue Cohosh and Raspberry leaves, will help the birth go easier and make sure the twins are well nourished. Any questions?"

"Nope. I'll be back in a couple of weeks."

Rosemary stopped in the lab to grab Fred's results, when a new thought bubbled up. *What if her moment of weakness gave Roger the idea she was ready to settle down and marry him?* She filled her lungs with a long breath and blew it out slowly with the intention of relaxing before she zipped into exam room two. "Guess what, Fred? It's a simple cure."

"Really? Nothing serious?" Fred put his hand up to cover a yawn.

"It seems you need some magnesium and calcium to turn on your brain's sleep centers. Your blood test showed you were extremely low."

"Huh, how'd that happen?" Fred twisted his mouth in confusion.

"Vampires are dependent on the quality of their blood sources. Here are some supplements that are specifically made for vamps. Take two now and two after every feeding for the next week."

"I should have known cheap blood is no bargain." Fred laughed and gave Rosemary a hug. "Thanks. Do I need to check with you after a week?"

"Only if you aren't sleeping normally."

"Thanks. As Mayor, I am grateful for you choosing to set up your practice in our city."

"I appreciate your support. Now, go get some sleep." Rosemary waved him to the door, just as another patient walked in.

Exhausted from the night before and the hectic morning, four hours later, Rosemary collapsed in front of the computer, head in hands, grateful it was lunchtime. She blankly stared at the computer screen, hoping it would give her the answers on how to navigate this mess. Roger or Bryce? Any question vanished after last night. She had no idea if she could trust another vampire, but she was sure she didn't want to give her neighbors anything more to gossip about. She glanced out the front window and caught a glimpse of a tall, broad-shouldered man opening the door and strolling in.

"Hi, Darling, have you got something for a love-sick wolf?"

Rosemary's face grinned, but inside, everything clinched. As casually as she could, she asked, "Who're you sniffing around today?"

Roger picked her up and swung her around the small waiting room, holding her aloft as he planted a big kiss on her lips. "You know

I've wanted you for some time. After our date yesterday, all I could think about was you." He lowered her into his embrace.

"You date a whole pack of girls." She put her hands flat on his chest, preparing to push away.

Grabbing her hands to hold her close, he said, "Yeah, but I want you as my main momma. Think of the cute little wolves we would make."

"And what if they turned out to be witches?"

"I'd love them too." Roger gazed into her face and sighed. "Rosemary, the sex we had the last night was great, but what I crave is you in the stands cheering for me and sitting at the dinner table sharing our fries. We've done this dance for a couple of years now. I love you."

"I love you too, but more as a friend. We've been over this." She tried to turn, but he held her.

"Yes, but I thought you'd come to your senses. You aren't seeing anyone, and we're both *weres*. Who's going to understand you like I do? Hell, I'd even let you have your occasional flings, if you don't mind mine." He dropped to one knee, kissing her hands. "Whatddaya say? Marry me?"

She jerked her hands free and whirled away from him. "I'm sorry. Last night was great, but as I have explained before, I'm not looking for anything long term with you." The silence was thick with frustration tinged with pain. "Besides, I am seeing someone right now."

He stood up. With a smirk, he said, "Knowing you, it's not serious."

Rosemary's brows came down and her mouth tightened.

"Come on; don't get mad at me for telling you the truth."

She took a breath and looked him in the eyes. "I think it might be serious this time. I want to find out."

"Who is it?" Roger barked.

"He's new in town. Bryce Gold."

"The vampire they brought in for the Community Blood Bank? Are you out of your mind? He'll want you completely to himself."

"I'm aware of that aspect of vampires."

"You should be. But are you aware he's just playing with you? Besides, you belong with the wolves."

"Roger," she said laying her hand on his arm, "I belong to the whole GDB community. I swore to heal and help everyone."

"Yeah, okay," He looked at her and sighed. "But, if he hurts you like Leon did, or you find you don't love him, you know I'll always love you, don't you?"

She wrapped her arms around his waist, hugging him as tears threatened to spill from her eyes. "I know, I know, and I will always love you as a friend."

"With benefits?" He pulled back, searching her face with his eyes and smiled.

"Probably not for a while."

He wrapped his arms around her and pulled her close. His lips met hers with an animal passion that frightened her as much as it aroused her. She breathed in his scent, finding herself not caring they were in her waiting room. Just as she realized what she was doing, he ended the kiss.

"Just to remind you of what you'll be missing." He grinned and headed out the door leaving her dazed.

Head shaking, Rosemary walked to her office and tucked into the chicken salad she brought for a quick lunch. What had she been thinking when she agreed to go with him yesterday? What lunacy possessed her when she invited him back to her place? She didn't know if he would keep his mouth shut or not. She hoped their friendship would mean enough to him. Still contemplating how to handle Roger, she listened as He-Who-Walks-The-Night-Sky came in the door. The shaman she called Night Sky for short, came highly recommended from a mentor at med school, and come to find out, he knew her mother. She took private lessons from him to learn trance work, remote viewing, and alternative healing techniques that came in handy with her diverse clientele. He also helped her develop her psychic and magical abilities.

"Hey, Night Sky, your timing is great. I just finished lunch."

"Ah! Timing is everything." His weatherworn face crinkled into a smile. "Speaking of timing, are you ready to work on your remote viewing this afternoon?"

"Ready and willing. Can I offer you some tea or water before we start?"

"A cup of your herbal mint tea would hit the spot."

Mint and magic wafted from the cup she poured, handing it to him, before she settled in a comfortable chair.

"When practicing the exercises that you gave me last time, I peeked in on my mom and stepdad making pancakes for breakfast. They looked yummy, but of course I couldn't eat any."

"The astral body has no use for physical food. You learn quickly," he teased. "Any other successes?"

"Not really. I had trouble staying completely in trance at times. In my dreams, I'm all over the place. I want to do this right." *And make sure Leon doesn't reappear.*

"You're doing fine. We will work on your focus to help you stay in trance. Are you ready to try it today?"

"Sure," she said as she leaned back in her recliner to get comfortable.

He rolled the desk chair to where he could observe her and sat.

"Relax and breathe deeply to clear your body of any negativity. Starting with one, take a deep breath and hold. Now, release, allowing the air to flow out, taking all the tensions, all the strains."

Rosemary's body relaxed and her mind released the morning's concerns.

Night Sky continued in his low gravelly voice that somehow soothed her. "Imagine you are walking on a sandy beach and with every step you take and every beat of your heart, you become more and more relaxed. You come to a gorgeous rainbow staircase and find yourself ready to walk up this staircase to meet with your guides. Step on the first step which is red and become the color red."

Rosemary's base chakra lit up and power flowed into her womb.

Night Sky's voice urged her on. "You embrace the energy and passion this color gives to you. Step on the next stair which is orange and become the color orange, full of creativity and sexual vitality. You are the color orange." He led her through the rest of the colors until she reached the top of the stairs. There she stepped into pure white light and began to talk with two of her spirit guides.

"Allow yourself to come to me, Rosemary." Amber, the spirit guide in charge of her trance work, held out a pale, slender arm motioning Rosemary to take her hand.

Jet, her spirit guide for scanning energies, took her astral arm in his strong grip and said, "Walk with me. I'll make sure nothing happens to you." She followed their lead while listening to Night Sky's instructions in the background.

"You made it," Amber exclaimed, blonde curls bouncing as she took Rosemary's other arm. "Now, imagine where you want to go next and concentrate on it."

Rosemary projected herself into Bryce's bedroom, where she saw him sleeping peacefully. She also saw by his bed an open jeweler's box containing a stunning sapphire necklace. Guilt struck her as she thought about last night with Roger.

Bryce twitched his nose and turned to lie on his back. With a start, she realized she needed to leave before Bryce sensed her astral body and caught her spying. Before she could project herself elsewhere, her curiosity took over. She glanced at his erection. His member reached to the ceiling in all its glory, hard, huge, and handsome. Her physical body responded with blood rushing to her lady parts. Unbalanced, her astral body struggled for focus.

She concentrated on the next destination. The last thing she wanted was to explain to Night Sky why she crashed out of trance.

Amber and Jet chuckled at her reaction.

"Okay, enough snooping, let's go somewhere else," Amber said. "You're good at this as long as you pay attention."

"My training started with me staring at a candle an hour at a time. Focus I've got, usually," Rosemary replied. "Bryce, he, well, he distracts me." Jet and Amber rolled their eyes and took her arms.

Night Sky's counting sounded faint to Rosemary as she fought to return to her body. "One, you are on your way back." When he reached five, she opened her eyes and took a moment to acclimate to her surroundings. "Are you okay?"

She sat for a moment, getting her bearings while rubbing her eyes. "I'm fine. I went deep into trance, for the most part."

"You held your own, but, I noticed you slipped for a moment. Were you visiting someone with whom you have an intense emotional connection?"

Rosemary blushed and simply answered, "Yes."

Night Sky winked and said, "I hope he was worth it. Eat a couple of oranges tonight to help with any fatigue. For our next lesson, you need to practice your remote viewing on someone new. You also, need to practice focusing your concentration."

"I can. I will."

"We've done enough today." Night Sky waved goodbye, allowing the quiet of her office to gather around her. Her brow pulled downward as she considered how much Bryce distracted her. This was new territory for her.

It was a quarter to six, and Rosemary was ready to go home and think about what she had seen in her trance, when the phone rang.

"Rosemary, it's Edward, Something's wrong with Jonathan. I can't wake him up."

"I'll be right there. Is he breathing? Can you find a pulse?"

"Yes, to both questions. He appears normal, but he won't wake up."

"Stay with him. See you in a few minutes." She grabbed her vampire emergency bag containing extra blood and headed to their home. Vampire's hearts beat slower than a human heart. Gratitude flooded her for Edward's exceptional senses finding Jonathan's pulse. She was raising her hand to the doorbell when Edward opened the door.

"Thank the gods you're here!" Edward said, and then swayed. She put a hand on his arm and had him sit down.

"Edward, tell me slowly, what led up to this."

"His was fine when we went to bed this morning around nine after having a late drink. This evening, around five thirty, I got up and tried to wake him, but he wouldn't respond. He was breathing and had a slow pulse. I didn't know what else to do."

"Let's take a look," she said collecting her equipment.

"I, uh, okay. He does sleep in the nude."

"I've seen nude vampires before. I know it keeps you more comfortable with your low body temperature." She tried not to think of the last vampire she observed sleeping in the nude.

Edward nodded and led her to a large bedroom lit by a small Tiffany lamp on a large walnut dresser. Her werewolf eyes helped her manage the shadow-laden room, and the scent of dark patchouli guided her to Jonathan. He was uncovered, lying face-up, on the large custom-made bed. She slowly walked over to him and gently said his name. When he didn't respond, she carefully lifted his lips to inspect his fangs. They were tucked up in their slots, indicating he wasn't hungry, mad, frightened, or horny.

Edward held Jonathan's arm in case he woke, while she took a small sample of blood.

"Thanks. While I run this sample, could you bring the blood you both drank before you went to bed?"

Edward headed to the kitchen at top speed and returned within seconds with two bottles of blood.

She opened the top of the small portable lab and unfolded the sections. The blood was processing in minutes. The vampire community made generous contributions to make sure she was supplied with equipment. The timer sounded, indicating the test was complete. Rosemary studied the results.

"Does Jonathan take sleeping pills, because that's what's in his blood?"

"No, not that I know of. He did drink some of this blood last night."

She reached for the bottle of blood Edward brought to her and read the card on it.

"It was a present from Victor at the morgue," Edward explained to her inquiring glance. "I finished off a bottle we had from the party, and Jonathan opened this one."

"How much did he drink?" she asked as she started testing it.

"A couple of glasses. He hadn't drunk much yesterday and was hungry."

In a couple of minutes, she read the results. "Well, it appears this blood is full of sleeping medicine. Did Victor mention the source of the blood?"

"No, and we didn't ask. Victor is usually careful. He did say it came from a suicide."

"The good news is Jonathan will be okay. The bad news is he will be very cranky when he wakes up. He may sleep for twenty-four hours at this point, but his vital signs are in a normal range for a vamp. I'll give him a transfusion that will help thin the sleeping medicine out of his system. If he does sleep for more than twenty-four hours, this extra blood will insure there's enough in his system to lessen the headache he's sure to experience on waking."

"Thank you, thank you, thank you," Edward said crying and hugging her at the same time. "I don't know what I'd do if I lost him."

"It's going to be okay. You caught it in time before he got too weak. Jonathan is a strong vamp, and he will be around for many years to come," she said as she patted him on the back. "Now help me set this up and we'll get the transfusion started."

She was there another hour, making sure Jonathan was okay. She went to do a last check on him and take out the IV when he stirred.

Red eyes glowing in the darkened room, he jerked awake. Jonathan paused, and then he moaned. "Oh-h-h shit! I feel awful."

Rosemary and Edward surrounded him, but they made no sudden moves. Both had seen the damage semi-conscious vampires could do.

"Don't move, you're hooked up to an IV," Rosemary's eyes scanned his aura for any problems. When it was obvious he recognized her, she continued. "We're just about finished. You got some bad blood last night. It had enough sleeping pills in it to kill a human."

"I don't mean to sound ungrateful, because I'm very thankful you're here, but how long will this headache last?"

"Lucky you're a vampire, and a strong one at that. I was afraid you were going to be out another twelve hours. Since you're awake now, I predict you'll be fine by tomorrow night. Now lie still while I get this needle out of your arm."

Edward stoked Jonathan's other hand. "I thought I'd lost you."

Jonathan managed a weak grin. "I'm yours for eternity, Baby."

Edward leaned in to kiss him on the lips gently.

A moment of wonder from witnessing the love and devotion between the two men sparked a deep longing within Rosemary. She let them have a second. Then she spoke, "Rest tonight and tomorrow. If you get weak, the headache gets worse, or anything you think isn't normal, call me."

"Thank you. I'm going to rest now," Jonathan squeezed her hand, and then closed his eyes.

Edward walked her to the door and gave her a big hug.

"He is going to be okay, isn't he?" Edward asked.

"He'll be fine. You need to get some rest now too," she said giving him a hug.

"How's things with Bryce?" Edward asked.

Rosemary paused, deciding how to answer him. Edward and Jonathan supported her not only because of their friendship, but also because of the asset, she was to the community.

"We are going on a supper date tomorrow evening. I'll call and fill you two in on how it went."

"He's being a perfect gentleman?"

"Absolutely. You have treated me with such kindness and respect ever since I walked into your CPA office years ago. Now, you obviously care enough about me to protect my heart, but I think this is a good thing with Bryce. I'm willing to take the risk to find out." She looked into his tired eyes.

"That's good. I'll be waiting for your call." The big vampire's hands shook as he kissed the top of her head. "Thank you for saving Jonathan."

She handed him a glass of blood and said, "Drink up. You've thanked me enough. Go take care of your man and get some rest."

With a goofy grin, he took the glass and headed back to Jonathan.

As Rosemary drove home, relief bubbled up in her at Jonathan's quick recovery. They were family to her. Now, she needed to get home and get some sleep. Tomorrow night, she needed to be awake for her date with Bryce.

CHAPTER 7

Can this day get any longer? Rosemary walked from the exam room to her office to grab her prescription pad. The patient, human, needed a regular steroid cream for a rash. The young man walked out the door with prescription in hand, and she grabbed a cup of coffee to go as she turned off the machine. Four o'clock and she wanted to be home. The clinic door clicked behind her as she headed to her car, shivering with excitement at the thought of her date with Bryce tonight.

At home, she jumped in the shower and lathered up her legs, shaving them as smooth as fine silk. After she dried, came a pair of khaki pants and a low-cut black sweater that showed off her girls as she shook them a bit to get them plumped and pretty. Next, she fastened her favorite blue moonstone necklace set in silver around her neck, followed with earrings to match. Both caught the color of her eyes. She finished with a perfume guaranteed to make a vampire's fangs drop at first whiff. The black lacy bra and panties with red trim insured his complete attention if they found themselves in the bedroom.

The doorbell rang, and she jumped in anticipation. Bryce was turned, staring off into space, when she opened the door. Treated to the sight of his tan slacks that molded to his agreeable-to-gaze-at butt, her breath hitched. He spun around revealing a golden-brown curl of chest hair peeking out of the open collar of his white shirt. Her eyes lifted to his face. They were met with eyes, crinkled into a smile, gracing a strong forehead, and a nose that curved down just enough to bring her gaze to his lush, sensual mouth.

His eyes drank her in before capturing her lips in a kiss. "Hello beautiful, are you ready to go?"

The scent of exotic oils mingled with sexy man brought on a quiver. She straightened her posture, her breasts coming to attention. "I'm looking forward to tonight. Where're you taking me to eat, Tall, Dark and Charming?"

"How do you feel about picnics?" He opened the car door for her.

"Love 'em!" She hopped in.

He slid into the driver's seat. "Good, I packed sandwiches and sides. What would you think about eating them on the lake while we bask in nature?"

"In the dark? All alone?" Rosemary raised her hand to her chest in mock horror.

"It's still twilight, although I do some of my best work in the dark." Bryce bounced his eyebrows at her, while a grin lifted the corner of his mouth. "Besides, this is at a lake house a friend loaned me for the evening." Bryce stopped and his brows came together in a way that endeared him to Rosemary. "That is, if you're okay being with me in a private place?"

"I trust you," she reassured him. *It's me I don't trust.*

"I trust you too," he said, reaching to smooth a curl of her red hair gone rogue. "Rosemary, I've been thinking. I… I want to get to know you better."

"You don't waste any time, do you?" She cocked an eyebrow in his direction.

"No, NO, that's not what I mean. I know you've been hurt in the past."

"Yes, so?"

"Well, I want to suggest we hold off on making love to give ourselves time to become acquainted with each other."

"You mean I shaved my legs for nothing?" Rosemary rubbed her hand down her thigh. Her smile covered her flash of temper. She had plans for that body of his tonight.

"Oh darling, you're killing me," Bryce groaned. "In my imagination, those long legs have wrapped around me in a variety of ways. But for tonight, let's see if we're on the same page before we end up on the same sheets." He glanced at her with a tight grin.

"If you think so," she said, shoulders dropping. *He wasn't serious, was he?* She planned to make him suffer. She squeezed her shoulders, making her cleavage increase.

Bryce moaned and then started the car.

She admired his willpower. However, the night was young and she came prepared for mind-altering sex.

The drive through the countryside was tense as her anger expanded with her thoughts. She needed to get laid. Damn it! How dare him not find her sexy. Long-established self-doubts wormed their way into her heart.

The too quiet car prompted Bryce to ask, "Are you angry with me?"

"Yes! No. Maybe. I think you've hurt my feelings." Confusion draped over Rosemary like a wet blanket.

Bryce shot his brown eyes towards her. "I'm sorry. Believe me, I want you, but I don't want either one of us to get hurt." He parked the car in the driveway of the lake house.

"I understand that and want to take it slow. I usually express myself through my physical interactions, forgetting to include my heart." Eyes downcast, she was afraid to look up.

Bryce reached across the car and lifted her chin. "Rosemary, I think you're hot. I also think you're smart, funny, loyal, and a good friend. Can we get past this and enjoy our evening?"

A single tear slid down her cheek as she nodded her agreement. "Just remember, vampire, I don't have all the time in the world." Her smile brought the release of a long-held breath from Bryce.

～

Arm in arm, they walked up the driveway and entered the house through a trellis- framed porch. Bryce unlocked the double glass-paned doors, allowing her to enter first. A wall of floor-to-ceiling windows offered a view of the serene lake. Rosemary walked to the windows, admiring the rich oak floors and the inlaid marble fireplace. She turned to comment to Bryce and noticed the open loft area.

"It's beautiful. Did I count right? Is this lake house three stories?"

Bryce beamed at her enthusiasm and answered, "Three floors and all the amenities." He joined her at the windows. "Don't you love the way the moonlight dances in little sparkles off the water?"

The realization that Bryce was a warrior with the heart of a poet made her rethink her earlier reactions. Determined to make it up to him, she wrapped her arm around his waist and kissed him on the cheek. "The moonlight is lovely, dancing on the water. Can we eat outside?"

He wrapped a protective arm around her, guiding her to the comfortable chairs on the private deck. "You're gorgeous this evening." He held her hands, looking with a penetrating gaze that shot all the way to her center of pleasure.

"You're going to make it hard to concentrate tonight!"

"That's not the only thing that's getting hard tonight." He winked at her.

"What a tease, you naughty vampire."

He leaned in close to her and whispered, "You like bad boys, don't you," as he breathed in her perfume and gently licked her ear.

For a split second, Leon crossed her mind. She pushed the memory of him making fun of shifters, not aware of her heritage. She didn't like all bad boys. Pulling back, she snorted. "Keep that up and there will be no hope of keeping our hands off of each other."

Guiding her into a chair, he kissed the top of her head as he reached for the wine.

"Red or white?" He held up a bottle of each.

"I always like white with my tuna and peanut butter sandwich," Rosemary said. "You obviously quizzed Jonathan about what I like to eat."

Bryce offered an amused grin and took a drink of his blood smoothie.

After they both were sated, she turned to him and asked, "I'm confused. Do you find me sexy?"

Bryce smiled while shaking his head. "I'm walking around with a hard-on like a teenage boy instead of a four-hundred-and-two-year old vampire. I think it's obvious how much I want to have sex with you. However, what I want more is a soul meshing, I-can-finish-your-sentences, you-are-the-love-of-my-life, long-term relationship. Relationships with that kind of connection take some time to grow."

"You may know what you want," she said hesitating, "but I don't. I admit it scares me because you're a vampire, but statements like that have me wondering if there's taxi service out here."

"I'll take you home anytime you're ready to go. However, I hope you hear me out." His eyes burned with the intensity of his feelings.

"My mission for the last couple of years was to set up my practice, and frankly, I'm not sure I can be in a monogamous relationship with anyone, let alone a vampire. Then, if you wanted me to turn, I'm not sure I could do it." She whispered.

Bryce stood up and pulled her towards him, "I wouldn't ask anyone to go through what I do as a vampire. There are advantages, such as immortality, but there are dangers too."

Rosemary considered his words. She cleared her throat and asked, "Would you bite me if we had sex?"

Bryce stroked the side of her face, his finger pausing at her throat. "Only if you asked me to. I often drink a glass of blood before sex to insure I keep my control. However, allowing a vampire to taste your blood is the ultimate gift of trust and love. Plus, it gives our partners one hell of an orgasm." He sat back down on a loveseat covered in white silk, pulling her with him. "Now, if you were to bite back and take in enough blood, you'd turn, but I suspect as a healthcare provider to GDBs, you know that."

"You're right. I would have to be drained of most of my blood and take in enough of yours or another vamp's to start the process. I've helped a few vampires through a messy change. I've seen cases where the person hasn't been completely drained of their blood, inhibiting the vampire virus from changing the body. They go back and forth with horrible spasms. Out of curiosity, if I asked you to turn me someday in the future, would you?"

"It depends on the circumstances, such as where our relationship is, how old you are, or why you want to turn. After being married to me for at least a couple of years, you will understand the pros, as well as the cons."

"Oh." She rubbed the smooth tassels of the loveseat between her fingers, unsure of what to say.

"I turned three of my wives. It's not something you can reverse. You'd need to be sure. Now, let me ask you a question. How will you deal with the fact I can't get you pregnant?"

"Good question." Rosemary frowned. "I don't think I could carry someone else's child if I was your wife, but I wouldn't mind adopting."

Bryce growled softly, "I don't think I could stand someone else getting you pregnant. However, if you really wanted a child, I would consider adopting."

"Knowing how you feel, that's a generous offer. With my work schedule and our circumstances, I'm not sure I could handle having a child. I'm also worried about what might slither forth from my genetic pool," Rosemary said with a nervous smile.

"Another reason to be cautious. Some vampires reproduce with help. I found it less than successful the few times I tried with a couple my human wives."

"Really, hmm, I want to go back to the women you did turn. Why did they decide to become vampires and where are they?"

Bryce paused a moment and then said, "You know about my first wife, Helen." Bryce stared off into the dark night sky for a moment. "A fiery redhead similar to you, I turned her on our twentieth wedding anniversary, which gave us another fifty years together."

Rosemary drew in a deep breath and finally released it.

"Shall I continue?" Bryce's eyes widened.

Rosemary nodded, hugging her midriff.

"Andrea, my second wife and I had issues because I married her on the rebound. She convinced me turning her would help our marriage. On our fifth wedding anniversary, I turned her. In less than five years, we divorced. Last I heard, she's still alive, but I'm not sure where."

"Do you hear from her at all?"

Bryce shifted uncomfortably for a moment before answering. "Yes, she pops in when I least expect it." Tears glistened in his eyes. "My last wife, Jeanne, was a kind and trusting soul."

"It's okay; you don't have to go on." Rosemary took his hand and squeezed lightly.

"Yes, I do. A couple of vampires were killing humans by feeding until they were drained. In a fight over territory and ethics, the female vampire, the wife of the other vampire was killed. Although I didn't kill her, he thought I did. Jonathan, Rhys, and I moved to the United States in an effort to put distance from him."

Hands entwined, her thumb made delicate circles on the back of his hand. Pain poured off of him as he sat, silent.

His eyes met hers, a tear escaping. "Nine years passed. We thought he'd given up. I married Jeanne in June of 1920, and for fifty years, we lived in bliss before he found us."

Bryce leaned forward, resting his face in his hands. "He stalked Jeanne, and eventually he raped and beheaded her."

She moved to stroke his back. "I'm sorry." She rubbed his shoulders, feeling his tight muscles begin to relax. What else should she say?

"Have you killed before?" She didn't mean for it to sound abrupt.

"Yes, I have." He lifted his head to look her in the eyes. "Without remorse, the first few years after I was turned. Then, I started to understand how to use my newfound abilities to help rather than hurt. I am trying to make up for all the killing and violence from my past."

She crossed her arms over her chest before asking, "Would you ever kill again?"

"I'm a vampire. It's possible." Bryce breathed in deeply while rubbing his hands over his face. "I'm sorry; I probably scared you off."

"You've given me plenty to consider, but no you haven't. Bryce, as much as it frightens me, I fear losing something extraordinary if I don't give this a try."

"You mean it?" He stopped, glancing over the lake as she considered her answer. Before she responded, he said, "Rosemary, I locked my heart away for the last forty years not wanting to take a chance on love. Killing is part of my life, which can be hard to accept. Now, I only kill if it's necessary. Please, be sure you can accept all of me, because I'm falling for you. Too fast probably, but there's something about you that calls to me."

"Bryce, it's obvious you're a decent guy. Jonathan and Edward respect you. I'd never lead you on, but I'm... I'm scared that I won't be able to live up to what you're looking for." *Especially, if I do something stupid like fucking Roger again.*

The breath she was holding flowed from her. "The killing does concern me, since I'm dedicated to preserving life, and there is violence in the vampire world. However, my biggest fear is that I've done my own thing for years, which makes being in an exclusive relationship a big change. I want to try. Can you be patient while I adjust?" She reached over and touched his shoulder.

"Sweetheart," he said, wrapping his arms around her, "four hundred and two years have taught me patience. I think we can work it out."

Rosemary leaned into him, her hand on his cheek.

"You make me hot," he said touching his lips to hers. "Does this mean we are going steady?" His face broadening into a grin.

"I believe it does." Rosemary smiled shyly.

"Good. I want to give you a little gift to let you know how much you mean to me." With twinkling eyes, he handed her a jeweler's box. Touching the box with reverence, she opened it.

"Oh my God! Are those sapphires? They're beautiful!"

"Jonathan told me they were your favorite."

"They are. Help me with it, please," she said, as she removed her moonstones. Bryce carefully draped the necklace around her neck, and as he fastened it, his fingers touched her flesh. She felt his hand tremble and sensed his rush of excitement as their bodies responded to each other. She led him inside to look in a mirror before the warmth spreading through her body got out of hand. Looking at her reflection, she saw the necklace from her trance. The cornflower blue stones sparkled surrounded by small diamonds placed to make the necklace catch the light. Her stomach fluttered when she saw Bryce's expression. He stood behind her, hands on her shoulders, and placed a kiss on her cheek.

"Perfect."

"Thank you. They're gorgeous, but not necessary."

"I can take them back, if you'd rather?" he said.

"I don't think so!" She smiled back and reached to kiss him. He gathered her in his arms, and they kissed. For a moment, they just held each other and didn't move or say a word. Then the kiss deepened, and the fire between them flared as their bodies pressed close and the room got hot. Their lips explored each other in a dance of passion. Rosemary reveled in his masculine spice as he buried his nose in the crook of her neck. Bryce backed off first.

"I want you, but only if you're sure." His low husky voice caught in his throat. Holding her at arm's length, he seemed to regain control. "Take time to think about what we've talked about tonight."

Rosemary raised her face, eyes half-closed and sighed, "Okay, I understand." They gathered their things and in a comfortable silence headed back to town. At her apartment, he walked her to the door and kissed her briefly on the lips. She felt his heat strike her womb, arousing her. The bulge in his slacks alerted her to his own fire.

"Would you be available for a date this Friday night?" he asked.

"I'm all yours, Mr. Gold," she smiled as his eyes twinkled.

"I'll pick you up Friday evening, my love." With a last, longing look, he closed her door.

She leaned against the door, watching him drive away. Her fears flooded her thoughts. Her career had always taken top priority. What would happen if things didn't work out with Bryce? Could she really afford to risk her reputation in this close community? Would she be walking into a nightmare where again she would not be enough or too weird for someone to love? Could she really afford to walk away from what might be her soulmate?

She turned and headed to the bedroom, sinking onto her bed lined with soft pillows. As she drifted to sleep, a small part of her soul reached for the love she never thought possible.

Now he was certain she was Bryce's new plaything. Time to teach him a lesson about sharing. Stringy brown hair whipped in the breeze as he disappeared into the night.

CHAPTER 8

Rosemary jumped when a spark of energy zapped down her arm.

"You're a powerhouse, aren't you?" She laid the clear quartz crystal with care on the black velvet cloth she created to hold her treasures. She needed a powerhouse right now. Not only did the training she receive from Night Sky assist her in her career by doing an astral check on patients, she hoped it would help on a more personal level. What was she thinking, dating a vampire?

In preparing for Night Sky's arrival, she had chosen a few of her favorites for him to use in her training as a healer. As a young girl, Rosemary spent hours collecting rocks that called to her from the beaches and gravel beds she visited. She favored what her mom labeled holey stones, or rocks with holes worn through them. The memory of her mom praising her treasures brought a smile to Rosemary's lips. Now her collection came from around the world in a variety of shapes, colors, and sizes.

The front door of her clinic opened and she greeted him, "How're you doing, this afternoon?"

"Excited to see your collection of stones. From your description, I suspect you have many helpful ones for your profession." His steps contained a bounce, following her down the hall.

She hung his well-worn denim jacket on a coatrack that resembled a silver tree, brushing off a couple of gray hairs. *He must have a dog.*

Once in her office, her favorites caught his eye.

With a nod of approval, he picked up a large stone. "Let's begin with the clear quartz crystals. They are the workhorses in any healer's collection. Their piezoelectric and pyroelectric properties can transfer, amplify, focus, store, and transform energy. As a physician or veterinarian, you can use them to facilitate healing by bringing your patients' energies back into balance." Night Sky's eyes sparked as he spoke.

"How do you know which crystals to use for what?" Rosemary's curiosity urged her to pick up one that came to a point at both ends. She planned to use a few in her healthcare practice and maybe a few more in dealing with her feelings with Bryce.

"Different crystals can produce different results. You can identify what purpose they serve by the shape of the crystal." Night Sky ran his long fingers over the stone she held, his touch following the shape.

Rosemary pondered on how to ask which crystal could help her understand Bryce. Goddess knows, her rules kept her safe, and yet her need burned with a crazy fire for him.

As if he read her thoughts, he said, "For example, this lovely is one of my favorites. Named a double-terminated crystal, energy can flow in or out of both ends. Put under your pillow, this gem will help your astral projection and intensify your lucid dreamtime in case you want to check on someone other than a patient."

Cheeks pink, Rosemary cupped the brilliant rock in her hands, her psychic talents humming. *Oh, you are definitely going to help me out with Bryce!* Her excitement flared as her energy intensified and flowed into her hands. "I can feel it! My remote viewing abilities are opening. This is incredible." *Mmm! The places I can go; the things I can find out.*

Night Sky leaned forward. "Keep that one close when you are going in trance, plus this valuable channeling quartz." He picked up a solid stone with a large seven-sided facet opposite a section shaped in a triangle. Placing it in her hand, he guided it to the center of her forehead. "What does your intuition tell you?"

For a moment, Rosemary's face scrunched in concentration. *Yes! This one will help me see my connections to Bryce.* Amazement flashed across her face. Night Sky must be reading her thoughts. "I can hear my guides more clearly. Other realms are opening for me."

"Good! This powerful crystal can help you connect with information when working in trance." With careful precision, he arranged the double-terminated crystal in her left hand and the channeling crystal in her right hand. "Are you ready to work on your remote viewing?"

"Yes." She sat, scooting down to cocoon herself in the chair, eager to experience the effects of her gems.

"Did you get permission from a patient to do an astral check in?"

"I did. He should be sleeping at this point." She bit her lip, hoping Jonathan had covered up today.

"That's good. Clients can be checked on more easily during sleep because they're usually relaxed." Induction starting, his words lulled her into a deep trance.

From there, she glided into the astral world. His voice, like a background noise, faded as she connected with her guides, Jet and Amber. The confidence of her improved skills sparkled as she navigated towards Jonathan's home. Her abilities as a psychic medium had always been evident; however, training with Night Sky had honed her control. She floated over Jonathan's bed, appreciative of his nude form while he slept. She chuckled, grateful for her increased regulation over her werewolf side. *Wouldn't you know he'd be naked? Good thing I'm a professional.*

Night Sky's voice became vibrant as he suggested, "Keep your focus on your subject, and notice any unusual color to his aura. Make a mental note of what you see." Night Sky paused. "Are any other entities around your subject? Are they attached?"

"No entities and his aura is robust, tinted a pure yellow with touches of indigo indicating a well-functioning mind and spirit," Rosemary reported. Night Sky directed her through more observations to make certain of her abilities and Jonathan's health.

"He appears healthy," she said.

"Time to return." Night Sky guided her out of the trance, nodding his head in approval of her skill.

"Amazing," Rosemary said, pushing off the chair. Too late, she realized her knees were like rubber, and Night Sky caught her before she fell to the floor.

"You are doing exceptionally well, but it would be good to remember the basics. Give yourself several minutes before trying to stand." He tried to sound stern, but the big grin on his face told her he was pleased with her progress.

"I didn't realize what a treasure I had in these crystals."

"You own many tremendously useful tools."

"Can you tell me more about these?"

"They are all quartz, but with different properties," he said, as his eyes ranged over the collection. Suddenly, he caught his breath. "Oh! What a fantastic Record Keeper." Night Sky's eyes gleamed as he lifted the crystal and pointed out the small triangles raised on its surface. "These triangles often hold important information on healing, among other things. You need to sit and meditate on this one."

Rosemary reached for the stone, eager to discover what the crystal could tell her about her feelings. She needed to protect herself from any attempts to put thoughts into her mind. Her being a witch helped, but not if she didn't use her magic. Night Sky amazed her by handing her the exact stones she needed.

"This pretty is a rainbow quartz, which can give your energy a positive boost." Tiny colored lights reflected as he held it up to the nearby lamp.

Rosemary touched the quartz and marveled at the surge of energy flowing through her. *I can use this one to keep myself in trance longer.*

Intensity grew in his voice as he picked up a dark brown crystal, roughened by the earth. "This darker one is an Elestial. During its formation, it was squeezed and then allowed to grow. Feel all the natural terminations and layers over the body of the crystal." He ran a finger over the surface of the stone before handing it to her. "This is a powerful healer that can help in restoring emotional and mental states."

This one will keep me from going crazy when in trance and will help me find information on Bryce.

He spent another few minutes giving her information on her assorted stones.

"You've opened my world to millions of stones." Rosemary reached out to caress her gems. "Is it safe for me to practice using these two crystals while I'm doing trance work on my own?"

"Yes, practice as much as you can and read chapter four and five in your book on crystal healing. We will work with other minerals besides quartz next time." Night Sky threw his jacket over his shoulder, turned and gave Rosemary a wink as he left.

Frustration escaped from Rosemary in a long sigh as she switched off the lights in her office. Fears and doubts ganged up on her in the quiet building. Would she be aware if he used mind control on her? Were the voices in her head her guides or her own insecurities?

By the time she arrived home, her curiosity blossomed into an obsessive need. She decided to use her newfound skills to discover anything that would explain their connection. After dimming the lights, she lit a candle and snuggled into a comfortable chair. Confidence radiating from the channeling crystal in her right hand and security from the double-terminated quartz in her left, she started counting herself into trance.

She focused in on Bryce. They stood on a road with a sign pointing to the past and to the future. She turned to the left, heading down the road to the past. A fence appeared with several red ribbons draped over the wood. One caught her eye with shimmering movement. Latching onto the end of the ribbon, she was drawn through a veil into a past lifetime where she walked on a gravel road.

Rosemary first saw a field with corn ready for harvest and tall trees splashed with gold and red. When she breathed, a hint of wood smoke filled her nose. With a sudden insight, she remembered her name was Mary. Excited, she swayed her hips, swirling the midnight blue dress around her shapely figure as she headed to a large home lit with lanterns and candles, decorated for a party. At the doorway, she saw Bryce welcoming guests into this house, his home.

On approaching the door, she looked around, searching for someone. When Mary saw she wasn't followed, relief poured through her as she walked in the door. Body swaying to the lively fiddle music, she blinked when Bryce approached her.

"May I have this dance?" His eyes searched hers. She blushed, casting her gaze down. He lifted her chin, her eyes meeting his, and said, "That's better." A shiver started at her feet and worked its way throughout her body, but Mary danced with him.

A man with hair the color of weathered wood interrupted their dance by staggering into Mary.

"Come here, tart, you belong to me."

She cried out when he jerked her away from Bryce, feeling the depth of the bruise sure to come. With narrowed eyes, Bryce watched them leave.

Months later in this lifetime, she saw Mary, as the same man lunged into her face, breath reeking of cheap whiskey and anger. "You're nothing but a stupid whore," he shouted, slapping her with a hand the size of a small ham. Her shock made her freeze. Dark hair covered her face as the blood flowed in scarlet streams, staining her dress. Dazed, she took an uneven step. He swayed trying to grab her. In spite of her pain, she swerved, avoiding capture. Straightening his body, her husband advanced on her with more focus.

"You're useless in the kitchen and the bedroom," he bellowed, grabbing her arms and flinging her across the room into a wall. A loud crack sounded and Mary lay knocked out. He snatched his bottle.

"I'll be home for supper, you witch. Make it something I like." With a chug of the whiskey, he headed out the door.

A man came to the door, picked her up, and took her to Bryce's home, where she slipped in and out of consciousness for two days. Eventually, Mary woke to a pair of deep gray eyes and a kind face treating her wounds.

"Who're you?" she whispered weakly.

The woman shushed her and said, "My name's Donalda. You're safe now; Mr. Gold has made sure of that. Now drink this to stop the pain." As she lifted the cup to her lips, a commotion erupted outside the house. Fear seized her like an iron shackle, freezing her mid-stride. She recognized the voice. Her body moved in small difficult steps bringing her to the window. Eyes wide, she peeked out of the window as her husband approached.

"Where's my wife! I know you got that whore. She's mine! You have a wife." His red face and jerky movements made her pull away from the window and sink out of sight.

The air crackled with a lightning strike across the clear night sky, as Bryce stepped outside and said, "You are mistaken." The man stopped, his confusion spreading before him. Bryce whispered, "You are calm and will forget all about Mary. You want to travel and never come back to this town." Her husband wandered away looking muddled. Mary sat down and drank from her cup, spilling drops when Bryce opened the door.

"Are you all right, Mary?" Bryce asked.

She nodded her head. "Did...did you use magic on him?"

Bryce paused, lips tight. "I can be very convincing when I talk to people. I don't think he will bother you again."

"However, you did it, thank you." She leaned back, exhaustion taking over her body.

"You are welcome to stay here as long as you need." Bryce's concern touched her.

"Thank you." The combination of the potion and exhaustion drew her into a deep sleep.

After a few weeks, Mary healed. Donalda, Bryce, and a pale woman whom Bryce introduced as Susan, his wife, sat with her in the living room.

"What would you think of working here for me?" Bryce asked in a soft Scottish voice. Mary looked at the two women, searching for their reactions.

Satisfied they approved, she said, "I'd like that, Mr. Gold. What would I do?"

"Donalda could use a hand with the cooking and herb garden. In due course, she can teach you how to mix different healing potions."

"I'm good in the kitchen and the garden." She paused. One hand rubbing the other, she said, "I don't know much about potions, but I'm willing to learn."

"Good, it's settled." Bryce and Susan stood.

"Thank you, Mr. and Mrs. Gold," Mary said.

The weeks flew by as she cooked and tended the gardens. Donalda taught her how to make basic healing salves and tinctures. One day, Donalda asked, "Mary, could I get a small amount of blood from you to make this potion for Mr. Bryce?"

Mary stopped, with her eyes wide. "Why do you need blood?"

"Mr. Gold has a condition that is helped by fresh blood. It's okay if you don't want to. I can get it elsewhere." Donalda turned to go when she stopped her.

"Wait, not only did Mr. Gold save me, he has been nothing but kind to me. I will give you blood now and later if he needs it." Donalda nodded and motioned her to sit while she prepared to take her blood.

"This will hurt," Donalda said, making a small cut in Mary's arm and holding it over a glass container. She flinched but held her arm steady as the scarlet liquid flowed.

"What kind of condition does Mr. Gold have that requires blood?" she asked, her eyes meeting with Donalda's.

Donalda clamped her lips together and started to say something, then stopped. "Help me by holding this glass while I put a dressing on that cut." She finished patching up Mary, and then took the glass of blood from her.

"Have you ever been called a name you don't understand?"

Mary paused a moment, then nodded. "Witch, because I know what herb will heal them."

"The same happens with Mr. Gold. His body is different in it can't always make the blood he needs, requiring him to drink it."

"You mean like a vampire?" Mary backed away from Donalda, her face a mask of horror.

"That's the label some people use. But he's still the same Bryce Gold who has never raised a hand to me, never raised his voice to me, never allowed anyone to harm me since I've worked for him."

"Does he sleep in a coffin?" Mary leaned forward.

"No, he sleeps in a bed, during the daytime." Donalda paused, considering her words. "He's sort of an insomniac."

Mary took a deep breath, blowing air out of puffed cheeks. "I guess he's not going to hurt me, is he?"

"No, he'll protect you with his life."

"I can live with that." Mary thought about this conversation for the next few months. She remembered how it stung to be called a witch even though she was healing someone. Witches were supposedly old, smelly women, who ate children and cursed the neighbors. However, she smelled of the fresh mint soap she and Donalda made and she mostly ate vegetables. If Mr. Gold was a vampire, she had not seen him tear out people's throats with his fangs or turn into a bat and fly into her bedroom. No. Everything she knew and everything she had seen, told her he was a kind and honorable man, no matter what people labeled him.

Over the next five years, Mary learned Donalda's healing secrets. When Donalda lay dying, Mary was the one who gave her potions to drink.

The older woman roused herself and said, "You need to take my place now as Mr. Gold's wise woman." Exhausted, Donalda settled back in her bed, pale as the snow wrapping over the landscape outside the window.

"I will in time."

"I... he's ah... different."

"But he is kind," Mary said, helping Donalda take another drink.

"Will you keep his secret?" Donalda's desperation clutched at Mary.

"That he's a vampire?"

"You knew?" Donalda's mouth hung open.

"Shh... I guessed years ago. Why else would he need blood? I'll keep his secret and make sure he and his wife have the potions and tonics they need."

"Thank you, child. You've made my life easier and now my dying too. I can go in peace knowing he'll be taken care of." Donalda sighed and closed her eyes.

Many tears were wiped away as Mary prepared Donalda's body for burial. Her sadness fell dark on the room. Bryce, sensing her grief, handed her a handkerchief and gave her a reassuring hug. "Thanks," she said as she met his watery gaze. He rubbed his face with his strong hands to hide the tears.

"Donalda knew all the names of the herbs in the garden and what they healed. She knew how to keep everything under control here when I was gone, but most importantly, she didn't judge me for being different. What about you?"

"Here's your tonic, Mr. Gold. Freshly drawn an hour ago." Mary handed him a glass of blood while making direct eye contact. "Donalda made sure I understood what was expected of me. And no, I have no issues with your being different."

Bryce reached for her and hugged her, placing a kiss in the center of her forehead. "Thank you."

As the years passed, Mary kept Bryce and Susan healthy. That time came to an end when Susan caught the flu. Bryce walked in the door from a trip to a somber house and gave her a questioning look.

"Mrs. Gold is very ill, sir. I'm doing all I can do, but she is having a hard time."

Bryce headed to Susan's bed with shoulders drooped. Mary followed where she put her hand on his shoulder and squeezed gently. He put his hand on top of hers and with a sigh said, "Thank you for all you do, Mary. This life may not be what you hoped for, but you'll always have my eternal gratitude."

"Sir, I thank you for this life. I would've been dead without your help. Now, drink your tonic and rest. We'll see how Mrs. Gold is this evening." Bryce's gaze softened as he nodded and took his glass to his bedroom.

She stayed close, as Susan and Bryce spent the evening sitting, talking, and laughing. A sad grin played across her face as she listened to the words of love they shared with one another. Love wasn't to be hers this lifetime. Ah...maybe the next.

The sun was still finding the energy to peek over the horizon when Mary heard a frantic knocking on her bedroom door. She opened the door to Bryce demanding she come quickly. Susan lay in a limp mass on her bed. Turning to Bryce, she searched his face, knowing there was nothing more she could do.

"I can give her something for the pain, but..."

Bryce bowed his head, and then nodded.

"I have to ask. Did she not want you to, uh...change her?" Mary continued to spoon the tincture into Susan's mouth.

Bryce answered in a voice choked with tears, "No. She couldn't imagine living so long that she would lose all her friends and family. She didn't want to be lonely."

Mary bounced her head up and down in understanding.

In a last moment of lucidity, Susan opened her eyes and said, "I love you, Bryce." She paused.

Bryce kneeled by the bed and took her hand in his. "I love you too, Susan."

She smiled and squeezed his hand with what strength she had left. Then, she lifted her eyes to Mary and said, "Mary, thank you. Take care of him."

Mary nodded, as the life force left Susan's peaceful face. Glancing up, she left to prepare his tonic.

In the last glimpse of this lifetime, the wise woman Mary had trained was spooning tonic into her mouth as Mary struggled for each breath. In those last moments, with Bryce holding her hand, she understood the longing for what never developed between them. He kissed her forehead and said, "Until we meet again."

With a sad smile, she nodded, emptiness enveloping her soul, and she faded from this lifetime, quietly passing.

Back at the sign, she drew on the last of her energy to go to the right. The road to the future looked much the same as it did for the past. Soon, red ribbons draped over the fence appeared. Her hand went for the one shimmering the most, allowing it to pull her into a possible future life. Her eyes glanced down at her feet to see they were in pale gold satin shoes peeking out from under the most beautiful wedding dress she'd ever seen. She caught her reflection in a mirror and gasped. The ivory gold color enhanced her red hair and pale skin. Her focus took in the room around her. She was in Jonathan and Edward's house. Russ, her stepfather approached her, wearing a black tux with a gold cummerbund and offered his arm. He escorted her down the aisle created in the guys' backyard. She could see the groomsmen and a groom, but couldn't identify them. Looking at her right hand, she saw an engagement ring with sapphires and diamonds. Could it be from Bryce? Closer now, she saw the groom dressed in a form-fitting tux that showed his broad shoulders. Bryce's shoulders. Russ guided her to stand by her soon-to-be-husband.

The opportunity to marry Bryce existed in the realm of possible futures. She could make that happen. Everyone possessed freewill.

Drained, Rosemary returned to the present with the help of her guides, aware there were more past and possible future lifetimes with Bryce to be explored. A moment passed while she stared into the candle flame, fighting to comprehend the importance of Mary's life. Tiny rivers of tears flowed down her cheeks powered by her discovery of their connections. Her heartstrings pulled her back and forth, as if she was panning for gold. Bryce Gold. For centuries, their souls had wandered in obscurity until that fateful night when he had flashed her. A smile lifted her mouth as the memories awakened inside her body.

Understanding hit her with a jolt as she headed to her room. Candles blown out, she grabbed the double-terminated crystal and crawled into bed. For a moment, she lay awake letting the thoughts twirl through her mind. She sighed, accepting her attraction to Bryce, the mate to her soul. Lips in a happy curl, she fell asleep within minutes, dreaming of the past, present, and future. She knew the answer to her fascination with Bryce and knew what she would do.

CHAPTER 9

Rosemary shoved a lock of her hair back into place with an impatient swipe of her hand and continued counting, "One, two, three, one, two, three." What was she thinking yesterday when she told Bryce she'd love to dance the night away with him? *I'll be lucky if I remember the difference between the waltz and the Watusi. Time to instigate plan B: knock his socks off with my sex appeal, distracting him from my lack of skill.* She smiled at her reflection in the mirror as she held the dress she bought this afternoon against her body. The dress flowed around her when she shook her bare shoulders. "Now that's a distraction."

The dress evoked the memory of her past life with Bryce. She stood lost in her own reflection as the feelings of that time made her question whether to tell Bryce about what she saw in her trance. What if she was wrong? She was still working on her trance techniques. Worse, what if he really still loved Susan and wanted to find her soul? She wasn't sure she wanted to marry Bryce yet, but she was sure she wanted to find out more about their connections.

An hour later found her running water in her large freestanding bathtub. The lavender scent of the candles on the bathroom counter calmed her as she slipped into the bath of warm, silky water, anticipating what the evening would bring. With her friends-with-benefits philosophy, she normally jumped right in the sex pool on the first date. Because of their choice to wait, her body hummed with desire. The rough sponge, slick with soap heightened her need as she imagined Bryce's touch.

She caught herself fantasizing about his hands when her eyes landed on the clock. *Crap! He'd be here soon.* She went into high gear, and soon she was sliding into a cloud of midnight blue satin that caressed her curves, urging even more desire to blossom.

After sitting down for a second to calm her jittery nerves, the doorbell rang. A deep breath comforted her, and she rose, taking measured steps to the door. She paused, with her hand on the door-knob. *This is it. I need to be sure I want this.* Pushing her fears back, she opened the door, rewarded with the sight of Bryce dressed in a bow tie black tux that emphasized his broad shoulders and trim waist. He stepped inside.

Her gaze started at his shoes and worked its way up to his strong jaw and amber gold eyes. "Well, you clean up handsomely."

His hand cupped hers and kissed it. "Come here, fantasy woman." Lips trailed up her wrist. "You're beautiful." Stopping at the crook of her arm, he inhaled. Body straightening, his eyes sparkled with passion. "And you smell delicious."

Rosemary's eyes followed him as he opened a jeweler's box to reveal the matching sapphire earrings to her necklace. *The man knows my weakness.*

"I want you to have earrings to match your necklace and your eyes." His fingers caressed each ear lobe while positioning the bright jewels before fastening them. Her body shivered in reaction.

"They're gorgeous, Bryce. Thank you." She turned, catching their reflection in the mirror above the table by the door. Muscular arms pulled her back to his broad chest.

Behind her, he reached down and began to kiss and nuzzle her neck. Without thinking, she tensed.

Is he going to bite me?

However, he only laughed. "I won't bite you. At least not without you asking me."

"I know. I'm...I'm just alive with energy tonight. That tux emphasizes every sexy muscle in your body. And that scent you are wearing is hypnotic."

"Many years ago, a woman in my employ created this scent for me. She was a wonder with herbs and potions."

Rosemary caught her breath. His scent had haunted her from the beginning. Now, her opened memories guided her to the source. Should she tell him about her vision or not? She decided she had to try.

"Do we have time for a drink? I've got a hearty blood chilled." Rosemary took his hand and led him into the living room.

"I always have time for you." He made himself comfortable on the sofa while she poured him a glass of blood and her a glass of wine.

She handed him his glass. "There's something I need—no, something I want to ask you." Her attention focused on the floor.

Bryce's face fell into a frown. "What is it?"

"I'm not sure how to tell you or if I even should."

"Rosemary, whatever it is, I've promised never to hurt you. Please trust me enough."

"Sometimes, we can hurt people without meaning to." She raised her eyes to his.

"I'm imagining the worst, here. Tell me what I can do to fix whatever I've done."

She laughed with no humor in her eyes. Taking a big swallow of wine, she said, "It's about your aftershave."

"What? If it bothers you, I'll never wear it again." He jumped up and stood locking his gaze with hers.

"That's not necessary, Bryce." She inhaled with her eyes closed. "Oak moss and nutmeg. Wild like the forest and spicy. I think I created it."

"Excuse me. I'm confused." He tilted his head to the side.

"Wednesday night, when practicing my trance skills, I discovered a past life of mine in the late 1800s in Scotland." She paused to take another drink of wine. Letting out her breath, she continued. "I believe you saved me from an abusive marriage and employed me to assist your wise woman named Donalda." She waited only a second before his eyes widened and his lips eased into a grin.

"Mary." Bryce placed his hands on her shoulders, regarding her with a look of recognition.

Nodding, she continued, "When Donalda died, I took her place and helped to care for you and your sick wife. I suspect I made this scent you're wearing. Does any of this sound familiar to you?"

"Yes, remarkably familiar." His face paled and his eyes grew soft, remembering that part of his life long ago. "Susan's death was hard for me. She brought light into my lonely darkness, but you helped me through. So, what's the problem?"

"I ...well. Are you sure you don't want to find Susan?"

"Are you telling me you want me to find Susan?"

"No, no. I don't want to become involved with you only to find you've settled for me." Her heart pounded out a tune of fear. *It's for the best.*

He stroked her pale cheek with his strong hand, wiping a tear that surged down her face. "I was hopelessly in love with you but married to a woman who I loved. I've often thought about Mary and what could've been, but I would never have hurt my wife."

Her heart beat in a joyful cadence. "I loved you, too." Rosemary paused, gauging his reaction. "That's why I want to explore our relationship this lifetime."

Bryce's face glowed as he pulled her to him. His embrace reminded her of a man returning home after years away. He wrapped his powerful arms around her, pressing her body to his. His hands, massive and strong, cradled her head.

"You had me going. I thought you had decided to break up with me." He rested his forehead on hers.

The joining shifted something within her. Dizziness flooded her senses, throwing off her balance. He steadied her when her hand reached for his arm.

"I love you, now, Rosemary," He brought his lips to hers, giving her a slow warm kiss. His eyes never left her face as he stabilized her.

"I love you, now, too, Bryce." Her eyes widened as the bond

between them grew stronger. Her hold eased. A shaking hand stroked his face. "I've always believed my soulmate existed, but I gave up trying to find you."

"I'm yours as long as you'll have me." Bryce lowered his lips to hers and slipped a hand behind her head to bring her close for the kiss. She rose to meet him with lips that sought to connect with him. Coming together, their souls joined and their bodies cried for the pleasure of being one. The kiss progressed to the parting of lips and tongues tasting tongues as the heat between them soared. Suddenly, he pulled back.

"Where're you going?" Rosemary looked up with eyes half-closed in passion.

"Our first time should be special. Full of love, like us. I want to experience what it's like to hold you in my arms while we dance and then sweep you off your feet."

She was ready to lay him out on the floor and ride him like a crazed cowgirl, but she had spent time and money on getting ready. Besides, she could use a breather to process everything. Grabbing her purse, she said, "Let's go dancing!"

Bryce led her to his car, putting his hand on the small of her back as he helped her climb in the door. Once in the driver's seat, he said, "Your dress is almost the same color of the dress you wore the first time I saw you when you were Mary."

"You're right. This dress appealed to me because of the color, and it complements the sapphire necklace you gave me too. Most of all, I love the way the skirt flows." He growled, running his hand down her thigh and under one of the layers.

Sparks of desire shot from her as she wondered how to keep her werewolf in check. Her fingers found the bottle of werewort in the outer pocket of her purse.

"Where're we going to dance?" she asked, trying to distract herself.

"I know this quaint little place you're going to love," he said, as they pulled up to a security gate that glided open at their approach.

Head turning in circles to capture the view, her gaze returned to him. "Quaint, yes. Little, hardly. Who do you know that lives here?"

"Actually, I live here. Are you up for a private evening of dining, dancing, and whatever else we can think of to do?" He smiled raising an eyebrow.

"Mmmm," Rosemary sighed, "I can't wait to see what your plans are, Mr. Gold."

"You're right at the center of those plans, Ms. Wolfe." The car rolled to a stop. He quickly got out and opened the door for her.

A woman with kind eyes greeted them as she opened the door and offered Rosemary a glass of red wine and Bryce something slightly darker. They walked through a wide entryway with white columns and tall cream-colored walls. She glanced into the gold framed mirror over the cherry sideboard, checking her hair.

Bryce clinked his glass to hers. "Cheers! We are going to need our strength tonight, sweetheart. Dancing can get quite physical." He took a drink and winked at the woman. "Rosemary, this is Donna. She runs my household."

"Nice to meet you." Rosemary smiled. Something about this woman tweaked a memory. An abundance of heartfelt emotion poured over her.

"You, too." Donna turned to Bryce. "I've set everything up in the ballroom as you requested, sir."

"Excellent. Thanks Donna." Hand on Rosemary's back, he turned. "We're going to dance."

Donna's eye's twinkled. "Have fun."

He led her down a long hall and into a room complete with flickering candles. She loved candles. Filled with shadows, the room seemed cozy to her in spite of the fact it could hold a hundred plus people. The rich brown wood of the floor reflected the flames making the floor undulate with light.

She listened to their steps echoing as they approached the center of the room. A shiver of anticipation ran up her spine. Bryce released her arm to set his glass down. The scent of orchids and roses filled her nose while waltz music played softly. Bryce turned in the low light and Rosemary's nipples pebbled as her body reacted to the quiet power coiled in his tall, handsome frame. Bowing and offering his hand, he asked, "May I have this dance?"

"You may." Rosemary gave him a mischievous grin as she took his outstretched hand. She set her wine down on a table laden with several small plates. "You kept Jonathan busy cooking all my favorites." She smiled up at him as he put his arm around her waist.

"I've been a very busy boy," A wicked grin spread across his face. *The Blue Danube* played as his arms encircled her, one hand in the small of her back, the other guiding her as they danced the waltz. Memories of their past life rose in a rolling cloud of emotions as Bryce twirled her across the dark wood of the dance floor. With his direction, her feet flew across the floor while her dress swirled midnight blue around her. Time bent in different directions taking her into his world of classic charm and culture. They were the ultimate couple, strong and yet vulnerable coming together in a dance that awakened their souls as well as their bodies.

The spicy aroma of the candles mixed with Bryce's blatant masculinity sent erotic sparks deep inside her center. She found herself staring into the eyes of the man, no the vampire she had fallen in love with. The dark hazel color changed to a glowing gold, the color of wild wolves' eyes.

The waltz ended, and they returned to the table where Bryce picked up a cracker spread with steak tartare. "Taste," he said as he held the morsel up for Rosemary to take a bite. The flavors of beef and capers and the crisp cracker burst in her mouth. Bryce finished the rest, closing his eyes to relish the flavor of Rosemary combined with the canapé.

Next, he rubbed a juicy pear slice down her neck, letting the juice flow down toward her creamy breasts. Starting at her neck, he licked the juice off her translucent skin down to her bodice. Rosemary quivered when his tongue ferreted out the pulse points in anticipation of the perfect spot to take the first sip of her red essence. Her trepidation at being bitten was replaced with a red-hot hunger involving his fangs.

As her excitement grew, Rosemary began to tremble, her body sizzling and sparking for him. The tingle in the soles of her feet traveled up her legs meeting deep inside her center. She nibbled on the pear slice he held in his mouth until she kissed his full and sensual lips. The sweet juice of the pear combined with the scent of nutmeg brought her passion to a new awareness. She licked his bottom lip and nipped it.

Amusement flickered in the eyes that met hers. A perfect slice of Brie came next. Scooping the cheese on his right index finger, Bryce held the morsel to Rosemary's lips. Her tongue started at the base of his finger and with a languid motion began to lick. Sexual heat flared in her eyes, and Rosemary pulled his whole finger in her mouth, sucking it and tonguing it to let him know what she planned to do to his erection later. The tang of the cheese and the warmth of his finger flashed images in her mind of taking him in her mouth. Brushing up against him, she felt his cock fighting to escape his pants.

"I'm hungry for something more," Rosemary managed to murmur.

"Me too," Bryce whispered. He downed the last of his blood and sucked on the lemon slice. He offered her his arm and they headed down the hall that led to the bedroom.

They ended up in a master bedroom suite that surprised Rosemary. She expected it to be oversized, overwhelming, and dark. Instead, she walked into a room painted in a soothing seashell white, dominated by a large bed covered by green satin. A candle burned, releasing a light vanilla scent. She hesitated.

"Expecting a coffin?" His mouth fought back a grin.

A flush crept across her cheeks. "No. I'm impressed with your décor."

"Another of Donna's many talents." He turned her toward him, not giving her a chance to look any further. Pulled to his muscular chest, his lips crushed hers as his long-controlled passion sailed from its moorings. His erection throbbed between them while Bryce's hands explored her bottom.

"I want you in my arms and in my bed." His hands played on her bare back, tickling and turning her into a pool of need. When his tongue slid between her parted lips, lemon and sexy man flooded her senses.

"I've never experienced this connection with anyone else. Are you sure you didn't use your vampire ability to control my mind?" She reached up and ran her fingers through his thick brown hair, pulling him closer. She had meant to tease, but there was a small, niggling fear in the back of her mind.

He pulled back for a moment. "I would never use mind control on you without your permission. It's important to me that what you feel is real."

His reaction said it all. Deep within her heart, the knowledge he would always protect her and never harm her settled in to stay.

"Teasing. I believe you." She pulled him back. "I want your skin on mine." She slid a hand to his chest, toying with a button on his shirt.

Rippling muscles reached for her.

The sizzle from his hands ran down her back as he unzipped her dress. The silky fabric pooled at her feet, revealing Rosemary dressed only in her high-heeled black shoes and long black stockings. The front of his slacks held evidence of his arousal going wild.

"Good thing I didn't know this was all you had on underneath that dress. I would've never made it through our dance," he moaned, and began to tear off his jacket and shirt.

"Trust me; what I feel is real for you. Really turned on at the moment." Her breath came in quick pants. Golden skin over muscles shaped in perfect hills and valleys drew her to explore his exquisite body. The defined ridges in his arms fascinated her. Bryce's centuries of hard work provided her with a playground of sensual enjoyments. He had the right amount of chest hair to tempt a woman to run her fingers through it. Rosemary gave in to the temptation, scraping his nipples with her nails.

His howl spoke of a combination of frustration and delight. He grabbed her hands, and kissing her palms, opened her arms, taking her left breast between his lips. He nibbled and sucked the nipple.

Rosemary's passion aroused her werewolf. Werewort taken, she was confident she wouldn't end up as a snarling hairy beast. However, her wolf wanted him inside of her now. He was distracted in sucking her right breast, when she grabbed his pants and tore them off. His hard penis proudly stood in front of her face.

"So thick, so long, so mine." Rosemary slid to her knees to take his cock in her hand, marveling at the velvet texture. Her thumb rubbed the wetness over the thick head before completely encasing him in her mouth.

His head fell back, eyes closed, long hands on either side of her head. Tongue circling around the head of his cock making his muscles to contract, she paid particular attention to the delicate area underneath. Desire flared at the scent of his dark manly spice. Mouth dropping lower to spiral around and around his length, her hands cupped his balls and occasionally massaged the small area directly behind them. She memorized his taste, the feel of his skin, and the spots that had him squirming in delight.

His ardent moan preceded him rapidly lifting her off the floor and his erection, spreading her on his bed.

"I wasn't finished." She heard his sharp inhalation of breath.

His pupils flared. "Anymore, and I would be."

He licked one of her nipples. Mouth tasting, teeth nipping, he drove her higher and faster into her need. After both nipples stood up, begging for more, he moved down her body alternating licks, kisses, and nips until he stopped between her open center.

"You are beautiful." He lowered his head. Instead of going right to her love button, he began to kiss her inner thighs.

"I must taste you." Strong arms under her knees lifted her legs back, giving him complete access. He started at her right knee and licked and nipped his way to her center. There he spread her to lick her sensitive jewel, making her jump. Then he started kissing and nipping his way from her left knee down to her center again.

She wriggled. "Bryce, I want you in me." Strong arms held her still as he bit down gently on her nub. The combination of being held and his intense attention to her core, wound tension tight within her body. All she could do was pant out his name in a breathless plea.

"I love your taste." His tongue explored her depths tasting, swirling, and plunging until she shook with the need to come. With a last lick and nip, she shattered.

The orgasm erupted in a wave she let carry her down the rushing river of desire. Bryce supported her using his enhanced strength. Her pleasure sparked Bryce into full vampire mode. Fangs long and hard, his eyes were a golden fire. His cock, thick and pulsing, was slick with pre-come.

She knew he was finally going to connect with her, so before he could slide into her warm wet center, she turned and quickly positioned herself on her hands and knees. Rosemary glanced up into the ornate dresser mirror and met his glowing eyes. "Take me wolfie style." With a playful wag of her bottom, she growled.

She craved the way her pleasure spots were brought to a raging flame in this position. And she bet Bryce had been around long enough to know the pleasures he'd receive from where he kneeled. She was right. His face took on the look of a man who had been handed a prize.

A low chuckle emerged from Bryce. Leaning over Rosemary's back, rubbing her breasts, he whispered, "Are you sure?"

"Yes, I want you, all of you." That's all it took. He impaled her with his cock. Even though she was warm, wet and waiting, she felt him stretch her as he filled her completely. Her heart stretched too, as he filled it with his love. Her body tightened around him as his cock pushed against her womb. Her gaze followed every scoop of his hips, stimulating her pleasure spots deep inside. His eyes flew open, allowing her to see the pure gold glow. There was no question, he loved her, wanted her, and would protect her. Nevertheless, she still wasn't ready to admit they were made for each other.

The scrape of fangs on her shoulder was enough to send her over the edge. She wanted, no needed him to take her blood into his veins. "Bite me!"

The empty parts of her filled with a connection to his powerful love. He thrust hard into her from the back and fingered her front with the delicate touch of a musician. A deep guttural sound came from Rosemary. Her release came as he found the perfect spot for his fangs and sank them deep within her. In the mirror, she watched with fascination. Deep spasms of her orgasm increased racing to her womb. Her core clenched, milking each of his thrusts.

On swallowing the first precious drop of her blood, his body started shaking as he drove harder into her slick opening until his cock exploded, claiming her. A low growl rose from his throat with his final thrust. They both had tremors for several minutes afterwards, collapsing on the bed still connected in body, mind and spirit.

Bryce put his arm over her shoulder and around her breasts and pulled her close. Rosemary, surprised by how much she liked the feeling, curled closer. For the first time in a long while, safety wrapped around her in the form of a vampire. A vampire she loved.

They lay there for a while, absorbed in the connection. Finally, they turned to face each other. His face stretched into a wide smile, Bryce kissed her on the forehead and climbed out of bed to get refreshments.

"You must keep your strength up, love," Bryce said holding a slice of sweet juicy peach to her lips. "I plan on a few more of these before morning."

"You'd better drink up then," Rosemary handed him a crimson glass of nourishment, before tonguing the peach as she sucked it into her mouth, "because I expect more than a few by morning."

Full of good food and feelings, Rosemary snuggled into Bryce and promptly fell asleep.

He pulled the covers around her, watching her sleep. She loved him. He had known back in Scotland all those years ago, Mary was his soulmate, but he had given up. Maybe not as much as Rosemary, but he just couldn't take the chance on love. Yet, here in his bed lay the woman of his dreams. After his last wife was murdered, he swore never to put another woman in danger until he could find that bastard, Stephan. For forty years, he made due with casual relationships and keeping his heart imprisoned. When he spotted her at Jonathan and Edward's party, something inside of him rebelled. He loved her. The warmth of her body against him lulled him into a peaceful slumber.

In a couple of hours, he woke. Figuring she had time to recuperate, he kissed her forehead, then neck, inhaling the scent of cinnamon and peaches. No response. He plucked up a silky red curl and twirled it around his finger, uncovering an ear. She stirred while he sucked in an earlobe, and then he sprinkled kisses down her neck.

Rosemary's long lashes fluttered open, cheeks flushed with excitement. His tongue made licking motions meant to tickle and arouse at the same time.

"Were you sleeping?" he asked, with a wicked grin.

"Not now," she mumbled.

"Well, since you can't sleep, maybe we could, oh, I don't know, fool around?" He didn't wait for an answer. He turned her toward him and started peppering her face and neck with feathery kisses. Rosemary giggled, hands stroking his shoulders and back until his front sprung to attention.

"We went a little wild and fast the first time. Let's take it slow and enjoy every second this time," Bryce whispered into her ear.

"Love to." Her breath caught as he covered one of her breasts with his mouth. He savored her flavor of cinnamon and sex, tonguing her nipples until they were firm beads of flesh. Her scent enveloped him. He couldn't remember ever being so attracted to a lover. Hand between her legs, his fingers dipped into the warm, slick opening and twirled her nub until it became a swollen ripe berry. His body responded with a million tiny flames of desire erupting at once.

"I love how responsive you are to my touch. You make me feel alive." He stopped a moment, realizing what he had said. Rosemary caught the sadness that flew over his face and then was gone.

"I understand. You are not dead, but not totally of this world. The virus and herbs that kill the infection but alters your genetics to cause vampirism is a conundrum. I can only imagine how you feel. However, I want you to know you've been the most vibrant lover I've ever had." She kissed his nose and forehead and then his lips.

He smiled and kissed her with more depth. The sadness was replaced with loving passion. Reaching for his cock, she took it in her hand. He flopped on his back and let her play. She knelt between his legs and spread strawberry lube over his towering erection.

At her touch, he let out a strangled moan, but stayed put. She took both hands and rubbed him up and down in a spiral motion, but when she took him in her mouth and gently began to nibble on his hard length, liquid fire gathered at the base of his spine begging to be released. A final scrape of his foreskin with her teeth had his fangs extending and eyes heating with the glow.

"Oh Sweetheart, I think you are ready for round two." She crawled on top of him and lowered herself down inch by inch.

"Ohhhh… grrr…" A possessive growl came from Bryce who was beyond words as his cock tunneled into Rosemary's depths. He reached up and grasped the soft flesh of her hips to help stabilize her position.

"Oh yeah." She held on to his arms, riding him with slow and intense thrusts.

His muscles contracted in time to meet her rhythm. She paused, eyes closed. A deep ache clamped onto his groin.

"Are you going to just sit there?" he asked, a grimace twisting his face.

"I'm just doing my tantric yoga and connecting to you."

"Did I mention I studied tantric yoga the last time I was in India?"

"No, you didn't. Are you able to go for hours without an orgasm?"

"After our last session of lovemaking, you'd think, but no, I'm unbelievably turned on by you right now."

"Let her blow!" she laughed, gyrating her hips. He grabbed her waist and increased the pace. She leaned down to offer him her neck. When he nipped her, Rosemary began to howl with her release. He drank her blood which initiated a low rumble deep within Bryce. A roar crescendoed from his throat as he claimed her with his climax.

Their release flowing away, they embraced one another, still connected and gazed into each other's eyes.

"That wasn't much slower." She gazed at him with sleepy, but satisfied eyes.

He managed to lift up his exhausted head. "Do we need to try again?" Physically making love again would be slow, but possible. Emotionally, he was wiped out with all the intensity.

"Not for a while." She snuggled into his chest.

"Whatever you say." He laughed at her expression. Grateful for the reprieve.

Rosemary dropped off, spooned in his arms. He held her, his mind working on how to hold on to this incredible woman he had somehow fallen in love with and keep her safe in his world.

CHAPTER 10

Bryce's firm ass and broad back provided a welcome good morning for Rosemary, even though it was noon. She sighed as she contemplated her decision to become involved with a vampire. Bryce was every bit the lover she imagined. During the night, he arranged a blanket over her, and slipped his hand under the cover to touch her. They had made love again early in the morning before falling asleep. The sight of him curled at her side filled her with warm fuzzy feelings and ice-cold fears. Possessive, loyal, protective, controlling, vampires could go to either extreme. This hunky vampire wanted her. Funny thing is she wanted him, but the thought of marriage still scared her stethoscope right off.

She quietly climbed out of bed and headed to the enormous bathroom with an oversized tub where Bryce had laid out a collection of scented salts and oils for her. *What a sweetheart.* She wanted to trust him, but she didn't trust herself. Then there was Roger. With a sigh, she turned on the water and grabbed a towel.

She took a long, luxurious soak and came out of the bathroom in a cloud of lavender to find him drinking a glass of his favorite red. He handed her some orange juice and a plate of pancakes with peanut butter.

"Thank you. Did you read my mind or have you pestered Jonathan and Edward about my every food preference?"

"You know I don't read minds. I just influence thoughts. The guys are extremely accommodating in helping me create a happy home here for you. Everyone should be blessed with such good friends." He pulled out a chair at the bistro table in their common sitting area.

She sat, unfolding the soft cloth napkin. "It's heaven here, but those lovely orchids will need water eventually."

His kiss landed on her temple. "I know."

She glanced up at him. "I'm planning to stay until Sunday morning or until you kick me out."

"You never have to go." Strong hands zeroed in on the tense muscles in her shoulders, massaging her until she resembled a limp noodle. "What do you want to do today?"

Rosemary decided to ignore the suggestion of staying. Why cause waves when his hands were doing such incredible things to her body. Between the pancakes, bath salts, and covering her with a blanket, let alone the massage, he caught her attention. Leon would have never done those things.

Her finger traced down his cheek. "Don't you need to sleep a little more?"

Catching her finger, he gave it a kiss. "Yes, but I want to be with you."

Goddess, he was thoughtful, but looking at his face, she saw lines of fatigue. "Your unused sunroom could use some company while I read my book. I'll wake you at five or six and we can grab something to eat."

"You sure you don't mind?" He held her hand in his.

"A little down time is a good thing. Speaking of, one of my patients told me there's a troupe of Japanese drummers in town that I'd love to see. How's that sound?"

"I'm in. I'll go rest awhile longer. Ask Donna if you need anything." He leaned in to whisper in her ear, "By the way, the sunroom has countless uses at night. Remind me to demonstrate sometime." He kissed her cheek and laughed at her shiver.

She was in such trouble. This vampire had her number. "I'll take you up on that offer."

With an eyebrow bounce, he headed back to bed.

Rosemary took her plate to the kitchen and ran into Donna. "Where would you like me to put this?"

Jumping up from the table, she took the plate. "Oh, I'll take care of it. Is there anything else I can get you?"

"This may be a crazy request in this house, but is there a possibility of rustling up some ice tea?"

"Bless you, darlin', you're a woman after my own heart! I always keep a pitcher of unsweetened made in the refrigerator. There's all manner of sweeteners in the pantry if you need that sort of thing." She poured her a glass.

"Thanks. I think I'm going to sit out on the sun porch and read."

"It doesn't get much use around here in the daylight." Donna smiled and went back to her work.

As Rosemary settled in on a padded chair on the sun porch, an intuition flashed in her mind. Donna and she were making tea in another place and time. Then it was gone. She would need to look into that.

"Rosemary!"

Looking around, she spotted Roger weaving his way through the crowd. She and Bryce had walked up the aisle to row H and had started the excuse-me-shuffle to their seats. *Oh crap! Why tonight?* She wanted to forget her last bedroom escapade with the werewolf. Best face him head-on.

Bryce frowned as she reversed directions landing them back in the center aisle.

"Roger, I wondered if you would be here. This sort of concert is right up your alley." *Please keep your mouth shut.* Her eyes implored him.

"I do love a lively concert. I'm Roger Rougarou." He extended his hand toward Bryce.

With an exaggerated politeness, he took Roger's hand. "Bryce Gold. Haven't we met somewhere before?"

"Maybe at Jonathan and Edward's party last week? Weren't you a flasher?" Roger stared at Rosemary's chest as he spoke.

Stepping in front of Rosemary, Bryce guided him to her side. "Yes, and you were the mad scientist. How do you know Rosemary?"

Bryce's voice was too polite and too controlled. *Crap.*

Eyes full of mischief, Roger reached around him and lifted her hand to his lips for a kiss. "We go way back, don't we?"

Bryce pulled her closer and she could swear he let out a small warning hiss.

Heart pounding, she fought back the fears from the past. Roger could be deceptively fast and vicious, but never toward her. She wasn't sure about Bryce.

"Yes, we've known each other for many years." She slipped her hand back from Roger's grip, giving him a clenched-teeth smile. Nothing like two alpha males in a small space. "It's good to see you, but we should head to our seats before the show starts. Who's your date?"

A tall blonde was headed their way with determined strides.

"Lucy, Lacy, I'm shaky on the name. First date with her." At her approach, he clutched her waist, pulling her in for a kiss. "Darling, this is Rosemary," he drew Rosemary closer with a hand on her shoulder, then waving at Bryce, said, "and her friend, Bryce."

The tick at the side of Bryce's mouth gave away his feelings about being labeled a friend. However, to his credit, he kept up a veneer of civility. Rosemary let out the breath she had held for the last minute.

The blonde held out a limp hand and gave them a tight grin.

"Nice to meet you. Roger, let's go sit down." She led him to their seat. He glanced back over his shoulder and winked at Rosemary.

Heat flooded her cheeks. Rosemary raised her eyes to Bryce. "Sorry, he's a bit much sometimes, but he's got a good heart."

Through gritted teeth, he answered, "And he wears it on his sleeve."

"Yes. I've made it clear I'm with you, but Roger doesn't always get the message." The tension in the air made her uneasy. Was Bryce going to react like Leon? This weekend had been perfect up to this point.

Serious hazel eyes stared at her. "Shall I make it clear?"

"No. He's a good guy. He'll find someone who will catch his fancy soon." She waited, hoping he would let it go.

"Shall we?" Bryce held out a hand to guide Rosemary to her seat. Grateful he dropped the subject, she started the journey around the knees of other patrons to their seats.

After they settled in, Rosemary ran her hand down the sleeve of Bryce's designer suit. "I like you in navy. Complements my dress."

Bryce leaned over to stroke the shoulder of her blue silk dress, and whispered in her ear, "Your beauty takes my breath away."

She blushed.

As the lights dimmed, he smiled at her reaction.

He seemed to have let the incident with Roger go. A small fear nagged at her. Should she tell him about their last encounter? She and Bryce had just agreed to date at that point.

Her gaze traveled over his profile. "You haven't let me keep my clothes on much in the last couple of days,"

"And I'm hoping to unwrap you from that dress tonight," he whispered.

With a lift of her eyes, she patted his hand and said, "Let's watch the show."

The curtain rose on twelve drummers beating their drums in a ritualistic fashion. The sound, banners, and bright colors they used wove a hypnotic spell over the audience.

Rosemary sensed the vibrations in her chair as Bryce kept time with the music with his entire body. The music snaked its way up her spine, filling her with primal energy. The beat, beat, beat of the large drums vibrated the whole auditorium, awakening her sensual desires. The heat of Bryce's hand holding hers slivered up her arm and landed in an explosion over her entire body. She snuck a glance his way and caught him staring at her. She lowered her eyes and caught a tent rising in his lap. Her eyes flew up to meet his with a lifted brow. With a smoldering look, he placed his coat over his lap and turned back to the stage.

The performers were full of humor and music. The finale was played on a twelve-foot drum called an Odaiko. Every time the performer struck the drum, electricity shot through them both. Bryce slipped their hands under his coat, resting them on the impressive erection. Her small feminine fingers traced the bulge, finally closing around it. She felt him jerk, but he held her hand there. His penis throbbed in her hand as the curtain fell. She and Bryce sat for a moment, taking in the experience.

"That was stimulating on so many levels. I need to sit here and absorb it all," Bryce said.

"That's not all you need to absorb," she said, giving him one last squeeze before bringing her hand out to retrieve her purse.

The theater crowd thinned out and Bryce quickly slipped on his coat before he stood and offered his hand to help Rosemary up.

"I'll admit to being tingly all over." She giggled as she placed her hand in his, the electric charge thrilling her. He helped her on with her wrap and guided her out of the theater with a protective hand at her back. In her covert searching for Roger, she found he and his date were heading out the front door. A breath flowed from her chest with the realization. Bryce was different from Leon, but a trickle of fear raced through her. *He can't find out about the last time I had sex with Roger.* She preferred that Bryce and Roger not meet again.

Gentle fingertips stroking up and down the back of her blue silk dress sparked a dizzying current to race through her. She shot Bryce a grin that told him she knew exactly what he was thinking and she approved. When they reached his silver gray De Tomaso, a vintage sports car she suspected he owned for the speed, he opened her door and gently steered her inside. He climbed into the driver's seat, paused, and then leaned over to kiss her gently.

His finger brushed her bottom lip. "That'll hold me until we get home."

She wanted more. "What? You don't have a secret place to go parking?"

"Good idea." He started the car and headed down the street.

She turned to study him. "Aren't you a little old to go parking?"

Her lover shook his head. "No, by this point, I know what I'm doing."

Excitement trilled through her. Bryce was different. He was funny, responsible, and caring. Another notch in the belt that held her back, slipped away.

Soon they pulled up to a wooded area off a county road where he stopped the car.

"Where are we?" She liked taking chances.

"We're on the backside of Edward and Jonathan's land," he said pulling her to him. He leaned down and kissed her with a rough passion that had her twisting in her seat. Masculine fingers fondled her breasts, pitching and squeezing her nipples with a nip of pain.

Her hand landed on his cock, massaging the length pressing against his slacks. Desire fired through her leaving a crazy need in its wake. She pulled on his zipper only to have him stop her.

He raised his head from nuzzling her breasts. "How do you feel about doing it outside?"

Her eyes lit up. "Between you and the music, I'm about to come. Out of the car."

"What's going on in that sexy mind of yours?" A vampire in a hurry, he was opening her door before she touched the handle.

She cast an amused smile his way. "I'm thinking someone might come down this road and see us."

He scrutinized her with a sidelong glance. "Does that bother you?"

With a quick turn, she bent over the hood and shoved her bottom in the air. He swiftly made the connection and came up behind her to kiss and burrow in the crook of her neck.

His touch blasted heat straight to her core. Her body shook with the craving of his primal connection. She needed him rough, hard, and now. "Fuck me!"

With understanding, he threw her dress off her hips to reveal a lacy G-string and black thigh high stockings.

His breath whooshed out. "Oh my God, you're hot."

Hands squeezed her cheeks, releasing more of her juices. Her underwear was ripped away and two fingers scooped up the liquid and filled her. She gasped with relief and then moaned with need. He taunted her with slow, shallow thrusts. Her orgasm was seconds from erupting when he stopped.

"No!" Her body quivered with the need to come. When the sound of a zipper opening reached her, she stilled.

"Are you ready, Wolfie?" Not waiting for an answer, he buried his engorged member into her waiting wetness.

Rosemary couldn't think in words as Bryce pressed into her. The chance that they might get caught had her bucking under him as he pushed into her with passion. He was having sex with her under the stars, not afraid to risk being caught with his pants down. She loved this man.

Suddenly, headlights topped the hill, and she let loose a long throaty wail signaling her climax. He picked up his pace and leaned in to nip her shoulder as he shot his pleasure into her. For a time, they stayed bent over the car, connected, trying to catch their breath. After the other vehicle drove on, they both started laughing.

"I can't believe they didn't see us." Bryce stood to pull his pants up.

"If they did, you could have just changed their thoughts," Rosemary said.

"True."

As their breathing began to normalize, Rosemary filled her lungs with the velvety night air scented with the grass and trees of summer. This aroma would be an erotic turn on for the rest of her life. Bryce breathed in deeply as he leaned over and kissed her softly on the lips.

"The scent of a summer night will always turn me on from this point forward," Bryce said, mirroring her thoughts.

When he gently cleaned her before slipping her dress down into place, a sense of being cherished settled over her.

Finger touching his lips, she smiled. "You took the words right out of my mouth. All the drumming tonight stoked my fire."

"Well, I think I got a pretty good rhythm going for you too." He smiled in that charming way that made her heart beat faster.

"You have a way with that drum stick that gave me great vibrations." Rosemary was laughing at this point. She reached up to hug Bryce and he embraced her pulling her close with his long strong arms.

Leaning her forehead on his, Rosemary whispered, "I love you."

"I love you too," Bryce answered. "Let's go home."

Her eyes sprung open when her hand brushed a muscular back. Breath catching in her throat, she tried to figure out where she was and whose hunky back she was cuddled against. As sleep abated and consciousness returned, Rosemary chuckled at herself. *I guess I'd better get used to waking up with someone in bed with me.* She kissed his shoulder, and then slipped out of bed. He didn't move. It had been a tiring weekend even for a vampire. They both needed a lazy Sunday. In search of the kitchen, she found Donna there drinking a cup of coffee. "Is there more of that?" Rosemary's night of drumming and other rhythmic activities had revved up her need for caffeine and food.

"Sure, do you need sugar or cream?"

"A little of both. Thanks." She sat down at the kitchen table.

"Here you are." Donna set a mug of coffee in front of her, followed by sugar and cream.

"Thanks." The warm liquid flowed over her tongue and into her stomach revitalizing her.

"Hungry? I can make toast and scrambled eggs for you." Donna's smile comforted her on a deep level she didn't understand.

"I am hungry. Can I help?" Rosemary pushed back from the table.

Donna put a hand on her shoulder. "No, relax."

Rosemary was still wondering why she sensed a connection with Donna, when she set plate of toast and scrambled eggs before her.

"Anything else?" Donna waited.

"Sit down and finish your coffee." Rosemary took a bite of the eggs and toast and shut her eyes and moaned. "These are delicious. Thank you."

Donna beamed from the compliments. "You're welcome." She sat down and picked up her cup. "You can tell me if I'm out of line, but you seem to make Bryce happy. It's been a long time coming for him."

Another flash of intuition hit Rosemary with a scene where she and Donna were pouring a glass of blood.

That's how I know her! Donna was Donalda from my past lifetime with Bryce. I don't know her well enough to say anything, though.

"I appreciate you saying so. He makes me happy too." Rosemary's curiosity was raised. "How long have you been with Bryce?"

"Ten years. Started working for him in Boston."

"Did you answer an ad or what?"

Donna's laugh relaxed Rosemary.

"My family has worked on and off for him through the centuries. We specialize in GDBs. The shifter I had worked for married his mate and moved to Spain. I like Boston, so I stayed."

"What all do you do for him?"

"The usual running the household and making sure he has the proper food and drink, if you know what I mean."

Rosemary grinned. "I do."

"Because GDBs need someone to trust, I often end up handling more emotional aspects of their lives. He and I have had some long conversations about whether he was ready to date again."

"Since I'm here, I guess he took the chance."

"I guess he did." Donna studied her for an instant. "He's a hard man to live with, but well worth the effort. If I can help you in anyway, let me know."

"I'm still going to be living at my apartment for the moment."

"We'll see. He's not a patient man." She stood and went to grab the coffee pot. "Refill?"

"Please." Rosemary waited until Donna sat back down and turned to her. "This may be out of line, but when you say he's hard to live with and not patient, are you telling me to run for my life?"

The look of horror on Donna's face brought a giggle to Rosemary's lips. Squelching that reaction, she waited for the older woman to answer.

"Oh my God, no! Bryce is one of the kindest, thoughtful, loving men I've ever known." Donna stopped to calm down.

Rosemary waited.

Donna composed herself before continuing. "What I mean is he will treat you with respect, honor, and love. The guy does his best to learn the culture and values of the time. He would never lay a hand on you in anger and would defend you from the world."

"How's that difficult?" Rosemary couldn't see any down side in the argument.

"Sometimes, you will need to back him off in order to be yourself. From what little I've seen, you're quite capable of doing so."

"Makes sense." She drained the last of her cup.

"Thank goodness. Bryce needs someone like you."

Rosemary liked Donna and thanked her lucky stars Donna seemed to like her. After switching to the subject of cooking, she realized Donna was quite accomplished in a variety of ways. *Maybe I'm in the right relationship, this time.*

"Thanks for the breakfast and the advice. I'll digest both." Heading out of the kitchen, she contemplated the influence Donna had on Bryce.

With her blouse tucked in her jeans, she emerged from the bathroom to Bryce's fine ass. Bent over, he was tying his shoes. "Nice view. How are you this morning? Shouldn't you still be asleep?"

"Hey, I'm a big boy. I'll catch up on my rest when there's not a beautiful woman around to keep me up." He waggled his eyebrows and smiled.

"I just showered. Forget it!" She attempted to walk away, when Bryce grabbed her and laid her on the bed with him on top.

"If you get dirty, I'll personally see to it you receive another hands-on shower." He began to kiss her ear, working his way down to suck her bottom lip. He nipped it before he slipped his tongue in between her parted lips.

"I want you," he whispered. "I need to feel you come around me one more time before you leave." His hand glided up her blouse and plucked up the mound of her breast, which he began to massage as he kissed down her neck. When he unbuttoned her blouse, he paused, taking in the view of her breasts as they quivered, barely contained in her white lacy bra. He put his mouth over one and breathed hot, humid air on her tightened nipple.

"Werewolves are known for their sex drive, but you're really putting us to shame," she whispered.

"I told you, Darling; I've been saving up for years. And I don't want just sex; I want to make love to you." With that, he slowly slipped her blouse off her shoulders and drew her left bra strap down her arm. He followed the strap with little kisses until he had reached her round orb where he flattened his tongue against her nipple.

His warm mouth suckling her made Rosemary desperate for the sensation of him inside her. His comment about making love rather than sex endeared her to him even more. She unbuttoned his shirt and the combustion of lust hit them. Clothes came off and Rosemary was soon on the bed with Bryce above her, anticipating his first thrust. His hands came around and lifted her bottom as he placed a pillow under her. At this angle, Rosemary was open and ready. He paused, as he positioned his thick cock at her swollen folds. Then he thrust it in deep and hard.

The bond of true love flowed over them in a golden mist. He reached between them and stroked her womanhood until she came, her contractions milking his penis. His tongue traced a path from the crook of her elbow to her wrist, stopping at the pulse point to complete the connection. Rosemary watched his face as his fangs came towards her in the heat of passion. The momentary pressure pinched, before warm tingly fire ran through her veins. A soft whimper escaped her lips. The blaze fanned through body building her pleasure ending in an explosion within her.

His gaze rose up, filled with love. The first jerk of his climax propelled him into her welcoming warmth with repeated thrusts. Bryce's eyes reflected with shimmering light, drawing Rosemary deep within the cocoon they created.

The afterglow settling, he raised up on one elbow. "I can give you that shower now."

"If I took you up on that offer, I'll never make it home."

"That's the plan," he laughed and pulled her up.

After a long, sex-filled shower, Rosemary headed to her apartment later than planned. The mountain of paperwork she lugged home from the office greeted her. The delay was worth every minute she would spend completing the forms.

CHAPTER 11

"An acquaintance of mine, Bryce Gold, recommended you. I understand you treat GDBs."

Rosemary tapped the speakerphone option and brought up her calendar. "Certainly, I can fit you in. Your name?"

"Idasson, Arne Idasson. I'm coming in from Sweden in a couple of weeks."

Following setting Mr. Idasson's appointment, she did the same for a vampire from Switzerland, and a werewolf from France. In the last couple of months, Bryce had informed many of his contacts from around the world of her services. Grateful for his support, she still was having a hard time keeping up with all the paperwork, training, and treating patients.

It's time to hire someone who can help me with all this. Rosemary flipped through the stack of applications of the candidates she had interviewed in the last two weeks. Either the applicants would have nurse's training, but no experience with GDBs, or they would be Genetically Diverse Beings with no medical training. Recently, she set up an interview with an RN who claimed to be a hereditary witch. Most witches whose gifts were passed down from their family were usually close-mouthed, but he had made the claim outright. Leery of his background, she decided she couldn't be too picky. The need of more time with Bryce was a big deal to her.

The doctor flipped the phone to voicemail and grabbed a notepad. Glancing up, she smiled at a tall young man with hair the color of a night fog with eyes to match coming in the door, right on time. His face broke into a bright smile.

Well, he does appear promising.

"Hi. I'm Dr. Wolfe. I'm hoping that's a résumé you're holding in your hand?"

"Why yes, it is! Good to meet you, Dr. Wolfe. I'm Owl Winterbird." His handshake was strong yet sensitive.

Another good sign, but something feels a little off.

His face was stretched in a wide grin. "I'm happy you made time to meet me, and you are going to be extremely happy that you found me. I'm the answer to your prayers."

She guided him to her office, wondering if he was confident or crazy. "What leads you to that conclusion?"

"I've been an RN at Happy Acres Mental Health Facility for the last year. Although they love me there, it's time to branch out. Being a witch is helpful because I can put spells on people and make them do what I, uh, you want." He sat in the blue cloth and wooden chair in front of her desk.

A warning bell clanged in her head. "Um, doesn't that interfere with free will?"

With a scoot forward, he perched on the edge of his seat, and whispered, "Sometimes in a health crisis, you must take extraordinary measures to save the patient."

"O...kay. You give the mental health facility as your address. Do you live there?"

"I do live on site." He glanced around the room and continued in a conspiratorial whisper, "I was going to volunteer to live on site for you, giving the security of knowing someone was always here. I don't need much room. You can consider it part of my pay." He sat straight up and said, "In fact, I can stay here tonight and ascertain if I'll be comfortable."

"You're getting a little ahead of me. I'll need to check your references before I make a decision." Rosemary's mouth dried up and her gut sank as it had many times for the last two weeks. This interview seemed to be going out even further on the nut tree limb than all the rest.

The absurdity continued from this young man. "I suggest you adopt me. You would know I'm family, and we all know family will do anything for each other." He pressed a hand to his mouth and his eyes shone with excitement.

Crap. No question he's an inmate. Desperation filled her. She needed help running her growing business, and most of all, time for her growing relationship.

"What a novel idea," Rosemary said through her clenched teeth. "Let me check on something in my office and we can look into that. Would you care for some coffee or tea?"

"O-O-O-h!" He squealed and clapped his hands. "It's tea time. Will there be cookies too?"

"Why certainly. Chocolate chip or peanut butter?"

"Could I have one of each? I'm a little peckish." He crossed his legs and threw his arms around them.

"Coming right up!" Rosemary grabbed his résumé. To give herself time to think, she slowed her movements retrieving the tea and cookies. Sliding the refreshments in front of him, she breathed in a sigh of relief as he started drinking and munching with the delight of a three-year-old.

"While you enjoy your tea and cookies, I'll step into my office to check on things for you. Okay?"

"You bet! I'll be right here." He looked up at her with a big smile that was framed by cookie crumbs.

"Great," she said with a wide smile stretching her lips thin. Once in her office, her lips went slack as she dialed the phone. *Good Goddess, she wasted another hour on this joker.*

"Hello, Happy Acres. How can we make you happy?" The receptionist sounded anything but helpful or happy when she answered.

"I wondered if you might be missing a patient named Owl Winterbird?"

There was a pause and then a giggle. "Yes ma'am, His name is Kevin White and he slipped out yesterday. He's harmless but confused. Give us your address, and we will come pick him up. By the way, if you have cookies, he will sit and eat those for hours on end."

"Not a problem. He's at my medical office at 2202 Main Street. How soon do you think you can be here?"

"Two of our orderlies will be there in ten minutes. Thank you for calling." She hung up.

Great. More cookies coming up.

When the nice young men in their clean white coats came to take Kevin away, Rosemary was relieved he went quietly with the bribe of more cookies.

She rescheduled a couple of patients and locked the doors. She was ready to give up on finding help. Tomorrow, she would be seeing a couple of patients that kindly agreed to be shuffled around from today. That meant she would be working on another Saturday. *Oh crap! It's a full moon tomorrow!* Not only did it affect the number of humans with health issues, the GDBs were twice as likely to have problems.

Time to tackle the paperwork. When the bell rang around eleven thirty p.m. startling her, she looked out the window on the front door. Sam Turner, a shape shifter, stood covered in blood.

She yanked the door open. "Sam, what happened?"

"Dr. Wolfe, I'm, I'm...sorry to come so late. My sister's torn up. Can you help her?"

"Of course. Is she conscious?"

"No. She's lost a lot of blood, but I think I can get her in."

"Let me go with you to the car and check her out first." She hurriedly followed him to the car where his sister lay in the back seat with blood everywhere. Rosemary recognized her instantly as Twylene, the woman she'd met at Jonathan and Edward's party. Rosemary gingerly felt for a pulse, then inspected the tourniquets around her left arm and left leg. "There's a gurney in my office. Let's get her on it and carry her in."

With eyes wild and wide, he nodded, trailing her to retrieve the gurney. They dashed to the car, where Sam opened both back doors.

"I'm going to crawl in the backseat and help support her as you carefully bring her out the other side. Then I'll come around and help you place her on the gurney."

"Got it!" Sam gently grabbed his sister's shoulders while Rosemary guided her legs and together they eased his sister toward the door. Rosemary ran to the other side and they both lifted Twylene carefully onto the gurney. They transported her using careful steps into the room set up for emergencies and laid her gently on a table.

"Sam, are you squeamish?"

"I'm a shifter. Blood and worse things don't faze me."

"Good, you can help me. Wash up and put on the large gloves to the right of the sink." With Sam's help, she cleaned and stitched Twylene up. "Her donor card says she's O positive. If you'll help me here, I'll start her on a drip and then head to the kitchen for a cup of tea with a shot of whiskey. Care to join me?"

"Just whiskey, please. It's been a rough night." Sam shook his head as he tossed his gloves in the trash.

They sat down with their drinks before Rosemary asked, "What happened?"

"She's been seeing this shifter, who commuted from East St. Louis to work at the hospital. She surprised him with a visit. The bastard was married to a particularly nasty shape shifter. Twylene took her usual form of a black panther. However, she met her match in this guy's wife. Not only was she pissed as hell about Ted seeing Twylene behind her back, she shifted into a tiger." He paused to take a gulp of whiskey.

"Damn, tigers are bigger than panthers. She's lucky to be alive." The doctor poured more whiskey in her tea.

"Steve, our brother, and I followed her, without her knowledge. Steve swore there was something off about the guy. We arrived just in time to see tiger woman attack Twylene. Ted just stood and watched.

Pussy whipped, I guess. Steve and I took her and Ted down and managed to bring Twylene back." Sam's brandy brown eyes welled up in tears. "Is she going to make it?"

"She's lost a lot of blood, but you got her here quickly. In a couple of hours, I will be able to tell you more. Do you need to call your family and give them an update?"

"Yeah, I'd better." Sam pulled out his phone.

She left him to call and went in to check on Twylene. Her face appeared deathly white. Rosemary checked her IV and made sure the drip was flowing correctly. When Rosemary touched her hand, she opened her eyes.

"Where am I?" she croaked, trying her best to sit up.

"Twylene, remember me? I'm Dr. Wolfe." Her hand supported her patient. "Your brother brought you in after another shape shifter attacked you. You need to stay lying down while you receive a transfusion to replace the blood you lost."

Twylene, relaxed back on the table, her face scowling.

Sam came in the room at the sound of his sister's voice. "You're awake." He grabbed her hand gingerly and sat down beside her bed. "Thank the gods you're alive."

Her brown eyes, full of gratitude and fear, searched his. "What happened to Louise?"

"She's not going to bother anyone again." Sam answered looking down at the floor. "Neither's her cheating husband." Sam's face hardened as he spoke these last words.

Twylene closed her eyes and let out a long sigh. Finally, she spoke. "Hindsight provides a clearer picture, but I sure wish I knew then what I know now. I loved him, but I'd never have gotten involved with him if I'd even suspected he was married. Especially if I'd known she was a tiger with a temper."

"She's going to need rest and probably more blood. I want to keep her here until at least tomorrow afternoon." Rosemary paused, knowing that Sam and Twylene came from one of the largest shifter families in the area. "This would be an opportune time for you to go home to report to your family and get some rest."

Sam stared at Twylene for a moment and patted her hand.

"I think I'll do that. Mom and Dad are going to be out of their minds. I also need to let the rest of the family in on what happened. I hope it ends here, but I fear it won't. Thank you again, Rosemary, for not only saving my sister's life, but doing it in the middle of the night." Sam got up and Rosemary saw him to the door.

"She's going to be fine. Please be careful, I don't want to have to patch up anyone else." She squeezed his hand. He gave her a short grin and was gone.

Rosemary checked on Twylene to make sure she was resting, before returning to her office to call Bryce.

"Hey, Sweetie, it's going be a long night." Rosemary stifled a yawn.

"I'll come stay with you." His voice soothed her even over the phone.

"Thanks, but the situation is under control. I have a patient who got torn up pretty badly. By the way, I'm going to need some more Type O positive."

"I'll send it over first thing in the morning, unless you need it tonight, then I'll personally deliver it."

"I *love* it when you personally deliver, however, it can wait until morning. Hearing your voice makes me feel better." Rosemary relaxed.

"How about I bring you some breakfast in the morning before I head home to bed?"

"Make it enough for two please; keeping in mind my werepanther patient needs food to start building up herself."

"Oh Gods! You have had a night! I'll see you with steak and eggs for two around seven a.m. And, Rosemary..."

"Yes?"

"Please try to get some rest, okay?"

"I'm setting my alarm for seven right now. See you later this morning, my love."

"Goodnight, sweetheart."

Grateful it was the weekend, Rosemary lowered herself in a recliner to keep a watchful eye on Twylene.

After a night of interrupted slumber, Rosemary forced her eyes open and quieted the chiming of the alarm.

Looking Twylene over, she checked her dressings. "How're you feeling?"

"Everything considering, like hell." She smiled.

Rosemary considered her smart-ass attitude a good sign.

"My vampire patients prefer blood for breakfast, but I've got steak and eggs on the way. Any takers?"

"I might go for a little bit. I'm still kind of queasy."

"Not to scare you, but you came close to dying. *Weres* heal faster than humans do, but not when they have too little blood left. You can thank Sam and Steve for getting you here in time. The fact they also can tie a mean tourniquet helped."

"Yeah, they learned that from me. When I was going through nursing school, I used to practice on them. They often turned the tables, though, and practiced on me. They gave the excuse they might need to be able to do it someday." Twylene smiled and shook her head. "Who knew?"

"You're a nurse?"

"Yes, I'm an RN with my Masters in Nursing. I've been working at the hospital here while I finish my certification for nurse practitioner. That's where I met Ted. He was the x-ray tech for many of the patients on the floor where I worked." She paused, with her lips pressed together.

"Could be hard to go back to the hospital." Rosemary checked her IV.

"I don't think I can go back to working where so many memories of us exist. It was time for a change anyway." Twylene blew out a breath.

"Would you be interested in working for me? It would be a change from the busy world of a hospital, but I could use someone with your background. Not everyone is used to seeing a shape shifter, vampire, and witch all in the same night."

"From what I've heard, it'd be busier." Twylene lifted her eyebrows.

"I couldn't pay you what I'd like, but I think we can work out some perks to help."

Twylene lifted up the hand that was not bandaged. "Stop, I'll do it."

Glee overcoming her, Rosemary asked, "When can you start?"

"Well, as soon as my doctor releases me for work and I give two weeks' notice. I should give a month, but I don't think I can take it."

"In my opinion, you'll need another week to recuperate. I can manage until you start. I consider myself exceptionally lucky to find someone with your skills." She paused. "As one of the perks, would you be interested in some of the specialized training courses I'm taking in alternative healing? I'd foot the bill."

"Definitely! I've always had a curiosity, but never the time or contacts to learn."

"I'm working with a shaman named Night Sky, who is teaching me some trance techniques and healing with different stones and energy. You could start sitting in on the Gemstones and Crystal Healing this next week, if you are interested?"

"I'd love to. As a kid, I always went to the creek and while everyone else swam, I dug up interesting rocks."

"Perfect! However, right now, you need to rest." Rosemary lifted her head at the front door opening. "I hear my love coming with breakfast. I'll be right back."

Rosemary went to meet Bryce, humming happily to herself. Her psychic sense ran up her spine in feathery fingers cluing her in on the rightness of hiring Twylene. That same sense also told her life was about to change for the better.

CHAPTER 12

"Hey! Werewolf with a foot wound waiting and a vamp with a silver bullet on the way!" Twylene popped into the lab where Rosemary was concocting a salve to remove a particularly ugly wart on a witch's pert nose.

"Thanks, on my way." Rosemary put the final drop of celandine extract into the jar before she screwed on the lid.

Ten days ago, Twylene was hanging onto life. Now, she sprinted across the waiting room headed to the operating room, where she barely avoided bumping into James, a young alpha werewolf. Engaged in a standoff with a cocky teenage witch, James, bones popping and claws growing, snarled at the longhaired guy chanting a curse in his face. Twylene stepped between the two and gave them an evil eye that settled any question of who would win this fight. James' mother caught up with her son, herding him through the exam room door Rosemary opened. Twylene escorted the witch in the direction of the exit.

Rosemary handed the wart cream to the young lady and made her way to the werewolf with the foot wound. Grateful that Twylene was picking up the slack, she considered the luxury of spending more time with Bryce. Her face curved into a thoughtful smile as she entered the exam room.

"James, that's quite a limp, what happened?" she asked as she grabbed him under the arms and swung him up on the table. *What a cute baby wolf.*

"He got his foot caught in a trap last night on our family hunt," his mom, Doris Weston, said. "We were running on our own land. I'm going to hunt the bastard down who set the trap and show him how it feels to be prey."

"I've treated more trap wounds in the last two months than the last two years. It makes it dangerous for the *weres* that enjoy a run. Setting traps on someone else's land is totally out of line. Did you contact the game warden?" Rosemary asked while examining James' foot. Nothing made her madder than animals being hunted and abused, unless they were kids, too. Little ones, like this pup had her biological clock ticking in double time.

"I called her last night. I'm not sure what the game warden can do." Mrs. Weston shrugged.

"You're lucky. The trap didn't break any bones, plus werewolves heal fast," Rosemary said. "James, you're a brave boy, aren't you?"

"Yes, ma'am," James answered with his eyes wide. They still glowed, but his claws had receded.

"I'm going to clean you up and put in some stitches. Can you show me your wolf strength by not howling?"

"I'm strong. I didn't even cry when they took the trap off me, Dr. Wolfe," James said, squaring his shoulders, showing some of the alpha *were* swagger.

The pungent smell of alcohol flooded the room as Rosemary prepared to clean the curved cut the trap's teeth had left. James turned the color of old bones left in the sun.

"James, you need to remember to breathe while I do this, okay?"

"Okay," James breathed out.

She stitched in quick movements, closing James' wound, wrapping his foot in a gauze pad held with bright blue tape.

"You are the bravest werewolf that has been in here today," Rosemary said, as she patted him on the back. "You need to stay off your foot for the next twenty-four hours and you'll be good as new."

"Thanks, Dr. Wolfe," James said, smiling as he hopped to the door where his mom waited.

"Take good care of him, Mrs. Weston. Keep me posted on what happens with the game warden." Rosemary smiled to herself and wondered if Bryce got her pregnant, how adorable their child would be. *Stop that! Remember the monsters-r-us genetic pool.*

~

During a break from the morning's rush, Twylene flopped down on the green corduroy sofa in Rosemary's office and said, "I'm glad the moon is no longer full."

"I'm glad to grab a minute to ourselves. It's been crazier than a werewolf during a lunar eclipse."

"You should know." Twylene cocked her head.

Eyes rolling, Rosemary asked, "Does your family encounter problems with poachers setting traps on your land?"

"No. why?"

The little werewolf you corralled in the waiting room had been caught in one on his family's land. Mrs. Weston was understandably upset."

"I'll call them tonight. Do you think it's humans or other GDBs?"

"Don't know, but either way, it's a problem. When is the wounded vampire due to arrive?"

"In the next fifteen minutes, the operating room is ready."

"There's been such a difference with you here today. I don't know how I ever got along without you," Rosemary said as she took a drink of her cold coffee. The bitter liquid made her grimace. However, the caffeine perked her up.

"This is much more exciting than sitting around the hospital waiting for someone to die. I don't think I could've taken the terminally ill wing one more day, that and being reminded about my ex." Twylene rubbed her finger over the cords in the couch.

"Do you think much about him anymore?"

"After his nasty-ass shape shifter wife tried to kill me, not really. Did I thank you recently for saving my life that night?"

"Not today." Rosemary chuckled. "There's no need. You working here is saving mine. You've made the transition very quickly. Are you feeling okay?"

"Werepanthers are as quick at healing as the wolves. Although, I believe your herbal supplements and trance techniques sped up even my quick immune response. And, working here is a dream after my last job. I've been around Genetically Diverse Beings of one variety or another all my life. This is nothing. I love it!"

"Good to know. With Bryce spreading my name to his contacts, our patient load is going to keep increasing. Say, where're you on your nurse practitioner's degree?"

"Gah...I forget to tell you. The courses are finished and I passed my test. I'm officially an advanced practice registered nurse."

"Sweet! I'm ready for you to start taking over more of the patient care. Seems like there's always someone in need."

"Speaking of in need, the vampire should be here anytime," Twylene said as she took a drink of her minty peach ice tea and headed into the operating room. "Where's the lodestone?" she yelled.

"I'm getting it, give me a minute," Rosemary yelled back. "Any sign of the vampire?"

"They just pulled in with him. He's unconscious, which is good. It'll be easier if he isn't fighting us." Twylene rushed to open the front door to allow the vampire to be carried in.

Two well-built vampires quickly carried a gurney through the door with an unconscious patient covered with blood.

"Put him in that first room," she pointed, "and lay him on the table." One of the vampires handed her a folder of the medical history.

"You guys brought him all the way from Chicago?" Twylene asked, reading the report.

"Yeah, and we're to wait and take him back." He raised his heavy-duty sunglasses revealing sagging eyes. "Is there somewhere we can get some rest until sunset? We're dead tired." The vampire had the good sense to smile with the last comment.

"Through that door at the end of the hall is a black out room with a couple of cots you guys are welcome to. We also have a refrigerator with liquid refreshment where you can find something just your type. Help yourself." Twylene ran to the operating room to prepare the vampire for the procedure.

"Is he out?" Rosemary asked Twylene, who was holding a mask over his nose and mouth.

"Like a light. He seems in good health other than the silver bullet. It's in his liver. He's already started to heal. We need to be quick." Twylene drew back his shirt swabbing the fast-healing bullet hole.

"Let's go get it," Rosemary said as she cut into the vampire and inserted the special lodestone vise.

"I thought silver wasn't all that magnetic?" Twylene asked.

"It's not, but many of the silver bullets are partially encased in steel, which is. It makes them stronger and the silver still does its number on the vamp." Rosemary adroitly maneuvered the lodestone, allowing it to pull the bullet out without her having to make a large incision. "Got ya!" She dropped it into the waiting pan.

Blood ran in a stream before Twylene jumped in to apply pressure while Rosemary started the process to clean and stitch the wound.

"Do we need to give him blood to help dilute the poison?" Twylene changed out a soaked pad for a clean one.

"That's a good idea. That bullet's been in there for a few hours. What type did his chart say?"

"O positive," Twylene moved the pad slightly to allow Rosemary to stitch. "We sure keep Bryce in business, don't we?"

"We do." A warmness blossomed in her chest. "I don't mind a good reason to see him. If you're okay, I'll go grab the blood and get our patient started."

"Works for me." Twylene put in the last stitch as Rosemary headed into the supply room. She finished cleaning him up just in time for Rosemary to wheel him into the recovery room and start his IV.

He hadn't moved a muscle when Rosemary inserted the needle.

The tape in place, she turned to leave when his eyes flew open, and he tried to grab his abdomen. In pain, he was not a happy vamper.

"Where the hell am I?" the vampire snarled. He tried to sit up, but fell back, body shaking.

Rosemary approached him with careful movements. He stilled. His eyes evaluated her. When he relaxed, she spoke.

"You were shot with a silver bullet that we removed. You're attached to an IV, which is providing you blood right now. You should be able to leave here in a couple of hours."

The vampire stopped and raised his half-closed eyelids. With a soft grunt, he drifted back to sleep.

A huge sigh escaped Rosemary's lungs. Every once in a while, anxiety would flood her. She knew there were good vamps like Jonathan and Edward, but Leon had taught her differently. *Would she ever trust herself to know the good from the bad again?*

The busy morning segued into a calm afternoon. Rosemary looked forward to a break from patients. Today, she hoped to learn about stones that would help her understand her feelings towards Bryce. Night Sky walked in the door at one on the dot.

"Good afternoon, Night Sky," Twylene sang out, her lips lifted in a grin.

"How's my favorite new student, today?" Night Sky's eyes twinkled as he smiled at her.

"Hey, what about me?" Rosemary asked with an exaggerated frown. She hung his worn denim jacket on the coat rack and led the way to her office.

"You're my favorite old student," he responded. "In fact, I wanted to compliment your trance work. Your accuracy is outstanding."

"Thanks, time and practice is my motto." She swaggered and then broke out in a huge smile.

"You're right, practice is essential. If you don't learn to control your gift, it will control you."

"I know. You don't want me to be a flake that can't handle this realm." Rosemary rolled her eyes. *Or a horny wolf that loses herself when remote viewing a certain naked vampire.*

Night Sky narrowed his eyes, and then grinned. "That's right. You aren't any good to anyone if you can't keep your focus."

A blush stained her cheeks. *Does that shaman know all my thoughts?*

Night Sky turned to Twylene and said, "You're coming along in this area, too."

"I'm glad you noticed. Rosemary has been a great mentor and inspiration."

"Just make sure she doesn't teach you any of her bad habits." Night Sky's eyebrows lifted as he gazed at Rosemary, making her squirm.

"Time to start," said Rosemary, sitting down at the conference table.

They followed. Gathered around a table, they took in the selection of stones he laid out on the light blue velvet cloth.

Held at eye level, Night Sky turned a striated column of stone. "Black tourmaline is one of the best for keeping you grounded and free of negativity from others." With a quick glance towards them, he asked, "Do you have patients who come in disoriented?"

They both nodded with set mouths and wide eyes.

"Put this in their left hand and a clear transmitter quartz crystal in their right hand and it will balance their energies."

Rosemary rested her chin on her hand. *I can think of other times I need to be grounded.*

"I thought I'd read somewhere that tourmaline could be used for dyslexia?" asked Twylene.

"Am I transposing numbers again?" Rosemary twisted her lips in frustration.

"Now that you mention it, yes!"

"Keep a big piece of it on your desk. The energy will help slow you down and allow your brain and body to coordinate better." Night Sky was tossing a small, pitted stone in his right hand.

"Are you concerned about tourmaline grounding your psychic abilities?" he asked.

"That could be disastrous for me." Rosemary sat up, eyes alert. *Especially around Bryce and his abilities.*

"A black stone that originates in the sky, tektite can keep you grounded and yet allow for you to use your psychic abilities." He tossed the small rock to Rosemary, who caught it.

"You take this one." He tossed another to Twylene. "Don't want to leave you out."

Night Sky picked up a shiny black ball, admiring the swirls of color just below the surface. "I love the sheen of the obsidian. Helping to remove diseases from the body and mind, it is one of the main stones used in shamanic healings." He handed it to Rosemary.

The sparkles of color drew her into the stone. She pulled back, not wanting to reinforce the idea she was unfocused.

"Use this gem with your remote viewing and astral projection. At the end of your session, make sure to dip the obsidian in large bowl of salt water, preventing negativity or disease from staying with you or spreading to someone else. Spiritual hygiene is as important as physical."

Rosemary ran her finger over the glass-like surface of the obsidian, as tiny sparks of energy tickled her hands. "I think we both need to invest in one of these," she said, handing the ball to Twylene.

Twylene held the obsidian to the light, catching the numerous rainbows reflecting deep within the gem. "Definitely."

Night Sky filled their minds with alternate healing options until Rosemary's head hurt. She rubbed the center of her forehead with the black tourmaline, dreaming of heading home and having a glass of wine.

"Okay, malachite was the last on my list for today." Night Sky's voice interrupted her daydreams. "Here's the homework for next time." Night Sky handed out assignments and carefully packed his impressive collection into a hand-sewn leather bag embossed with the profile of a howling wolf.

Rosemary locked the door behind him in preparation to close for the evening and returned to her office.

Twylene was gathering up her stones, when she turned to Rosemary and asked, "Are you interested in getting together to study this material sometime this week? I think it would help me to have an actual person to lay the stones on."

"Yes, love to. I was thinking the same thing but didn't want to intrude on your personal time. With you sharing the load here, I've had more time for my personal life, which includes Bryce. He appreciates you being here too."

"Are you going to spend time him tonight?" Twylene asked.

"For the last couple of months, I've met him for my supper, his lunch, and then we lock the office door to have hot, quiet sex."

"Quiet sex, with you two? Is that even possible?" Twylene laughed.

In the last couple of weeks, spending time with Twylene had Rosemary enjoying a friendship with a smart, funny, and sincere person. The last time she had friends like this was in college.

"It's a good thing there aren't many folks at the Blood Center that time of night," Rosemary said with a guilty grin. "Of course, I usually visit on Thursday. Tonight will be a surprise."

"Enjoy yourself, and don't worry about coming in until one tomorrow. I can handle the appointments until then."

"Really! Are you sure?"

"Positive. Now go surprise that handsome hunk and everything that goes with him."

"Thanks. See you tomorrow." Rosemary walked out the door, trying to ignore the psychic poke at the back of her brain.

Rosemary headed home worrying that she and Bryce had become predictable in the last few weeks. She sensed he wanted things to speed up, but he kept his word and let her take time to get used to the idea of being in a monogamous relationship with a vampire. His subtle stop at a jewelry store to look at watches somehow turned into a production of wedding ring shopping. They left with neither.

Fear of losing him tugged on her while fear of his alpha male turning into a control freak crept over her. He would have lunch delivered for her and Twylene when he knew the clinic was over-booked on patients. He'd have Mitchell take her car to be washed and detailed. Too nice. Damn! She was waiting for the other shoe to drop. Pulling into her driveway, she shook off her dark thoughts and headed into her home to plan her surprise.

Showered and dressed in her favorite blue jeans, she added the sapphire necklace and earrings from Bryce. She nodded her approval in the mirror. A quick stop in the kitchen yielded a picnic basket with sandwiches, wine, and blood.

Smiling to herself, she started her car and headed to his office. She was proud of herself for breaking out of their routine. She couldn't wait to see the surprised look on Bryce's face.

Each step she took up the sidewalk leading to the Community Blood Bank building rubbed her tight jeans in a caress of her private parts. The friction sparked an excitement she hoped to feel soon as Bryce massaged the same areas. Rosemary carried herself confidently; aware of the appreciative glance the lab tech on duty gave her when she strolled into the reception area.

"Hey, Rosemary, you meeting Bryce tonight? He'll be surprised." He greeted her with a big smile.

"I brought him some supper. Can I go on back?"

"Sure. He's got someone in his office at the moment, but he should be finished soon, especially if you walk in front of his door."

He winked at Rosemary, releasing a flood of confidence in herself. She was totally committed to Bryce but liked the attention from good-looking guys.

"I'll just read one of last year's magazines he keeps in the waiting room." She said waving her hand in dismissal.

"Yeah, that'll keep you entertained!" He laughed and opened the door for her.

She wandered down the hall to the waiting room outside Bryce's office and briefly peeked in the partial glass of his closed door. Bryce sat studying a stack of papers on his desk. Behind him and bent over him, mashing her considerable breasts into his back was Marie, the blonde shape shifter from Edward and Jonathan's party.

Rosemary realized she must have gasped, because Bryce's vampire ears seemed to prick up and his eyes rose to lock on her face through the glass in the door. Marie was too busy trying to seduce him to notice. Shock yielded to fury as Rosemary turned to leave.

All she could see was Leon flaunting a string of beautiful women past her at every opportunity after he gave up on getting her back. Embarrassment stained her face red when Jonathan and Edward reluctantly confided Leon had been cheating on her with a variety of hot, classy dates. Once again, her cheeks burned with the fire of her humiliation. She sprinted out of the waiting room and through the front door in record time.

By the time she got to her car, Bryce was leaning up against her driver's side door with his arms crossed and looking at her with luminous eyes. Rosemary just stared at him for a minute, mute with hurt and betrayal.

"Rosemary, I know you're hurt and angry because of what you thought you saw."

"I think I saw you enjoying Marie grinding her boobs all over you. I should have known when I first saw you at Jonathan and Edward's party you were a player." Her voice caught fighting back her sobs.

Bryce exploded. "I don't know what you think happened with Marie that night, but it didn't involve us having sex in any fashion. I was already captivated by you."

She stilled. "So, you didn't have sex with her then or tonight?"

"No. If you had stayed a half a second longer, you would've seen me move away from Marie and explain to her I was in love with you." Bryce stopped, seeming uneasy under her scrutiny. He uncrossed his arms and ran his hand through his dark brown hair.

"Bryce, I want to believe you." To her dismay, her voice broke slightly, "In fact, on some level I probably do. However, on an emotional level I feel like I've been a fool." She was doing her best not to break into tears. He moved to hug her, and she stopped him with a glare. "Don't. I'm going home."

"Can I come by after work?" Bryce's face was iced over.

"Don't bother." Her tears threatened to well up in her eyes.

"I'll see you in a couple of hours." His face cast with detached inevitability, he turned and stalked off toward the building.

Rosemary crawled in her car, biting her lips to control the sobs and headed home. She made herself drive slowly instead of pressing the gas pedal to the floor. What had she been thinking dating a vampire? Worse, she fell in love with him. Her anger turned to her past actions. She'd kept a lid on the guilt she felt over her indiscretion with Roger. Now, the lid flew off and her guilt spattered everywhere. *She was no better than Leon.*

On arriving home, she turned off the car and sat, tears making pools on the front of her blouse. Resolved to tune in to her true feelings, she made her way into the house. Passing her collection of stones glittering on her black velvet cloth, she plucked up a piece of malachite. Well, she needed clarity and healing. Night Sky had emphasized it was helpful in those areas. She held the stone up to her chest and breathed deeply, allowing its energy to enter her heart. Immediately, the tight band of fear squeezing her eased.

The realization she wanted to commit to Bryce on another level filled her thoughts. *When had she actually begun to think of marriage? No, she craved it.* Soul-wrenching sobs spilled out of her at this revelation. *Too busy. I let it sneak up on me. I took too long. And Roger...*At this, her wails echoed from the walls. She'd trusted Bryce with her heart. Had he betrayed her with that freakishly big-breasted shifter?

After thirty minutes of misery, she decided to try breathing in the energy of the gem again. The tears had cleared out the rubble of her broken heart, allowing her intuition to kick in. Her astral body floated out of her physical body and connected to his past. Her psychic centers opened to allow her to view Bryce's life.

The first vision showed him making clear boundaries with Marie throughout the last couple of months. After Bryce returned to his office this evening, he firmly explained to her she was to keep her breasts to herself. Marie stormed off and Bryce turned his lights off in his office. Then he shut the door. Rosemary experienced his disappointment and pain at the thought she didn't trust him.

When he broke down into tears, Rosemary's heart cracked open.

Every cell in her body was aware of their connection, aware of their love that extended beyond lifetimes. At that moment, she knew she had to make things right with him, because to lose him was unthinkable.

~

Slivers of fear worked their malicious magic through Bryce as he rang Rosemary's doorbell. His mind spun from all the fires he'd put out at work and now he was afraid he'd lost the love of his long life over a stupid misunderstanding. God, he wanted to throttle Marie, but as a representative of one of the largest clients of the blood bank, he had to play nice. Not, that he didn't spell out his feelings for Rosemary and set firm boundaries with her. Marie made it clear she didn't care.

Rosemary eased the door open. She lifted red, teary eyes to stare at Bryce. He stood there unsure of what to say.

"Hi," Rosemary sobbed, her tears glistening on her pale face.

"Hi?" Bryce's eyes searching her face for any indication of her feelings.

For a long moment, she held his gaze. "I'm glad you're here," she whispered.

"Rosemary, I know you're hurt, but I've done nothing wrong and…"

"I know." She swung the door open, backing up to let him enter.

Frustration coated Bryce in impatience as he walked into the entryway. "Why did you run away, and why the tears?" He stared back in waiting silence.

"I, I guess I was taken off guard when I saw Marie's huge boobs pressed up against you." She shut the door and turned to face him. "And, I'm…I'm not as beautiful as she is."

"But you are"

"Stop, let me finish." She held up a small hand. Bryce shut his month. "I realized tonight after I came home that you've tried in every way you know to tell me how much I mean to you and how much you love me. When I saw Marie with her pointy chest stuck to your back and what appeared to be you allowing it to happen, I assumed I'd been foolish in trusting you. I came home and thought about it. I did a meditation with a healing stone and my spirit guides helped me find the truth I've been hiding from myself. You have been true to me and set boundaries with Marie."

"Oh, Rosemary, my sweet untrusting Rosemary," Bryce said, his voice shaking. He gathered her into his arms, her curves melting into him. She hugged him tight as tears came bubbling up to the surface. "Why are you crying again, darling?" he whispered into her hair, thanking the gods for the second chance.

She leaned her head back and gazed into his eyes saying, "I want you by my side for the rest of my life. I can't imagine living without you. I love you, Bryce, and I'm committed to making our relationship work for both of us."

He searched her face, finding her blue eyes full of love. "Me, too," he said. "What can I do to convince you I'm not like Leon?"

"You already have. I need to tell you something that happened in the past."

His body stiffened. "Does this have anything to do during the time we were dating exclusively?"

"Not exactly."

"Then I don't want to know. I get you have trust issues and a lively past. I understand you are wired differently. That's what makes you perfect for me. Not everyone can trust a vampire who influences minds, and in your case trusting vamps in general is a challenge." His gaze searched her face.

"Do you love me?"

"I do."

"In that case..." He reached into his jacket pocket bringing out a small white box. Bending on one knee, he took her left hand in his. "Will you make me the happiest vampire in the world by becoming my wife?" The box cradled an engagement ring with a clear corn-flower-blue sapphire set in a platinum rose with diamond leaves accenting the sides.

He didn't breathe while she gazed at the ring. His heart sank as tears formed in her eyes. The dread of her rejecting him filled him with a cold loneliness. He knew he should slow down, but he couldn't seem to help himself.

"What a perfect ring." She blinked her eyes, stopping the tears. With a ragged breath, she said, "Yes, I want to share my life with you."

Bryce rose up and slipped the ring on her finger, silently sending another prayer to the gods.

The stones sparkled in the light reflecting the magic of the moment. Her eyes twinkled in pleasure at the sight. "Recently, I learned that sapphires are supposed to bring peace and joy to a person by opening their mind to beauty and intuition."

"They certainly let me see the beauty in you." His kiss landed softly on her forehead. "I swear to you to always protect you to the best of my ability and always love you."

"I don't know if it's the sapphire, but I've not felt this peace and joy, well ever."

Bryce picked her up holding her close to his chest and headed to the bedroom. She was the part of him that he had missed for too long. The part that made him want to be a better person. The part that made him want to be compassionate and kind. He gently placed her on the soft French blue and purple bedspread and started to kiss her in little feathery kisses all over her face, neck and shoulders.

Her response, a purr of pleasure, intensified his love for her, making him ready to brand her as his own. She kissed him with a touch of her lips and reached to unbutton his shirt. Warm, eager hands slid down his chest, evoking twitches from his solid muscles.

His heart craved her love. He had lived a long time, never believing he could find another soulmate. The loss of her now would condemn him to an eternity of nothingness.

She undid his slacks, allowing his cock to push out, still imprisoned in his tight, bright red underwear. When she glided her hand over his taut silk-bound penis, his head dropped back, and his eyes involuntarily closed. The motion of her fingers exploring his arousal shot waves of desire through his body. When his need for her built to a furor, he opened his eyes to drink in her beauty.

He would never let anyone or anything come between them again. Her face filled with lust as his cock jumped in delight.

"Oh, darling. You've had me going all night, don't torture me now," he begged, grabbing her hand. The need to claim her overcame any gentleness he possessed. Rosemary's sweater flew over her head landing on the dresser's mirror. With eyes focused on her chest, he released her succulent breasts from her red lacy bra in a blur of speed. His talented mouth was sucking at her breasts, making them into hard pearls of lust. He had her jeans off, leaving her in silk thong. "Great minds think alike," he quipped.

"If that's true, then what am I thinking," she asked with a laugh.

"Let's peel off our red silky underwear."

"You are a mind reader!" They both slid their undies off and fused together from the lips down. Bryce lifted Rosemary's knees up with his arms then pressed his cock into her slick core.

Rosemary moaned against his lips and Bryce kissed her harder. The anger they had generated earlier, now erupted into white-hot passion. His insides burned with the need to brand her as his. Her panting from the pleasure of their lovemaking inspired him. His tongue traced a path down her neck to the vein in her shoulder. Her eyes followed him, sparking in anticipation as his fangs touched her skin. He paused and then bit, drinking deeply. Her wail filled the room as she tightened around him, pulsing with her climax. He continued to drink, not because he was hungry, but because he wanted Rosemary in his veins.

Soon, he lifted his head from her shoulder. The need to claim her blazed a path to his penis, jerking his body as he spilled his essence deep within her. "Mine," he said.

Collapsed on top of Rosemary, he basked in their connection.

She began to wriggle about.

"Am I too heavy for you or are you trying to get another rise out of me?" He smiled as he touched his nose to hers.

"I need to breathe. Turn us on our sides, keeping us connected until I get that rise from you." She grinned as Bryce repositioned them with a quick movement.

"That better?" he asked.

"Much. Are you staying the night?"

"I'm behind on my sleep, I think I'll curl up with you and then head home and sleep tomorrow."

"Bryce?"

"Yes?"

"I truly love you. I'm ecstatic we're getting married." Her voice shook.

His eyes met hers, and then he smiled. "I'm sorry Marie caused you such pain. The fact you trust me enough to marry me makes me the happiest I've been in a long, long time."

She wrapped her arms around his neck and kissed him lightly on the lips. They cuddled up next to each other and fell asleep.

A beam of sunlight squeezed through the shade waking Bryce with an uncomfortable heat.

Short on blood and sleep, he cringed when Rosemary sang, "Rise and shine, love."

"What? That light is killing me!" He shaded his eyes from the light.

Closing the curtains, she handed him a scarlet glass of breakfast.

"Yum, thanks." He took the glass and downed it in four swallows. His eyes cleared and skin lost the pale sheen. "I guess I was hungry," he said as he sat on the edge of the bed, naked.

"Hungry for many things is my guess."

"I'm still hungry for you, my sweet," he reached for Rosemary and kissed her soundly on the lips. "When shall we set the date?" He waited, gauging her response.

It took her only a second to answer. "I'll need about six months to plan and send out invitations. I assume it will be an evening wedding?"

Relief spread through him. *She hadn't changed her mind.* "That would make it easier. How many people are we inviting?"

"My family and friends, including Jonathan and Edward. How would you feel about having the wedding at their house?"

"I'd like that."

"How many people would you like to invite?" She crossed the room to pick up a notebook and pen.

"Well, there are the people from work, and my brother, Rhys. Let me get back to you with a better estimate."

"Don't take too long," She jotted down a note. A flash of concern struck her face. "Do you want to invite Marie?"

Do I have fool tattooed on my forehead? He stood and put his hands on her arms. "Even though she is a representative of one of the largest clients of the blood bank, she has been nothing but trouble. I don't want to deal with her on my wedding day."

She searched his face. "I agree. However, if you need to invite her, I would love for her to watch while I marry you."

"You're just a touch evil." He cocked an eyebrow.

"Better remember that." The corners of her mouth lifted and her eyes sparkled. "How do you feel about a May wedding? The thirteenth is a Friday."

"Humm... Friday the thirteenth has always been lucky for me." He searched his calendar. "That'll work just fine. I'll take some vacation time and we'll go on a lovely honeymoon. Let me know some locations you would like, and I'll make travel arrangements." He laid his calendar down on the nightstand.

"Okay. Um.... Bryce, what about our living arrangements?"

"I was hoping you would move in with me. I designed the house with two adjoining master suites, because even though I'd given up on love, I always had a secret romantic hope I'd meet the woman of my dreams. You can redecorate it to your tastes and move in as soon as you're ready."

"I'm fine with the décor you have."

"I'm not. You should have your suite reflect your tastes. I will pay to have whatever you want done."

"That's a generous offer, but I don't want you to use your money. I'm beginning to make a decent living."

"I'm doing it to insure you will be close and safe. We haven't discussed money, but after my four centuries of investing, neither of us would need to work if we didn't want to."

"Again, I appreciate your generosity. However, I do my work because I want to help people like you and me who end up receiving either incorrect treatment or none at all from the regular medical profession. Many GDBs die due to their ignorance. I love what I do and want to continue."

"I thought that's what you'd say. Hell, it's one of the reasons I fell in love with you. Would you let me remodel for you and look into moving your regular offices to a better location? I'll consider it money well invested."

"Give me some time to research my needs. I do believe a move will be necessary for my office, but let's look into the options."

"I also want us to meet with my brother, Rhys, to set up trusts and make sure everything with our money is spelled out. In case something happens to me, I want to make sure you're set up for the rest of your life. We can work out the details later."

"If something happens to me, I want to make sure you get everything of mine that you deserve. Right now, we both can't imagine reaching that point, but who knows. I wouldn't want to take you for everything, but I do want my practice to survive for the sake of my clients."

"Rosemary, I recognize my issues with jealousy, possessiveness, and territorial tendencies. Therefore, I'll do my best not to jump to conclusions and interfere with your work." He paused for a moment. Reaching for her hands, he said, "I can tell you understand after what happened with Marie last night. After some thought, I realized I might've been worse if the tables were turned."

"I hope we never find out. Promise me we'll always talk and work things out. Let's keep the lines of communication open, especially as we plan our wedding!"

"Agreed." Bryce kissed her and said, "Why don't you call Jonathan and Edward and tell them the good news, and see if we can hold the wedding at their house? In May, we could do it in the back yard."

She dialed the number. "I like that idea."

On hearing Edward's voice, she turned her attention back to the phone. "I hope I didn't wake you. This is Rosemary."

"You're psychic! We were still up. In fact, we were sitting here wondering how Twylene is working out for you."

"Perfect, she's smart and charming. You know how shape shifters can adapt to fit the situation."

"Yes. They're entertaining to be around, but Twylene's also a bright cookie. We were also wondering if you and Bryce would join us for dinner Friday evening."

"Now you're being psychic. Let me ask Bryce." She got his nod of approval. "We want to share some big news with you both."

"You two are getting married, aren't you?"

"You will find out Friday night. Is there anything I can bring?"

"Just you and that handsome soon-to-be-husband of yours. See you on Friday around eight. Kisses."

"Kisses to you and Jonathan." Rosemary hung up and glanced at Bryce. "Shall I meet you there?"

"My meeting should be done in plenty of time for me to pick you up," he said as he finished dressing.

"Okay. I'm heading into the office to try to get my life caught up today. Please, get some rest, my love." Rosemary kissed him then headed for the shower.

Bryce put on his sunglasses before he headed out the door with all intentions of catching up on his sleep. Walking to his car, a big smile broke out on his face. Rosemary was going to marry him.

Stephan's eyes followed Bryce to his car. *Soon. Very soon.* In the meantime, he planned to do a little breaking, entering, and entertaining himself with Rosemary. No turning or torture, yet. On the one hundredth anniversary of Bryce and Jonathan murdering his wife, his superior skills would claim justice for his Kate.

CHAPTER 13

Twylene grabbed Rosemary as soon as she opened the door. "The walk-in sitting in our waiting room thinks she's a human, but I think she's fae."

"Is she my one o'clock?" Rosemary hung up her coat and stashed her purse.

"No, that'd be Karen Crow." Twylene snatched her electronic tablet and brought up the schedule.

"Oh, Goddess!" Rosemary threw her head back and sighed. "It doesn't take a psychic to figure out what's going on with her. Let me guess, her eyes are muddy green?"

"You are psychic!" Twylene chuckled.

"Damn, a cheater and possessed. I'll try not to ruffle her feathers."

"What? Aren't you up for a therapy session with the old gal on why you shouldn't cheat on your partner?" Twylene rolled her eyes.

"Not today." Rosemary flashed her engagement ring,

"Nice! Bryce?" Twylene held Rosemary's hand up to get a closer look.

"Yes. I'll tell you more later."

"Can't wait."

"Show the fairy changeling into exam room two. Gather her basic information and I'll be in with her soon." Rosemary booted up her tablet and headed into the first exam room to meet with Karen. After last night's run-in with Marie, she put in extra effort to project a professional demeanor towards the crow shifter. She wasn't in the mood for repeat cheaters. Karen often tested every nerve she possessed. Rosemary knocked on the door and a raspy voice said, "Come in."

"Good afternoon, Karen. What's going on today?"

The petite woman perched on a chair, her dyed blonde hair a contrast to her dark eyebrows and lashes.

"My head hurts. It starts in the back here," she said, touching her neck, "and travels over my head to my eyes."

"Are you nauseous, or does light hurt your eyes?"

"No, no, I just experience this sensation of the pain traveling and then concentrating in the center of my forehead."

"Okay, let me examine you." Rosemary used her hands and eyes in the manner she had learned from Night Sky to scan her patient. Right over the top of Karen's head a cold spot caught her attention, alerting her to possible blockages. *Ah ha! We have a problem.*

Not for the first time, Rosemary asked questions that Karen responded to with incomplete answers or out-and-out lies. Rosemary's lack of patience with women who flirt with other women's husbands rose up again, forcing her to take a deep breath. "Do you experience more problems around a full moon?"

"Yes. My husband is not interested in going on full moon hunts. He just wants to roost at home in front of the TV." A bitter smile graced her lips.

"You stay home with him?"

"Not exactly." She laid a hand against her breastbone, clutching her gold necklace in mindless strokes. "I've been flying with a guy with a sharp eye for shiny things, but the headaches started after our first hunt."

Compulsive liars who cheat on their husbands. Ahh! She was being tested. Still raw from last night, Rosemary reminded herself Bryce asked her to marry him. A secretive smile broke from her lips. *He had chosen her.*

Back to business and out of medical suggestions for Karen's promiscuous ways, she asked, "Would you be up for something I learned from my shaman?"

Clapping her hands until the numerous gold and silver bracelets clanged, she said, "Yes! That sounds so mystical."

Rosemary positioned her on a padded table and pulled a thick blanket over her legs left bare by her short skirt. In the dim light, she guided Karen through a meditation while using hands-on-healing on her head. She stopped, sensing the heavy, bone-chilling block and said, "Karen, an imbalance in your system exists that allows for outside influences to manipulate you easily. Do you feel the energy of my hands?"

"I do! Right above my forehead." She drew in a quick breath. "Black icky stuff is trying to burst out of my head. Oh God, it hurts!" Karen squeezed her eyes shut. Dark clouds of a sticky substance like sooty hairspray poured out of Karen's head covering Rosemary's hands.

Rosemary raised the energy, her hands glowing with healing heat, burning hotter and hotter.

"My head is tingling and itching. They're leaving." Karen opened her clear forest green eyes. A good sign, since they had been a muddy beastie green when she had laid down.

Hands washed to remove any leftover negative energy, Rosemary helped Karen sit up. "How do you feel?"

"My headache is gone for the first time in months!" Karen flew off the table and put on her black stiletto heels with red soles.

Maybe I should consider turning into a vampire. I will not be one of those old women who try to look twenty years younger.

Rosemary handed her a booklet outlining exercises to help her. "You had some negative energy blocking you. Here are some techniques to help keep yourself positive."

"Thanks. What else can I do?" Karen danced in place with joy.

Words considered, Rosemary said, "Well, if you find yourself telling someone something that's not true, then stop yourself and stick to the truth. When we expand too much on something, we fill our heads with doubts and fears."

"I always tell the truth," Karen avoided looking at her.

"Good to hear. That will help with any problems." Rosemary sucked in a calming breath, aware of the lie. She needed a good psychologist, but the first time, Karen got upset and shifted into a crow there would be complications. She slipped in some spiritual hygiene when she could.

Rosemary finished up with Karen and headed to exam room two. *Definitely need to consider becoming a vampire.* She skidded to a stop. *Where had that come from? She was just now accepting happy ever after for one lifetime, let alone forever or until ...* She shook her head and walked down the hall to her next appointment.

When she opened the door to exam room two she was met by a pair of the most incredible aqua eyes taking her measure. "Good Afternoon, I'm Dr. Rosemary Wolfe, what brings you here today?"

The pale young woman let out the breath she held. "Hi, I'm Sylvia Worth, and I'm not sure why I'm here. My regular doctor says he has conferred with you on some of his patients and suggested I make an appointment. I took a chance you might squeeze me in today, because I don't think I can go another night without sleep."

"Tell me more about your sleeping patterns."

"I seem to fall asleep fine, however, I wake up around four A.M. after having the same dream. I'm enormously disturbed to the point, I can't go back to sleep."

"Let's start with the dream. Can you tell me what it is?"

"Sure, the dream starts out with me sitting in my backyard reading a book. The day is warm, and I'm relaxing in a chair in the shade. Convinced someone is staring at me, I look up from my book to see a winged female creature about four inches tall looking at me with an intense stare. I ask her what she wants. Come outside, she says. I tell her I'm outside." Sylvia paused, shivering.

"You're doing fine." Rosemary covered her with a blanket and handed her some water.

Waiting until the blanket and water calmed her, Rosemary jotted down her observations.

Sylvia's eyelids quivered, and she started relating more of her dream. "She again states she wants me to come outside. She's standing between two large oak trees and motioning me to follow her through them as if they were a door. Taking a step that way, I hear a voice behind me telling me it's a trick. I freeze, and the fairy starts yelling to hurry because the monster behind me is going to kill me. Cold sweat pouring off of me, I wake up screaming." Wide aqua eyes searched Rosemary for answers.

Patting her hand, Rosemary nodded. "Thank you for sharing your dream."

Sylvia drew in a deep breath, settling. "It feels almost real, but how can that be?"

"Your subconscious is trying to tell you something. Your primary doctor probably sent you to me because I do some alternative healing that involves dream work. First, what do fairies mean to you?"

"I'm not sure. As a child, I was convinced a fairy would come and save me when my mom was in one of her alcoholic rages. As I grew older, I guess I thought it was silly to talk to fairies and I convinced myself that they were figments of my imagination. In fact, I was frightened of them in high school. I'd have a nightlight on and still feel their eyes watching me."

"I think you might have some fears that hypnosis could help. Would you be willing to try that?"

"You aren't going to make me cluck like a chicken, are you?"

"No, unless that's something you would normally do," Rosemary answered with a twinkle in her eye and a laugh. "Hypnosis is an altered state of consciousness where you're highly focused and highly relaxed at the same time. But, you're always in control. You're aware of everything that goes on. However, you're focused on what we are doing. It's sort of like watching a good TV show or reading a good book. You may be aware of a neighbor mowing his yard or kids playing outside, but unless there is something like a fire, you pay no attention to them. I'll record the session and give you a copy. I can also reschedule, if you need to bring someone you trust. I have time right now, if that would work for you."

"I trust you already. What do I need to do to get ready for this?"

"I'll send Twylene in with the paperwork while I set up the recording equipment. Will that work for you?"

"Yes, Dr. Wolfe, I've got to get some sleep."

"Please, call me Rosemary." Rosemary left her to Twylene while she set up her office for a hypnosis session. She suspected Twylene was right about Sylvia being a changeling. Rosemary would soon find out. She met Sylvia in her office and got her relaxed in a comfortable recliner. Rosemary induced hypnosis, grateful she was an easy subject.

After listening to the dream, she realized Sylvia possessed more than a few markers of a fae genetic makeup. Her pale skin and big aqua eyes were the most obvious. After a long hypnosis session that confirmed her theory even more, she sat down across from Sylvia. "How are you?"

"Better. I remember everything I experienced. It's a little weird, but it makes much sense with everything that's happened in my life. I've had many experiences where I'd swear I changed a situation by focusing on it. Usually, I'm in a very agitated state when that feeling overtakes me. The room goes dark and time slows down. In a few seconds, everything is back to normal, but the situation has changed to my liking."

"Sylvia, you are not the first person who has come to me with fairy DNA. Are you interested in visiting with others who are like you?"

"I don't know. Can that help?" She shifted in her chair, a frown marring her face.

"Talking with others who have experienced some of the same things can help you feel you are not alone. They also have workshops on how to handle fae abilities." Rosemary paused, allowing the information to sink in.

Sylvia raised her eyes and smiled. "I'd try a couple of meetings."

"Let me give you the contact information." Rosemary handed her the brochure.

Her face glowed with a soft light. Brochure in hand, she nodded. "I think I'll actually sleep tonight. Thank you so much."

"If you do find yourself restless, I gave you a post-hypnotic suggestion described in this handout. Give it a try. Make an appointment with Twylene. I want to check on how you're getting along in a couple of weeks."

"I'll be looking forward to it. Thank you again." Sylvia flitted out the door.

Rosemary reached for her phone. She needed to talk to someone normal like Bryce. Well, she laughed to herself, more normal. He should be awake by now. Just as she picked up her phone, the front door jerked open to allow Roberta, in labor, to waddle over the threshold.

"Ahh..." Roberta was bent in a contraction, leaning on a rugged man, who supported her as though she was a precious flower. A flower with brambles.

Twylene and Rosemary glanced at each other with a when-it-rains-it-pours look.

"They're coming! The twins, they're coming! She's in labor," Lester tried to pick up his expanded wife, who growled at him.

Twylene grabbed a wheelchair, positioning it under Roberta to transport her to the delivery room.

"Thanks. Mercy, that hurts!" Roberta moaned, easing into the wheelchair.

"How far apart are the contractions?"

"About five minutes."

"Let's position you quickly then," Rosemary said, joining Twylene to help Roberta into a birthing chair that allowed her to sit in a semi-squatting position using gravity to help push the babies out.

"Breathe, that's good! Breathe deeply, you're doing so good, honey," Lester said, holding her hand.

"Grreat! Mercy! Awwwol!" Roberta was using her wolf strength as the pain shot through her. The strength of her wolf clamped her hand around Lester's.

The only clue to his pain was the way he was biting down on his lower lip. Lester was a good husband.

Rosemary heard the popping sounds of Roberta's bones, as she wavered between human and wolf. Better to deliver them as humans than wolves. She caught Roberta's attention.

"Let's start the hypnosis like we practiced. Breathe deep and imagine the pain is a twisted rope." Rosemary guided Roberta into a trance, easing the pain.

"Lester, keep Roberta breathing and visualizing that rope slowly relaxing while Twylene and I go grab some more supplies." Rosemary motioned for Twylene to join her.

When they returned, Roberta was completed dilated and the top of a little dark head of hair could be seen.

"Keep breathing, Roberta. Now imagine that each contraction feels like a pressure with no pain. The baby is flowing out of your womb easily and quickly. Breathe deeply, that's perfect." Rosemary turned and whispered to Lester, "You're doing great too."

Lester gave her a part grin and grimace.

Rosemary switched back to guide the first baby out of the birth canal.

Lester let Roberta squeeze his hand as he urged her on. "You're a champ, honey, keep pushing."

"I...I...am!" Roberta's face relaxed a bit as she continued pushing with Twylene and Lester's help.

Soon the head of the first baby was being held in Twylene's hand. In the meantime, Rosemary gradually guided the child's shoulders out of the birth canal. She glanced up to made sure Roberta had stopped shifting. Satisfied she was stable, she checked on the position of the second baby.

Covered in blood and other fluids, she realized she was going to be late going home. Good thing Bryce understood the demands of her job.

The clock read 10:00 p.m. when Rosemary finally had a chance to look. Both human baby boys were born, cleaned up and resting in their mom's arms.

"They're beautiful," Roberta said.

"They're perfect." Twylene straightened the blanket covering Roberta. "Lester, are you ready to hold one?"

"Oh yeah!" He stopped a moment, and then looked down at his family. "Honey, thank you for birthing our babies." He touched her forehead with a tender kiss and with a grace unexpected of such a large man, let alone a werewolf, he took one of his sons from his wife.

"What are you going to name them?" Rosemary was captivated by the red, wrinkled cuties.

"Robert and William, after our fathers," Roberta said.

"You'll be calling them Bob and Bill, right?" Twylene cocked her eyebrow.

"Unless they're in trouble, and then it'll be Robert and William." Lester laughed. "This is Bill. What a face! I think he's smiling at me."

Rosemary figured Lester would soon discover Bill's smile resulted from his digestive system filling his diaper. She gave him a smile and nodded.

"Time for Twylene and me to clear out and let mom and babies get some rest," Rosemary said, placing the babies in cribs near Roberta's bed. "Lester, we've set up a cot if you want to stay with your family tonight. I arranged for a temporary night nurse to stay for this evening. Since the little guys are in human form, I don't think there will be any problem. However, here's my card with my cell number written on the back. Don't hesitate to call."

"Thanks. I'll be right here," Lester said, with a big, silly grin.

Rosemary finished filing the last of her forms for the day and turned to Twylene to say, "Can you believe how busy it was for a Tuesday?"

"Not really. Roberta was not on the schedule." Twylene locked the door to the supply room.

Walking beside her, Rosemary turned to her. "What are your plans for this weekend?"

"I'm going out on a date," she said, her eyes downcast.

Twylene is many things, but shy is not one of them. "You're finally up to seeing a new man in your life?"

"Not exactly."

She's not coy either. "Come on, spill it, what are you hiding?" Rosemary stood in front of her.

"Fine, never try to keep something from a psychic witch. There's someone I really like." Twylene paused to lick her lips.

"That's fantastic."

"And, she's not married."

"She! That's the big secret. Where'd you meet? What's she like?" Rosemary held Twylene's hands, jumping with joy.

Twylene cleared her throat. "It doesn't bother you that I might be dating a woman?"

"Are you kidding me? You do know about my past loves and about my current friends, don't you?" She guided her nurse to chairs and they both sat.

"Well, there are rumors, but..."

Her hand released Twylene's in a dismissive wave. "At least half of them are true. The only thing I care about is your happiness. Now, tell me all about her."

"She's a pharmacist at the hospital. We've known of each other for years, but we met at a horseshow last weekend. Her son was barrel racing, and my brother was showing a new quarter horse. We starting talking and realized we had lots of things in common. She confessed she had broken up with a woman last month who was a shape shifter. I told her about Ted, and we became fast friends."

"Wow, she sounds perfect. Is this your first time dating a woman?"

"Yes. Frankly, I'm confused about how sexual I feel towards her, but I believe the best way to deal with confusion is to find out more. Have you really been with another woman?"

"Yes, several times. It's different from being with a man. Both are enjoyable, but what really matters is how I feel about the person." Rosemary waited for Twylene to continue. A warm glow filled her. She liked having a girl friend who trusted her to share the more intimate details of her life.

"I know this sounds crazy, but I think she's my soul mate. Her name is Liz, by the way. I want you to meet her and tell me what you think." Her face was flushed with color.

"I'm happy for you! I'd love to meet her. Let's see how this weekend works out."

Twylene threw her an expectant glance. "You want to tell me about that shiny rock on your left hand?"

She held out her left hand to show off her ring. "Bryce and I are officially engaged. The wedding is May thirteenth."

"Congratulations! You two are a picture-perfect match. Where are you going to hold the wedding?"

"We hope at Jonathan and Edward's house. We'll ask them Friday night when we go there for dinner. Would you be interested in being a bridesmaid?"

"Of course! You aren't going to have ugly dresses, are you?" She smiled and hugged Rosemary.

"You can help me pick them out. That way, you can make sure the dresses are up to your standards."

"How about your mom and sister? Will they be helping?"

"They'll be coming up to help on occasion, but I need someone here who'll be in my corner." They both nodded their heads and chuckled.

They walked out the front door, Twylene turning her key to lock it. "I bet you didn't get much sleep last night."

A guilty smile spread over Rosemary's face. "I was in bed for at least eight hours."

"Sleeping?" Twylene checked to make sure the door locked.

"A little. I plan on making up for lost time tonight. I glanced at tomorrow's schedule. See you bright and early." Rosemary headed across the parking lot to her car.

"Congratulations, again." Twylene closed her car door and started the engine.

Rosemary, reaching for her car door, spotted a cream-colored piece of folded paper tucked under her windshield wiper. Her head whipped up, drawing in the frosty November air in an attempt to scent out the author of the note. Too many GDBs and humans had been in the parking lot today. She turned to her psychic senses. Nothing out of the ordinary, she plucked up the note. The spidery handwriting read; *You're next.* Eyes wide and heart racing, she climbed into her car. Doors locked, she alternated between wanting to kill the joker and feeling the icy fingers of fear dance up and down her vertebrate.

I'm a witch and a werewolf, for Goddess sakes. I could run to Bryce, but wouldn't that make me weak and dependent on him? That's one of the many ways I got in trouble with Leon. Yet, this feels like more than a joke. Maybe Jonathan and Edward? They would tell Bryce. No. I can handle this myself.

She put the car in gear and contemplated what to do while driving home.

CHAPTER 14

"Oh crap," Rosemary said flinging open her apartment door. The Friday afternoon appointment with the teenage witch/wolf, Marcie, had run late.

Jumping in and out of the shower, she headed for the bedroom. In front of her closet, she smiled remembering Marcie's new slim body and increased confidence. She listened to her talk nonstop about the difference the werewort tincture made in helping her control her shifts. With that thought, she drank her own dose down and reached for her flowing black pants followed by a silky red blouse topped with a black sweater.

Was she doing the right thing? She grabbed her watering can and watered her cheery red orchids from Bryce. They calmed her. The decision to show him the note left on her car troubled her. *He's different from Leon.* The doorbell rang, just as she finished. *Good timing.*

Bryce stood on the porch holding a long-stemmed blood red rose. Perfect in color and shape, the flower matched the ones embroidered on her sweater. He smiled down at her and brushed the soft satin petals of the bud along her cheek.

"Hi, beautiful, are you ready to go?"

"I am." Nose buried in the petals, she took a long whiff. "What a lovely gift, thank you," She located a vase and slid the stem into water. "Now I know why this outfit spoke to me. Why a rose instead of orchids?"

"This lovely blossom reminded me of you. Redheaded, sweet fragrance, and thorns where you least expect them." He chuckled while putting his hand on her shoulder in a possessive gesture to guide her out the door.

She stopped, putting a hand on his arm. "Do you have a minute for me to show you something?"

"Sure." He led her back inside and closed the door.

The piece of paper she held in her hand shook as she passed it to him. After reading the two-word warning, his eyes flashed up to hers. "Where did you get this?"

"It was tucked under my windshield wiper when I left work on Tuesday night."

"Who left it there?"

"I'm not sure. I'm not even sure it's a threat. It could be someone playing a sick joke, but, I'm uneasy." She bit down on her lower lip trying to keep her face calm.

Bryce's nostrils flared and his head jerked up to meet her gaze. "This is more than a sick joke."

She steadied herself with filling her lungs with air, then slowing releasing the breath. "I'd hoped you could give me some perspective. Going to the police seemed like a bad idea."

He reached for her, wrapping her in a blanket of comfort. "I doubt it's anything but let me keep the note and show it to a detective friend who is aware of GDBs. If you are okay with that?"

She nodded, afraid to speak.

"You're safe with me tonight. I'll have it checked out tomorrow."

"Okay" She lifted a brave face and smiled at him, gratitude pouring through her. "Thank you."

"I will be your personal body guard until we find out who put this on your car. Let's go enjoy our evening with our friends, and I will worry about this tomorrow."

Her arm slipped around his waist, and arm-in-arm they walked to his car, breathing in the chilly, late fall evening, admiring the full moon. The moon's energy strummed across her nerves. Her hands rubbed the pouch containing a tektite meteorite and rose quartz in her pocket immediately calming her down. Excitement churned through her at the thought of telling Jonathan and Edward about her engagement. A welcome thought after seeing Bryce's face when she showed him the note. Even though he smiled with reassurance, his eyes revealed he knew more than he said. She would worry about that tomorrow. Tonight, she prayed Jonathan and Edward would be okay with Bryce after all the issues with Leon.

On the drive to Jonathan and Edward's, Rosemary studied his taut expression. "How was your day?"

Bryce filled his lungs with a deep breath of air. Blowing it out his mouth, he said, "Representatives from the American Association of Blood Banks gave us an update on testing blood donations for hepatitis C and talked to us about submitting our donor information electronically."

With a disbelieving shake of her head, she asked, "Are you having problems with bacteria or viruses?"

"No. We're small enough, and my personal interest in the quality of our blood assures us of very clean products."

"That's good."

He glanced her way. "We are short on donors. Therefore, I'm going to need to travel and train on some recruitment methods in a couple of weeks."

She made a disapproving sound. "How long will you be gone?"

"Only a couple of days. Traveling tires me if my schedule includes too many daylight hours. Thank goodness, Mitchell does most of the traveling. By the way, he thinks you are adorable even soaking wet from the shower. He mentioned several times if I ever do you wrong, he will be right there to make sure you are not lonely."

"He is pretty cute," she said, "but I don't think you need to worry about him replacing you. Of course, if Marie is still brushing her boobs up against you, Mitchell might get lucky." She grinned.

"I don't suppose anyone ever mentioned what a smart ass you are?"

"Often. Don't tell me you are just noticing, Mr. Gold?"

With a chuckle, he stopped the car in Jonathan and Edward's drive, and reached over to kiss her on the lips. "Notice? Hell, it's one of your best features!"

With narrowed eyes, she smiled. "I'll take that as a compliment."

"By the way, when we marry, how are you going to handle your name?"

"I'm thinking I'll hyphenate. Is that okay with you?"

"I've lived in times where women usually took their husband's name, but I don't care what you do." He stopped and shook his head. "Well, I do care a bit. If you decided at least to hyphenate, so everyone recognizes you belong to me, you would make me extremely happy. But I don't want to be possessive." He looked sideways at her and grinned with those oh-so-sexy lips.

Rosemary would have called herself Doodles the Clown if he'd asked, but she wasn't going to let him in on that little fact. Vampires' advantages were too many already.

They got out of the car and headed to the door.

Edward answered the door with a gleam in his eye. "Good evening. Come on in and let me take your coats and learn your secrets."

"All in good time." Bryce clapped him on the back.

Rosemary admired the view of the fireplace that lit up the family room. The touch of Bryce guiding her to the sofa filled her with warmth that had nothing to do with the fire.

Jonathan came out of the kitchen to greet them wearing his, *Kiss the Cook* apron.

"Welcome. What's your pleasure in drinks tonight?"

"I'll take a glass of red wine." Rosemary wrapped her arms around him in a hug.

Jonathan turned to Bryce. "A good red for you, too?"

"You know me well." Bryce handed Edward his coat.

Coats hung in the closet, Edward turned to the happy couple. "Good week?"

"Tiring week. Somehow, a unit of blood tested positive for hepatitis C." Bryce shook his head. "Damn thing is I have no idea how that happened."

Edward's handsome face frowned. "You suspect it's more than an accident?"

"Don't know, but I will be checking out that angle. Anyway, tonight is about the good thing that happened this week. We are officially engaged." Bryce put his arm around her and planted a kiss on top of her head.

"I'm thrilled for both of you." Jonathan did a happy dance.

"Congratulations. It'll be great having my two favorite people, outside of Jonathan, in the same house." Edward handed Rosemary her wine and Bryce his blood. "A toast to the happy couple."

They all clinked their glasses and took a drink.

"Is the date set yet?"

"We are thinking about May thirteenth." Rosemary hesitated. "We want to ask if we could hold the wedding here in your backyard."

"Of course, and I insist on catering the food and cake." Jonathan kissed her lightly on the cheek.

"Thank you. You two are a blessing." Rosemary clutched both in a hug.

"I can't thank you enough for helping me relocate here from Boston and believing in me enough to give me Rosemary's address. I admit I'd given up on finding love again. However, she is the light and love in my life." Bryce's golden hazel eyes softened.

"We'd both given up on love. You guys are the greatest!" Rosemary couldn't remember ever being so happy.

"While we are making plans, would you both consider being my best men?" Bryce glanced at Jonathan and Edward.

"Love to, old man. You know how I feel about both of you," Edward said, with a catch in his voice.

"I'd be honored. I'm excited about this marriage. You two are such a perfect match." Jonathan hugged his friend and guided them to the table. "The wedding business is settled, let's eat. I fixed a French dish I think we all will enjoy: Boudins Noirs Aux Pommes."

"I don't know about the apples, but blood sausage is always tasty to me," Bryce said as his fangs started to extend. He took a healthy portion of the dish Rosemary handed to him and passed it on to Edward.

"Jonathan can make an incredible array of dishes using blood." Edward took a big-man portion of the concoction.

"I'm flattered you two enjoy the variety, but I love making the more normal food for Rosemary. Even though eating it would probably give me digestive trouble and absolutely no nutrition, I still love the smell of good food cooking. Thank goodness for your healthy appetite and active life." Jonathan sat the dish down. "I use Calvados in the sauce which I think brings out the apple flavor."

"That's what I'm tasting." Rosemary tasted the sauce, contemplating the flavor. "I think this is one of your best dishes ever."

Rosemary watched Bryce. His eyes closed, she could tell he enjoyed the gourmet flavors of the meal. A perfect evening with her two best friends and soulmate.

Everyone sighed as the meal ended. Jonathan and Edward headed to the kitchen carrying dishes, giving Bryce an opportunity to stand behind Rosemary and carefully place his hands on her shoulders. He leaned down as she looked up and kissed her on the lips.

"What's that for?"

"I love you and wanted to show you." He burrowed his nose in her hair.

"Hey, you two, only Edward and I are allowed sex on the dining room table," Jonathan teased as he came in carrying a large decorated cake. Edward followed with champagne for Rosemary, and blood and tequila to make Vampire Sunsets for the guys.

"This cake is for your birthdays, Bryce, and Rosemary. However, since Rosemary is the one who will enjoy it the most, I used all her favorite spices. You'll also notice there's only a representative number of candles on the cake, as four hundred and three might set the house on fire and we won't bring up Rosemary's age. Of course, no chocolate either. We wouldn't want to cause your wolf side any problems." Jonathan set the cake down.

After Jonathan and Edward sang *Happy Birthday* to both of them, they held up the cake and said, "Make your wishes and blow out the candles!"

Laughing, Bryce and Rosemary did their best to outdo each other blowing with childlike abandon.

"Come on, Rosemary, you can blow harder than that!" Jonathan winked.

Rosemary smirked. "You're just jealous." Then she and Bryce blew out every candle in a single united breath.

"You're good for him." Jonathan patted Rosemary's hand.

"You think?"

"I do. He hasn't laughed this much in a long time."

"Time to cut the cake. Is it age before beauty or beauty before age, I forget?" Jonathan put a finger to his lips and lifted a perfect eyebrow as he held up the knife.

"I have her on the age, but she certainly has me on the beauty. Therefore, I'll acquiesce to my sweetheart." Bryce waved his hand to Rosemary. Jonathan turned and handed her the knife.

"I love it when we agree." Rosemary set a plate with a piece of cake between them. "Shall we share? You usually don't eat much of it anyway."

Everyone sampled the cake, but Rosemary savored her first bite like a delicacy she would never have again.

"This is the best cake! Is it Betty Crocker or Pillsbury?" She pressed her lips together to keep from laughing.

Jonathan did a double take and then laughed. "You're evil! You know good and well it's homemade, Miss Rosemary!"

"Yes, and it's a masterpiece as usual. Thank you so much." She laughed as she offered Bryce a bite.

He leaned forward, closing his mouth around the morsel. "Thanks."

She noticed he had slipped into a quiet mood. Planting a kiss on his cheek, she held up another bite.

With a big grin, he took the piece and washed it down with a swallow of blood.

Okay, he's done.

Turning to Jonathan, she asked, "So, how're the restaurants doing these days? I went to lunch with Twylene last week at Jonnie's Downtown. I love the new honey balsamic vinegar dressing you created."

"Thanks, I worked on that one for a while. The restaurants keep busy."

"And Edward, how's your CPA firm doing these days? The rumor is your hours are long, and it isn't even tax time yet."

"We've been busy setting up trusts for a couple of families in town and working out accounting procedures for a couple of big businesses in St. Louis. There's nothing like job security." He smiled.

"I don't mean to talk shop, but I need you to check some records for me at the Blood Center. I think we've gotten off somewhere. Nothing serious, but I don't want it to blow up, either," Bryce sighed.

Rosemary followed Jonathan into the kitchen to refresh the drinks. His eyes met hers over the glass of wine he poured for her. "So, you and Bryce are all better after the incident with Marie?"

"How'd you find out about that? I didn't get a chance to call you." Her back tensed, remembering that night.

"Oh, sweetie, Bryce called before he went to your place." He stepped behind her and rubbed her shoulders. "He was worried sick that you would break up with him that night. He's told her to back off several times, but she doesn't take the hint."

"She still makes me insecure." She relaxed.

"She's a cow, and I don't mean that's her preferred shape to shift into. She just tries to run over people." Jonathan turned her to face him. "Bryce hasn't been a player for centuries. The day after you met at our party, he confessed to me you were the only woman he wanted for as long as you'd have him."

"I know, I know, I'm just not a trusting sort."

"Well, trust me when I say Bryce Gold is a man of his word. He saved me many times when we knew each other in Scotland."

"What happened?" Rosemary directed a questioning gaze his way.

"There were times I was starving, and he would share his stash of blood. Always compassionate, in spite of his circumstances, he makes a point of doing charity work in any community he lives in."

"Why relocate here from Boston?"

"For twenty years he lived there without aging. He casually dated a plastic surgeon at the hospital. Suspicious and jealous, she started asking too many questions about who'd done the nip and tuck on him. Even though he loved it there, Bryce decided to move on before she caused him any serious problems. When this position opened up, I told him about it. I put a good word in for him, but after looking at his résumé and references, the hiring committee was ecstatic about him."

"Very interesting. Thanks for cluing me about his past. We'd better take the drinks back to the boys." Rosemary held Bryce's glass in one hand and hers in the other while she walked with an energized stride to the dining room.

"Yes, our guys need their blood before we go to bed," Jonathan winked.

"Did you miss us?" Rosemary's expression was thoughtful as they came back into the room.

"Always," Bryce beamed.

"It's been so lonely without both of you. What've you been up to?" Edward wrinkled his brow.

"Just talking wedding plans," Jonathan shot back with a smile.

"Guess what we're going to hear about for the next six months?" Edward rolled his eyes towards Bryce.

"Yeah." Bryce's face reflected pure joy.

"Jonathan and Edward, thanks for the magnificent food and hospitality, but my bed beckons and rest awaits." Rosemary yawned.

"Your bed may beckon, but I don't think you are going to rest any tonight." Jonathan giggled as he hugged her good night.

"Are you staying tonight?" Rosemary led the way inside her apartment, leaving her love to shut and lock the door.

"Of course." Taking her hands in his, he lightly touched his lips to her forehead. "I want to see you every morning, every evening, and every day." He paused, gauging his next comment with care. "Honestly, I'd feel better if you would move into my house. My security is top of the line, and someone is there all the time."

Rosemary leaned back, her face locked into a determined grimace. "I can take care of myself. Besides, I don't have security going to or from work, or even at work."

"That can be arranged."

Her jaw was set in a firm clinch. "Thanks, but no thanks. I appreciate you looking into the note, but Bryce, I'm a big girl. Make that a big wolf and witch."

"A wolf that's afraid to shift and a witch who hasn't practiced in several years." One glance at her face told him he had gone too far. He held up his hands. "I'm sorry, that was out of line."

"It was, but you're right. I'll never mature if I don't learn how to deal with my abilities."

"Please, let me help." *Gods! She's headstrong.*

She stared at him for a moment. Shoulders rising with a breath of resignation, she nodded. "Because I love you and want to live with you, I will give notice and move in when the time is right. I do not want any other security. Understood?"

"Very well, you can bring your stuff over anytime. Would you consider talking with Donna tomorrow? If you did, she can start redecorating your room?" Bryce shot her an earnest look. Still, a little niggle of doubt tried to sneak up on him, but he pushed it away. He had won most of this battle.

Turning to head to the bedroom, she nodded. "We'll start the process tomorrow."

"Perfect, but for tonight, I want to make love to you all night long." Standing behind her, crossing his arms over her chest, he drew her into his embrace. Strength covered with velvet, he sensed her muscles shift under her smooth skin as he swayed with her, inhaling her cinnamon-honeysuckle scent. So hard, his erection hurt, but he continued the dance, his hardness rubbing her soft, round bottom. A quick kiss to her left ear, made her shudder. Little bites followed. Her hips squirmed against him and she let out a deep moan.

"Let's take this to the bedroom where we can get comfortable."

"I'm pretty comfortable here." He bent down to nibble her right ear.

"Fine, I'll be in the bedroom, enjoy yourself." She started to pull away, and then laughed when he picked her up and headed down the hall, still nibbling on her ear.

With a quick flip of the switch, the lamp lit the bedroom. He put her down facing him, continuing to kiss her with a slow, sensuous hunger. He planned to make love to her all weekend.

"God, I love being with you," he whispered in her ear.

"I love being with you too." She unbuttoned his shirt and ran her hands over his chest.

He jumped and then snorted. "Those hands are colder than some zombies I know. Let me warm you up." He held her sweater up while she slipped her arms out. Next, he undid each button of her blouse, his tongue teasing open her mouth. Her blouse eased off her shoulders while he deepened the kiss. Her tongue explored his mouth, exciting him with her uninhibited lust. A soft, sexy sound escaping his lips, he pushed her pants down and moved back to allow her to step clear. He stood, staring at her, puzzling over the ivory satin bra with lace that revealed her taut pink nipples. Matching ivory panties showed off her delicate folds. Her outfit led him to believe she wore black or red instead of an innocent ivory. A dizzying revelation struck him.

"How's this going to get me warm?" Her face holding the question.

"Let me show you." He pulled back the covers on the bed and tucked her in. The purity of the ivory lace occupying his thoughts.

"Are you going to join me?"

"Let me undress and I'll be right there." He slipped into the bed a moment later cuddling his naked body next to hers. The ivory lace underwear fascinated him. Over and over, he fondled her bra by cupping her breasts and squeezing them, the lace fanning out over her creamy skin. The silky fabric triggered a deep reaction within him. She had let him see the vulnerable wholesome side of her she normally hid.

"When I saw your ivory lace tonight, I felt as if you let me see the genuine you. I know it doesn't make sense, but I believe deep within myself, I can completely trust you." He traced small circles around her nipples.

"Bryce, it makes perfect sense. You might be strong and powerful in many ways, but we all need someone we can trust to be in our corner and watch out for us. I promise you I'll be that person for you." She gave him a quick peck on the nose and he smiled.

His eyes blazed down into hers. He released the front hook of her bra. "Strong women turn me on." Warm, tempting breasts fell into his waiting hands. He stroked them like precious jewels. "Your breasts are perfect. They are an exact fit for my hands." He ducked his head under the covers to suckle. "And, my mouth."

Pleading for more, her hips bucked as he licked and sucked, turning her nipples into velvet nails. She reached under the sheet and wrapped her small hand around his cock. Fingers running over his sensitive head caused him to shudder with desire. Laughter rang out when they found each other's ticklish spots. Bryce reached down and pulled her panties off.

The laughing stopped. Passion exploding, they grabbed one another with frantic actions. Rosemary touched his hand to still the rubbing of her aroused clit.

"What?" A puzzled expression on his face.

With a shy smile she said, "I want you wolfie style."

"Whatever Wolfie wants, Wolfie gets." He helped her turn around and position her on all fours. His arms reaching around her to play with her breasts ignited her need. His tongue brushed her shoulder in delicate spirals and ended delivering intense swipes on her pulse by her ear.

The rough touch of his tongue pressing on her vein drove her to craving the orgasm caused by his fangs. "Go ahead and bite me."

"Not yet. Maybe later. I want your blood humming when I taste you. Mmmm... do you own any massage oil?"

"Try looking in the top drawer of my nightstand. Are you going to give me a massage?"

"In a way. I want you to experience something I think you might find titillating. Trust me?"

"No kinky vampire stuff?" She said, turning and looking at him over her shoulder.

"No, just a mind-blowing orgasm. You game?"

"Okay," she said, swallowing with unease. Behind her, he opened the bottle to squeeze oil into his hands. "You are going to warm that up a bit, right?"

"Of course. I'm warming it now as we speak. I'm just going to rub it on your back and hips, okay?" The soft swooshing of his hands calmed her.

"Sounds great," she said, with a little hesitation.

Bryce chuckled. "I'm starting on your shoulders." He guided her to lie face down, his hands doing relaxing circles on her upper back. With a lover's touch, he caressed away the tension she carried.

"Oh, right there, yes." Rosemary sighed as she let go. He continued down to her lower back, working out all the knots and tension. "This is going to get me aroused?"

"Let me show you. Relax while I massage lower on your hips now." The small intense circles he made on her pear-shaped bottom opened and closed her cheeks as he moved closer and closer to the lush valley of her sex. A gentle finger caused her to tense when he began to explore deeper into the valley.

"What are you doing?" She jerked up a bit.

He paused but did not move his hands. "Trust me; I'm not going to do anything that you don't want. Just lie back down and let me rub your cute little butt, okay."

"Okay, but if I say stop, you will?"

"Absolutely." His experienced fingers began to slide down the length of her twin globes invoking pleasure at every spot. He rubbed some lube on her anus, her muscles tensing, but she didn't stop him.

In her past sexual experiences, she never trusted anyone to touch her there. Her heart told her he would stop if she asked, but as he continued traveling deeper into her opening, the beginnings of a new kind of excitement caught her attention.

A slow insertion of his finger in her dark rosebud made her clench. He paused as she adjusted. Pain awakened her desire in little bursts. In and out, he moved his finger, pausing, until she accepted all of it.

"Do you like that?"

"I...I...do. I didn't think I would, but I do." As the pain subsided, an unfamiliar rise of sexual fire kindled within her. Soon, two of his fingers plunged deeper and faster into her secret tunnel preparing her. Every nerve ending he touched burned with secret cravings she sought to feed. His hands caressed her sensitive openings, turning her on to the point she couldn't lie still.

Trusting him with her unknown erotic feelings, her need to connect physically surged. "I need to feel you in me."

She rose into her favorite position allowing him to push his thick, lubed member into her virgin opening. She caught her breath, grateful he paused to allow her to adjust to his thickness. Holding her hips, he let her push back to take him deep within her. A low rumble escaped her throat signaling her readiness. Slow and steady, he drove himself balls deep into her. Trust for him grew as he took his time and allowed her to experience this new level of intimacy.

Her body vibrated at his increase in speed. Soon, her warm slick flesh hugging his cock catapulted him into vampire form. When he leaned over sinking his fangs in her shoulder, a deep moan escaped her throat. The pumping of his arousal deep within her dark tunnel had her coming in wild spasms of joy. He pulled out of her and they fell into bed, she on her back and Bryce on his side with his leg over her.

He kissed her cheek and said, "You never cease to amaze me with how you respond." He wrapped the covers around both of them, putting his arm over Rosemary. "Are you warmed up?" he said tilting his head.

"As a matter of fact, I'm very warm." She smiled and put her arm over his and squeezed his hand. "You never cease to amaze me when you make love with me. Want to tell me how many women taught you those skills?"

"Rosemary, my long life has included many times I was wild and wanton. Are you sure you want to hear all that?"

"Are you telling me you were a tramp of a vamp?" She grinned.

"Yes, Wolfie, I am. Honestly, I don't remember. I did learn some interesting things. However, the most important thing I learned is sex with someone you love is more satisfying and more exciting compared to casual fucking. With someone you love, you care about the outcome. Therefore, you put more into making love. What the other person does means more to you."

"I admit sex with you is some of the best of my life. And, I've had lots of casual sex."

"I hope you are planning on giving sex up with anyone but me, now that we're together," he said, his face pinched with concern.

"Bryce Gold, I told you at the beginning I am aware vampires are possessive and jealous. In agreeing to marry you, I assumed you knew you were the only one from now on. I want this relationship to work, and by the way, weren't you listening when I said this was the best sex of my life?"

"You're not the only one who feels insecure on the rare occasion. I know you're in this relationship one hundred percent, but in discussing my past, I feared you would assume something different. I intend to be faithful to you as long as we're together."

"I kinda got that the night you proposed," she laughed. The glitter in his dark eyes silenced her laugh.

"One whisper of your scent brings me to my knees. You hold my life in your small, miraculously healing hands. Never has any of my other lovers held me in such a loving way. I'm the one who is always in control. I'm the one who always calls the shots, but not with you.

Please be careful with my heart." He tucked her under his arm. Beyond words, she fell asleep with her head on his chest.

~

The wolf paused, her eyes following a rat scuttling across the path of fallen leaves. Sneaky creatures. She didn't trust them. The instinct to hunt and kill the rodent swelled in her. The scent led her to a clearing where she honed in on the creature, preparing to strike. Suddenly, it turned to her. Blood oozed from his mouth as he shifted to a man. He stepped aside, revealing the body of a woman with her neck torn.

His eyes fixated on her, a maniacal laughter filled the forest. "You're next."

Her wolf fought to attack, but Rosemary dragged them both into consciousness with her screams. Her arm reached out for Bryce but landed on the cool sheets. A second later, he ran into the bedroom.

"Wolfie, you okay?" He sat down beside her and held her hands.

"Yeah, just another nightmare. What time is it?" She turned to her nightstand. Her distraction worked. She didn't want to get into the meaning of this dream, but she suspected this one would haunt her.

"Four o'clock. You can jump in the shower before we move the boxes I packed for you tonight." The excitement in his eyes cautioned her to behave.

"I'm headed for the bathroom. Do me a favor and start the coffee pot." After a quick shower, she gratefully accepted the cup of coffee and bagel he set in front of her.

"Shall I take a load of clothes over now?" Rosemary opened her closet door. At this time of morning, she could care less about clothes when her body craved caffeine and carbs.

"As long as we're inside before sunrise," he said with a hint of impatience. "Sunlight is not my friend."

"Let me grab my suitcase." She packed what she needed for the weekend. Traffic sparse, they managed to walk in Bryce's door a couple of minutes before the sun peeked over the horizon. He made his way to bed and left her with Donna to discuss the redecorating.

"I guess you're right," she paused, "I'm going to be living here."

"I guess you are. I'm glad. I was concerned about the move here from Boston. The last woman he dated hurt him, but you're another matter altogether."

"I hope so." She studied the older woman's expression, hoping to pick up a psychic clue on what she thought of her.

Donna tilted her head and looked her in the eye. "I'm pretty sure you're aware of his lifestyle demands and are okay with them."

"I'm aware and okay with them. My lifestyle comes with requirements too."

Eyebrows lifted, Donna stared at her for a moment. "They must be different than his."

"They are. I'm part werewolf and witch. Using my medical background to alter my body chemistry enough, I can control when I shift, but I have my moments. Will that bother you?"

"Honestly, it depends on what those moments entail."

"If I forget to take my werewort, I can shift into my wolf form. That in itself is not bad, but often I black out. It just depends on my stress level at the time I shift."

"Are you dangerous during these blackouts?"

Rosemary filled her lungs, pausing before letting the air rush from her lips. "Not usually, but I'd be lying if I said there was no possibility."

"I like your honesty. My job has involved taking care of folks like Mr. Bryce for years. Just like my family did for centuries. Shifters have been part of that job. I think I can handle a little werewolf shift."

"Are you sure? I mean two people with special needs can be overwhelming."

"I've worked for a whole family of shifters. Big cats. I think I can handle a civilized old vampire and a smart young shifter/witch. Speaking of taking care of needs, what color do you want in your bedroom?"

Rosemary's face lit up as she picked up the paint chips and spent a delightful afternoon with Donna planning her décor.

∾

"Did you and Donna figure everything out?" Bryce emerged from his room that evening, seeing the two of them working together.

"We did. I like the thought you put into the arrangement of the bedrooms. We can feel connected, even though we might be sleeping separately and at different times. My favorite is the sitting room with a window into each of the bedrooms. Watching you sleep is comforting to me."

"Yes, I'll have to adjust to that. It's a touch creepy." He shivered.

"Really? With all you've been through as a vampire, you find me watching you sleep creepy?" Rosemary raised her hand to stifle a laugh.

"Oh, fine, if you're going to make fun of me." Bryce feigned hurt. "I will still sense when someone is watching me."

"If you know it's me, I think you'll relax." She rubbed his shoulder.

"Maybe." He shrugged.

"Let's have some dinner, or breakfast in your case, and then go grab another load of my things. I think I'd like to sleep here tonight with you, if you're up for that."

"Always," he said. *I can make sure you're safe.* He smiled.

They had just gotten into the car when Rosemary's cell phone rang. "Hi, Pauline. Are you okay? You sound funny."

Grateful she turned on the speaker, he tuned in to the conversation. Rosemary mentioned Pauline had been kicked out of her apartment by her paranoid snake shifter housemates. He prayed they weren't back in the picture. He knew Pauline was part of her past, but she still roused a jealous streak in him.

"Candy left me." Pauline sobbed in hysterics. "I...I think I tried to commit suicide, because, well... I drank some whiskey and took some pills, but I...I don't want to die."

"Pauline, where are you?" Rosemary used her best calm-doctor voice.

"I'm at home," she whimpered.

"Stay right there, I'm on my way. Are you in the same apartment I helped you find?"

"Uh huh." Pauline was quiet. Too quiet in Bryce's opinion.

Rosemary's gaze met Bryce's, hitting him with her concern. She mouthed, "Overdose."

He nodded his head. She gave him the address, and he floored the Lexus. *Pauline's trouble.* Her manipulative nature was obvious to him the night he met Rosemary. His Wolfie was a soft touch, but it was also one of the reasons he loved her. An unwelcome burst of anger at having to deal with Pauline tonight spread through him.

A few minutes later, they knocked on the door.

The door opened slowly. Bryce barely recognized the pale woman who stared at them for a moment before breaking into sobs. Rosemary guided her down in a chair to examine her.

"Hey, it's okay. Let's see what's going on with you. Where are the pills you took?"

Indicating a bottle on the table, Pauline swayed, catching herself on the chair's arms. "Those blue ones. I took... I don't remember how many I took."

Rosemary picked up the bottle of pills. It was a prescription for ten mg of Valium. She pointed to the fill date, a week ago and counted out twenty pills left from the thirty.

Bryce nodded, admiring Rosemary's quick thinking. He reminded himself she was a physician/veterinarian, and a damned good one. He waited to see what she would do next.

"Your usual dosage is one of these a day?" Rosemary attempted to calm Pauline by thinking rather than panicking.

"In the...ah... morning." Fresh sobs erupted from Pauline. "Candy and I had a fight. She left me. So, I took another one." She started wailing at this point.

"Bryce, please go brew some coffee and then come back and help me walk her around. She has had just enough to make her loopy, but not life-threatening."

"Okay, do you need help to get her up?"

"No thanks. I've got it." Rosemary glanced his way, gratitude on her face. She slipped him her bottle of werewort, indicating to add two full droppers to Pauline's coffee. He nodded his understanding and headed to the kitchen.

Bryce's issues with Pauline were assaulting his memory, especially since she and Rosemary had been lovers. He never asked the details, and she had not told him much, but doubt had him in a headlock. Had she been seeing Pauline on the side?

"I drank whee…iskey. I-e-e-e think a bottle of it." Pauline's body was cracking and popping as it tried to shift into her bat form.

Rosemary hauled her to her feet and started walking her around the small apartment. "Why did Candy leave?" Rosemary hugged Pauline's shoulders close as they walked.

"I-e-ee think sheee went back to Lucine, her girlfriend before me. She said I…I tried to control her too much. I don't do that, do I?"

Bryce nodded his head, as he listened from the kitchen.

"You're a strong woman. It takes someone who's your equal to be a good partner. Maybe Candy isn't that strong?"

She stopped a moment and sobered a bit. "I don't think she was."

"Well, perhaps you'd be better off looking for someone who's your equal, don't you think?"

"I don't know if I could put up with them." She chuckled.

Where did his love find the compassion to deal with her patients? Bryce walked in and handed Pauline a cup of coffee. "Here we go."

Grateful eyes met his. "Thanks." Rosemary steadied the cup in Pauline's hand.

"I put some cream and sugar in it to help your stomach, but I can switch it for a cup of black." Bryce waited for her response.

"This is fine." Pauline took a drink. "Rosemary, I'm sorry, I'm embarrassed that I called you. Honestly, I didn't know who else to call."

"I'm the person you should've called."

"Bryce, I, uh, I want you to understand I'm happy about you and Rosemary getting married. I hope you realize we're just good friends, now." Pauline clutched the coffee cup like a shield.

"Thanks, I'm glad to hear that." Bryce pasted his best fake smile on his face. *What does she mean? Why did she feel the need to say that? Rosemary and I need to talk.*

"Drink up and let's keep walking." Avoiding eye contact with

Bryce, Rosemary rushed Pauline to her feet. They walked another twenty minutes until Pauline appeared sober and her body stopped the shifting process.

"Pauline, you look better, how are you feeling?" Rosemary completed a check of her vitals.

"I'm fine. I'm a shifter, not some puny human. You and Bryce need to go on with your evening."

"I'm not sure you should be alone. I can't send you to the hospital. Is there anyone I can call?"

"My older sister moved to town a couple of weeks ago. I think she wouldn't mind coming over. I didn't call her because she wouldn't have known how to handle an overdose."

Rosemary soon had Pauline's sister on the phone and on the way.

"Okay, your sister will be here shortly, but you call me if you need me. I'll check on you tomorrow. You aren't going to try doing this again, are you?"

"No, I give you my word I'm not."

"Okay. I don't mind if you even need to talk, just call me."

"Thanks, I will. Thanks for everything." The doorbell rang announcing the arrival of her sister. Pauline gave Rosemary a big hug and kiss on the cheek before opening the door.

Bryce's insides twisted into knots. *That's my mate!* He headed out the door to wait for Rosemary.

Rosemary wrote down instructions for Pauline and her sister. Her face was a mask of concentration.

Pauline, supported by her sister, held the door open for Rosemary. "I'm going to bed and get some rest, before I have to face Candy tomorrow. Good night and thanks again."

Outside, Rosemary watched Bryce's face frown and lips purse.

"What'cha thinking?"

"What did Pauline mean about being just good friends, now?" He opened the car door for her.

"Bryce, we've known each other for years, and in some of that time, we've been friends with benefits. I thought you knew that." *Pauline was way too chatty when high.*

He leaned his arms on the car. With a grim expression, he shot back, "That I knew. Have you been *friendly* with her since we've been together?"

"I've been *friendly*, but no, I haven't had sex with her since the night you and I met." Rosemary waited for that to sink in.

"Let me see if I understand this. You were all upset about me being *friendly* with Marie and I didn't even kiss her, so you went home with Pauline and fucked her?" Bryce threw his arms in the air, turning away from her.

"That's not exactly how it happened. I didn't know you were seriously interested in me, and we weren't together. You're blowing this way out of proportion." She stood in front of him. "I think you're afraid I might be interested in her now. Well, you're wrong."

"Are you sure there's nothing between you, now?" His eyes glowed with a jealous light.

"I will not be in another relationship with a vampire that doesn't approve or trust me ever again. Leon was bad enough." She stood her ground, shaking on the inside from the fear raising up in her body.

"You didn't answer my question."

"For Goddess's sake! No. We're just friends with no sex. The only person I have sex with is you since we agreed to be exclusive. Unless you want to count the times I masturbate, and even then, I'm fantasizing about you."

"Do you want to have sex with her or anyone else?"

She stepped forward. "No. Back off and calm down. I love you, and I'm marrying you."

He looked at her. Both faces set in frowns, as they contemplated the other. He started laughing.

"What are you laughing at?" Her frown deepened as her incredulousness grew.

"Us. I'm sorry, you're right. I will never hurt you like Leon did. But,

I can be jealous. You're right. I'm overreacting and I'm officially backing off." He held both hands up and stepped back.

Studying the ground, she said, "I'm sorry I didn't tell you before. It didn't seem important."

"Do you really fantasize about me when you masturbate?" His face held a proud smile.

She rose amused eyes to his and shook her head. "Yes."

"Does this mean I get one night with Marie?" Bryce smirked, helping her into the car.

Head jerking up, she glared at him. "You're always free to do what you wish. However, there will be consequences."

"I'm not brave enough to risk discovering what those might be." He grabbed her and kissed her soundly.

"Good choice, vampire." She shook her head, but her lips quirked up in a grin.

"Yes, I like my choice." His gaze sparked little fires of passion as it traveled up and down her body. He headed the car in the direction of her apartment.

"Let's use those muscles and see if we can move a load of my clothes and personal things tonight. Tomorrow morning, I promise to massage parts of your body until you go to sleep." She ran her hand over his bulging thigh muscle.

"I don't think massaging them will make them go to sleep."

"Oh, eventually it will," she said, as they rode in companionable silence back to their home.

"Open it!" Rosemary handed him a box wrapped in satin white paper tied with a blood red bow. They had unloaded the car and settled in for the evening. "I wasn't sure what someone who was four hundred and three years old would want." She stood waiting by his chair in the area connecting their bedrooms.

"Rosemary, I want whatever birthday gifts you bring me." He tore into the perfectly wrapped package like a little kid, flinging the bow across the room. His tentative smile slowly widened as he held up two crystal goblets with Bryce etched on one and Rosemary on the other. "They're perfect. Thank you."

"I thought they would be nice for our evening drink." She poured him a glass of his favorite red and a glass of her favorite white. "Look further."

Next, he pulled out a cd of The Five Browns, *Browns in Blues*. His eyes got wide, and he laughed.

"How'd you know?"

"Donna has been very helpful in informing me of your musical tastes, and I happen to like the Five Browns."

"Well, isn't that interesting? I got you a gift for your birthday, too."

"No need. You've already given me way too much as it is."

"Indulge me and open it." Bryce handed her a package wrapped in pale blue paper and topped with a fluffy pink bow.

She lifted the bow off first, laying on the table before carefully opening the immaculately wrapped package. "It's tickets to the Five Browns next Friday night!" Rosemary was doing a dance as she jumped up and hugged his neck. "What're the odds? We are soul-mates." The awakened knowledge of how bonded they had become spread through her heart.

"Happy Birthday, darling. I'm ecstatic you're here." Bryce lifted her to his lap while cradling her in his arms. He kissed her with a slow tenderness that sparked a warm glow that flowed through her.

"Me too." Enfolded in a silken cocoon of euphoria, she laid her head on his strong chest. He closed his arms around her, generating in her the sense of being loved and protected. "Am I sleeping in your bed tonight?" She softly whispered in his ear.

"Yes, my sweet. I'll tuck you in and then go work in my office for a while." He set her down and hand in hand, they walked to his bedroom. He lovingly undressed her, stopping to explore her body. She slipped her satin gown on over her head, catching him gazing shamelessly at her naked body.

"See something you like?" She twirled.

"As a matter of fact, the whole package." His kiss flowed across her lips igniting her deep feelings she had for him at this moment. He held the covers back for her to slip in between the sheets. Bryce curled around her, gently holding her with his large hands around her waist and his broad chest shielding her back. She was asleep within minutes. He smiled and kissed her tenderly on the top of her head and went to work in his office.

CHAPTER 15

Like a wolf in a chase, Rosemary dashed to exam room one. Twylene exhibited her panther agility by directing patients into exam room two and three. She had circled back to consult with the human in room two by the time Rosemary greeted her vampire in room one. "Good morning, Fred, are you sleeping any better?"

"I was, thanks to you and investing in better blood. However, I'm developing nausea which distracts from my sleep."

"Hmm, any other symptoms?"

"I've been tired, but I assumed I was catching up on my rest."

"Let me run some tests. You didn't happen to travel to the east coast recently? A potent virus is affecting other vamps in the area."

"As a matter of fact, I was in D.C. last week visiting with some old friends."

"Let me guess, those old friends are vamps?"

"You guessed right."

"Let me draw some blood and I'll see what's going on. The cure is simple. I'll prescribe a sleeping pill that will allow you to catch enough Zs to utilize your own natural immune system. This virus works by preventing the deep sleep that heals vampires." She got him the meds he needed and hurried in to her next patient.

When both women finished with their morning appointments, Rosemary seized a moment to talk to Twylene in her office.

"Hey, how was your weekend with Liz?"

She glanced up from her desk, face beaming. "It was grand. We went to a horse show with her kid and then dropped him off with his father for the weekend. We went back to my place, and I fixed dinner and she stayed the night."

"I assume you had pleasant dreams," Rosemary grinned.

"Yes, very pleasant. You're right; it's different with a woman. There's a different feel to the connection." Twylene entered information on her last patient into her electronic tablet.

"I'm glad things are turning out so well for you. When are you going to let me meet Liz?"

She raised her eyes, meeting Rosemary's gaze. "She's kind of a night owl. How do you feel about a late supper with you and Bryce?"

"That'll work. What do you mean when you say night owl?"

"Ah, well…" Twylene rubbed her forehead. "Let's say she and Bryce have more in common than working in the medical field."

"She's a vampire?" Her brows lifted.

Twylene glanced out her door, before quietly saying, "Yes, but she prefers only certain people to be aware of her status. She works the overnight shift at the hospital pharmacy, which is perfect for her. Not for me. Any suggestions?"

"How about we change the hours of the office here? I've been thinking of how to rearrange our schedule. Bryce and I need more time together."

"That'd sure help us too. Do you think if we opened at eleven and closed at eight we could take care of everyone?"

"That's a start. I suggest we hire an office manager/medical assistant. Don't you think we've become busy enough to do that?"

"I might bow down and kiss your feet! Yes. The paperwork alone is a full-time job, and someone with those skills could take care of some of the more routine procedures."

"We'll need to find just the right person to work here. I did tell you the horror stories when I was interviewing for your position, didn't I?" A shudder passed through her remembering Owl Winterbird.

"You did. I worked with a nurse at the hospital that would be perfect." Twylene had a gleam in her eyes.

"Really? Do tell."

"She works on the psych ward."

"Are you sure she's qualified?" The scowl on her face deepened. *The psych nurses I deal with are often just as insane as their patients are.*

"Hear me out. Bunny is a nurse whose expertise is exploring people's heads, but trust me, she can hold her own with GDBs."

"Let me guess. Bunny is a shape shifter who happens to take the shape of a rabbit." *Oh, Goddess. Twylene is a sandwich short of a picnic to recommend a fluffy bunny to deal with some of the GDBs.*

"Yes, Miss Smart Mouth, you're exactly right. Have you ever been attacked by a wererabbit?"

Rosemary howled with laughter. "No. They tend to run from wolves."

"Well, not this bunny. In fact, she and her husband had just bought a new home a couple of months ago and decided to do what rabbits do best to celebrate the purchase. Apparently, the real estate agent unknowingly interrupted their private party. Thank goodness, he was known for having too much to drink at lunch. He tells a tale of being chased out of the house by two seven-foot-tall rabbits with extremely sharp teeth."

"Really? They get that big?"

"Yes. He never did convince anyone he was telling the truth. Bunny and her husband, Jack, got out of there before the real estate agent could bring anyone back to check it out. They are a legend in the shifter community."

Her brow beetled. "I'm listening. Let's see if she is interested in working with us. She may not want to leave the benefits of a hospital."

"You'd be surprised. The new director wrote Bunny and the security officer up after he pulled a patient off of her who was trying to gouge out her eyes."

"They need a new director with some common sense, don't they?"

"Desperately. That's why I think we can convince Bunny to join us."

"Okay, you've convinced me. Can you set up a time for us to talk with her?"

"Sure. It may take a bit due to the holidays coming up, but I'll arrange an interview with her in the next couple of weeks." Twylene made a note to remind herself.

"Back to changing the hours, let's send out a mailing and make sure we change any appointments we can." She turned to go, and then whirled back. "Wait, you know Bryce and I've talked about moving the practice. Maybe we can include that in the mailing?"

"I'm all for moving. Are you thinking of a larger space?"

"Yes. The supernatural community has been very generous with money and equipment, so the more I can offer, the more pleased they'll be. Are you aware of any locations that you think would work for expansion?"

"Hmmm...when I picked up Liz the other morning, I noticed a space for lease near the hospital. For our patients that can use the hospital, it would be convenient, and you can slip away to visit Bryce at his office down the block. I'll copy the number down when I pick Liz up in the morning."

"That sounds perfect. You'll be close enough to visit Liz there too."

"Of course," Twylene said, blushing.

The first blush of love, cute. With an easy walk, Rosemary headed to her office.

"Hi. Are you Rosemary? I'm Wanda." Rosemary reached for the extended hand of the real estate agent she called after Twylene brought her the number yesterday. She picked up that Wanda was a GDB of some kind. No matter, she was just looking today.

"I am. It's nice to meet you. Thanks for arranging an appointment this soon. With Thanksgiving coming up, time next week is limited." She hurried to follow Wanda's quick stride into a structure with tall windows. She loved the natural light pouring into the lobby of a building four times the size of her current space. So far, so good.

"No problem." Wanda waved a hand with manicured nails and slim gold bracelets and proceeded inside. "This is a great location for a clinic. The group of ophthalmologists that occupied this place for several years just moved into a new building."

"I love the entryway. How many offices are there?" She peeked under the granite counters of the reception area. Perfect, they wouldn't need to update the wiring.

"Let me show you the offices. I suspect you'll love them." Wanda smiled as she proceeded to point out all the features in an obvious attempt to sell Rosemary on the space.

"Does it include a fenced yard?" Rosemary envisioned the needs of her shifters in their various forms.

Wanda opened the back door that led to a privacy-fenced yard. "I should tell you the building changed hands recently, too. Last month, a new holding company bought the property. They seem eager to work with any new lessee."

On further inspection, Rosemary was picturing which office she wanted. The building proved to have the right bones. With some minor remodeling, they could move in. No need to let Wanda in on her delight. She jotted down a note and turned to her.

"Can we go back to your office to check out the figures? The place has possibilities."

"Sure, I'll meet you there." Wanda held the door open for Rosemary to pass before she locked it and headed to her Mercedes.

Settled in Wanda's office, Rosemary asked, "Can you tell me more about the holding company?"

"Here's a brochure with all their info. The Gold Financial Group, out of Delaware, has been around for a long time. They are known for being excellent to work with."

The brochure shot a tingle from her hand all the way up to the center of her forehead instigating a psychic response in her third eye. Raising her head, she caught Wanda studying her intently. In an effort to cover her reaction, she placed the brochure on the desk, determined to discover the cause later.

Her eyes locking onto Wanda's, she said, "I'm dreaming anyway, but give me the price, and I'll discuss the options with everyone concerned."

"The Gold Financial Group indicated with the right lessee they'll ask a very reasonable price." Wanda handed Rosemary a piece of paper with the fee printed in Wanda's precise handwriting. "How does that sound?"

"Really?" Confusion weighed her down. "That's below market value. What's the catch?"

"No catch. The terms are generous and reasonable." She bent forward, removing her dark-rimmed reading glasses, and in a hushed tone said, "Between you and me, I think the new owners bought this as a way to keep their money invested and manage their taxes. If I were you, I'd jump at it."

Dizziness engulfed her. At that price, they could afford to move and hire an office manager/medical assistant. Catching Wanda studying her again, she focused. "I am interested, but I need some time to plan."

Wanda put together a packet of information and handed it to Rosemary. "Understood. Take this home, think about it, and call me tomorrow, okay?"

"Sure. Thanks, Wanda, I need to head to work. I'll consider the terms, talk with my partners, and call you." Rosemary left the agency deep in thought.

Driving back to work, alarm bells clanged in the back of her mind, but she was too overwhelmed to listen. The building was perfect, the rent incredible, and the timing curious. Perhaps she shouldn't look a gift horse in the mouth, but everything was too convenient, too impeccable.

In her office, she glanced at the brochure from the holding

company, Gold Financial. Surely, a coincidence. They were in Delaware, not Missouri. Still, her psychic senses shouted for her to pay attention.

She caught Twylene in the hall as they were both headed into different exam rooms. "I saw the property this morning. Can you carve out some time today to talk about it?"

"Definitely! How about after my four o'clock? That will give us an hour before my next appointment." She was juggling an electronic tablet, stethoscope, and a bottle of meds. She carefully balanced the pills on the tablet and opened the door to exam room two.

"Perfect, I'll meet you at four." Rosemary walked into exam room one to a werebear with diarrhea, leaving no doubt about what bears do in the woods.

At four, Twylene bounced into Rosemary's office and plopped down on the sofa, almost spilling the herbal ice tea in her hand. "What did you find out? Do you like it?"

"I do. I'm hoping you and I can figure out how we can move and afford an office manager/medical assistant. By the way, did you contact Bunny to ask if she would be interested in working here?"

"She's very interested in working with us. There was another incident last week where the director struck a nurse and then fired her. Bunny's concerned the woman is losing her mind."

"You think?" Rosemary decided that the director's loss was their gain.

"I do. In fact, I took the liberty of checking your calendar and made an appointment to interview her," Twylene said.

"Perfect. Bunny joining us will be priceless when we move."

"I think she's going to be a treasure. Do you have an idea on how much this is going to cost us?"

"That's what I wanted to talk to you about. A new company just bought the place and they're willing to rent it for half the going rate." Rosemary sat down across from her.

Twylene's jaw dropped. "What's the catch?"

"I can't find one. Maybe Bryce or his attorney can."

"I say go for it. Who is the holding company?"

"Here's their brochure. The Gold Financial Group out of Delaware."

"Gold huh? Any relation to a certain vamp you know and love?" Twylene cocked an eyebrow.

"I don't think so. The company is in Delaware after all." Rosemary's brows pulled forward in a frown.

"Actually, I think many corporations are formed in other states due to the legal advantages even though the folks may live elsewhere. Is there some way you can discover who's involved in this company?"

"Bryce and I will talk tonight. First, I'll do some research on my own this afternoon. Other than that, what do you think?"

"I think moving right now is smart. How do you feel about my investing some of my savings in the new clinic?"

"I love the idea." She paused, considering her next comment. "Let's set everything up with an attorney for our protection. Is that okay with you?"

"Very much so."

"Good. To our success!"

"To us!" Twylene clinked her glass of tea to Rosemary's coffee cup.

That night at home, Rosemary researched Gold Financial in hopes of linking Bryce to them. Giving up on the internet, she turned to her psychic channels. The brochure in her hand, she went into a trance. In her quiet spot, her guides gave her the information she sought. She counted herself out of trance. Her sneaky lover was involved in Gold Financial. This will be fun. Almost midnight. He will be home soon.

"Hi, handsome, how're you tonight?" Rosemary greeted him at the door and helped him hang up his coat.

"I'm fine, and you?" Bryce put down his briefcase and gave her a hug and kiss. He had just hung up from a call with Wanda who was excited to inform him Rosemary had toured the building.

"Perfect. Donna is serving us supper in the dining room. She poured you one of those synthetic bloods that relax you with a type AB chaser."

"That sounds good. Makes my mouth water and my fangs drop. What's the occasion?"

"No occasion, but I would like your opinion on a building I considered today."

Her eyes were glued to his every move. Something was up.

"Love to share my opinion, but I do need some down time. I've been through a hell of a Wednesday at work. Between problems with lab equipment and the distribution software, I'm beat." Bryce headed to the bathroom to wash up.

The table was set with fresh flowers, his two glasses of blood, a rare steak, and her grilled salmon. He enjoyed his meal and sharing the details of their day.

"Thanks for letting me unwind. Now, what building did you want my opinion on?" He leaned back and sipped the AB from a deep belled glass.

"I looked at the property that Twylene recommended at 3443 Dogwood today. By all appearances, it would be perfect for my clinic. Are you aware of the place?" She casually took a swallow of her wine.

"I am. My opinion is that location could be a real fit for you. What can I do help you decide?" He settled back in his chair. Maybe she was just being nice.

"Well, I see possibilities with the building and location, but the holding company wants an arm and leg for the rent. So.... should I explore other options?" Rosemary shrugged her shoulders.

Bryce kept his face calm as he ascertained what went wrong. Wanda was to offer her half the going rate. He rubbed his face with both hands. His right hand ended up tugging on his right earlobe in an effort to clear his thoughts.

He moved forward in his chair. "Would you consider negotiating the rent? Sometimes holding companies can be persuaded to give a good tenant a break."

"You don't say, like half off the going rate?" Rosemary regarded him with an I-gotcha grin.

Bryce went still, and then his shoulders sagged. "When did you know?" He shook his head. He was caught.

"You confirmed it when you pulled on your earlobe." She beamed. "I don't suggest you play poker with people who could spot that tell."

"Damn! Sneaky little wolf. Are you upset or grateful?"

"Honestly, a little of both. Bryce, I appreciate what you've done. What upsets me is the fact you didn't tell me up front."

"My only excuse is I love you, and I want you successful in a safe setting. The truth is I was afraid you wouldn't accept my help. Please consider it as somewhat selfish support of you and for what you do for our unique population. I know all the *weres,* vamps, and others in the GDB community appreciate and depend on you."

"You're lucky I agree with you. Tell me, was Twylene in on this?"

"No. she happened to give you the number before I could get Wanda to contact you."

"Glad she wasn't being a snitch. She wants to invest in the business as well. I'm not sure how to handle that."

"Let me confer with my brother, Rhys. He can help set up everything in a legal and fair fashion. The reduced rate can be considered an early Christmas gift." Bryce gave her a crisp nod.

"Uh...I don't mean to sound ungrateful, but will there be anything actually under the tree? I always like something to unwrap." Rosemary's eyes lifted up to meet his.

Bryce walked over and clasped her delicate hands in his, placing a kiss on each one. "What do you think? Apparently, you know me better than I thought."

She twisted in her chair to raise her amused face to him. "I predict you will spoil me appropriately by having something delightful for me to unwrap."

"You are psychic! Who knew?" Bryce tipped his head to the side.

"Thank you. I could use your help to get this going. By the way, how does the rest of the Gold Financial Group feel about the rent being below market value?"

"We'll break even. As you grow, we'll all meet and decide what is a fair price. If we lose a little, we'll recoup on our taxes." Bryce hoped she would let him protect her.

"Who's we?"

"My brother, Rhys and I, have the controlling shares with some other money coming from some older, well established vampires we've associated with for years. Jonathan and Edward being a couple of them."

"They're okay with this?"

"Yes. I passed it by everyone via email and they've agreed to a year of the reduced rate in consideration of what you're doing. We don't have many options when it comes to healthcare."

"Alright. I'll make this work. This move is already keeping us too busy. We have an interview next Monday to hire an office manager/medical assistant which will help tremendously."

"I've complete faith in you and Twylene. Who's the nurse you are interviewing?" He tucked her under his arm, guiding her towards their bedrooms.

"Bunny Rabbit. She's a nurse Twylene knew from the hospital." She fell in stride with him.

"She's the wererabbit?"

"That's her. Apparently, everyone knows about her but me."

Bryce's face relaxed into a grin. "Oh, she'll be good, if you can hire her."

"Chances are, we will."

He settled her in his bed before heading to his home office. Confident she was sound asleep, he clicked on the email. The private security guard he had hired to follow her reported no suspicious activity in the last two weeks.

A relieved breath flowed from his body. Maybe Stephan wasn't the author of the note. His detective friend didn't find any connections. He concentrated on relaxing but felt a nagging chill settle in his bones. Surely, things will be calm for the next few years. The exhaustion of the last couple of centuries was as if a lead blanket draped over his thoughts. He prodded himself to stay in the present.

He poked at the paper, reading the chilling words: *You're next,* for the hundredth time. Of course, it could be someone else. He had made some enemies throughout the last four centuries. For that matter, Rosemary dealt with some questionable beings, too.

He deleted the email and locked the note in his safe. She would be protected the next two days while he was out of town.

∾

Five thirty already? It had been a Monday all day long. Rosemary used the last few minutes to glance over Bunny's résumé before Twylene escorted her in.

"Hi, I'm Dr. Rosemary Wolfe. Come in and take a seat." Rosemary shook Bunny's hand and indicated a chair at a small table in the office. Twylene sat in-between Bunny and Rosemary.

"Thanks, I'm happy to meet you, Dr. Wolfe." Bunny's voice was soft but firm.

"Can we offer you a cup of coffee or tea? And, please, call me Rosemary."

"Thanks, Rosemary. A cup of herbal tea sounds good. Caffeine this late in the day makes me jumpy."

"I understand." Twylene went to fix the tea.

"Your résumé tells me you are a registered nurse with over twelve years of experience. The last five in the psychiatric ward at the hospital. What's prompted you to change?" Concerns about Bunny's experience milled about in her mind.

"I'm sure you are aware psych nurses can burn out after a time, and I possess some other skills I'm interested in utilizing." Bunny leaned forward.

"You're right." *Good answer.* "What are those other skills?"

Twylene set a steaming mug of tea in front of Bunny.

With a glance up, Bunny nodded her thanks. "On the medical side, I have experience in labor, delivery, and operating room procedures.

Before working in the psych ward, I managed the office of a large family medical clinic."

"We could certainly use some help in those areas." Twylene sat down. "How well do you multi-task?"

"I like to hop right in and finish the job. If I don't know something, I'm a quick study." Bunny nodded.

Rosemary and Twylene were nodding their heads in agreement at much of what Bunny was saying. After an hour, they had all learned a great deal about each other.

Rosemary decided to ask the obvious question. "Will you be comfortable working with Genetically Diverse Beings?"

Bunny paused, a perceptive glint to her eyes. "I wondered when you'd ask that question. I've thought about it long and hard, and yes. I'm ready to do something different that'll help others who face some of the same challenges I do. I know you're aware that I'm a wererabbit, which means I have to be careful of not turning at inopportune times. I've never slipped. In fact, I think it might give me extra insight into caring for others in your patient base."

"Agreed." Rosemary glanced to Twylene. "If Twylene doesn't have any more questions, I want to discuss with her what kind of salary and benefits we could offer you and talk with you again."

"I'm good," Twylene said.

"I'm interested in working with both of you. Your reputation is sterling in the community. I'd like to make as much as I'm making at the hospital. However, the working environment here will be worth plenty to me."

"Thanks, Bunny. We'll call you in a couple of days." Rosemary stood and shook her hand as she left.

Twylene turned to Rosemary. "Do you feel like she can do the job?"

"Yes. If we can afford her, she'll be just what the doctor ordered."

"I think we can. Have you given any more thought on my investing in the business, by the way?"

"Yes. Bryce's brother, Rhys, is setting up forms for us. I suggest we meet with him and come to some agreements after Thanksgiving. Okay?" Rosemary picked up her electronic tablet.

"It's more than okay. Thank you. I'm excited. Did you find out if Bryce was connected to Gold Financial?" She gathered the teacups.

"Yes, he is, as is his brother, Rhys, Jonathan and Edward too. They've all agreed on a year at a reduced rate to help us establish the new clinic."

"That is sweet. Their help will give us a running start. By the way, are you and Bryce going to Thanksgiving at Jonathan and Edward's?"

"Yes. I offered to bring mashed potatoes, but I'm always nervous cooking around Jonathan. He never criticizes outright, but there's always a look in his eyes when it's not up to his standards. Of course, the big event is my family is coming up to meet Bryce for the first time."

"Uh-oh, is Bryce ready to meet your family?"

Rosemary nodded, flashing a smile. "I think it has him concerned, but not worried. I think my family is grateful I'm engaged."

"I can see that. Liz is making sanguinaccio dolce for the vamps and a pumpkin pie for the rest of us." Twylene rolled her eyes and smacked her lips.

"Liz is a brave vampire. Jonathan will be judging any blood dessert with his sharp tongue."

"She comes from a long line of Italians that have made that blood and chocolate pudding for years. I admit to eating a bit last time she made a bowl."

"I might try a taste. I'm also bringing a case of that synthetic blood that the vamps rave about. I find myself giggling when they let loose."

"As long as they control their powers, it's fine." Twylene wrinkled her brow.

Sounds like tension in paradise. Rosemary laid her hand on her shoulder. "How are things between you and Liz?"

"They're fine. We're going through an adjustment period as all couples do. Plus, we are stretched thin for time. When are we going to change the hours here?"

"Christmas week is always slow. Want to try then?"

"The sooner the better. I can't get enough of Liz, but she really takes her beauty sleep." Twylene sighed.

"Let's call Bunny tomorrow. She's in our price range, and her help will more than offset the cost."

"I agree. I'm dragging my tail. Let's head home to our loves." Twylene gathered up her belongings and with a half-hearted wave headed out the door.

Rosemary checked on the exam rooms, arranging supplies. She checked her purse for the canister of mace and headed to her car.

Her car was free of notes. She controlled her movements to appear unafraid, but the drip of fear agitated her. Her eyes scanned the inside of the car, finding it clear of dead bodies. Slamming the door and pushing the lock button too quickly, she let out the breath she had been holding.

There was no new note, no one in the parking lot. When had she become such a 'fraidy cat? Time to admit living with Bryce would feel good.

Two days before Thanksgiving, Goddess, she needed a break.

CHAPTER 16

A couple of cases of synthetic blood, the good stuff, rested in Bryce's arms, and a content Rosemary walked by his side. A smile spread across his face. She had agreed to move in with him completely in the next couple of weeks. This was going to be one of the best Thanksgivings of his very long life. Rosemary rearranged the mashed potatoes, trying to hold on to her purse. Bryce never understood women and their purses but was smart enough not to comment.

Thanksgiving at Jonathan and Edward's house in the past had a Norman Rockwell quality, only with a bit more camp and vamp. Black candles in gothic-style candelabras lit the dining table casting flicking lights on the delicate black china rimmed in gold. Red napkins popped against the snow-white tablecloth. The silverware, (gold-plated stainless steel), looked like something that would be found on the Collins' family table in the television show *Dark Shadows*.

A perfect place to meet Rosemary's family, especially her mom. Sadie had quite the reputation. His feet froze in mid-step. His happy mood faded for a second at the thought of meeting her. Not many things scared him at this stage of his life, but she did. The woman told a whole pack of werewolves to piss off and proceeded to raise her werewolf daughter with a stepfather. Rumor had it she was working with a daemon. He would love to hear more. Rosemary glanced over her shoulder with a question in her eyes. His feet started working again allowing him to catch up. His attitude brightened again at the realization of where Rosemary acquired her spunk.

When they rang the bell, the Jeopardy tune sounded, bringing a harried Edward to open the door. "Oh, thank the Gods you're here! Jonathan is driving me crazy. Rosemary, you can handle him better than anyone I know can. You have kitchen duty while Bryce and I set up the dining room."

"Happy Thanksgiving to you, too!" Rosemary gave him a quick peck.

"Forgive my manners. Happy Thanksgiving," Edward's eyes widened as he took in the cases Bryce carried. "If that is what I think it is, it's going to be a very Happy Thanksgiving."

"Some Rosie's Red and White Night." Bryce held it up for him to inspect.

"Is it warm?"

"Body temperature."

"Give me one now, please." Edward's eyes rolled upward as he chugged half the bottle.

"Boys, don't drink too much." Rosemary, attempting to sound stern, chuckled all the way to the kitchen where she found Jonathan in a tizzy. "What can I do to help?"

"I'm glad you're here. I need someone who actually appreciates the flavor to tell me if this gravy is too salty." He held a spoon of gravy to her lips.

Sampling the sauce, she smacked her mouth a moment. "No, the saltiness is perfect, but I bet some pepper would help."

"Of course, I forgot the pepper!" He started grinding at vamp speed over the pan of gravy.

"Slow down, let me taste before you go wild with the pepper." She snickered. Jonathan was cute when he was wound up.

"Okay, I'm a bit manic. I've made two turkeys, a big ham, and a few divine blood-based dishes for those of us who appreciate that sort of dish. Today must be perfect with your family coming to meet Bryce, and for that matter, Edward and me."

"Relax; they're going to love both of you. Bryce is another story. My mom is a hard sell." She grimaced. She loved her mom, but more than one being had underestimated the petite redhead. Mom always had her back. Sadie could drive her crazy, but Rosemary never questioned her love.

"He's a good guy. He'll win them over." He draped an arm over her shoulder and squeezed.

"He will, but even at thirty-three, I'm still their little girl."

"We all want to protect you, if you'll remember."

"How can I forget? Poor Bryce. It's a wonder we ever got together with Edward standing guard. Let me thank you again for giving Bryce my address." She kissed Jonathan on the cheek taking the hint from his *Kiss the Cook* apron.

"All clear in here?" Edward poked his head into the kitchen.

Bryce hung back to see if Rosemary had subdued Jonathan's dither. He loved his friend, but not when he had one of his crazy cooking fits.

"Everything's under control, sweetie. How's the set up in the dining room?" Jonathan patted Edward's hand.

Good. Bryce followed Edward into the kitchen.

"The table is set for ten people with the good china and the special gold goblets." Edward raised his fist in a victory pump.

"Fantastic. Thank you. Can I offer anyone a drink?" Jonathan grabbed a couple of glasses.

"I'm going to have a White Night. Would you like that or a Rosie's Red?" Bryce held up a bottle of each.

"Yum! Where did you find those?" Jonathan removed the cap of a Rosie's Red, taking a long swig.

"Rosemary has her connections." Bryce put the cases down on the counter.

"Let me put those in here." Jonathan made room in the blood warmer as the doorbell sounded.

"Got it." Edward's long legs made the trip to the door in a short order, followed by a tentative Bryce.

In anticipation, Bryce scanned the energy signatures with his vampire senses at the front door. Rosemary's family had arrived. Edward opened the door, leveling his gaze at the petite red-haired woman with wise green eyes escorted by a tall muscular man. The man smiled, while guiding a young woman away from inspecting the intricate detail on the porch railing and onto the welcome mat. Bryce stood to the side, gathering his courage.

"You must be Edward. Rosemary described you, and you're just as handsome as she said." Sadie focused her unwavering gaze on him.

Edward tucked his chin slightly. "You're definitely Rosemary's mother. You have the same red hair. Come on in, she's in the kitchen."

"This is a beautiful home." Sadie let Edward lead her inside.

"Thank you, Jonathan does the majority of the decorating." Edward motioned with a sweep of his arm.

"Is he a professional decorator?" Sadie took in the cream-colored walls accented by dark moldings and high ceilings.

"I own a couple of restaurants, but I decorate for fun." Jonathan entered the room to welcome them.

"Mom, Dad, Greta…" Rosemary rushed out of the kitchen, wiping her hands on a towel. She hugged all three at once. "I'm glad you came."

"We're excited to meet your fiancé and friends, besides seeing you. You're too busy!" Russ gave her a peck on the cheek.

"Guilty as charged. I'll try to do better. Come on, I want you to meet Bryce." Rosemary led them over to where Bryce was standing.

It's now or never. Bryce shielded his mind and projected friendliness as much as a 400-year-old vampire could.

Rosemary put her arm through his. "Mom, Dad, Greta, I want you to meet Bryce Gold, my fiancé, and Bryce, this is Sadie, my mom, Russ, my stepfather, and Greta, my sister."

"Nice to meet you, finally," Bryce held out his hand to Russ.

"Rosemary talks about you a lot." Russ took his hand.

Bryce shook his hand. *If I can win this guy over to my side, maybe I'll have a chance with her mom.* Sadie waited, her eyes following his every move.

"I'm glad to meet the man who finally won my daughter's heart." Sadie took his hand in hers. The flash of energy flowing from her hand to his caught his attention.

"I'm happy to meet the woman who gave her such a spark." Bryce watched for any sign she approved of him.

She lifted her brow and smiled. When she let go of his hand, the warmth lingered. He turned and reached for Greta's hand.

"Looks like my sister has good taste," Greta shook Bryce's hand.

"I can see the smart mouth gene runs in the family." Bryce enjoyed the sparkle of her aura.

"Oh, I like you! Have you got a brother?" Greta's brows flew upward.

"I do, but he couldn't make it." Bryce lifted a shoulder.

The Jeopardy tune announced the arrival of more guests. Edward headed for the door.

"Come in." Edward herded Twylene and her lover, Liz, inside with Bryce's assistant, Mitchell, close behind.

"Hi, Mitchell. What? No red orchids today?" Rosemary hugged him.

"I considered bringing you some, but Bryce might have noticed." Mitchell winked at Bryce, who hurried over to introduce him to everyone.

After introductions were made and food put in place, Jonathan walked in from the dining room and announced, "Dinner is served. Please join me in the dining room where Edward will say the blessing."

Breathing in and releasing it slowly, Bryce offered his arm to Sadie. "I believe you're sitting by me. May I show you to your place?"

Out loud, she said, "Certainly, thank you." Her mind punched into his with, "*Oh God, an old-fashioned type of vampire.*"

Realizing she had no idea he could pick up her broadcasted thoughts, he helped seat her. Bryce made sure she was comfortable before he scooted her to the table. "You're welcome. I think manners are always in fashion." His mind slid into hers with, "*Don't you?*"

Her green eyes shot up meeting his amber ones in surprise. She nodded with a knowing smile.

He tipped his head and sat down. *Round One, Bryce.*

Everyone else located their place card and settled. Then Edward in his lovely low voice began to pray.

"Let us be thankful for all the families at this table and hold each person in divine reverence. May the nourishment we receive give us the strength to carry on the graciousness to all we hold dear in our lives. May we show our gratitude in a thousand different ways as we leave this table and go back into our worlds at the end of this day. May we share abundance, love, and spiritual community with each other. For all this, we give thanks."

During the prayer, Bryce lifted Rosemary's hand to his mouth and kissed it. Her face beamed. His eyes slid over to watch Sadie tracking their every move. He bowed his head and mentally spoke to her, "*I love your daughter.*"

Her mental response came quickly. "*And, so do I.*"

After a pause, Edward clapped his hands. Holding his glass of AB high, he said, "A toast to our engaged couple. Dubious when Bryce first wanted to date Rosemary, I now see they're truly soulmates. Therefore, I invoke blessings of shared love, laughter, and strength to survive tough times for both of you."

Everyone clinked glasses. Bryce touched his glass to Rosemary's and turning to Sadie, he saluted her with his glass. "Cheers to you, Ms. Wolfe. I look forward to being your son-in-law."

"I'm touched." Sadie followed with the mental afterthought. "*Not yet, vampire. Leon thought he was in, too. We all know how that turned out.*"

Bryce fought the anger from showing in his eyes. Face plastered in a smile, he nodded then mentally threw back, *"I'm nothing like Leon."* He stopped, aware Sadie was grinning at him. *Round two, Sadie.*

"Okay, the blood and the food are getting cold, eat." Jonathan smiled as he winked at his partner. Edward started carving the turkey and ham which he piled high on a serving platter for those who ate meat. Servers brought in bowls of deep red soup for the vampires and tomato for everyone else.

"Jonathan, this soup is to die for. What makes it so good?" Liz grinned at her own joke, as she winked at her lover, Twylene.

"Vietnamese seasonings." Jonathan deadpanned. "You give me the recipe for that luscious sanguinaccio dolce dessert you brought, and I'll gladly give you the soup recipe after dinner."

"By all means, yes. This beats opening a bottle and sucking it down. You raise the vampire diet to an elegant and civilized dining experience. Three cheers for our hosts!"

Bryce appreciated her enthusiasm for being included in their close-knit community. The synthetic blood, good food, and dear friends were just what he needed especially after Sadie's last comment. *Good thing I can block her if I want.*

He leaned over to Rosemary and marveled at the way she was enjoying her soup. He kissed her on the cheek.

"What's that for?" Rosemary paused in between sips.

"Just because you're you." He went back to his food. Sending Sadie the mental message, *"And, I love her just the way she is, warts and all."*

Sadie's eyes flashed as she yelled into his mind. *"Look who's talking. You can't walk in the sunshine or have kids."*

He studied her then. She wanted grandkids. They both were losers in that respect. With a resigned sigh, he mentally whispered, *"You're right. I can't. But, I can give her everything else in the world, plus my love."* *Round three, draw.*

After the soup, all the traditional foods were served alongside some more exotic dishes for the vamps. Jonathan paraded out a platter heaped with Swedish blood pancakes and Spanish morcilla with a spicy red sauce. Four diners sported toothy grins in response.

"Oh my God, Jonathan is that the same Spanish morcilla recipe you made last time?" Bryce ran his tongue across fangs that edged out of his lips.

"Good memory, that was over a hundred years ago."

"You don't forget a sausage like that. It ranks up there with one of the most incredible things I've eaten as a human or vampire."

"I'll take that as a huge compliment." Jonathan's wide smile revealed his growing fangs. He passed the morcilla Bryce's way and everyone enjoyed the food and company.

The last bites of dessert were being savored, and happy faces ringed the table. Mitchell produced an amber wine bottle with a peeling label. He poured a libation in each of the golden goblets that had sat empty throughout the meal. Raising his glass of the honey-gold liquid, he said, "I want to share this mead in a toast to us all. The comfort I experience with this group is a blessing for me. When Bryce asked if I'd be interested in moving here from Boston, I thought he was nuts. He changed my mind by creating a magical and lovely journey."

Bryce couldn't help the pride that spread across his face.

His moment was interrupted by Sadie's mental comment, *"How much did you pay him to say that?"*

Bryce wasn't looking at her at the time, so he slowly turned to her and raised an eyebrow. In a quiet whisper, rather than a mental connection he said, "Not a thing."

Rosemary tilted her head in their direction, about to question him, when he took her hand in his and kissed it. She tweaked an eyebrow, letting him know they would talk later.

Mitchell swirled the liquid in the glass. "This wine was blessed for a full month by a coven of witches in England."

"Tell me more." Sadie cocked her head to the side in rapt attention.

"Yes, Sadie, I thought you'd particularly enjoy this treat. The legend is this brew will bless those who drink of it and help them open doors to their wishes. I suggest we go around the table and everyone toast to the door they wish to open and give thanks to the forces making that happen. I'll go first. Here is to the door of abundance opening for me and thanks to the forces keeping money flowing in my life."

Liz sat next to Mitchell. With eyes directly meeting Twylene's, she said, "My toast is to open the door of time for love. She is in my life, but I don't seem to find enough occasions really to enjoy her."

Bryce nodded in understanding to Liz.

A blushing Twylene went next. "I toast to healing. Love has arrived on my doorstep. However, I need to open the doors to healing my fears from the past."

Edward stood and held his glass high. "I want to open my door to my adopted family gathered at this table tonight. I ask the forces to help keep all of us connected through our shared love. And, I ask a special blessing for my soul mate, Jonathan." He sat down, but his dark eyes never left Jonathan's blue gaze.

Greta looked at Bryce and then at Rosemary. "I'm not sure is this is correct, but I want to open the door to love. After seeing what my sister has, I want the forces to help me find that someone."

Bryce's longing for a peaceful, loving family increased. He had to find a way to win over Sadie.

"In setting my Medical Practice, I intended to open doors to help all sorts of fellow beings similar to myself. What I'd given up on was finding true love. With my crazy schedule and my interesting genetics, it didn't seem worth the effort. Then Bryce walked into my life. I hope those doors keep opening in our relationship and the forces to help us not only be husband and wife, but a team for good." Rosemary, smiling at everyone at the table, fixed her gaze on Bryce, who fell even deeper in love with her.

"When those doors opened and allowed Rosemary into my life, I prayed I'd find some way to make this work. Now, I pray those doors will stay open to allow safe and sound times for all sitting here at this table." Bryce elevated his glass, looking directly at Sadie, and then slipped his left arm around Rosemary's shoulders. *"Especially, keep my Rosemary safe."*

Sadie's gaze fell on Russ and her two girls, before she raised her glass. "I want to open the doors to this new extended family and ask the forces to help me be an integral part of it all." She turned to Bryce and patted his hand. She mentally spoke to him, *"I heard that."*

Bryce fixed his eyes on her, raising his brows, but said nothing.

"I would like to open the door of belief." Russ inclined his head to his family. "I have found the love of my life in Sadie, Rosemary, and Greta. I would like the forces to help me in expanding and using the magic that is available for me."

"Ah, we saved the best for last." Jonathan's face reflected his humor. "I ask the doors keeping Edward and me able to bring everyone together and help form the bonds of community to stay open and the forces bless all of us with health, wealth and the wisdom to use our knowledge correctly. Living long periods of time gives us a perspective that can benefit others and ourselves. May the forces keep Edward and me alive and well and in love for many, many more years."

Mitchell raised his glass in a toast. "Here's to us, our doors to open, and the forces to help us! So mote it be!"

"Hear, Hear to us!" Everyone joined in, drinking the mead.

"Oh, tasty!" Sadie looked at the golden liquid still in her glass.

"I feel it working," Liz giggled.

"I think that might be the synthetic blood Rosemary brought." Twylene's eyebrows crept towards her hairline.

"I think we're experiencing the powerful and delightful energy in this room." Bryce winked at Sadie, finishing his mead. The tilt of her head and the look in her eyes gave him hope.

The rest of the evening went by pleasantly and soon it was obvious that Rosemary and her family were tired. Bryce came over and whispered in her ear, "I think the time's come for us to take you and your family home."

"I think you're right. I'm exhausted and my family must be." Rosemary stopped a yawn from becoming fully formed. "Jonathan and Edward, thank you for this divine Thanksgiving. We human and witch sorts don't keep the nighttime hours you guys do. If you will excuse us, we're going home and to bed." She reached up and hugged and kissed them both.

"Rosemary, we're glad to have met your family. Russ, Greta, and Sadie, you are always welcome here." Jonathan hugged them too.

"We can't thank you enough for watching out for our little girl." Sadie beamed, as Rosemary rolled her eyes.

"Okay, time to go. Follow us and we will lead you to Bryce's house." Rosemary guided them to the door.

"She means our house." Bryce pulled her close to his side, and they walked out together. A sense of well-being flooded him as his hand rubbed up and down her side. Sadie seemed to be softening to him, he hoped. He had much to be thankful for this year.

"Okay, our home." Rosemary's eyes twinkled.

"Thank you for letting us stay here tonight. We could've rented a hotel." Sadie walked around the family room.

Bryce was grateful they were alone while Rosemary helped Russ and Greta put their bags in their rooms.

"You're family, like it or not." He grinned.

"Yes, I suppose I am. Pardon my directness, but what does a centuries old vampire, who obviously possesses advanced mind powers want with a young witch/werewolf who is still finding herself when it comes to her magic and shifting?"

"Good question." Bryce decided how to best phrase his answer. "First and foremost, I love her. I have loved her soul for centuries. She is more than a woman I am fond of; she is my soulmate."

"Um, do you know my daughter?" Sadie's tone gave away her disbelief.

"I know she takes werewort tincture. She developed it to prevent her shifting into a stronger version of herself that frightens her to the point of losing consciousness. I know she needs to spend time practicing her magic, but instead, she practices her medicine. How am I doing so far?"

"Surprisingly well. Those don't bother you?"

"Of course, they do. I want to keep her safe as she grows into her powers, but unlike Leon, I accept her the way she is right now and hope she accepts me on the same terms."

"That's something. The first time she strays with someone else, are you going to try to kill them?" Sadie waited for his answer with a smug expression.

"I trust she's a woman of her word. However, if that happens, I will not kill anyone." Bryce stopped at the bar. "Drink?"

"Do you have a good red wine?"

He handed her a glass. "I regret there will be no grandkids, but I'm willing to adopt."

Sadie took a long drink and pursed her mouth. "It's probably for the best, considering her father's side of the family."

"Is she aware of that?" He took a swallow of scotch.

"Not entirely." Sadie's pupils contracted to hard pins.

"Don't you think she should be?" Eyes wide, he studied her.

She turned to stare out the window into the dark landscape. "Sometimes, it's best to protect those you love."

"I see."

"You've never lied to her?" Sadie turned to meet his eyes.

"Sometimes, it is best to protect those you love."

Sadie's eyes shimmered as she tried to read his mind, but he easily blocked her. "You are good, but if anything happens to my daughter because of you, there will be a coven of witches who will make sure you won't hurt anyone again."

"Threatening to turn me into a toad, are you?" He suspected she could, but he was not going to give her the satisfaction of his fear.

"Don't tempt me."

Bryce sighed. "Threats aren't needed. You're aware a vampire's life can be filled with risks. For that matter, Rosemary deals with some GDBs that are unstable. I am dedicated to protecting her with my resources and helping her develop her own. I hope you are too."

"Well, something we can agree on." Sadie's shoulders rose and the fierceness in her eyes stilled Bryce.

"Do you intend on turning her into a vampire?"

There it was. The big question he expected sooner than later. He gave her a nod to indicate he understood not only her question, but also her fear.

"No, she did ask about the procedure, but I told her I will only consider it after we've been married for a couple of years, and if she understands what's involved." Bryce hesitated, not knowing what else to say.

Sadie released the breath she was holding. "She's already a mess with the werewolf and witch genetics, so I am concerned what turning her would do."

"She said something very similar when we first started dating. Neither one of us will go into that lightly."

"I suppose that's all a mother can ask." She tilted her head toward the stairs. "They're coming back."

"We can always talk." Bryce couldn't help the smile lifting up his lips.

A grin eased the frustration from Sadie's face. "Yes, there are not many beings who can converse with me on so many levels."

"What are you two talking about?" Russ twisted his head first to Sadie and then to Bryce.

Sadie greeted Russ by wrapping her arms around one of his. "How much we missed you."

Russ shook his head. "That's fine. I probably don't want to know."

"Are your accommodations satisfactory?" Bryce stepped over to the bar.

"Perfect, thank you." Russ hugged Sadie.

"Drink anyone?" Bryce opened the wet bar.

"I could go for a glass of red wine." Rosemary joined him at the bar to help pour.

"Me, too." Sadie held out her empty glass.

"Make it three." Greta held up her hand.

"Have you got scotch?" Russ perked up.

"You bet. A nice old one." Bryce poured drinks for everyone, with another shot of scotch for himself. He was grateful he tolerated drinking alcohol in small amounts. He needed the relaxing power of a good scotch after talking with Sadie.

"A toast to my whole family." Rosemary raised her glass and everyone followed suit. A quiet pleasantness fell over the group.

"I'm curious. Bryce, how do you manage to work at the Blood Center?" Sadie fixed her penetrating green eyes on his.

Ah! The interrogation continues. Bryce blocked his mind before answering. "That's a fair question. My normal schedule is from around four p.m. until midnight. With my laptop, I can do almost anything I need to from here. If I can't manage it, Mitchell, my Medical Director, steps up."

"He's the Mitchell we met this evening?" Russ placed his glass down on a coaster.

"That's the one. In case you didn't notice, he's a character and quite the accomplished mage. What I admire the most is he sincerely wants to help others," Bryce said.

"I'm grateful you're all here, but it's been a long day for me. Can we pick up this conversation tomorrow at breakfast before I fall asleep?" Rosemary's eyes drooped with the weight of a full day of family and friends.

"Of course, we're exhausted, too." Sadie stood up.

"It's been a long day for all of us, but we need to be up early to catch all the Black Friday sales." Greta hugged Rosemary.

"I know Mom is going. How about you, Dad?" Rosemary touched his sleeve.

"Thanks, but Bryce belongs to a vampire-friendly racquetball club. Not only are they open during the day, they're lit up all night. He said I could go alone as his guest tomorrow, but I'm going to sleep a few hours and join him at 4 a.m."

Bryce nodded at Russ. *I need to get him alone to find out more about Sadie.*

"That's about the time we'll be headed for the sales. Naps for everyone tomorrow." Rosemary hugged her mom and dad, then everyone headed to bed.

Rosemary and Bryce walked with arms around each other to their suite of rooms. "I like your family. Do you think I passed your mom's inspection?" Bryce met her sleepy eyes with his.

"I hope so. She was certainly giving you the evil eye at dinner. What was going on?"

"It seems she and I can send and receive mental messages to each other." He hesitated.

She stopped, tilting her head. "What? No kidding? What did she say?"

"She was determined to protect you." He wrapped his arms around her. "Which is good, because so am I."

"You do comprehend she was a wild woman before she met my stepdad?"

"If the rumors are true."

"Then be prepared for more questions tomorrow. With her reputation of scary-good intuition, she can pick out a scoundrel when she meets one."

"Uh-oh! Let's hope a couple hundred years of being good has cleansed my aura." Bryce kissed her on the lips, breathing in her scent of honeysuckle and cinnamon.

"We'll find out tomorrow." She shrugged. "I'm truly glad we found each other. You've made my life better just by being in it."

"You flatter me." Bryce put his hand to his chest and fluttered his eyelashes. Then he laughed at her reaction. She made his life worthwhile. She almost made it tolerable to deal with Sadie.

"Come cuddle with me until I go to sleep, okay?" Rosemary slipped into her bed and Bryce sat on the edge. Rubbing her shoulders, the day ran through his mind. He was guarded, but hopeful Sadie would accept him as a mate for her oldest daughter. *At least we understand each other.*

His instincts told him Russ hid something much more powerful than just human genes, but he seemed friendly to him. Greta was a cutie with powers she had yet to discover. What impressed him the most was the way they cared for Rosemary. At that moment, she let out a noise consisting of part snort and snore. *She was adorable.*

CHAPTER 17

Saturday morning, the aroma of pancakes caught Bryce's attention. A sigh escaped his lips. He remembered the sweet taste of blueberry pancakes melting in his mouth as he accepted the glass of his usual scarlet smoothie. "Thanks, Donna. Is everyone finding something to eat?"

"Everything is delicious as usual. Honey, come sit down by me." Rosemary patted the chair beside her.

"Donna's an excellent cook." Russ took another pancake from the platter he was holding. "After yesterday's racquetball and shopping, dinner last night was perfect."

"You're very impressive on the racquetball court."

Russ smiled and shrugged.

Very impressive. There was something more to this guy. I swear his eyes turned a bright silver when I made a point. Bryce tried to take another sip of his smoothie.

"They're a fun bunch, Mr. Bryce. I'm headed to the kitchen for more coffee. Do you need anything else?" Donna paused at the door.

Bryce questioned if he'd done too much yesterday, as a wave of dizziness and nausea hit him. "Is there any of that synthetic blood in the refrigerator?"

"I believe there is. Rough night?"

"Yes, I don't feel good this morning. I'm hoping the synthetic blood will help me relax enough to sleep." Bryce rubbed his head and sat down. The room had become a carnival ride and he an unwilling rider. *Vampires are not supposed to get sick.*

Rosemary inspected him. "You don't look good. Did you drink some blood last night?"

"Yes, I had a couple of glasses." Bryce recognized the cold, empty fatigue taking over his body.

"He is pale, even for a vampire." Sadie studied him with a concerned gaze.

"Where did you purchase the blood you drank last night?" Rosemary touched his forehead.

"It was some I picked up from work. It should be fine. Take a sample and check it out." He held out his glass in a shaking hand.

"Hang on while I grab some supplies from my bag." Rosemary took the blood to run a couple of tests.

Greta glanced at the others with concern. "Do you have many problems with contaminated blood at the blood bank?"

"No, not really. We did have some problems with our lab equipment recently, so that could have compromised some bags." He struggled with his thoughts. *Must stay upright.*

"This blood is very low on erythrocytes. Your organs aren't receiving enough oxygen. Is there another bag? This one's not going to do you much good." Rosemary continued her exam of him.

Lifting his melted brown eyes to look at her, he shook his head. "This batch was run through the tests at the lab." He paused to catch his breath. "I need to call Mitchell to check the equipment. Donna, could you pour me a glass of blood from the unopened bag in the refrigerator?" He slumped on the table.

"Certainly, Mr. Bryce. I'll be right back." Donna ran to the kitchen.

"I planned to stay up and show you around today, but I think I'd better follow my doctor's orders and rest. Rosemary will delight in taking you around the estate, and perhaps tonight we can all enjoy dinner together." Bryce attempted to remain gracious in spite of his failing energy

"We don't want to disturb you," Sadie started.

"You won't. I designed this house so I can sleep even though a rip-roaring party might be going on in the next room." Bryce smiled and then accepted a fresh glass of blood from Donna. "Thanks. Did you slip some of the synthetic blood in here?"

"I did. I think you need some rest." Donna whispered.

"I happen to agree. You two can stop whispering." Rosemary put away her instruments. "Okay, let's put you to bed and then I'll come down and show my family around. If you will excuse us?"

"Certainly, we'll meet you in the family room when you're ready." Russ stood as he spoke. "Do you need help walking to your room?"

"Thanks, but I think I'll make it. One thing about being a vampire, I heal quickly. Good day, everyone. I'll see you around dinnertime." Bryce slowly walked towards his bedroom, grateful for Rosemary by his side.

Rosemary helped him dress for bed and tucked him in. "Bryce, I'm not used to seeing you like this. Are you sure nothing else is wrong? I can do more tests." Rosemary sat on the side of the bed and rubbed his hand.

"I can feel the fresh blood already working. Let me get a good day's sleep and then, if I'm not better, you can test away." Bryce's eyes were closing as he spoke.

"Sleep well, my love." She said as she leaned down and kissed him.

Bryce will be okay. Concentrate. Her racing thoughts slowed. She had checked everything, and he was improving rapidly. She put on her physician's best face to show to her family, while the part of her that belonged to Bryce swallowed an uncontrollable sob. *She had to pull herself together. Donna will call her if something happens.* She calmed herself and faced the four faces covered in questions.

"Is Mr. Bryce going to be okay?" Donna stopped clearing the table.

"Yes, I think so. He's tired from lack of sleep and that bad blood." At that moment, Rosemary realized Donna was family to Bryce and her. "I'm planning to show my family around the estate and after, drive into town. Could you check in on him while I'm gone?"

"Oh, certainly. Are you going to drive by your new clinic?" Donna's eyes shone with pride.

"Definitely. After viewing the clinic, we'll have lunch. We will return later this afternoon to let me check on Bryce while you finish dinner. Does that work for you?"

"Works for me. You have fun. Where are you taking them for lunch?"

Rosemary looked over at her family. "Well, I haven't asked, but I thought they might enjoy eating at one of Jonathan's restaurants."

"Well, if his food is anything like Thanksgiving, yes!" Greta chimed in.

"It is, trust me." Donna smiled.

"Grab your coats," Rosemary said. "Thanks, Donna. Call me if you need to."

Stopping at the location for her new clinic, she was pleased at the support her family showed for her expanding practice. *Jonnie's* Downtown was the next stop. As they walked up to the restaurant, the breeze blew the smell of fresh baked bread combined with steaks on the grill.

"Oh man! That smells good." Russ closed his eyes and breathed in the aromas. "After you," he said as he opened the door for the ladies. The hostess took them upstairs to a private room to seat them. The tinted glass windows revealed a stunning view of the city.

"Wow! Did you reserve this for us?" Sadie raised her well-formed eyebrows.

"I just asked Jonathan to reserve us a table, but I think he's been his usual generous self." Rosemary arranged her napkin on her lap.

"Oh, you're too kind." Jonathan's voice came from behind her.

"What're you doing up in the middle of the day?" Rosemary stood up, pulling him into a hug.

"What's sleep when I can be with you and your lovely family?"

Jonathan returned the hug and greeted everyone. "Who wants white wine and who wants red?" Jonathan started pouring as a server took their orders. The orders taken, and the wine served, Jonathan joined them at the table. "Did Rosemary show off her new space?"

"She did. She's going to have plenty of room to expand." Sadie's eyes sparkled.

"I understand you and the others are giving her a break on the rent. We really appreciate that," Russ said.

"We appreciate what she's doing. She's saved Edward and me at least once in the last couple of years, and there are countless others grateful for her services." Jonathan flashed her a smile.

"Thanks for the vote of confidence. I hope I can live up to everyone's expectations." Rosemary's cheeks colored.

"Yeah, she even checked out Bryce this morning. He looked bad," Greta said.

Jonathan's hand flew to his chest. "What's up with Bryce?"

Rosemary held tight to the panic raising in her chest. She turned worried eyes towards Jonathan. "He drank anemic blood from the blood center. He was pretty weak this morning."

He grasped her hands and squeezed. "That's not good."

"No. I had him drink a fresh glass of blood and sent him to bed. Donna is keeping an eye on him until we return. I think there are problems with his lab." Rosemary leaned into his touch.

"He'll need to correct that. Bad blood can cause all sorts of problems with not only the vampire community, but the human as well." Jonathan gave her a final squeeze before he refreshed everyone's wine before the food arrived.

As he poured white wine into Greta's glass, she tilted her head. "Jonathan, can I ask you a sort of personal question?"

Jonathan's eyebrow shot up and he grinned. "You can ask me anything as long as you can deal with the answer."

A blush blossomed over her face. She gathered her courage in a quick breath. "How do you stay awake during the daylight? I thought most vamps just sort of shut down?"

"Oh that! Whew, I thought it was going to be much more fun."

Jonathan teased her. "It's simple. Think about when you stay up late at night. Your natural rhythms want you to sleep, but you can override them for a while. Now, being in the sunlight requires good sunglasses and clothing to cover, but once I'm inside, I'm fine. I might have to nap during the evening or sleep an extra hour or two tomorrow during the day, but I'll be fine for today."

"That makes sense. Thanks." Greta smiled.

Everyone ate, laughed, and adored Jonathan's stories of his restaurants and parties. He was telling them how Rosemary and Bryce had met at his party, when Rosemary stole a glance at her watch and said, "Speaking of Bryce, I'd like to go check on him."

"I'm sure he's fine. Donna is a great caretaker and they need to be clued in to what a wild child you really are." Jonathan winked at her.

"Oh fine, wrap it up then." Rosemary rolled her eyes.

"Sweetie, we're aware you're no angel, but we do think it's romantic he sent you red orchids." Sadie clasped her daughter's hand.

"He's a sweetheart. I lucked out when he came into my life." Rosemary exhaled. She reminded herself Donna hadn't called and Bryce was doing better when she left, but she still worried about him.

"You did. I do think we should go check on him. He didn't look good this morning. Jonathan, thank you for such a lovely meal. Are you sure we can't pay?" Sadie reached for her purse.

"No. I love Rosemary and Bryce. They both have been there for Edward and me. Please let us do something in return," Jonathan said.

"Thank you." Rosemary kissed him on the cheek. "Now go home and go to bed. Doctor's orders."

"Will do. Let me know how Bryce is."

"I'll call later this evening." Rosemary nodded.

He signed the credit card slip for his meal with a large, spidery *Sean James*. Stephan Johansson no longer existed. *What a productive afternoon.* Almost worth the harsh daylight. Jonnie's menu included some of the best dishes he'd ever eaten. He could still taste the impressive Polish Czarnina. Duck blood was thick and rich.

Jonathan had always been a great cook. Vampires needed to stick to blood. He served humans. That was one of the many reasons he'd enjoyed tormenting Jonathan with the headache from hell. He had slipped sleeping meds into the blood bags at the hospital lab. Victor never even sensed his presence. Just as Bryce never suspected he had messed with his lab equipment at the blood center. The bastard had become too complacent since the murder of his last wife, Jeannie. This time, he would do something far worse.

He let a hard smile split his face. Bryce was too weak to be out today with his fiancée. *Good.* He wanted Jonathan and Bryce both to be taken off guard. Worn down. Giddy, he didn't let his laugh escape. Jonathan hadn't recognized him, but he was taking no chances.

Soon, they would both be aware of how much he hated them. When he raped and turned Rosemary, they both would suffer. Jonathan should have never helped Bryce murder his wife. Patience. He had to have patience. The day was coming that would mark the one-hundredth year of Kate's murder. He would have justice for his wife.

He placed his hat on his shaved head and adjusted his designer sunglasses over his blue eyes. Contacts were such a great invention. Out the door, he pulled on his gloves to shield his hands.

His eyes lit up at the sight of a man holding a young boy's hand as they approached. *Dessert!* Unfolding a white cane, he tapped his way toward them.

"I seem to be lost. Can you tell me the way to the bus stop?"

The man stopped, beetled his brows and pointed. "Go back a block that way and turn left."

"Sorry, which way?" Stephan stared off into space.

"Oh my gosh, forgive me." Taking Stephan's arm, he turned him in the correct direction. "Should I walk with you?"

"No, that's not necessary. I'm just a bit turned around." Stephan pushed his hypnotic power into the man's mind and directed his steps.

"I insist." He tucked his arm in his and started walking down the sidewalk only to turn into an alleyway.

"Stop. Stay." The man nodded at Stephan's commands and stood with glazed eyes. The boy cried for his dad, reaching for his hand. Stephan felt his fangs tingle at the child's fear. He squatted down as to comfort him.

"Come here, young man. It's okay." The tone in his voice quieted and drew the boy to Stephan. A quick turn of his head assured him they were alone. His mouth opened to reveal the needle-sharp fangs. The boy's eyes urged him on. He drank in gulps, cutting the boy's cry short. *Delicious.*

He dropped the body to the pavement and using wet wipes, cleaned his face. *Cleanliness first.* He tossed wipes into a dumpster before he altered the father's memory. In five minutes, the man would wake, believing they had been mugged. Maybach sunglasses in place, he tapped his way out of the alley with the white cane and down the street. *What a perfect, productive day.*

When they reached the house, Rosemary left her family to freshen up and went to Bryce's room to check on him. She met Donna coming down the hall from his bedroom. "How is he?"

"He's much better. Warmer with a bit of color. I'm glad you caught that diseased blood. It might not have killed him, but it would've set him back." Donna patted her arm.

"Thanks for checking on him, Donna. I'm going to peek in on him and then let him sleep as long as he can. We ate late. I think we can push dinner back to seven if that's okay with you?"

"That'd work out fine." Donna continued on to the kitchen and Rosemary to Bryce's room.

Rosemary stopped in the adjoining office and peeked in the window to see if he was still asleep. She stood, looking at his peaceful body breathing softly.

Treating vampires had taught her many things. Like humans, they breathed and their heart beat. When exposed to the vampire virus, the humans died. The ones who were able to, for whatever reason, came back to life when fed vamp's blood. It was a miracle and magic rolled all in one. He was her miracle and magic. Tears welled up in her eyes. She knew he was blessed with amazing vitality. However, he wasn't indestructible.

He sensed her and stirred. He opened his eyes, looked at her in the window, and smiled.

She walked into his bedroom and said, "How's my favorite patient doing?"

"I'm fine. You just wanted to play doctor with me, didn't you, sweetheart?" Bryce winked.

"Oh, you! I'm grateful you heal quickly." She ran into his arms and kissed him.

"Did you have a good time showing your family around and having lunch at *Jonnie's*?"

"Yes. They loved the new clinic space. Thank you again for setting that up. And Jonathan surprised us by joining us for lunch."

"Jonathan got up in the middle of the day to meet your family? It's a good thing he's gay and attached to Edward or I might be jealous." Bryce raised an eyebrow.

"Well, it's obvious you are feeling better. I was going to let you sleep until supper, but it looks like you are ready to get up." Rosemary stood up.

"I'm ready and up. Why don't you crawl in bed with me, and we will have a quickie before supper?" Bryce threw back the sheet to flash her his impressive arousal.

"You're a bad, bad vampire tempting me like that. I can't. My family is downstairs waiting for us. Rain check?" Rosemary reached out and stroked his length just to watch him shudder. With a wink, she walked toward the door.

"You'll pay for that, and you better believe there's going to be a storm when I collect on that rain check." Bryce shook his head and headed to the bathroom to shower and dress.

Rosemary smiled and clicked the door closed on her way to set the table and check if Donna needed any help.

In the family room, she set out wine, cut a sharp cheddar cheese, and arranged whole-wheat crackers for her family. She was grinning remembering her interaction with Bryce.

"How's Bryce?" Russ gave her a quick hug.

"He's much better. Thanks for asking," Rosemary squeezed his arm. "Would you like a drink?"

Russ nodded his head in enthusiasm. "Gin and tonic."

"Coming right up! Are Mom and Greta primping as usual?" Rosemary joked with him.

"Now you know what your mom says," Russ started.

"Good looks don't just happen, they're cultivated, I know, I know. They both think I could do with some more cultivating," She laughed and handed him his drink.

Bryce followed his nose to the dining room. The vampire menu was impressive with soup, sausages and pancakes all made with Bryce's favorite type B. "Is everyone hungry?"

"You wouldn't think after our lunch, but yes." Greta walked toward him. "How are you feeling?"

"Perfect. My physician is excellent." Bryce laughed as Rosemary blushed. Her modesty endeared him to her even more.

The table groaned under the dinner of roast beef, potatoes, carrots, and onions. There were also homemade dill biscuits, a green salad with walnuts and cranberries, and peach cobbler for dessert. Bryce nodded approval of Donna's skills.

"Donna, you've outdone yourself." Sadie put down her fork. "Where'd you learn to cook such tasty dishes?"

"Mr. Bryce often has guests who dine on more traditional menus, and I worked for a werepanther for a couple of years. Let me tell you, it's always a good thing to make sure those shifters are well fed." Donna laughed.

"She's also a vampire's dream," Bryce said. "She has learned to cook a variety of blood dishes I didn't even know existed. These pancakes are a real treat."

"Thanks, Mr. Bryce, I'm glad your taste buds are pleased." Donna went back to the kitchen.

"What's on the agenda for tomorrow?" Bryce turned to Rosemary's family.

"We're heading home. We've had the best time, and we love your home and hospitality, but we all need to get back to our lives come Monday. And I suspect you two need a little alone time too," Sadie said. *"Don't you, vampire?"*

Bryce smiled at the mental message. "Oh no. We love having you here."

"The soundproofing is excellent." He had to stifle a laugh at Sadie's wide-eyed reaction.

"Oh, Mom, you're welcome to stay longer. It's been a comfort to have you all here." Rosemary hugged her.

"We've loved being here, but we need to get home. Maybe you'll come see us soon and bring Bryce?" Sadie gave Rosemary a pointed look. Mentally, she poked him. *"That way, I can keep an eye on you."*

"I'd love to come visit. I bet you could tell me all sorts of good dirt about Rosemary." Bryce put his arm around her shoulders and pulled her close. Then he prodded back into Sadie's mind. *"That's a two-way street."*

Slapping his hand, Rosemary turned to him. "I think you're out of luck, buddy. My mom isn't going to dish anything on me."

"Well, not much, anyway." Sadie's face held a genuine smile. "I'm headed to bed. Bryce, I hope to see you in the morning before we leave, but if not, thanks for the hospitality and being the love of my daughter's life. I think you two will be very happy together." Her mind slipped in his. *"Just for the record, I mean that."*

"Thank you. That means a great deal coming from you. Rosemary's a very special woman because of her family." Bryce smiled and kissed Sadie on the cheek, slipping into her mind. *"Just for the record, I mean that."*

~

"I owe you a rain check, don't I?" Rosemary played with Bryce's collar as they stood arm-in-arm in her bedroom. Seeing family was wonderful, but she needed this.

"Oh my, was that tonight?" Bryce smiled holding her in his arms.

She tilted her head. "What a tease."

"Does this feel like a tease?" His lips touched hers like a whisper. They were more persuasive than she cared to admit. He lightly traced his tongue along her lower lip and then continued to explore her mouth with quick little licks. She quivered at the flick of his tongue. Savage hunger flared up from her center. She pressed her lips to his in an urgent connection, communicating her burning desire for him.

Fear tripped a trigger in her. *I could've lost him.* A vampire. What irony. She'd come a long way. Her vampire slid his talented tongue into her mouth. Need demanded he be inside her, to be possessed by him, held by him, loved by him. She curled her arm around his neck, urging his tongue to slide against hers in a dance of passion.

The bed dipped as he eased her down, his hand outlining the circle of her breast. Rosemary lifted up a moment and with a wicked glint in her eye. The zipper on his slacks made a sound as she managed to free Bryce's cock, only to capture it firmly in her warm hand.

"Well, hello my little friend." Rosemary stroked him.

"Uh… I don't think he likes being called little."

"I suppose not. How ya doin' big boy?"

"Are you going talk to him or make love to us both?" His voice a strangled whisper.

A smirk was his only warning as her mouth slowly lowered onto his hard length. The seductive scents of oakmoss, nutmeg, and her man released wetness that flooded between her thighs.

"OH, O… kay, Yes! Oh my God. Yes!" Bryce's body instinctively arched as Rosemary worked her magic.

She drew him deeper into her mouth, savoring not only his spicy scent, but also his shudder as she pleasured him. *Delightfully hard.* Lost in his taste and feel, she didn't stop when he put both hands on her.

"Stop. No, stop!" he panted. "I need to be in you. Feel you, please!" Bryce eased himself around so Rosemary ended up sitting beside him. "Let me undress you."

Eyes heavy with passion, Rosemary stood as Bryce unbuttoned her blouse. On the second button, she caught his finger in her mouth and sucked it down to the knuckle.

He pulled it out with a pop and shook it at her. "If you keep that up..."

A giggle filled the air as she ran her hands under his shirt to tease his nipples lightly. Their sensitivity fascinated her.

He captured her hands in his, using his vampire-modified reflexes and wrapped them around his waist. "Keep 'em there."

"Or what?" She pushed her way down the back of his slacks, admiring how the solid muscles in his ass filled her hands while she pushed the slacks to the floor.

Buttons flew across the room along with the rest of her blouse. "Or that." He stepped out of his pants.

"That was one of my favorite..." She bit her upper lip. His eyes were glued to her little black lacey bra that allowed her nipples to peek out of frilly slits. "See something you like?"

"Uh huh." He opened one of the slits enough to allow him to press his mouth around her perky nipple.

Her arms pulled him closer, and she couldn't imagine being more turned on by him. Then his hand reached up, found her other nipple, twirled and twisted it as he sucked on the first. Inside she was unraveling, opening, needing him.

A whimper sounded from her throat as she tore off his shirt. Her hands touched the column of steel his neck muscles formed, massaging them all the way down to his arms that melted her core.

A frustrated huff issued from him as he pulled her slacks off. At the sight of her panties, he stopped, staring, again.

"Excuse me, if you don't know what to do, I can show you." She arched an eyebrow.

"Are those crotchless?" He delicately ran a finger over the pink bow before pushing it slowly into her wet center.

The smart-ass answer left her brain. Her hunger for him spread from her womb to every cell in her body. A second finger joined the first. She welcomed his hard body as it wrapped around her and his hand as it pumped into her.

Bryce inhaled. "Honeysuckle." He nipped her shoulder. "And cinnamon." His tongue slid over her earlobes, his fangs out in full force.

His arousal thumped against her belly. She moaned with anticipation at the thought of connecting with him. The mirror above her dresser reflected her aura shimmering with small silver lights of magic casting an enchanted glow in the semi-darkened room. A thrill shot through her. The image of his sculpted body supporting hers awakened her desire to connect with him completely.

Bryce stared in the mirror at her. "You're so beautiful. I know I don't tell you that enough." The brush of his lips against hers sent a tingle down to her core.

"Thank you, but that's not true. Every time your eyes run up and down my body, or you worry if I'm safe, or you hold me close, you tell me how much you love me."

His eyes touched her soul. "I want you. Now."

"I wanted you since before supper." She rubbed her rigid nipples across his chest enjoying the feel of the lacey bra and rough chest hair.

His muscles lifted her as if she weighed less than a feather allowing her to wrap her strong legs around his waist. The mirror reflected her body, small compared to his, cradled in his dependable arms. He penetrated her folds with a thrust, and she arched to meet him. She savored the way he stretched her tight. Her vampire was a perfect fit.

She clung to him. The sensation of his solid length raised the molten need to come until she was panting his name. His aura shone with a bright gold sparkle as it melded with her silver lights. The blending of their auras fascinated her. Silver and gold created a bond of their souls. Connected, she felt the passion pound through their bodies.

She offered her throat in a gesture of love. Bryce moaned in response as he lightly scraped her neck with his fangs. "I'm going to lick that drop of blood off your milky white skin."

Her sex tightened, anticipating the surge of pleasure that came with his bite. His tongue left a trail of sizzling heat, driving her closer to her climax.

"You want me. I can taste your desire." He leaned in, fangs fully formed. She made a small noise of submission combined with desire.

His fangs sank into the sensitive junction between her shoulder and neck resulting in her whole body to vibrating with a forceful energy. She gave in to her orgasm, relishing in the way he held her as her body shook and her soul blossomed.

Her cry of bliss faded. His thrusts penetrated her in rapid succession, going on and on until a powerful orgasm ripped through him followed by a roar. Finally, the last shivers of his member ceased.

Her eyes rose to the mirror. He stood tall with her still wrapped in his arms. A red mist swirled around them in a spiral. His glowing eyes met hers in the mirror. Captured in his gaze, she savored the love and connection.

He buried his nose in her hair, her smell overloading his expanded senses. *Mine.* Need poured into his cock, arousing him again before even leaving her warmth.

"Bryce, are you..." Rosemary's breath caught.

"Hard as rock." He nuzzled her neck. "You do that to me." The vision she created when he laid her back on the bed, legs still wrapped around him reminded him of the red orchids she loved. Exotic. Erotic. Exciting. He slid deep within her body meeting her arching hips. He loved the way their bodies were in exquisite harmony. Eyes closed, he soaked in the silk of her skin while he relished the little moans of excitement escaping her.

What the hell? His reverie disturbed by a sharp pain, his eyes blinked open.

Her eyes rose to meet his. She had scraped her small teeth along the curve of his neck.

"I want to taste your blood."

Desire to bond with her completely flooded through him. *She wanted him!*

"Not yet." Bryce pulled away. How to explain his fears without upsetting her?

"Why not? You said I won't turn unless I'm drained of most of my blood." She stopped, confusion showing on her face.

"That's right, but once you drink my blood, you will bond to me forever. Let's save that for our wedding night." Bryce stopped moving. The expression on her face gave him hope she would drop the subject.

The push on his chest from her small hands took him off guard. He rolled to the side and off of her. A thundercloud had taken over her face. "When you drank my blood, you bonded to me?"

Not dropping it. "Partly. I don't want to put you in a permanent position until we have said our vows." A stroke of his fingers on her cheek had her sit up, turning her back to him.

"You think I might change my mind?" The stiff little back of his love made his heart heavy. How could he explain to this determined and intelligent woman that he wanted to give her time? He'd been down this road before.

His legs slid in beside hers, and he put his arm around her shoulders. "Not at all. However, if you do, I don't want you fighting an unwanted bond."

The spark in her eyes tipped him off she wasn't going to let this go.

"I won't." She turned her neck to him. "In fact, why don't you change me now? That way I can prove to you I'm ready to be yours forever."

He stared at her smooth white neck. The pulse visible beneath the skin. Mesmerized by the vibration with each beat of her heart, his fangs dropped. The fight to protect her from his lifestyle suddenly seemed unnecessary. He couldn't help himself. His tongue followed the vein from her collarbone to her ear. Her too-white hands were clenched in preparation for his bite. Turning was violent, bloody and permanent. He stopped.

"I will not do it just to prove a point."

Her eyes snapped open. "Why not?"

"Wolfie, you're not thinking. Being a vampire is a tricky way to live. I love you enough to want to give you the option of having the best of both worlds." The desire to turn her still clung to him. He could smell her fear. Not the right motivation to turn someone.

She jumped up, breasts bouncing. "How?"

He reached for her hand. "You can remain a witch/werewolf and yet enjoy the advantages of my wealth and influence."

A pout appeared on her pink lips. "What happens when I get old and wrinkled and you still look forty?"

He pulled her onto his lap. "I'll still love you and be by your side." Bryce sighed. "Look, Rosemary, our wedding is only five months away. Bite me that night and bond to me. You will be able to read my mind and sense my feelings."

The anger in her voice plowed through him. "You can read my mind and sense my feelings, and you neglected to mention that to me!" She tried to wiggle away from him, but he held her in his solid grip. *Damn, she's strong!*

"No. That will happen only after we both have sampled each other's blood. I didn't mention it, because I love you and want to protect you from my world." His shoulders rose and relaxed as he released the breath he had been holding.

"I don't need protection!" This time, she jumped up and twirled around, hurt morphing into anger on her face as her brows beetled and her mouth tightened.

Well, hell. This wasn't the night of lovemaking he had planned. Carefully choosing his words, he stood up and said, "Wolfie, we all need protection in one way or another. Jonathan, Edward, and I take responsibility for our lives and for each other. I know they have watched over you now for a time. Why won't you let me?"

The fierceness faded from her face leaving behind a woman with red cheeks, creamy white breasts, and a body that brought him to his knees. He almost missed her whisper. "I don't know."

Because her body was shaking, he wrapped a blanket around her and guided her to the bed. "I swear to you I didn't keep this from you on purpose. If you had asked, I would have told you. I assumed after being engaged to Leon, you would have known about the bonding."

"He probably never mentioned it because if we had bonded, I would have known he was cheating on me." The defeat was plastered on her face like mud on a shoe.

The bed creaked as he sat down beside her and turned her face towards him. "Are you afraid I'll cheat on you?"

"No, but..." Her face reflected her thoughts as she processed what he had said. "Will you tell me why you and my mom can talk to each other telepathically?"

That'll teach me to be transparent. He took a deep breath and met her eyes with his. "I'm not quite sure, but with your mother it's different. I hear only her thoughts not sense her feelings."

He could almost hear the wheels turning in her head when she asked, "Did you know my mom when she was younger?"

She surely doesn't think I bonded with her mom? "I knew of her."

She pinned him with those ice blue eyes. "But you never had sex with..."

He leaped up and turned to stare at her. "Stop right there. Ew. No." He couldn't believe she went there.

The vision of Sadie and him doing the nasty was still plaguing his mind, when she asked, "Has that type of mind-reading happened with anyone else?"

Thankful for his will of steel, he dismissed the frighteningly inappropriate thoughts of his soon-to-be mother-in-law and concentrated on the present. "Throughout my lifetime there have been others on my wavelength."

Her voice choked with tears, "Why am I not on your wavelength?"

He wiped a tear from her cheek. "Is that what's bothering you?"

Her lips drew down as she nodded. He shook his head. How could he have been so dense? She was a genius when it came to treating her patients, but insecure when it came to her desirability as a mate.

"You are on all my wavelengths, but because we are soulmates, those gates won't open until we both taste each other's blood. That's a good thing. Otherwise, we would be overwhelmed."

The worry in her face relaxed. "Are you sure I'm good enough for you?" Her eyes searched his.

Bryce let out an incredulous chuckle. "You risk yourself to treat us all, monsters or not. You're a big heroine in my book."

She stood, wrapping her arms around him. "You're not a monster."

He embraced her, welcoming the warmth of her body against his. He had been a monster. One of the worst at the time. Her declaration was a song of joy to his ears. They stood that way for a moment.

His kiss on top of her head caused her to tilt her head up.

"Thank you for saying I'm not a monster."

She landed a playful swat to his arm. "Well, you're not."

With a quick motion, he grabbed her hand in his. "Others can be monsters, giving the rest of us a bad name." The feel of her strong hand in his inspired him to make sure he always protected her.

"Trust me, I've met them. I've even been engaged to one."

His lips caressed her fingers. "I'm truly sorry about your relationship with Leon."

Eyes wide, her attention was held by his kisses to her hand. "Thanks."

The slow swipe of his tongue across her palm filled him with her own distinct flavor. "But I'm glad you're with me. I assure you there are more of us that are decent beings than not."

Her pulse was pounding and her breathing came in pants. "Well, when you put it that way..." She glanced down. "I can't believe you're still hard."

His arms pulled her into his embrace. A whisper from his lips into her shell-pink ear produced a squirm. "What can I say? You make me hot."

Face shining with joy, she wrapped her hands around his neck. He kissed her lips with a slow, slide of his mouth, urging them open with his tongue. When she let him in, he plunged deep in her mouth, tasting, exploring, and connecting.

She moaned in an awakened response that opened him up to her. He had been afraid to love her, to risk her being a victim of Stephan; he had kept himself at bay. Meeting her family gave him hope.

He burst into action again. The raw emotions had raised a fire within them, and soon ecstasy possessed them both. Sated, they found comfort in each other's arms.

Her eyes closed in a deep sleep. His eyes followed her breathing. He was at peace for the first time in a long time. *I pray to the gods I blocked my thoughts from Sadie.*

∼

"We need to talk." Sadie put her arm around Rosemary guiding her into a bathroom off the family room and closed the door.

The tone in her mom's voice made her frown. "Okay. Why?" She backed out of her mom's arm. For her to want to talk right before they planned to leave this morning raised a red flag.

"Do you think Bryce is your soulmate?"

Her mind was churning over the possibilities of what her mother had in mind. "Of course, why do you ask?"

"You're a spirit witch who's just about to find her power." Sadie made herself comfortable on the edge of a large marble ledge surrounding the tub.

"Hang on. I remember studying about spirit witches years ago, with Grandma Rosie, but I didn't realize I was one." She racked her brain for the small amount of information she absorbed.

Her mom crossed her legs, swinging them as she held Rosemary in her stare. "We weren't sure if it passed down to you. The best way to find out is when a spirit witch finds true love, she will also find her true power. She'll be tested."

Breaking the stare, she took a deep breath. *Crap.* "How do I know I've passed?"

"A mark appears on your body that will look similar to a witch's hat."

She tried to control the rolling of her eyes. "Let me get this straight, I'm going to have a witches' party hat tattooed on my body?"

Sadie narrowed her eyes. "I sense an attitude."

Whirling around to face her, Rosemary said, "I bet you do. I can't deal with all the information and studying you want me to do with my magic and be a successful healthcare provider." She held up her hand to stop Sadie from speaking. "And now, I'm getting some tattoo that signifies something I barely understand."

The look her mother shot her had leveled many a badass. "You would if you studied your grimoire."

The hint of sarcasm colored Sadie's voice. "That's your personal book of rituals and spells, in case you've forgotten. You would understand if you practiced your magic on a consistent basis." Sadie took in a breath. "And it's not a party hat. A witches' hat is a cone of power with the sign of infinity below it."

"Very funny. I know what a grimoire is." She relaxed her stiff stance a bit. *I know I need to listen to this.* "You mean like a triangle on top of a figure eight?"

"Close enough. The witches hat shows up when you've tapped into the infinite power of the universe, and you are using your power and wisdom together in harmony."

Her curiosity propelled her forward "Do you have one?"

Sadie stood up and lifted her blouse. "Yes, right below my left breast."

Leaning in, she nodded. "I always thought that was a birthmark. When did it appear?"

"I've told you about the night you were conceived." Sadie lowered her blouse.

"Yes, you sidled up to this good-looking guy and said, 'That's quite a head of hair. What do you do to get it so thick?' He took one look at you, gave you a wolf whistle and a night to remember."

A grin spread across Sadie's face. "You remember."

"How could I forget? My mixed genetics have been a big factor in my medical studies." Rosemary shook her head. "Anyway, about the witch mark?"

"Instead of staying with your father and his pack of werewolves, I decided I wanted to have a better life for you. The alpha of the pack decided you were to be brought up as a werewolf only. He wanted me not only to permanently bind your powers, but mine, too."

"Seriously? What a jerk." Rosemary's brows beetled.

"So, I struck out on my own. They banished me forever from their pack. I've had no contact with them since that day and no help either."

"Mom, I'm sorry. I didn't realize… Why haven't you told me this before?"

Sadie drew her into a hug. "You were already a troubled child between developing magic and shifting without control, but now, I see a young woman who has matured and has grown strong through her challenges."

"Ah, Mom, you got me through it. You always help me through the rough times."

"With some help. I met your stepfather and things worked out. Right after I married Russ, my witch mark showed up. I was freaked out. I asked my mom if I was dying. She explained that not only had I connected with my true love, I'd made a courageous action that lead up to the mark appearing."

"Thanks, Mom." Rosemary hugged her. "I'm glad you told me about the witch mark and about my biological father."

"You're welcome."

"Do you know where he is?"

"Yes, but please don't go looking for him." Sadie's eyes pleaded.

"I hadn't planned on it. Why not?"

"Russ and I have hidden you all these years with a combination of magic and common sense."

"Dad knows all about this? Must be hard on a human."

"That's another thing I need to tell you." Sadie hesitated. "Russ isn't exactly human."

"Hm. Well what is he?" Rosemary's eyes met hers.

"Do you remember studying the difference between demons and

daemons?"

"Russ is evil? I don't think so." Rosemary shook her head.

"No, he's a d-a-e-m-o-n. He's a lesser god from Ancient Greece. A good god." Sadie waited, watching Rosemary.

"I... uh...I... don't know what to say." She stared at her mom.

"It's a lot to take in. Give it time to settle in your brain and then email or call with questions. Remember, Russ loves you like his own. We both lucked out." Sadie smiled as she kissed Rosemary on the cheek.

"We did, didn't we?" Rosemary released her and turned to the door. "I will try to be better about my magic. School and setting up my practice has eaten up all my time, but things are beginning to settle."

"Your Grandma Rosie was just getting to all of this when she died. I feel bad for not insisting you continue to learn magic." Sadie smoothed Rosemary's hair.

Her mom's touch brought tears to her eyes. "I'm beginning to understand how important it is for me."

Sadie cupped her cheek. "It's important for both you and Greta."

"Greta is part witch part daemon? She's never mentioned it." She glanced out the window to see Russ and Greta loading up the car.

"Uh... there's a good reason." Sadie's gaze landed on Rosemary. "She doesn't know."

Rosemary's chin lowered and jaw dropped. "Mom! How could you and Dad keep this from her?"

Breaking eye contact, Sadie waved her hand. "She's attributed all her powers to being a witch. We plan on telling her as soon as she's mature enough to handle the implications."

The worry she had for her little sister had her stomach tied in a knot. "I would think so. She needs to learn how to handle it."

Her head moving in agreement, she glanced out the window. "You're right." Her attention returned to her daughter. "Darling, I'm sorry if I didn't make the best choices concerning your biological father, but I always did what I thought was best for you, and that's what I'm trying to do for Greta."

Gratitude for her mom filled her voice with emotion. "You've always had my back, Mom. I promise to start studying and practicing my magic." She paused. "I feel like with Bryce, I can."

Sadie smiled. "I'm sure you can."

A glint of curiosity appeared in Rosemary's eyes. "Is that because you can read his mind?"

Shock flashed across Sadie's usually controlled face. "He told you?"

The smirk on her face took every bit of her will not to end up in a guffaw. She rarely surprised Dear Old Mom. "We don't keep secrets from each other."

The placid face Sadie normally wore returned. "All couples keep secrets. It's the reason they keep them that can make or break a relationship."

The smirk on Rosemary's face dissolved instantly. "What secrets is Bryce keeping from me?"

With a shake of her head, she took one of her daughter's hands in hers. "I honestly don't know, but for what it's worth, I'd bet he has honorable reasons. What secrets do you keep from him?"

Her head jerked up. "None. Really. No, none."

"I don't need to know. Does he?" Sadie kissed her daughter's cheek. "Promise me Bryce and you will find some time to come visit soon, okay?" Sadie's eyes ignited the guilt only a mother could spark.

"Promise." Rosemary kissed her back and walked out of the bathroom bumping into Russ.

"Here you two are." He looked down at Rosemary with eyes that flashed with a silver gleam just for half a second, then returned to the warm brown.

Rosemary recovered her surprise with a big smile. "Dad, we were just talking about you."

"Nice, I assume?" Russ enveloped her into a hug.

"Always, Dad, always." She kissed his cheek inhaling his fresh, comforting scent of pine. She walked them out to their car, saying her good byes.

"We're headed home. Call us if you need anything." He winked as he slid into the driver's seat.

CHAPTER 18

"Watch it!" Bunny caught a box that tumbled off an overfull dolly Twylene wheeled out to the waiting room of their old offices.

Rosemary nodded to her in appreciation. They were packing up as much as they could in anticipation of moving into the new offices tonight.

"I'm so glad we hired Bunny. She's been amazing." Twylene grabbed the box as she and Rosemary walked to the parking lot.

"I'm so glad you convinced me to give her a chance. Who knew a wererabbit could be so tough?" Rosemary opened the back-cargo door on her SUV.

The box barely wedged in between two others. Twylene double-checked the sturdiness and shut the door. "She made this Monday morning much easier. She'll keep those moving men hopping."

They left Bunny to lock up the old office and drove to the new clinic. Goddess, she was grateful for Bunny and Twylene. They had enabled her to have the clinic of her dreams. She was grateful for Bryce's financial help, but those two had made the day-to-day process of growing the clinic easier. The last few months had gone fast. She couldn't believe it was the last of November. Things were going great.

The first steps into the new building excited her senses. The smell of fresh paint and the shine of new flooring reinforced her vision. Her hard work and negations with the medical community were finally paying off.

Twylene stopped and turned to take in the improvements. "Wow, that color of paint made it much brighter in here."

"Green is such a healing color, it only made sense." She walked behind the reception desk to check out the updated wiring. "They did a nice job on the set up for the computers, didn't they?"

"They did. There's plenty of room for everything up here." Twylene waved to her. "Come on! Let's go check out our offices." She opened the door to her office. "Oh yeah, Sunset Pink is perfect. I can so work in here."

Rosemary enjoyed the way Twylene spun around telling her where she would place everything. "Let's go peek in at my office. I want to make sure the blue and green colors I chose work together in that space."

The satisfaction Rosemary felt after the long day of planning for the move that evening had her humming a song as she and Twylene made their way to Jonnie's Downtown to meet their significant others, plus Jonathan and Edward for dinner.

Twylene spotted Liz when they stepped into the entrance. She pointed to a private room. "Jonathan's put us in the Lover's Lair around the corner."

After everyone's order had been placed in front of them, Rosemary let that feeling of contentment swell up inside of her again. Of course, that little voice of self-doubt had to ping in her brain. At least she hoped it was self-doubt and not her psychic senses. She was going to ignore them all tonight and have a good time.

The large order of fries Rosemary and Twylene shared prompted a bump on

Twylene's shoulder from Jonathan. His long, slim hand pointed to the greasy treats.

"Do you know how many calories are in those?"

"Yes. Do you know how many calories a werepanther will burn

moving stuff tonight?" Twylene popped a ketchup-laden potato in her mouth.

"With four vampires, all you two will need to do is direct." Edward pointed with his bottle of Iron City Red.

"He may be right, but we've packed all day and will pack more tomorrow, so I'm not worried about fries." Rosemary gave Jonathan's shoulder a friendly shove. "Hey, are you having unnatural cravings for potatoes?"

"Um…with a little blood instead of catchup…" He swirled the last of his Blood on the Beach drink and pretended he was going to pour it over their fries.

"Ew!" The girls' faces were drawn in mock-horror.

With a twinkle in his eye, he downed the last of his drink.

"Alright, let's get this show on the road. I'd like to get Ms. Rosemary back home and in bed." Bryce stood offering her a hand.

His mouth in a smirk, Jonathan said, "Notice he mentioned nothing about letting her sleep."

The lift of his eyebrows and slow smile left no question what Bryce had planned. "That's right."

The sight of Twylene holding Liz's hand as they walked in front of her and Bryce, elicited a sense of gratitude. Maybe this being in love with one person had some merit. She looked up at Bryce and grinned.

"What?" He opened the car door for her.

"I love you." She scooted into the car.

Shaking his head with his lips turning up at the corners, he climbed into the driver's seat and kissed her. "Love you, too, no matter what you're thinking."

"That's good." She enjoyed the warm silence as they made their way to her old offices to pick up the packed boxes.

Rosemary was amazed that, even with four vampires, they ended up working late into the night. At one in the morning, Jonathan and Edward unloaded the last of the boxes from the rental truck while she and Twylene guided them to the correct locations.

"Let's call it a night." Rosemary closed her office door and headed to the reception area.

"No argument from us." Edward, followed by Jonathan, hugged Rosemary and said their goodnights. Twylene and Liz followed them out the front door.

~

"I'll bring in the last box from your SUV, and then let's go home, my love." Bryce left by the back door as Rosemary nodded.

She had her hand on the handle of the front door in preparation to turn the lock when it swung open, and a very drunk Roger stumbled inside.

"Hi, gorgeous, what'cha doing here this late?" Roger's unsteady gaze did nothing for the sexy look he attempted to give her.

The breath she was holding whooshed out of her lungs. She had to get him out of here before Bryce came back in with that last box. "Moving into my new office. What are you doing here? Are you ill?"

"Just love-sick." Roger came towards her with arms outstretched.

She stepped back and put the reception desk between them.

"You've been drinking. How about some coffee?" She turned to go to the kitchen area, only to be stopped when he lunged towards her catching her around the waist.

"How about some sugar," he said as he tried to kiss her.

Frustration fought with fear as she struggled to free herself from his werewolf vice grip. "Roger, Stop! Let go of me. I've told you it's over between us."

"Oh come on, you can't tell me that old stuffy vampire can make you come like I can." He pushed her against a wall, groping her breasts.

"Get. Off." She tried to shove him back but failed. The fact she couldn't turn into her wolf to protect herself sparked her anger combined with her fear. She could tell Roger wanted love and comforting, not to rape her, but Bryce wouldn't see it that way. Roger kept on trying to undress her.

The stress of the situation flared her wolf in to action. Although she didn't shift, the familiar strength rushed through her body as she kneed him. He barely managed to howl and grab his crotch, before in a blur of vampire speed Bryce rushed into the room.

She heard his roar. Roger, in his drunken state, was no match for an angry vampire. Eyes flashing golden red, Bryce lifted him up, fangs extended. Roger hung limply, not even trying to fight.

"Bryce! No!" He paused inches from Roger's throat. Rosemary pleaded softly with him. "He's not worth it." The fire in his eyes flared as he held his beast in check, then, with a disgusted grunt, Bryce flung him against the opposite wall.

The wall shattered and Roger moaned, lying on the floor, clutching his crotch.

Bryce stood, staring at the werewolf. "You heard the lady, it's over. This old stuffy vampire has no problem protecting what's his." Bryce started for him, when Rosemary laid a hand on his arm.

"Roger, I'm calling your brother to come pick you up." Rosemary dialed the number as he crawled to his feet, keeping his eyes on Bryce the whole time. She looked away, folding her arms across her chest.

"I'm sorry." Roger whispered.

"I know." Rosemary drew in a ragged breath. She turned towards him. "Rex will be here in a couple of minutes."

"Okay." Roger nodded, then lifted up his head and looked at her with eyes that revealed a broken heart.

"Let's wait out front." Bryce grabbed Roger's arm and ushered him out the front door. He deposited Roger on a bench, sitting down beside him. He gave himself a second to calm down.

"Rosemary and I are getting married. She's mine now. You need to move on, because if I ever find out you have harmed her in any way, I will come for you." Bryce glared at him, fangs still prominent on purpose.

Roger shook his head. "I love her. I didn't mean to hurt her. I just miss her." He buried his head in his hands, but Bryce still caught the shine of a tear.

Bryce took pity on him and backed off. "I love her too."

"You wouldn't consider sharing?" Roger looked over at him.

"Really! No. You need to find your own mate." They sat in silence for a moment.

"Okay, but you'd better be good to her, 'cause I'll come for you if you hurt her."

"Understood."

"That's my ride." Roger limped to the curb before falling into his brother's car.

Bryce walked back through the front door with precise strides, locking it with a loud click. Rosemary stood with her arms around her middle. She should have told him more about Roger, but what was there to tell? Yes, she slept with him after their first date, but they weren't exclusive at that point.

Waves of anger still flew off of him. He walked to her and bent down to meet her eyes. "Are you okay?"

She could hardly meet his gaze. Her wolf was rattling the bars of the cage she kept her in. She just wanted this to all go away. "I... I am." She swallowed. "Bryce, I'm sorry."

He stood up and let out a long sigh. "Rosemary, I know there were others before me and it's not like you've had sex with him since we've been together."

"Well, not exactly." Rosemary's wild eyes overtook her pale face.

"What do you mean?" His voice was clipped and sharp.

She glanced up at his face. "After our first date, I spent the next day with him, and... and the night."

"Oh." His face hardened into a cragged stone.

The blood that carried her witch powers ran up her spine, straightening her stance. "I realized then, I didn't want to be with him. I'm sorry."

Bryce stared at her, his eyes glowing. "I'm sorry too. I tried everything I know to help you feel safe, and you go fuck a werewolf."

He just crossed a line.

"I had one date with you. I didn't know if I would ever see you again."

The pained look he threw her way caught her off guard. "You ran scared. Don't you think you could have trusted me enough to discuss your fears with me?" He turned to pick up a box.

Her wolf and witch stood ready for battle. Her voice hardened. "You're damned right I was scared! You've had seven wives and at least one has been beheaded because of you."

He put the box down with slow, particular movements and turned to face her. "Every day, I regret Jeannie's death." He closed his eyes,

A tear slid down his cheek. Suddenly, all of her anger drained out. She had hurt the man she loved.

Opening his eyes and not bothering to wipe away the tears, he whispered, "This is too much for me right now. I need some time. I assume you can drive yourself home." He didn't spare her a glance as he walked to the back door and slammed it shut on his way out.

Hugging herself into a ball, she dropped to the floor, her sanity on the edge.

"One twenty, one forty, one eighty, two hundred! Yes!" Bryce pushed down the accelerator on his red Ferrari 458 racing against his thoughts. Why didn't Rosemary tell him about wolf boy? Maybe her mom was right. He had no business being with a screwed-up witch/werewolf who couldn't even shift to save herself and ignored her magic. *Damn! Does she even love me? She's so fucking screwed up, how would she even know?*

How many other lovers has she not told me about? He hit the steering wheel with too much force, denting it. *Gods! I'm acting like a child.* The dark landscape whizzed by as his hurt and anger begin to abate. The car slowed down in time with his thoughts.

A gnawing sensation wore at his gut. He hadn't told her about Stephan or the extra security. Wasn't he just as guilty as she was? But he was trying to save her from worry. He stopped. Wasn't that what she was trying to do? She was right. They hadn't agreed to anything beyond dating at the point she went out with Roger.

He pulled the car to a stop in a gravel driveway. He had left his Rosemary, his soulmate alone at night when Stephan could have easily hurt her. *I'm an ass.*

Turning the car around, he gunned the engine, going back to the clinic in hopes he wasn't too late.

~

A crash reverberated in the operating room, scaring Rosemary enough to jump off the floor. She grabbed a flashlight she had tucked in the reception desk and carefully made her way back to the noise. "Who's there?"

No answer. *Great.* She could only hope it wasn't the crazy person who put a note on her car, or worse, Roger returning. Should she turn on the lights? Wasn't she already a moving target holding a lit flashlight? *Ah Hell!* She flipped the switches lighting the whole clinic.

Nothing. She grabbed a scalpel from an open box and made her way to the back. A small box lay on the floor. She recognized it as one she had packed. It had been balanced on a stack of larger boxes. Gravity was her big monster. For the first time in minutes, she took a full breath.

She grabbed her purse and turned off the lights, making her way to the back door. The scalpel held in her left hand shook as she fished around for her keys. *I'm being a big chicken. It was just a box. A teeny tiny box.*

She couldn't believe Bryce left her here alone after Roger's intrusion. *Well, I'll show him. I'm a big bad werewolf.* Spine straight and head held high, she turned the doorknob and pushed outward, only to have the door jerked away from her. A battle cry shot out of her and the scalpel found flesh.

"Ouw! Why did you do that?" Bryce caught her hand with the scalpel, but not before she sliced across his upper arm.

"No. Oh God, no." Rosemary pushed away the shock and went into doctor mode.

"Come on, let's get into my office, so I can clean that and dress it." She flipped on the lights and sat him on a chair.

"I know you're mad at me, but slashing me with a scalpel?"

Her head jerked up in horror. "I thought you were someone trying to get me." Then she noticed he was laughing. "I ought to let you bleed." She got his jacket and shirt off and started the cleaning process.

"You probably should, but you won't."

He was right. The mix of gratitude and horror jerked her feelings around like a rag doll. The touch on her arm from his shaking hand stopped her. A quick inspection of the wound told her all she needed.

"You're already healing. I'll dress it for protection for the next few hours." She measured out gauze. "You're right. I won't."

His smooth, deep voice touched her core. "Is that because of the Hippocratic Oath or the fact you love me?"

The tape to hold the gauze in place held her attention for a moment. Lips quirking up at the corners, she tilted her head. "A little of both."

He placed his hands lightly on her arms. "I realized while I was getting some air we both are trying to protect the other, by not always being completely honest."

"Is that so? What secrets are you keeping?" Fear shot through her like a flaming arrow. Yet, better to find out now rather than later.

She caught the concern in his eye when she started to shake. "I have reason to believe the vampire who beheaded my last wife is stalking you." He paused.

"That note on my car, you think was him, don't you?" Shock filled her again for the second time that night.

He shook his head. "I don't know. I've had some of the best private investigators as well as friends on the police force looking into that possibility to no avail."

"Does that mean you've put extra security on me?"

His eyes squinted as he worked up to the answer. "Yes."

She blew out a long-held breath. "Thank goodness."

He reached for his shirt, inspecting the cut across the sleeve. "You aren't mad?"

"Are you crazy? There's a vampire stalking me. If I had been aware of that little fact, there couldn't have been enough security." She helped him on with his shirt. "I'll buy you a new shirt."

He waved away the idea. "Not necessary."

"I'm miffed you didn't tell me this from the beginning." She held his jacket for him.

"Would you have been so agreeable to date me?" He put his wounded arm in the jacket sleeve.

"We'll never know, will we?" She zipped him up. "Do you know this vamp's name?"

"Stephan Johansson. He has long brown hair, greenish yellow eyes. I'll show you a picture at home."

"That is a vague description, but I will be on the lookout." She closed her office door, and they headed to the back door.

His low voice touched her heart. "I swear to you I will do everything in my power to keep you safe."

"I know." The gratitude she felt for him set off a chain of reactions. Roger had been more than enough of an issue tonight, but to find out a crazy vampire was stalking her sent her over the edge. Her hand that tightened across her mouth did nothing to hold in her sobs.

"Do you trust me now?" His eyebrows rose.

She looked up at him with tears spilling out of her eyes. "Yes. Do you trust me?"

Bryce sighed, and walking to her, he pulled her into his arms. "You were honest with me in the very beginning about your lifestyle. You asked me to be patient while you adjusted." He leaned back, meeting her eyes. "I would've preferred you confess your doubts and concerns at the beginning."

"You do understand why I didn't?"

"I do. I trust you. Being aware of your past, I understand you better, too."

She responded by hugging him and burying her face into his chest, sobbing with the release of her feelings. She wanted to believe he could protect her from this Stephan Johansson, but her stomach was knotted in fear.

He rubbed her shoulders and held her until she cried herself out.

"Let's go home," he said, kissing her in the center of her forehead.

CHAPTER 19

"Taste this!" The festive red liquid caught the attention of Bryce's guests. He loved sharing the Yule season with friends. This year, sharing old traditions with Rosemary brought a special warmth to his heart.

"Dessert wine?" Rosemary held up a bottle towards Twylene.

"Sure." Twylene inspected the bottle.

Rosemary uncorked the bottle. "This is a raspberry wine from Tomasello Wineries. It's sweet, but not so bad your teeth feel like they're wearing little sweaters."

"I love raspberries and dessert, so pour me a tall one." Twylene held out her glass.

Bryce cleared his throat and held his glass high. "A toast to our friends and family for Happy Holidays and a New Year filled with abundance and joy. Rosemary and I are pleased to be able to share this Christmas Eve and our home with all of you."

The clink of his glass on Edward's started everyone laughing, as they made sure they clinked glasses with one another.

Twylene's face reflected pure bliss after one sip. "MMmmm. This tastes so much better than plain raspberries."

Rosemary nodded and guided her friend to the dessert table.

Jonathan tipped his head to the side. "Oh, hm... Bryce, is this what I think it is?"

"What do you think it is?" Bryce grinned.

"I don't know what he thinks, but this is sweet, almost fruity. How does that happen?" Liz whirled her glass, inhaling the aroma.

Jonathan nodded. "It's from a diabetic, isn't it?"

"Unfortunately, at this time of year with all the sugary sweets, there'll be someone whose blood sugars will spike. We all feed on death one way or another. However, this is one of those treats that only comes along once in a while. I knew a vamp who would follow diabetics around hoping to catch them nearly in a coma. But, I can assure you this came from a poor soul in a morgue," Bryce took another taste, enjoying the bouquet.

"This's one of the best I've tasted." Edward took another drink, closing his eyes and letting the crimson delicacy roll around in his mouth before swallowing.

"I bet you paid a pretty penny for it too." Jonathan's eyes followed the legs as he swirled the blood expertly in his glass.

"I'll never tell." Bryce handed each of them a bottle with a festive bow around the neck. "In fact, I purchased each of you a bottle as a gift. Drink it in good health."

Bryce searched the room for his love. His face broke out into a smile when he spotted her. The ridiculous Christmas sweater she wore was decorated with a reindeer whose nose lit up. She lit him up from the inside out. The proof was in the sweater vest he wore over his normally somber slacks and white shirt. A Christmas tree twinkled across his broad back.

"You're giving vampires everywhere a bad name wearing that sweater." Jonathan clapped Bryce on the shoulder.

Bryce gave him a sideways glance. "Tell that to Rosemary. I dare you."

Tilting his chin and raising his eyebrows, Jonathan shook his head. "Uh uh! My momma didn't raise no fools."

Edward joined them. "Why are you talking like that?" He put his arms around Jonathan from the back and pulled him into his big body.

"Why? Do you like it?" Jonathan glanced over his shoulder, meeting Edward's eyes.

"Not particularly." Then he pinched his ass.

With a jump and a yelp, Jonathan laughed.

Bryce rolled his eyes at his friends and looked back at Rosemary. "Gentlemen, I need your opinion on something." He motioned for them to follow him to the kitchen.

He'd hesitated involving them up until now. He should've been able to capture Stephan and do away with him years ago, and yet, he hadn't. His breath came out in ragged bursts. "I believe someone is stalking Rosemary. In fact, I fear he's the same vampire who killed Jeanne." He paused. The mention of her name reignited the horror of her death by evil monster's hands. His summoned all his will to clear the lump in his throat.

Jonathan's sharp voice finally broke the silence. "Stephan Johansson?"

Still trying to control his grief, Bryce nodded. Jonathan's presence in the community that had dealt with Stephan and his wife had been a blessing.

Gathering his focus, Bryce answered, "I believe so, but I'm not certain. I hired an investigator to follow Rosemary after she found a note on her windshield."

Frowning, Edward moved beside Jonathan. "What did the note say?"

"*You're next.*" He inhaled slowly to allow the quiver in his voice to subside. "Neither the P.I. or my contacts with the police have found anything. One of her patients could be the culprit. Who knows?"

"Still disturbing." Edward's dark eyes were cold, flinty stones.

"Stephan was a cunning hunter. No morals or ethics." Jonathan's gaze locked with Bryce. "What can we do to help?"

"That's the thing, I'm not sure. For the last forty years, I've made casual dating a fine art, but Rosemary has changed me. I want to marry her without fear he will kill her. I want her safe...forever."

"We'll do some investigating of our own. Between my contacts and Jonathan's staff, something is bound to show up." Edward leaned forward to hug Bryce.

"Thank you." His voice just above a whisper. "I owe you guys."

"We've protected each other for decades. Out of all of us, you have plenty of good karma built up." Jonathan reached out and squeezed his shoulder.

Bryce hoped so. Things had been too quiet. Stephan was known for lulling his victims into a false sense of security before striking hard and fast.

Rosemary peeked into the kitchen. "Hey, guys, time to open gifts."

Bryce hoped she didn't catch the look the three shared as they flashed smiles her way and followed her into the living room.

Twylene and Rosemary placed colorful bags and brightly wrapped boxes in front of the intended recipients. Rosemary settled her warm body beside him. Her hand slipped up to rest on his thigh, and he let the air whoosh out of his lungs in a satisfied sigh.

He hadn't felt this happy and this worried in a long, long time.

Rosemary shut the door after the last guest left. "I'm worn out." Her lips curved into a tired smile. "I'm going to bed. What's on your agenda tonight?"

Inside Bryce, there was a little kid waiting for Santa. "I was hoping we could exchange gifts before you go to bed."

"I can find some energy to do that." Rosemary reached under the tree and handed him a small box wrapped in gold paper with dark red ribbon. He loved the way she bit her lower lip. She didn't need to worry. He would love whatever she gave him.

He handed her a gift wrapped in silver paper with dark blue ribbon.

"Open yours first." His gaze focused on her every move. What if she didn't like it? His nerves shot up a notch.

Hands shaking, she tore off the bow and paper discovering a

jeweler's box. With a quick glance, up, she opened the box finding a delicate ankh necklace set with blue and black stones. "It's beautiful."

"Do you really like it?" A beam of happiness spread across his face.

The light in her eyes cheered him. "I love it! Ankhs are one of my favorite protective charms. I admit I've never seen one quite like this."

Pleasure surged through him. *She likes it!* "Chances are you won't. It's specially made with blue and black sapphires set in platinum. It wouldn't do to have it set in silver."

"You think of everything. Thank you." She fastened the necklace around her neck. "Now, open yours."

The way she fondled the ankh as she waited for him to unwrap his gift assured him that the gift was perfect for her with everything that had happened recently.

"Okay," Bryce turned the gold package around, searching for the taped ends. Inside was a wooden box created from dark walnut, polished to a deep sheen to organize cuff links. "Rosemary, darling, this is lovely. You've seen the mess my cuff links are in."

"Open the box." A grin stretched across her face.

His little wolfie intrigued him.

He raised the lid and paused. She never failed to surprise him. "Oh, Darling, these are incredible." The cuff links caught the light, sparking a warm glow within him. "You remembered."

"How could I forget? When I revisited that lifetime in Scotland in trance earlier this year, I saw them on you. Black rubies with stars of red in the center surrounded by a circle of red rubies on the outside. Set in platinum, of course."

"I loved those cuff links. Their loss drove me crazy. They were one of my most protective charms." He pulled her into his arms and kissed her. "Thank you."

"You're welcome. I have to keep you protected, too." She rested her head on his chest. With her in his arms, he relaxed and enjoyed the connection in the quietness of the house.

A soft rumble came from her. He chuckled and pressed his lips to the top of her head. "Shall I go tuck you in bed? I think I heard you snore."

"I don't doubt you did. My bedtime was hours ago. I'm glad we've got the new office set up and have taken a week's vacation." Rosemary smiled as they walked arm in arm to the bedrooms.

Bryce headed to his office to find a good book. At least, that's what he told Rosemary. His computer screen lit up, showing he had an email from his security guard following Rosemary. Each word he read drenched him in a shower of icy fear. A vampire somewhat matching the description of Stephan Johansson had been spotted outside Rosemary's old office today. Thank goodness, it was empty, but she had left the new address on the door. The suspect had disappeared before they could confront him.

He stood at her bedroom door, watching her sleep. Her hand curled around the sapphire ankh. He had a week. *I'll deal with Stephan once and for all.*

CHAPTER 20

"Good evening, Mr. James. What brings you in tonight?" Rosemary searched her memory. Something about her new patient rang a bell. Maybe it was the way he gazed around the room with his untamed blue eyes. Unstable vampires were unusual, but not easily forgotten. Her ex, Leon, came to mind.

"Evening, Dr. Wolfe, I'm carrying extra metal in my body."

"I trust that metal isn't silver." The sensation of hairy spider legs at the back of her neck distracted her. *Not now!* She tried to shrug off the psychic warning. Her day had started out at the new location with new hours, and it was mid-January. There was the possibility she was just tired.

"It's not. I got caught in a spray of bullets last week and healed before I could dig them all out. I've heard you have a gentle touch and drugs that make it almost painless to remove them. By the way, you can call me Sean." A smile slithered across his face.

The spider legs kicked up a notch. Her hand reached to rub her neck involuntarily. "Okay, Sean, what happened? Vampires usually move fast enough to avoid bullets." A twinge of suspicion poked her consciousness.

"I was sloppy. A jealous ex shot me in the back and backside too." He shook his head, disbelief flicking in his eyes.

"Let's take a look," Rosemary said, as she had him lie down on his stomach in preparation for an x-ray. *I wonder why he shaves his head. I don't think the bald look does a thing for him.*

After the exam, she sat down with him in her office. "You're right. I found several bullets."

He gave her a dismissive nod. "I'm sure you did."

What an odd response. Whatever. "Sean, I'll need to schedule you for surgery tomorrow afternoon. Will that work for you?"

"Sure, that's why I'm in town." He raised both hands, flinging them outward.

Maybe it's a cultural thing. She scanned his file. "I see you came from Savannah, Georgia."

His eyes narrowed as he cocked his head to one side. "Correct. I'm a shaman there."

"What a coincidence. I'm working with a shaman." *That may be why I pick up such weird vibes. I know Night Sky can block most of my psychic probes, if he chooses.*

"I'd love to do a session with you before I leave town."

"That'd be great. You should be up and around by tomorrow evening. At that time, we can compare notes." Something still sparked a memory she couldn't quite grab. *No way was she trusting him to do a hypnosis session, but she would like to talk to him while the anesthesia wears off.*

"Certainly, I'll put it on my calendar." He held her hand a second too long and her gaze even longer.

Taking her hand back, she wanted to slather it in alcohol. An odd odor she couldn't place struck her nose as she guided him to the exit. "I'll see you here tomorrow at one o'clock. We'll have you finished and up by sunset." Rosemary smiled and tried to blame her suspicions on a long, exhausting, first day back.

∾

Rosemary ran into Twylene, who had finished with a pregnant shifter, a rabbit. Bunny was referring all her friends and family, which meant even more business. She poured a cup of coffee and asked Twylene to meet her in the conference room for a quick check of the schedule.

"We're done for the day, unless there's an emergency." Twylene blew on her coffee before taking a small swallow.

"I can tell you, I'm sure done. The last vampire wore me out, and I can't decide why."

"Any ideas?"

"He seemed charming enough, but I had creepy-crawly sensations on the back of my neck around him. He's scheduled for surgery tomorrow at one to remove a slew of bullets from his backside."

Twylene raised her eyes from her electronic tablet. "How did he end up with so many? Vamps usually move fast enough to avoid gunfire."

"I asked him. He mentioned something about a jealous ex." She paused to take a drink of coffee. "Come to think of it, he didn't say if it was his ex or someone else's."

"Well, at one in the afternoon, we can hope he'll be sleepy enough not to give us much trouble." Twylene grabbed her electronic tablet and her cup.

"I'm counting on that. I still sense something funny about him. Another thing, he made this appointment a month ago, and yet, he said the gunfire didn't occur until last week." Rosemary followed her out the door.

"That's weird, even for our clientele." Twylene paused outside her office.

"I planned on doing the surgery alone, being that it is simple, but would you mind being in the room with me tomorrow when he comes?"

"I think that would be a good idea."

Stephan ran a hand over his smooth scalp. *I miss my long hair.* As did the security guard Bryce hired to protect his precious Rosemary. *Idiot.* He looked right at the guard and was waved on inside. He swaggered down the sidewalk, twirling his dark glasses. Some might say having her do surgery on him was risky. The thrill of being hidden in plain sight caused him to do a little dance. Besides, the good doctor was just that: good. Too good. Well, tomorrow, she would help him by getting these damn bullets out of his ass and having his revenge on Bryce, and as an added bonus, Jonathan.

෧

He had enjoyed his meal tonight. Well, until Rosemary mentioned her new patient.

"He's a strange one." She handed him an after-dinner drink of plasma with a twist of lemon.

"I think you need to tell him to go to someone else." Bryce worried Stephan was in the area, but his security team had not seen him since the end of last year.

"He's odd and a little arrogant, but I think he's okay." Rosemary brushed a kiss on his lips.

"I don't care! Please don't take any chances. Besides, he might want more than surgery from you, and you know I don't share well." He pulled her down on his lap.

"Oh Bryce, he's a patient who is bald with blue eyes. He looks nothing like the description or picture of Stephan. In fact, he offered to stay and talk about his shamanic work after his surgery tomorrow. I think you're over-reacting."

"Fine, but what if this guy is bad news? If you'd tell me his name, I could have him checked out." *Of course, I can't imagine Stephan seriously pulling off being a shaman.*

"No names. HIPAA patient privacy auditors would throw all sorts of hissy fits about that." Rosemary gently kissed his ear and playfully nipped at the lobe.

"Hey, are you trying to distract me?"

She met his eyes. "Is it working?"

He answered her by possessing her lips in a kiss that drove her to distraction.

~

The mournful howl rose out of the mist. The sound made her shiver. Where was her wolf? Usually, she was her wolf, but they were separated. Rosemary stumbled over an exposed root in the dark forest and barely managed to catch herself.

"Child! You need to pay attention!" Grandma Rosie pointed down a path with her staff, before fading away.

She shivered awake, tired of dreams she didn't understand. Sleep would be elusive now, so she hopped out of bed early and started her day.

Twylene caught Rosemary before they operated that afternoon. "Mr. James is prepped for surgery. He told me about his work as a shaman and praised my knowledge of gem healing, but I'm with you on the funny feeling. He's covering something up."

"We'll see what comes out of him other than bullets." Rosemary deposited her rings in her desk drawer and led the way into the operating room. "Good afternoon, Sean, are you comfortable?"

"Yes, yes I am. I must admit, this is the middle of the night for me, so I'm ready for a rest." Pointy white teeth gleamed from his big smile.

I'm just being paranoid. Yesterday, she had discovered Sean was arrogant. Rosemary was ready to get this over with. "Can you sleep on your stomach?"

"Not a problem. Once you give me the drugs, I'll be out like a light. Speaking of which, will you be turning on more lights?"

"Yes, but we provide a blackout mask for you. In fact, let's turn you over, and I'll put it on." Twylene helped position him. "Now take a deep breath for me and count backward from one hundred." He was out before he hit eighty.

"Going in." Rosemary steadied her hand. The first incision was always the hardest. In Sean's case, she wanted to finish quickly. She couldn't find any reason to mistrust him, and it was her duty to heal the sick, no matter how annoying they might be. However, he made her nervous.

The ten bullets they retrieved brought out Rosemary's curiosity. The patients she served had their share of gunshot wounds. She glanced at Twylene as she studied the bullets in the tray. "Four 9mm, two .45 rounds, and four .25 caliber rounds. This vamp's been shot by at least three different people. I suspect two guys and one woman, but you never know."

Twylene frowned at the bullets and smirked. "All these shots in the back and none in the chest. Vamp, huh. Are sure he's not a big chicken?"

She rolled her eyes at Twylene. Her irreverence helped cut the operating room tension. This was one of the many reasons they were a great team. She checked her work and gauged how quickly the incisions were healing. No need for stitches for this operation. "Even for a vampire, he's a fast healer. You can start taking off some of those butterfly band aids."

"Nice ass for an old man." Twylene removed another Band-Aid.

"Are you noticing men's asses? What would Liz think?" Rosemary winked at Twylene.

"Trust me, there is no comparing to Liz's ass, and she's well aware of how I feel." Twylene's soft eyes glowed with joy.

"I enjoy being around her. It's different having a female vampire among all the boys." Rosemary laid her instruments in a pan and peeled off her gloves.

"Why don't you check with Bryce and let's do a late dinner this Saturday evening?" Twylene prepared Sean for a transfer out of the operating room.

"It's a date. Let's roll him into the recovery room and sterilize everything." Rosemary wanted to find out what this vampire was hiding. His offer to talk about his work could give her some answers.

Fog surrounded him in a shroud of quiet death. He fought through the dream in hopes of waking before seeing her body. Too late. The crimson pool of blood flowed over his boots causing him to choke. Kate, his wife, lay on the ground, throat slashed, eyes frozen open in shock. Stephan clawed his way to consciousness and tried to sit up.

"Whoa, you're probably healed enough to do that, but go slow and let me help you." Rosemary took his arm and supported his back.

Her touch brought him the rest of the way back and he realized he was in the bitch's recovery room—just as he planned. "Thanks, I'm a little shaky." *That was close.* He took a moment to steady himself. He hadn't anticipated the nightmare, but it made him even more determined to avenge his mate. "I do feel lighter. How many bullets did you take out of my back?" The comforting kick of his vampire strength spread through his body.

She inspected his incisions with gentle hands. "We found ten. You were lucky you weren't in more pain. Did you get all of those last week?"

"No. I had another batch or two before then. That's why I made the appointment earlier. I was lucky, or is that unlucky, to catch another round of bullets last week." He swung his legs off the table and stood up, staggering slightly on purpose, pretending he was still weak. Truth of the matter was, as an old vamp, he would be up to full speed in the next few minutes.

Her sharp eyes assessed his condition. He gave Bryce credit for attracting smart women.

"You must have a lot of exes shooting at you," Rosemary said, raising an eyebrow.

A wave of his hand dismissed her comment. "Not really. These were from folks who've been involved with clients of mine, who for one reason or another didn't agree with my advice. Especially when it led to them getting dumped." He moved toward his clothes, needing to dress before she noticed he didn't have in his blue contacts. Not that she was likely to recognize him from any of Bryce's descriptions. He had made more changes than just his eye color. However, he was so close to his goal and didn't want anything to stop him.

Finally, she opened the door. "We'd love to hear more about your work as a shaman while we wait to make sure you've completely recovered. Let me grab you some refreshments and we can go into my office and visit. How's your pain?"

"Tolerable." No way was he going to be drugged up for the next part of the evening. "I'd love to tell you about my work. Have you got any type A? It's my favorite."

Twylene, who had locked the front door behind their office manager/medical assistant, Bunny, overheard his request. She made a quick turn to the supply room, saying, "Coming right up." A few minutes later, she joined Stephan and Rosemary in Rosemary's office with drinks.

"Let's hear about your shamanic work." Twylene dropped to the couch.

Curious little panther. He liked her. "I work with my guides to pass on information and provide guided meditations to balance their chakras, discover their guides, or remember their past-lives."

"How'd you learn all of this?" Twylene leaned forward, hands on her knees.

He found himself wanting to answer her questions. "My mother was a psychic junkie, who took me with her to events. As I got older, I hooked up with women who could teach me how to use the gifts I had." The scowl on Rosemary's face told him she was starting to suspect him. Time to use his mind control to hypnotize these shifters before they caught on to his plan. He was amused her next question played right into his strategy.

"We've been working with a shaman on remote viewing and remote healing. Have you done much of that?" Rosemary watched him.

"Some, but there's not much call for it in my regular day-to-day work. Say, I'd love to demonstrate my trance technique. I bet you both could use a little relaxation after the day you've had." He started pouring on the magical energy that was his gift.

"I'm relaxing just learning about everything you do." Rosemary crossed her arms and leaned back in her chair.

"Of course, what else would you like to know?" He gazed into

Rosemary's eyes. Her body started swaying while her eyes became unfocused.

She shook her head and shifted her gaze to Twylene for a minute. Twylene nodded, not seeming to sense a problem. Rosemary was a strong one. He'd have to put more effort into putting her in trance.

"Ah, okay...Tell me more about the guided meditations you do." She seemed to revive.

A burst of energy exuded from him. Every word vibrated with his intent. He made sure the energy reached both women. "Interesting subject. I love the classic start where I have my client imagine that each part of their body is becoming heavy, very heavy, so heavy they can't move it."

"I...I...can see where that would work." Rosemary's head dropped forward only to jerk up with wild eyes.

The fight she put up made his obsession for her increase. Her strength as a vampire would be phenomenal. His voice surged with his power. "It works quickly. They find themselves going deeper and deeper into a pleasant and safe sleep. Much like you are now."

Her eyelids fluttered. "I'm..." Rosemary slumped in her chair.

Sean looked over at Twylene who had dropped off much sooner. "Charming. What shall I do with you while I tend to your boss?"

Cold. So, cold. Rosemary tried to cover herself up but couldn't quite move her arms enough to find her blanket. A fog enveloped her brain. She fought to open her eyes, to understand where she was. Moist air hit her face tainted with sickening sweet rotten fruit. Where was that stink coming from? Her stomach lurched, jerking her to consciousness. The first thing she saw when she got her eyes to cooperate was Sean James leaning over her with a frightening stare.

His smile chilled her. She identified the source of the stench. "What're you doing?" Those overhead lights were in her operating room. "Where's Twylene?" The hard steel under her back was her operating table. "Why am I naked?" Rosemary struggled against the steel-reinforced restraints. "And strapped to my table?" *Shift. I need to shift, Damn it!*

He came closer. "I wouldn't worry about Twylene, right now. You're soon to have the honor of being my vampire slave. Do you know what that is?" Startling her, he lightly touched her bare breasts with his cold fingers, making them contract to hard points.

The burn of vomit hit her throat as she choked it back. "I do. But that's not going to happen."

He stopped, giving her a moment of hope. "I've planned this for years. Lie back and enjoy. At least you'll be alive as a vamp when I'm finished." The laugh that emitted from him was a cold crackle that made her freeze.

She studied him. His rank smell increased turning her already nauseated stomach and told her more. *Insane. Completely off his rocker.*

Any hope she had flew out the window.

Mom was right about learning my magic. Crap! What spell would she use? She struggled to twist away from him.

With a rough grip, he held her head. "If you're a good girl, I'll make sure you enjoy the sex and the turning is quick."

She answered him with a silent glare.

"Guess what happens to vampires who are starved?" Coarse hands slowly explored her breasts and started down her torso, rubbing and pinching her, seeming to size her up. "They go mad."

The touch of his hands left a trail on her body she desperately wanted to wash off with rubbing alcohol. She rammed against the metal restraints cutting her arm in a useless effort to avoid contact with him.

The pain in her arm and the fear the blood would excite him more, caused her to still. "Why are you doing this? Your surgery went fine."

He snarled and grabbed her throat. "You naïve bitch! This is about Bryce Gold. He killed the love of my life. Now, I'm going to show him how it feels."

Her heart was beating faster if that was even possible. This psycho vampire was the one her love had warned her about. "Your name isn't Sean James, is it?"

That interrupted his tirade. "As a matter of fact, no. Doesn't matter. He'll know who I am."

"You left that note on my car."

He stood, releasing her throat. "Yes, among other things. Ever since the night you met that murderer at Jonathan's party, I've watched you." His face held a smirk.

"Had to work up the courage?" She couldn't help the snark in her voice.

He paused, studying her. "No. I wanted to kill you on the one hundredth anniversary of my wife's death. Which, by the way, is today."

She waited. Oh Goddess, this would be the perfect time for Bryce to be able to connect with her mind. *Bryce! Mom! Can you hear me? Please help.*

He narrowed his eyes. "Trying to mentally connect? Cute. Can't do it, can you?"

She held her breath.

"As you are probably aware, vamps have different gifts. Mine happens to be mind control through my voice. Didn't you wonder how you got here?"

She released her breath and nodded.

"I'm also scrambling any messages you might try to send out. So, save your energy. You're going to need it." He proceeded to adjust the straps so her legs were spread. "I'm fucking you because I want him spitting angry, and you're hot. I'll call him in a few minutes. He'll be here in time to see everything. I'll make damned sure of that."

Disgust rolled through her as she tried to distract him from touching her. "I'm sure if Bryce killed someone he had sufficient reason. Let him explain and work it out."

He answered by directing his attention between her legs. A long cold finger played with his target. She tried to squirm, back away from the pain, only to be held in place by the steel straps cutting into her flesh. Panic flooded her as the dam on her control sprung another leak. No way would she let him penetrate her.

His voice took on a hypnotic tone. "You want me inside you. Find your body excited at the thought of me fucking you."

Repulsed by his stimulation of her through the use of his mind and hands, she jerked her arms against the fastenings, ignoring the blood and fought her worst fear. *What if he bit her? With her messed up genetics, what kind of creature would she become?* In hopes of distracting him, she asked, "Where's Twylene? Is she hurt?"

Stephan stopped and considered her statement. "You're worried about that cute little blonde, huh? I wouldn't. I'd worry more about yourself." He propelled a scalpel along her inner thigh, releasing a stream of blood.

The pain seared in sharp points throughout her. She used her self-hypnosis to try to control the pain and panic. She had just arrived at her happy place when he started again.

"Of course, one of your first duties as my slave could be to turn her while you fuck her. You'll be so hungry and horny; you won't be able to resist. Yes, that's a fine idea, one more little show for your boyfriend's enjoyment."

His cruel laugh sparked her anger.

"He's a better man than you will ever be."

"You have no idea what kind of monster he really is. You'll be better off with me!" He lunged forward, latching on one of her breasts with his mouth.

"I'll never be your slave!" She screamed as he assaulted her body with his mouth and mind. *Sick bastard.* His stench clung to her. The bulge in the front of his pants brought her to the realization her anger and terror turned him on. She pushed down the vomit threatening to spew from her mouth.

He lifted up from sucking on her breast. "Fight me, fight me hard." His eyes lit up in glee at her struggle.

When she wore down, he surprised her by licking the blood from her thigh and sinking his fangs in the flesh, taking a long drink of her blood. Her roar of fright filled the room.

"Tasty," he said, licking the blood from his fingers. "I think I'll drain you while I do you. Don't go anywhere."

Fear morphed into anger as she fought against the restraints. Blood soaked into the sheets on the table from his abuse and her cuts that resulted from her attempts to break free.

He leaned in so close to her face, she could see her blood clinging to his fangs. "But you can start imagining how it's going to feel when I put my big dick in you and suck you dry. I'm turned on just thinking about it." He followed through with rubbing himself against the blood on her arm.

She paused, disgust taking a hold of her, and curled her lip. "What makes you think I could get turned on by a low-life bloodsucker like you?"

He stared at her with cold eyes. The wet wipe he used to clean his mouth dripped her blood on the way to the trash. The level of crazy he had reached jacked up her adrenaline higher. She held perfectly still, his face darkening with rage. Her instinct to duck did her no good as he hit her with a backhanded slap.

"Quiet, bitch. I'm calling your fiancé."

Pain sliced through her as her head bounced against the metal table. Still grasping for focus, darkness surrounded her as she lost her grip on consciousness.

Sometime later, she fought through the cold haze once again.

Stephan's voice shook with anger. "Why, I'm hurt you don't remember me. The memory of my wife's death has kept your face in my mind for decades."

Who was he talking to? She lifted her pounding head and realized he was on the phone. *Oh, no. He's talking to Bryce.* No! She had to warn him.

"No, I'm not dead. Maybe undead." His laugh panicked her.

"Actually, Jeannie is dead and Rosemary's next. What a beauty. How do you trick them into falling for you?" He paused, listening intently to his phone.

Goddess! He was a sick bastard. She shook her head in hopes of clearing her vision. He turned and walked back to her. She stilled, trying to make herself small.

His hand lifted her chin. "Let's see, I'm here with your fiancée at her clinic having a lovely time. Would you like to talk to her?" Dropping her head, he rattled a restraint. Pain shooting through her, she cried out. "Oh, but by the looks of those sturdy restraints, she'll literally be tied up for some time."

Every ounce of control she possessed helped her to quiet herself and the pain. However, when he continued, she realized Stephan was setting a trap for Bryce.

"Uh-uh. I might let her talk to you after I've fucked her and turned her, that is, if she still wants to talk to you."

She couldn't hear what Bryce was saying, but she had to do something.

"I'll wait for you. Come alone. Try anything, and I'll fuck her in every possible way until she bleeds to death. Then, while you are frozen from my voice, I'll make sure you have a front row seat at her turning."

She couldn't have Bryce put himself in danger. Surely, she could do something. Some spell that she would remember. Stephan's harsh voice caught her attention.

"Don't be such a hypocrite because you don't kill for your blood! You're a disgrace to vampires everywhere. The way you treat humans, you'd think they're something more than our next meal." He stopped and took a breath. "Although, your little sweetie will make a hot slave as well as a hot meal for me."

The terror she had kept at bay finally broke free. Her body shook. Pushed over the edge of her sanity, she screamed, "Bryce! It's a trap!"

He looked at her with his lips turned up at the corners. A low chuckle started in his chest. "She's right, but what are you going do?"

She noted his every move. Quiet now, she tried to stay still. But, when he bent down to lick the blood off her breast, she steeled herself. It didn't matter. He bit down hard and drank with a savage noise. Her anguished cry reverberated through the room.

"Revenge is sweet." A smack of his lips brought a smile to his face as he hung up.

∾

Terror coiled around his gut. His fangs dropped, ready for battle. Bryce stood with the phone in his hand and his eyes closed. The monster had his little Wolfie. Stephan Johansson was one of those mistakes he should have killed. "This time, I will."

The serpent of terror crawling up his spine motivated him forward. With precise movements, he dialed his friends.

Even though he did his best to hold it together, his voice trembled. "I need your help."

"What's wrong?" Edward's deep voice exuded concern.

"Stephan Johansson is holding Rosemary at her clinic. By the sounds of things on the phone, he's torturing her and has plans to rape and turn her. Can you and Jonathan meet me there?" He let out a long breath, praying he could figure out a way to stop Stephan and save Rosemary on the way.

Edward responded quickly. "Shit, man, we'll be there."

Within minutes, the three were outside the clinic, scanning the energies. The enhanced vision and hearing of his friends gave him hope to find his love before Stephan hurt her any more or worse. Each vampire had taken a section of the building and met back by the front door.

"The body heat in Rosemary's office is warm, like a shifter." Jonathan peered in the glass on the locked front door.

"Think he's left her there?" A bubble of optimism floated up in Bryce.

Edward appeared around a corner headed toward them. "I can't get a clear read on the back side of the building."

Bryce took in this information. "The extra sound proofing and reinforcements would make it hard."

"We need to get in there." Edward started to break down the front door.

A hand held up by Bryce stopped him. "Wait. If the alarms are set, that will alert him."

"Could we climb into the office through the windows?" Jonathan glanced back and forth between the others.

With a motion, Bryce indicated the guys to follow him. "I've got a plan I think might work." His speed and strength enabled Bryce to scale the wall and with a tug, he removed the glass and jumped in, the other two following behind him. "Remind me to have alarms put on the windows. Just because they are ten feet off the ground and sealed, they obviously won't stop a vampire."

The three took a moment to scan the office as their night vision adjusted to the dark. Edward located the light switch and flipped it on.

The sight of Twylene panicked Bryce. Tied to an office chair and gagged with a handful of surgical masks, her head hung forward with her eyes closed.

Jonathan raised his eyes to him. "What's wrong with her?"

The used syringe he picked up told him the answer with one sniff. "Valium." The drug cabinet provided him with the needed stimulant while the other two freed her of her bindings. With a slow and gentle hand, he injected her with a small amount and waited.

A low growl was the only warning they received as she shifted into her panther and came to slashing. The fact she was still a bit woozy saved them from some serious wounds.

"Twylene, it's Bryce. I'm here to help you." A tight grip to the nape of her neck held her at bay while he prayed Edward and Jonathan had a solid hold on her legs. Another yowl from her again alerted the vamps. Golden eyes promised violence as she struggled.

"Twylene, come on, kitty cat. Where's Rosemary?" Jonathan shook her paw.

The wild look in her eyes convinced Bryce that Jonathan was a goner, but suddenly, the panther's body went limp, only to start to shift. One minute she was going to kill them, and the next, bones cracked and claws retreated leaving a pale, blonde woman limp in their arms.

Bryce checked her pulse and jumped when she grabbed his hand.

"Operating room." Twylene's voice was a raspy whisper.

After a quick check revealed she was fine, Bryce's mind filled with hate. With every bit of his control, he focused on what he needed to do. His imagination of what Stephan was doing to Rosemary caused his body to shake. The long-held breath he released calmed him. He would do as Stephan asked. He would be the bait. His friends would also be there, not part of Stephan's plan. This time, he was going to make sure he never hurt anyone again. His anger gave him the concentration to explain his plan. All in agreement, they headed out.

"Time for me to go distract Stephan in the operating room, since that's what he expects, while you gather the supplies and take your positions." A thought stuck him. "Remember, if he uses his voice, he can control you and worse, he might kill Rosemary if he realizes I didn't come alone." All three heads nodded in agreement.

The back door opened quietly, allowing Bryce to slip into the observation room above the operating room. The sight that greeted him was Stephan fondling Rosemary's naked bloody breasts, while playing in the gore that covered her chest and dripped in a pool on the floor. Her legs lurched against the restraints as she let loose with a string of curses that would make an old shifter blush. The anger that threatened to overtake his senses was put on hold. He couldn't influence Stephan's mind, but he could distract him. Grateful his love was conscious and spitting mad, he opened a connecting window.

Suspicious that Stephan heard him open the window, Bryce paused. The leer he tossed over his shoulder at him confirmed his suspicion. The torture Stephan inflicted on Rosemary was a show to hurt him.

Dread washed over Rosemary's face. "Monster, I can't believe I helped you."

He moved away from her breasts to the junction of her spread thighs and stared into her eyes. "Admit it; you like it rough, don't you?" A quick tightening of the restraints spread her legs more. He ignored her cry.

"Your lover is a real pansy in bed, aren't you, Bryce?" Even though he spoke to Bryce, Stephan remained focused on Rosemary.

The spike in his temper made it hard for Bryce to remain calm. His fangs dropped as he prepared for battle. "My definition of a pansy is a vampire that has to tie up a woman to make love to her."

Stephan turned to face him. "That's where you and I differ. I will not make love to her. I will fuck her. Hard. Then feed on her blood until she's on death's doorstep. If you behave yourself, I will spare her life by feeding her my blood and turn her."

His fangs lengthened. Stephan had already killed one woman he loved. Now, it was his fault he had Rosemary. A dark cloud of abhorrence filled Bryce, focusing his anger and controlling it at the same time.

Hand covered in blood, he smirked and licked his fingers. "She will make a delicious slave. Humans aren't for loving. They are to fuck and feed upon." An evil sound disguised as a laugh emitted out of him as he turned back to Rosemary, unzipped his pants releasing his cock, and positioned himself between her legs. "I'm honored you're here to watch the show." His eyes met Bryce's as he advanced.

Time for him to die! The hope everyone was ready urged Bryce to slap the light panel. Intense full-spectrum light flooded the small room, reflecting off the quartz embedded in the seamless floor. Jonathan and Edward, clad head to toe in full body LightNight protective gear, burst into the room and grabbed Stephan's arms, dragging him away from Rosemary. He thanked the gods the fabric-lined vinyl suits fitted closely yet allowed for the movement the two men needed to get to her quickly.

An unholy sound hissed from Stephan as Edward closed his white gloved hand around his throat, effectively shutting down his gift of hypnosis.

"Ha! Caught him with his pants down, didn't we?" The humor usually present in Jonathan's voice was replaced with a deadlier seriousness.

The light left burns on the malevolent vampire's skin, leaving him weakened as he struggled to free himself from the two strong vampires. His mouth moved, but no sound emerged.

In a desperate move, he landed a head butt to Edward's chin. The crack of bone sounded through the suit's thick material covering their faces. The deep glow of Edward's eyes showed through the eye guard as he jerked Stephan's face up to a light. "Here, I think you need some enlightenment."

In a desperate move, Stephan twisted away. Edward's hand slipped from his throat.

Screams echoed off the walls as he thrashed. "No! He killed my Kate!"

Jonathan grabbed for his throat and missed as Edward attempted to shake off his injuries.

Stephan dropped his voice into the unnerving timbre. "You can't move." The vamps froze. For a moment, he slumped. The skin on his face bubbled with burns.

The doors to the room crashed into the walls as Bryce rushed into the room. Reason had long left him. Afraid Stephan would escape, he ignored the light that burned his skin. Long, sharp fangs sank into Stephan's throat. The swipe from the other vampire's hand caught Bryce off guard. The bastard had a scalpel he plunged deep into his shoulder. Blinding pain shot through him as he managed to pull it out. His fangs aimed again to Stephan's throat, and tore out bloody flesh. In a last-ditch effort, Stephan dragged the scalpel through the tendons on his hip. A roar of anger laced with pain flew from Bryce as he flung the scalpel across the room and proceeded to destroy him. The sensation of the hated vampire's flesh shredding and his body releasing life triggered rage in Bryce. He had waited for years to do this. For Jeannie and now Rosemary, he ripped the monster's body with savage glee. Blood splattered crimson streams over the operating room adding to the pool from Rosemary. The acrid, metallic smell of burning vampire filled the room.

"Leave before you burn more!" A wave from Twylene's hand brought the guys back to attention. Heads nodding in understanding, they pulled the out-of-control Bryce off the mangled bleeding pieces of Stephan scattered across the floor.

Somewhere in the back of his mind, Bryce realized he had snapped and was burning, but he couldn't stop. The taste of Stephan's blood gagged him, and yet, he craved the kill, the violence. That monster had hurt the women he loved. Jonathan and Edward tightened their grip on him when he lunged towards Rosemary. He just wanted to see if she was okay.

Her scream vibrated the walls. Rosemary fought the restraints. Bryce slipped out of Edward's grasp and dropped to the floor when Jonathan tripped him.

"Got'm," Edward yelled as he grabbed Bryce's arm.

"Damn it! Let me see Rosemary!" Bryce twisted and jerked, ignoring his burning flesh.

"Bryce! You're burning and scaring her." Jonathan finally broke through the crazed vampire's insanity, stopping Bryce in his tracks.

The last thing he remembered was the pain as his tears ran over his burned cheeks. Strapped to a bed in an exam room, he passed out.

Twylene used her panther speed to turn the full-spectrum lights off on the way to Rosemary's side. Worry shot through her. The sight of Bryce covered in burns and blood, fangs flashing, had sent her friend into a blackout.

The fasteners were tricky to undo. She worked as quickly as the blood-soaked straps would allow. Her rising panic had to be controlled. Rosemary had lost enough blood to put her in real danger. How fast could she get her on an IV?

Her patient stirred when the last restraint was loosened.

"No!" Rosemary fought her.

Trying not to hurt her, she held her still. "Rosemary! It's Twylene." She stopped flailing.

"Twylene..." The exertion took over, and she lost consciousness, again.

Afraid her friend was going into shock, she grabbed a blanket. "Oh honey, let's cover you up." Twylene continued to examine her. *No broken bones. Good. Gashes, bruises, blood loss. Bad.*

She had to keep her cool. *Rosemary first, Bryce, then Edward.* She lifted her unconscious friend and positioned her on a table in the closest exam room. Sure she was stable, she started an IV of blood and pain meds on her and then Bryce. Edward and Jonathan joined her, having shed the LightNight suits.

"How's the chin?" She looked up from treating Bryce's burns.

Rubbing his massive hand over his lower face, Edward nodded. "Damn asshole broke it. Good thing I heal fast."

Jonathan put his arms around Edward's neck and pulled him close. "Let me kiss it and make it all better."

With a weary grin, Edward accepted his lover's kiss. "As much as I would like to be covered in your kisses, we have a body that needs to disappear."

Jonathan, one eyebrow arched high, gazed up to him. "I know just the place." Stepping out of his arms, he lightly touched Twylene. "Will you be okay, or do we need to stay?"

"Things are under control here. Don't you think we need to dispose of what's left of Stephan's body, before someone notices?" Their offer to stay reassured her, but she and Rosemary couldn't afford any scandal with their new clinic.

"We'll clean up the operating room and dispose of the trash." Edward guided Jonathan to the door. "You have your cell?"

"Yep. I'll call if I need anything. Here." She tossed them each a bag of blood.

With a nod, they headed to the operating room.

The IV in Bryce's arm was secure. The pain medicine she injected in the IV should help keep him immobile as he healed. She needed to finish Rosemary. The usually strong, confident woman lay pale and broken. Twylene stood for a moment in the doorway to the exam room and released a breath. She wiped the tears streaming down her face and gathered her supplies.

The wolf walked through the inky landscape, raising her nose to sniff the air. No vampires. She had to keep going. Too many monsters. The cuts on her legs and chest hurt as she moved. The wolf's mournful whine flowed from Rosemary. The dream faded as Twylene's face came into view. She jerked up, stopped by the IV and a light touch from Twylene.

"Stay still." Twylene helped her lay back down. "I'm going to stitch and dress some of your more serious wounds. Okay?"

She nodded her head.

"He really did a number on your breast, didn't he?" The cleaning and bandaging Twylene performed felt comforting in spite of the pain. Her eyes searched the exam room. She was safe, right?

A sob bubbled up from Rosemary. "I...I...why?" She had taken an oath to heal and yet he tried to rape her. The memory plowed through her bringing more images of Stephan's leering face and his stink as he bit her breast. The panic rising in her shot out of control as she relived the feel of his sharp fangs piecing her flesh and the terror of how close he came to raping her and turning her. Her body thrashed from one side to another trying to escape the monster in her mind. Her sobs morphed into screams. In the back of her mind, she heard Twylene's voice and slowly responded.

"You're safe now, sh-h-h, shhh, he can't hurt you again." Twylene rubbed her hand until she settled, then injected her with what she assumed was pain medicine. The memory of Bryce's body being slashed had her fighting the numbness. Remembering the madness in his eyes as he fought to get to her sent cold fingers of horror up her spine.

"Where's Bryce?" Fear had her wolf on alert. Was the violence too much for him? Had he gone rogue?

"Bryce's strapped down in another exam room receiving blood and pain meds while he heals from his burns and wounds." Twylene checked her bag of blood and started in on a gash on her thigh.

"He's not..." Tears spilled from her eyes.

"Sweetie, I'm not sure. I don't think so. He's an old vamp with incredible control. I think what appeared as him going rogue was him desperate to see if you were okay."

"Will the burns heal?" The physician in her kicked in, giving her a sense of stability.

"His body will heal." Twylene concentrated on her stitching.

Her imagination went into a crazy place. "But not his mind?"

She stopped stitching and met Rosemary's gaze. "I haven't allowed him to be conscious, yet."

"Probably best." The physician in her returned. "Are you okay?"

The tremor in her voice gave away her reactions to the trauma they both had experienced. "Yes. Stephan hypnotized me and put me out with a shot of Valium. The sting of the needle woke me for a moment. The creep had the balls to brag about where he was taking you and what he was going to do. Then, the drug knocked me out. When I came to, the boys had a scare when I shifted."

A half hiccup and laugh tumbled out of Rosemary's mouth. "I bet."

"I need to go check on Bryce and call Liz. Will you be okay for a few minutes?"

"Go call Liz." Rosemary waved a hand in careful little movements. For a time, she lay floating on the numbness the meds provided. Alone, the horror of the night trod back into her mind. She couldn't do this, could she? Why did she think a relationship with a vampire would work? She loved Bryce, but was he even sane at this point? Bloody battles could tip even old vampires back into a life of carnage. Hell. She was on the thin edge of sanity herself. The chance she could shift into her wolf and not come back would certainly put an unwelcome kink in their relationship. She didn't remember when her body started to shake or her tears began to fall. Her wolf wanted control. Forever. But the healer in her couldn't live that way. A scream burst from her lips.

Twylene must have heard her from the other room. She rushed to her side. "Oh honey! I'm here. You're goin' be okay. Sh-h." Tucking the blanket loosely around her, she held her hand as rivers of tears flooded down her face. Rosemary welcomed her warm touch and low whispers that finally comforted her on a deep, primal level.

"How're you doing?" Twylene's touch to her forehead swept back her hair.

She continued her exam for other wounds.

With a soft grunt, she sighed. "Not so good."

"Want to talk about it?"

Rosemary pinched her lips together in concentration and because

Twylene was working on her upper left side. "Eventually." She touched her chest. "My left breast hurts like hell. How many stitches did you put in it?"

With a grim twist to her lips, she answered, "As you know, vampire bites heal quickly, and you being a were increases healing even more. However, I put several in to hold the flesh together while it knits back to form."

"Oh God! I'm not hairy, am I?" Rosemary reached up with frantic movements to run her hands over her face and arms.

The nurse practitioner's lips curved upward. "Apparently, your vanity's unaffected. Werewort came with your pain meds." She eyed the IV. "You will be ready for a second bag in an hour or so. We both are aware the soreness and weakness will lessen as you build up your blood supply."

She settled under the cover. "I'll eat plenty of red meat in the next couple of days and be fine."

"Well, someone's feeling more like themselves." The last wound dressed and covered, she started the cleanup.

"How's Bryce?" She had argued with herself about asking, but she needed to face it head on.

Her friend came over and stood by her. "He's awake and his body is healing."

"And his mind?"

She pressed her lips together, pausing. "He saw your reaction to him in the operating room."

What blood was left in her face drained, leaving her a white sheet. "When he came at me?"

"He was coming to rescue you, to release you."

She gazed into her friend's eyes. "He wasn't trying to kill me? He didn't go rogue?"

"I don't think so. Right now, he's fighting being embarrassed, hurt, and afraid."

"Afraid?"

"That he's lost you forever."

"Oh." The vision of him tearing the other vampire apart inundated her mind. Terror crawled all over her like a herd of mad spiders. Spasms and screams racked her body and mind.

"Stop! Don't go there!"

Barely aware of Twylene's effort to reel her in, she fought the panic. After a few minutes, she took a deep breath and returned.

"Sorry. Stopping it is tough."

"Understandable. Do you think it would help to talk to him, now that he's back in control of himself?" She wiped Rosemary's face and glanced at her IV.

"Maybe in the morning. I just want to sleep." She suspected the drugs and the exhaustion were hitting her at the same time.

"I made a bed up for you tonight in the recovery room. I want to monitor you for a day or so."

"Not necessary." The attempt to sit up resulted in her falling back onto the table like a ragdoll. "Well, if you insist."

"I do." Twylene guided Rosemary into a wheelchair and rolled her to the waiting bed.

"Did I thank you for saving my life?" The tears spilling onto her face had Rosemary scrambling for a tissue.

"Not recently, and you're welcome." Tears clouded her eyes. "I thought we'd lost you." She supported Rosemary so she could stand.

"Yeah. Well, I have to admit I thought I was a goner. Fear had me in a crazy place when he was torturing me, but when he stopped, I was praying he hadn't hurt you." Rosemary grabbed the railing on the bed and with her friend's help, climbed into the waiting bed. She had to find a way to increase her strength other than shift to her wolf.

She assisted her in adjusting into a comfortable position before covering her with a thick blanket. "He was more obsessed with you. Me, he put out and tied up. You can thank your fiancé and friends for figuring out how to save us both. Liz is pretty grateful too."

With a lift of her heavy eyelids, she met Twylene's gaze. "What did Liz say?"

Twylene enveloped one of Rosemary's hands in hers. "Once I convinced her I was fine, she promised to come over as soon as someone replaced her at the pharmacy. She'll probably come back and visit you, too."

Rosemary jerked back against the pillow. "I look awful."

"You look alive. She'll understand." Twylene attached a call button to her bed. "I'll be in my office rearranging the schedule so you can take time off. Press the button if you need me."

"Thanks, I'm going to sleep now." Her eyelids closed as she finally relaxed.

CHAPTER 21

The burns on his skin were healed, but his heart still felt as if someone had sliced it open. Bryce stood at the open door of the recovery room watching Rosemary sleep. Twylene had told him she was still having panic attacks and was not ready to talk to him. His night vision revealed she was covered in gauze and tape, and still receiving blood. Guilt cut through him. Stephan's methods were familiar to him. The woman he loved was always the target. After Jeannie, he'd not dated anyone seriously. Old feelings of her death surrounded him in a shroud of grief. *How did I let this happen, again?* The breath trapped in his lungs escaped in a whoosh.

A small cry from her caused him to freeze. Twylene had told him of her nightmares and panic attacks. He couldn't help himself. Each step he took was calculated to bring him close enough to comfort but not frighten her. He stopped a few feet from her bed.

Her eyes were closed, but she thrashed and the deep moan she released ripped at his soul. She was having a nightmare. *Damn it! I can't just let her suffer.*

His voice soft, he tried to insert himself into her consciousness in hopes of calming her. "Are you okay?" The glow of her opening eyes told him her wolf was on alert and could see him. He watched as his love regained control, pushing the wolf in submission.

"B-b-bryce?" She was shuddering like a leaf in a windstorm.

"Yes. Do I need to leave?" He took a step back.

"N-n-no, stay." She flicked on a light and raised the bed to a sitting position.

Every cell in his body urged him to wrap his arms around her in a protective hug, but Twylene's words of caution slowed him down.

The raw wounds that covered her did something to him nothing else had in centuries. Once, any blood appealed to his dark, primal nature, now, his stomach constricted. "I thought I'd lost you," he whispered.

Calmer now, she stared at him with those intense blue eyes, not making a sound. He'd done the very thing he promised he wouldn't. He'd put her in deadly danger, not only from Stephan, but also in her mind, himself. *Gods! What kind of man, let alone vampire, was he?* His control returned. "I just wanted to make sure you're okay." All he could manage was a dip of his head before turning to leave.

The barest whisper caught his attention. "I know."

Grateful for his enhanced hearing, he faced her. "That goes for now, and in the operating room. I would never…"

"I know. Now, anyway. I was pretty messed up then." Her hands still shook slightly as she adjusted the blanket, revealing the yards of gauze covering her body.

"Would you be okay if I came and talked to you for a while?" His throat closed up as fear choked him.

Tears welled up in her eyes. Her head nodded.

His body pained him with each careful step he took. The tears in his muscles and joints were healing in the rapid time of all old vampires. However, Stephan had managed to inflict serious damage to his right leg and shoulder. He lowered himself carefully in the chair beside the bed. "Thank you."

The *doctor* look crossed her face, cluing him in on her next question.

"How badly hurt are you?" She started to move toward him for a closer look, but when the IV tugged on her arm, she stopped and leaned back.

"I'm healing. Twylene has the commanding presence of a nurse practitioner down pat."

A smile snuck across her lips. "That she has."

"Can I get you anything? Fresh water?" Now that he had made it to her side, he searched for the right words.

"No, thank you."

The need to touch her overcame his caution, and he held out a shaking hand to her. She hesitated, and then slipped her small hand in his large one. Pain squeezed his heart as he caressed the cold fingers that trembled with his touch. The gauze on her arms gaped, allowing him to view the damage done to her. Guilt and fear from his failure to stop Stephan burned like a hot coal in his gut. The knowledge they needed to talk moved Bryce to gather her other hand. Touching her skin between the many bandages settled his nerves as he ran his hand carefully up and down her arm. "I'm so sorry my past caught up with you. Can you ever forgive me?"

"You had no idea Stephan was around. He didn't match the past photos or descriptions. There's nothing to forgive." Her stare never left the floor.

"I have a confession." Bryce searched her face.

Head jerking up, she met his eyes. "What?"

"The security guard watching you reported seeing a man that matched Stephan's description around your old offices on Christmas Eve."

She sat still, her face a stone. "Why didn't you tell me?"

"It was weeks ago, and I didn't want to worry you. I wasn't even sure it was him." A gentle finger stroked her face.

She turned away from his touch taking her hands with her. "This isn't a good idea."

"What's not a good idea?" Bryce froze.

"Me being with you. I can't trust you to be completely honest with me."

He stared at her for a moment, contemplating what to say. "I'm trying to be honest now. What will it take for you to trust me again?"

Her face fixed like a deer in headlights, she swung her head back and forth. "I don't know. I don't know!" The ragged sobs led to tears and gasps for air.

Twylene's warning of her panic attacks became a reality for him.

He shushed her, trying to calm her as she flailed. "Wolfie, I'm sorry. Please stop crying." The lights flooded the room confronting him with the pissed off eyes of a black panther. Twylene glared at him as she rushed to Rosemary's side, injecting a bolus into the access port on her IV.

"What part of *she's not ready to talk to you* did you not understand?" Twylene pulled the syringe out and soothed her until the medicine helped her fall asleep. Checking her over, she started a new bag of blood and motioned him to follow her out of the room.

Sadness enveloped him as he took a last longing look at his soulmate. How could I lose my control around her? I should probably lock myself up like my brother and never love anyone again. Turning to follow Twylene out the door, he shook his head in defeat. *I've lost my reason to live.*

The chair in Twylene's office creaked as he tried to get comfortable. Perhaps it was the fact she was still gazing at him with those eyes. He ventured a glance up to her face which had softened.

"She will get better."

"Are you sure?" He took in a deep breath.

"Rosemary is a one of the strongest women I know, but she's had some horrific things happen to her in the last twenty-four hours." Twylene opened her computer.

"And, it's all my fault." He clamped his jaw down hard to ward off his own rising panic. He did lose control with Stephen. After forty years of hating the vampire, he had killed him in a blind rage. The thing that nagged at his conscious the most was he would do it again in a heartbeat.

"Listen, you and I both know that's not true. Stephan is the one at fault and you eliminated him."

He grunted, "With a lot of help from my friends."

She finished entering something on her computer. "That's right. We're your friends, and as your friend, I want you to trust that I will do everything in my power to help her heal. She's not only my boss, she's my best friend."

He shook his head. "Sorry, I'm being selfish. You're losing a good friend if she shifts to her wolf on a permanent basis."

"We all are. Jonathan, Edward, her family, we need to help her through. At her request, I called and talked with her mom and step-dad, and they are on their way here." Her eyes narrowed.

"Do you really think that will help?" He was already berating himself. He didn't need Sadie's help or judgement.

"Yes. Her body is healing, but her mind is stuck on panic."

He swallowed the lump in his throat. He would do anything for his Rosemary. "What can I do?" He didn't like the gleam in her eyes.

"Rosemary needs to stay close so I can monitor her and her parents are wanting to take her to their home." Her mouth curved up on one side.

"I see where this is going." He dropped his head.

"I need you to talk them into staying with you." She trained her cat eyes on his.

He slumped into the chair. "I will do my best. Will Rosemary come home or stay here?"

"I hope to release her in the next day or so and then send her to her home."

"You mean with me?" He tried not to appear like an eager kid on his birthday.

"With you, if she agrees. Well, if everyone agrees."

The thoughts running through his head made it spin. Rosemary would be home, but with her parents, a high-powered witch and a minor daemon. His lips curved up in a smile. The first one in days. "Okay. I'm in. Tell me what I need to do to help her."

She reached behind her to a notebook and handed it to him. "Here you go. Instructions and rearranged schedule for time off are all there." She paused, and then pulled out a small plastic baggie from her desk drawer.

Rosemary's engagement ring caught the light. His throat tightened while he fought to breathe.

Her extended hand held the package in front of him. "I trust you will make sure these are returned to her?"

Breath skidding out of his lungs, he reached for them. "I will. Thank you."

Her warm smile relaxed him. "I'll need your help in convincing her to take time off."

Glad for her humor, he raised his brows in mock surprise. "You think?" They both laughed. A knock on the front door jerked both of them up from their seats.

"I'll be right back. Read through that and let me know if you have questions." Twylene stood up. He started to go with her and then remembered her black panther. *She can handle it.*

"Just a minute!" On her way to answer the persistent visitor, she peeked in at Rosemary who still slept. Outside, she saw a welcome sight. Her girlfriend's mass of dark hair was falling over her cell phone as she punched in a number.

The door flung open. Liz glanced up. Even with her shifter speed, Twylene couldn't run to her fast enough. Strong arms held her close to her lover's soft body. The realization hit her right then how much she needed someone to be there for her.

The tight grip eased as they walked into the clinic.

"Are you okay? I got here as soon as I could. Are you hurt?" The questions were accompanied by Liz's hands exploring Twylene with a delicate touch from head to toe.

"I'm fine. Stop tickling me." Twylene giggled and then without warning, she was crying hysterically. "I'm so glad you're here." Her eyes shining with tears met Liz's. "You've just come into my life, and I was afraid I'd never see you again."

Twylene's face in her hands, Liz brushed away the tears. "Sweetheart, it's okay. I was terrified. When you didn't call at ten, I assumed you had a late patient. After you called, I convinced the day pharmacist to come in early." Liz leaned her forehead on Twylene's, and then kissed her. "You know I love you, don't you?"

"Yes, and I love you, too." The warmth and comfort from her lover calmed Twylene as they held each other close for a few seconds. "Rosemary is in the recovery room, but I just gave her a sedative."

"Problems?"

"Yeah. Bryce is waiting in my office. Let's go talk with him." Their steps had only moved them down the hall when the door rattled. Both shifter and vampire turned ready to destroy the intruder.

"Hey, good-looking ladies, can you spare a bag of blood for a couple of hungry vamps?" The grin on Jonathan's boyish face and the wide-eyed wariness on Edward's had Liz turning a questioning face to Twylene.

Shaking her head, Twylene unlocked the door. "I guess you two deserve a tasty meal in payment for cleaning up around here."

The guys walked in. Jonathan nodded to Liz before addressing Twylene. "Thanks. We have made creative use of the barbeque pit in our backyard. Ashes to ashes and all that. The trash has been burned."

At the confused expression on Liz's face, Twylene decided they all needed to confer, so she directed them back to her office.

CHAPTER 22

The pale sunlight teased her eyes open. One sniff told the wolf she was alone and safe, for the moment. The wounds on her body had begun to heal, finally allowing her to rest. Sleep. An older woman stood, staring at her, shaking her head. Unsteady, she managed to stand.

"Young one, study your magic. Next time you might not be so lucky." Grandma Rosie rubbed under her chin. Her wolf faded. She needed food. *Food... Was that a hamburger, no a cheeseburger?* Rosemary opened her eyes, brushing the dream back to her subconscious. *God, I must be so hungry I'm hallucinating.*

"Ready for breakfast?" Jonathan followed by Edward made an entrance into the recovery room with a tray laden with a meal fit for carnivore.

"Is that a Jonnie's special cheeseburger?" She licked the drool off her lips.

"Just the way you like it. Two quarter pound bison patties, cheddar, Swiss, lettuce, tomato, pickles, mustard, ketchup, and mayo." Jonathan positioned the tray in front of her chair.

She couldn't help herself. A squeal emanated from her. "Fries with your homemade béarnaise sauce." A sauce-covered fry disappeared quickly in her mouth, followed by a long moan of happiness.

"You guys are the best. I was dreaming of cheeseburgers, but this is so much better. Thank you." She leaned back to let Edward tuck a napkin under her chin.

"There you go. Now, dig in." He stepped back and winked at his lover. "Jonathan's food has mysterious healing powers."

"You appear much better, today. Do you think Twylene will let you go home?"

She swallowed and nodded. "We talked about it last night. I'm done with blood transfusions and injectable pain meds, and grateful for my werewolf healing abilities. Even though it's been only a couple of days, I think I'll heal better at home."

"Are you going to stay in town or go home with your parents?" Edward patted her foot.

The food turned to lead in her stomach. "I...I...don't know." Her heart beat faster and sweat covered her face.

Edward grabbed her foot. "Stop. Breathe. You know you are more than welcome to stay with us."

Warm brown eyes met hers. *Calm. Control.* "I'm sorry. The attacks are coming less often and don't last as long."

"You're doing great." Jonathan pulled up a chair and sat, facing her.

"Not really. How am I ever going to provide any sort of healthcare if I'm scared of my patients?" She played with a fry, creating little circles in the béarnaise sauce.

Edward squatted down in front of her. "Are you afraid of us?" His face winced.

"No. I trust you with my life." She paused. "I'm afraid of the GDBs I don't know or trust."

"You know Bryce." Jonathan's voice cracked.

"I thought I did. But..." Her voice choked with tears. He had been perfect. Safe. Strong. Loving.

Edward slid a warning glance at Jonathan. "Do you not feel safe staying with him even with your parents there?"

"What if he loses it and tries to hurt them?" *Control. Breathe. I can do this.* Calmness settled into her core. "Or me?"

Edward cupped her shaking hand in his. "I understand your fear and why you have it, but do you think he would do that?"

"Probably not." Her eyes met his and serenity flowed in her. One of Edward's gifts.

"But he did. When it came to you, he killed Stephan, didn't he?" Jonathan always cut to the chase with her. That was one of the reasons she loved and occasionally hated him. She nodded, afraid to trust her voice.

"From my perspective, you can call it quits right now, and you both can try to regain balance in your lives, or you can find that balance by engaging your magical wolf warrior. She is amazing. Fight for this man you love and who loves you." Jonathan brushed back the strands of hair from her face, comforting her.

"You seem awfully certain I'm not broken beyond repair." Lips pursed, she listened to her inner wolf laughing incredulously.

"You're not." The familiar voice warmed her right to her core before bringing on a quivering she tried to halt. In the doorway stood the one person who possessed her heart, body, and soul, and terrified her. His black silky slacks stretched over the muscles in his thighs, his shoulders filled the entry. Oakmoss and nutmeg mixed with his masculine scent triggering her wolf to pace in anticipation.

"Bryce..." In a gesture of universal longing, Rosemary extended a hand his way.

He came to her side and pressed his lips in a careful kiss to her forehead. "How's my Wolfie this morning?"

"Better." She started to reach up to him and stopped when the jagged reminders of her mistakes came into view. The raised flesh circling around her arms where the restraints mangled her, now uncovered, caused disgust to plow through her. She tried to hide her arms.

He took her hands in his and kissed both of them. "I can see that."

He kissed her scars. The ugly, gross reminders of Stephan's insanity. She still wondered how he managed to trick her, bypassing her intuition. How could she have been so stupid? As a physician, she had told many a patient the scars wouldn't be that noticeable and would fade in time. Hell, she created ointments that helped the fading. Would Bryce ever be able to look at her breasts, her whole body without being reminded and turned off? Would she? But, he kissed her scars. In that moment, she decided her relationship with him was worth saving.

Bryce packed up her things, handing them to Jonathan and turned to Twylene who entered the door with a wheelchair.

"Here are her meds and instructions in this bag." The bag was placed over the handle of a wheelchair. "Let's load her and roll."

Golden brown eyes sought answers from her. "Are you coming with me or are you going with Jonathan and Edward?"

The spark of fear that flew across his face, tugged at her heartstrings. Yes, she had to give them a chance to work this out. With bravado, she didn't feel, she said, "With you, of course."

The gratitude that settled on his face told her she had made the right choice. Even if they still had issues to solve.

He moved the wheelchair closer to the bed. "Your chariot awaits."

"I can walk," The first step propelled her forward in a wobbly gait, which triggered Bryce's quick reflexes as he picked her up and carried her to the car.

She caught her breath. Jonathan's words rang through her head. If she wanted to regain her balance, she needed to push her panic aside and deal with her fears. Her lover's strong arms cradled her body. Could she trust those safe, loving feelings again? Goddess, she wanted to. Needed to. She glanced up at his determined lips uplifted in a smile and nestled her head in the crook of his neck. She inhaled, letting his scent fill her and calm her wolf.

A stolen glance at Rosemary revealed nothing to Bryce on the drive home. Eyes staring out the window, she didn't say much. Weariness surrounded her, but he feared more.

"How're you doing?"

She trained her gaze on him. "Physically weak, but better. Otherwise, still unsure."

The car was quiet for a moment. Sadie had generously offered for him to pick up her oldest daughter. She had told him they needed to be alone. *Gods, I don't want to waste this opportunity.* He concentrated on steering around a curve, giving himself time to think. "Anything I can do to help?"

Mouth twisted in concentration, she sat, head bowed. "Did you have to kill Stephan?"

A sudden coldness hit him leading to his back stiffening into a straight column. He hadn't known whether to expect this question from her, but hoped it would never be asked. "Yes, I did. There's no way in hell I would let him hurt you again."

Eyes, lost in the memory of the horrors she'd seen, locked onto his. "There was no other way?"

He gathered himself. "By the time we could've handed him over to the VIEW authorities, there's no telling how many others he would have killed or tortured with the use of his gifts, particularly the hypnosis."

"You lost control." Her voice was flat.

How could he make her see what he did was the best choice for everyone? Frustration slipped into his voice. "I was angry, terrified, actually. The moment I saw what he was doing to you, nothing would have stopped me from eliminating him. I *swear I* would not have harmed you." He paused in hopes of not losing his temper. "I didn't hurt Edward or Jonathan. The desperation that you were dead or worse drove me to you. I got close enough to see you were alive. That's when I let them take me out of the room." He gave her and himself a moment. What could he do to convince her? He understood her fear, but he had to prove to her that he would protect her to the best of his abilities. *Like with Stephan?* He hated that little voice in his head that brought up valid points.

Lost for words and needing to calm down, he pulled over in a parking lot. They stared at each other, silent. He extended his hand in a gesture of friendship. She considered it for a long moment, and then placed her small hand in his.

She stared at their joined hands. "I wanted him dead."

He nodded slowly, encouraging her to continue.

"I'm a healer and he was a patient. I can't feel this way." She turned her watery eyes to him. "What if I'm never able to work again?" Her voice quivered.

"I'll be right beside you, doing whatever I can to help."

"The last several years has been about me becoming a physician, veterinarian, a healthcare provider for those who didn't have someone with the understanding and skill to heal them. I'm letting them down." Her hand grasped his with a tight grip.

His thumb stroked her pale fingers in an effort to calm her. "I won't push you. Consider the fact that if you and I do go our separate ways, Stephan wins. Not only does he win, the good we can do together for all the decent GDBs is lost."

Her fingers were ice-cold when he planted a kiss on them. "No matter what happens between us, I will always love you and do my best to protect you, but you need to come home to me so I can."

The terror in her eyes struck him like a left hook. What was he thinking? Obviously, he wasn't using his brains.

"I appreciate your efforts, but it's too soon for me." She withdrew her hand from his, leaving him in a cold panic. The darkness of a long life without her closed in on him. The expression on her face told him she was contemplating what he had said. He hoped his words had touched her heart enough to awaken her love for him. Pushing back the knots of tension in his body, he pulled the car on the road. The rest of the ride was silent and cold as a midwinter's night. All of his power and experience hadn't prepared him for dealing with a wounded soulmate. He hated it when a life lesson hit him over the head like a psychic two by four.

After he parked the car in the garage, he came to her door and started to pick her up.

"No, please, let me try to walk." Her legs were unsteady, but she managed to stand, with his help. With every step, her strain to walk made him uneasy, but he let her take the lead. After several minutes, they stopped in the mudroom. The fact she leaned on him almost completely by that point concerned him.

"Do you need to sit?" He motioned to a bench, nearby.

"No. Do you think you could carry me into the living room?" Her exhausted little face troubled him.

"Well, just to the living room. I know you're just doing this so I'll feel useful."

The giggle that bubbled from her lightened his mood. He carefully carried her to where her parents waited.

She tolerated her mom's hands running up and down her body touching her wounds. She had been frantic when she and Russ arrived at the clinic that first night. Their constant presence even when she lay unconscious gave her a sense of safety.

"You're healing." Sadie nodded her head.

"Thank you, Mom and Dad, for coming. I...I'm sorry you're missing work."

"With technology, we can work anywhere. You, we are here to protect." Sadie's eyes fell on Bryce. From their reactions, Rosemary assumed there was some telepathy going on between them.

"Excuse me. If you two have something to say, we would all like to hear it."

Sadie turned to her and shook her head. "You're certainly my daughter. I was nicely asking Bryce to leave us and take Russ, so you and I could talk. Okay with you?"

If only she had her mom's confidence. Hands braced on the couch, she turned to Bryce. "Fine. I'm sure my dad would like to see your collection of cars, or something."

He kissed the top of her head. "We were just on the way out. Let me know if you need me." She saw the wink he gave her mom. They were forces to be reckoned with all on their own, what chance did she have when they were working together?

The men gone, her mom took her hands in hers, rubbing them absent-mindedly. "Are you hurting?"

"Not much. Well, not physically." She met her mom's concerned eyes.

She shrugged a shoulder. "I blame myself."

Rosemary jerked back with her face in a frown.

Sadie hesitated, appearing to find the right words. "I probably overprotected you from my world, our world."

"I don't think so. You never lied to me about what Genetically Diverse Beings were or do."

The grim twist to her mouth softened. "But, I never exposed you to the ones who were truly evil, either."

"Thank goodness. I was a child. A sensitive one, at that. No, this one's on me. I've tried to distance myself from our world by concentrating on my career and ignoring my magical abilities." She stopped. Her mom sat there holding her hands and fighting the tears trying to slide down her face. *Oh crap.* No one had seen Mom cry in years. The burst of strength surprised her, allowing her to hug her mom. "I'm sorry I'm such a screw up."

Her mom wailed at that statement. She held her mom and rubbed her back at a loss for what else to do.

Finally, her mom lifted her head and her red eyes searched her face. "You are the farthest thing from a screw up. You're smart, kind, and compassionate. You deserve people around you who appreciate that and support that. I was too busy being the best and baddest witch to insist on your magical training. I left it up to your Grandma Rosie. When she passed, well…"

She touched her mom's face. "Mom, I decided while strapped to my own operating table by a crazed vampire that it might behoove me to study my magic more."

"Really?" Sadie paused.

"Really." She took a deep breath, ignoring the pain in her ribs, and relaxed.

"Perfect. I have something for you. Your Grandma Rosie left me her grimoire when she passed. Greta and I have had a few years to copy into our own magical journals the spells and rituals we felt we needed. I think this would be a good time for you to expand your own journal into a grimoire while making time for your magic again," Sadie said this as she handed Rosemary a very old and beautiful book.

"Mom, are you sure?" Rosemary asked, gingerly reaching out to take the book.

"Grandma Rosie was a very powerful witch and she always had her eye on you. Does she come visit you as much as she did when you were a child?" Sadie looked at Rosemary intensely.

"Oh, Mom, you know she doesn't! But she came to see me in a dream last night and pointed out that I'm not making time for her or my magic. Because if I had been, I would've been more aware of the danger I was in." Rosemary hugged the book to feel the connection to her grandma.

"I think you'll find some very helpful information in this book. Hold tightly to your own connection to powerful magic though," Sadie hugged her and planted a kiss on her forehead.

"Thank you, I will. Can I ask you something?" She placed the grimoire on the gleaming walnut coffee table.

"Anything, especially if it's about you and Bryce." Sadie elevated her well-shaped eyebrows.

The right words evaded her. The nap of the amber colored couch held her attention as she ran her hand over the cushion. She raised her head and stared at her mom. "How do I learn to trust again?"

A wrinkle crossed her mom's forehead. "You mean Bryce?"

"I mean everyone. He's at the top of the list, but I panic at the thought of treating anyone I don't have a complete history and background on. Do you think it will go over well if I chain all the new patients to the exam tables?"

Her mom waved in her direction. "Let's start with Bryce. Do you think he meant to hurt you?"

"No, but he still did."

"And, you hurt him." She held up a hand to stop the comment coming from Rosemary. "Not in any way like Stephan, but in rejecting him, you wounded him. When you love someone, you become vulnerable to them."

"You're making my point, Mom."

"Trust is built back bit by bit, day by day. No magic wand exists that will bring it back. You can make someone think it's there, but that's an illusion. You both will need to learn to trust each other again."

Her attention fixated on her hands. "Okay. What about my scars? I'm hideous."

Scooping up her daughter's hands, she inspected them. "Between your werewolf genes and our magical abilities, we can make those better."

Hope blossomed in her for the first time since that horrid night. The scars grew lighter every day, but she feared they would never disappear completely. "Tell me more."

Her mom held her hands between hers and gave them a shake. "First, promise me you will give Bryce a chance. Russ and I will stay as long as you need us."

She couldn't help the silly smile that stretched across her face. "I promise, but tell me, aren't you angry with Bryce?"

Sadie released her hands and looked down at the plush beige carpet for a moment. "I was, until Twylene explained the circumstances. After talking with her, I now understand Bryce was trying to protect you in the best way he knew how. He could have been a bit more forthcoming, but he's a man. Trust me, vampire or not, alpha males can be a challenge when it comes to communication."

"Do you really think he's worth my time and energy?" The old doubts along with the new fears collided within her.

Her mom shook her head. "Only you can decide that, but if you don't take a chance on love, don't be surprised if you never find it."

He'd hoped on the ride home this morning, he and Rosemary would have settled things. Not hardly. Now, he sat in their mutual sitting room this evening, waiting for her to join him. He downed the glass of blood Donna had brought so he could go on to work after talking with his love. He still loved her. Still needed her like the blood that kept him alive. It fed his body, but she fed his soul.

The scent of honeysuckle and cinnamon floated into the room a second before she entered wearing a blue flannel nightgown covered with a fluffy robe to match. The belt was cinched tightly, preventing any glimpse of skin other than her face and hands. In spite of her best efforts, she was sexy as hell. Auburn hair fell to her shoulders in graceful waves, calling for him to run his fingers through it. He didn't, but a man could dream.

She stood, hands holding the collar of her robe together. "Hi."

"How're you doing?" Her too-quick smile put him on alert. The tension in his arms relaxed as step-by-slow-step she made her way to her chair and dropped onto the seat.

"I'm tired and in pain, but I'm here." She loosened her grip on her robe and leaned back.

"It's good to have you home." The nervous flash from her eyes made his gut drop. *Might as well get this over with.* "When I return from work in the morning, will you be staying here or returning with your parents?"

Her gaze remained on the floor for so long he thought she'd not heard him. He kneeled and looked up into her face. "Rosemary?"

Her eyes squeezed shut as she shook her head. "Sorry."

The wind was knocked out of his sails. Waves of emotion threatened to spill from his eyes, but he refused to turn from her. His voice whispered, "No, I'm sorry. Sorry I didn't protect you from my life. Sorry I put you in danger. Sorry I tried to control you. Sorry…"

Her chilly hand cupped his cheek. "Stop. I'm sorry I reacted the way I did in the car this morning."

His large hand closed around hers. "You mean when I tried to tell you what to do?"

Her snort made him smile.

"You could have been a little less pushy."

"I promise to work on that." He wiped a tear that had ventured down her cheek.

"Good. Because, I want to try to work things out between us."

He held his breath. Slowly, he nodded. Every muscle in his body stilled. His control trembled with the need to shout his joy from the rooftops, but he listened.

"But, I still have a long way to go."

"I will do whatever you need, Wolfie." He sat on the floor holding her hands.

"What I need is to find my way, without you doing it for me. My magic and abilities as a werewolf need to be cultivated." She let out a breath.

His hands brought hers to his lips for a kiss. Gratitude blossomed within him at her growing self-awareness. "Okay, tell me what to do."

"First, can my parents stay here with me for a couple of weeks?"

He liked Russ and Sadie, but he wanted Rosemary all to himself. *Doesn't matter. She needs them here.* He nodded. "Certainly. What else?"

"I'm...Well, I..." Her voice died.

"You don't trust me completely and want time to rebuild our relationship?" A part of him balled up in pain even saying it, but he wanted to acknowledge the elephant in the room.

He barely heard her whisper.

"Yes." With her head hung, she didn't meet his gaze.

Unable to help himself, he guided her chin so her eyes met his. "I will always want you."

Her eyes widened. "I need time. I want to be with you, but not the way I am. Can you understand that?"

Eyes narrowing and brows pulling down, he concentrated on his answer. "You've been through horrific things nobody would come away from unscathed. I am dedicated to giving you the time and support you need to heal." He held up her engagement ring. "When I see you wearing your ring, I'll know you're ready."

The look of gratitude in her eyes struck him to his core. The belief she would heal and be his Wolfie again, kept him going.

The ring sparkled in the light as she held it in her hands. "Yes, thank you." The tension she had carried all day seemed to flow from her as she stretched her mouth in a yawn. "I'm going to go to bed, now. Have a good night at work, and I'll see you in the morning." The tentative lift of her lips made him want to pick her up and carry her to bed, however, he restrained. Instead, he offered his hand to help her up.

"Would it be acceptable for me to tuck you in?"

"I'd like that." The acceptance of his help warmed the cold places fear had camped in for weeks. Her slow steps into her room reminded him of how much her body needed to heal, too. He helped her out of her robe and made sure the covers were pulled up to her chin. A quick glance around the room assured him both of her nightlights were lit.

"Goodnight, Rosemary, pleasant dreams." He kissed her on the forehead like some old, doddering uncle. It was worth it.

A genuine smile crossed her face. "Have a good night at work. I'll tuck you in tomorrow morning."

"It's a deal."

The scented smoke rose in spirals around the people in the room spreading a sandalwood fragrance that calmed Rosemary. Excitement glimmered from her. After almost two weeks of studying her spells with her mother and learning to control her wolf with Night Sky, the time had arrived for her to be dedicated into the craft of her family's tradition. On Saturday evenings like tonight, Grandma Rosie would tell her stories of the witches in their family. As a child, she imagined what she might be capable of when older. This ritual signaled her leaving behind her old life and being what they called *twice born* into the ways of her ancestors. Sadness moved through her as she regretted Grandma Rosie couldn't be here for this ceremony, although she suspected she would watch from another realm.

She turned her attention to the ritual room Bryce had constructed on the top floor of his mansion. A quick glance upwards brought a gasp to her mouth. The domed skylight that covered most of the roof over this room allowed the crescent moon to beam light into the floor. Planets added their illumination, while stars twinkled in happy little bursts. The wonders of nature always humbled her. Returning her gaze inside, a sense of security wrapped around her. Each of the four directions of the room was occupied by either her family or friends ready to call in the magickal elements to form the circle.

Her mom in the east quadrant of the circle lit the yellow candle after calling in the element of air. The flame stirred from her mom's enchantment. Jonathan called in the south's element of fire, the candle crackling when he lit it. The soft mist that resulted from Russ calling in the water element of the west brought a smile to her lips. Really, her daemon stepdad loved to show off his demigod abilities. As if he read her thoughts, he turned after lighting the aquamarine candle and shot her a wicked grin.

At the northern quarter of the circle, stood Bryce. Tall and solid, he called in the element of Earth. His voice quiet, still reverberated throughout the entire room. A thrill erupted in her core as his energy enveloped her. How had she missed the fact he was so impressive in the magickal arts? With a small grunt, she acknowledged the paradox in his personality. As a lover, he went after what he wanted with focus and confidence, rarely taking no for an answer. However, like most powerful beings, he understood the need to keep hidden the magickal abilities he possessed.

As he sealed the North with a pentagram, Sadie's clear voice started the call for the goddess, Morrigan, to join the circle. Amazement opened her to the power her mother drew into the circle. Not everyone could handle the energies of Morrigan, but Sadie channeled the essence of the warrior goddess with perfection.

She possessed that ability but was afraid to use it. Time to change that part of herself. She owed it not only to her mom, but also to her grandma.

With the goddess present, Russ crossed his arms over his chest in a traditional pose and invoked the god Cernunnos. The god of the animals flowed through the connection he made, adding his wild grace to the circle in Russ's body. Like Cernunnos, Russ protected her, loved her like his own. Deep within her chest gratitude swelled up with love for him.

The power that came from her parents as high priest and priestess astonished her. How did she not comprehend before what treasures they gave her? Her neglect of her maternal family's magick and her complacency about Russ's part in her life made her swear to be better.

Edward offered her his arm. "Are you ready?"

His warm brown eyes held tears that threatened to fall. Such a dear friend, Edward came from a family that practiced a longstanding version of Voodoo. Before becoming a vampire, he had been a High Priest in the Voodoun religion when he lived on the West Coast of Africa. Giving him a hug, she fought her own watery eyes. "Thank you for being my escort. I can't think of anyone more appropriate to present me to my ancestors."

He kissed the top of her head. "Shall we?"

She nodded. He tied the blindfold gently around her eyes and took her arm in his to direct each step. The authority of his experience calmed her as he guided her into the circle.

The cool floor vibrated under her bare feet. The beat of a drum sounded in slow, soft beats. The aroma of the incense wrapped her brain in peace. Edward's tall body guiding hers added a sense of protection. Psychic abilities opened, she immersed herself in the experience.

The sound of the drum sped up, increasing her heartbeat. Night Sky had used the drum in his guided meditations to help her reach deeper states and begin to take charge of shifting into her wolf in the last two weeks.

Focus. Edward had stopped and had positioned her in front of what she assumed was the entrance to the circle. The heat of candles cautioned her to stay still. Her mom had given her the basics, but not the specifics when planning the ritual. Her stomach fluttered with anticipation. She recognized her mother's scent just before she spoke.

"You stand between the worlds. The one of the mundane and the one of the magickal. Do you have the courage to cross into the world of your ancestors?"

Her wolf stayed on alert but allowed her to answer. "I do."

A hand grasped the front of her white cotton robe and pulled her forward. A hard metal point rested against her chest. The newly found concentration and trust between her and her wolf held, barely.

"It would be better to rush on my blade and perish than enter this world with fear in your heart."

With all the calmness she could muster, Rosemary said, "I come in perfect love and perfect trust."

"With those passwords, you are welcomed. I will give you my guidance through the door."

Her mother walked behind her and kissed her on the cheek. Then using her body, she helped her into the circle. Arm around her, her mother presented her to the four directions, and then returned them to the center.

"In other religions, you would kneel while the priest would tower above. Here in the Craft, we are humbled by your courage, and therefore, kneel before you. May you be blessed as you walk our path." She stood and kissed her on the lips. Steady hands removed her blindfold, revealing her friends and family.

"Thank you, Priestess." The candlelight reflecting off the smoke of the incense added to the already otherworldly perceptions she experienced.

Her mom's hand reached for her shoulder, steadying her. "Are you ready for your challenge?"

She grounded herself using the energy her mom transferred to her. "I am."

With a nod, her mom released her shoulder and backed away, giving her room. "So be it."

The drumming started again, with Night Sky's mellow voice guiding her to change into her animal. *Focus.* The room slipped from her consciousness as her body began to twist and transform. The snapping of bones and the spouting of hair shot burning pain through her.

"Relax. Breathe. The change can go quickly and smoothly."

Night Sky's words touched her subconscious somehow, giving her relief. The fact she fought the shift caused her more pain than most. Her wolf worked with her, panting as the pain hit her. The robe split in pieces as her other self took shape. Her legs shook with the effort, but she stayed conscious.

The room was silent as they gazed at her. She gathered her bearings, then walked to her mom and nuzzled her hand.

Tears of happiness ran down her mom's face as she petted her. "You did it!"

She licked her mom's hand and then her stepdad's before sitting in front of the altar and howling her delight. After everyone had greeted her, she prepared for the rest of the challenge, changing back.

Perhaps her confidence helped make the shift back easier, because in half the time it took to become wolf, she was a witch again. Grateful for the new robe Edward slipped on her, she accepted her new magical knife, an athame.

Holding it in her right hand which crossed her chest, she repeated the vow of secrecy and protection of others in the Craft. The ancient words connected her to ancestors past and relationships of the future. The knowledge of her place in the cosmic fabric clicked in her. Her strength and confidence returned on a soul's level.

The odor of frankincense and myrrh wafted her way when her mom touched the center of her forehead with the anointing oil. "I consecrate thee with this oil as a new witch and priestess. So mote it be."

She stood glancing around the room, her eyes locking with the golden-brown eyes of Bryce. He radiated love and pride to her in his glance. He had seen her wolf and unlike Leon, remained, supporting her. Time to reclaim him. She smiled back at him and then prepared to finish the ritual.

Worry surrounded her like a cloak. Shifting into her animal had been easy compared to the magick she prepared to perform next. Before the altar, she drew in all the energy from the Earth she could, concentrating and forming it into an extension of herself. Her parents stood guard in the High Priest and Priestess roles, protecting her from harm. The room echoed with silence as she concentrated. Rivets of sweat ran down her back and her muscles trembled. Chanting the words in fevered whispers, she watched her silver athame jerk in tiny motions lying atop the altar. A wave of energy rolled through her hands and another through her eyes, bombarding the knife. Sweat dripping off her arms and face, now, she raised her arms in slow, smooth arcs bringing the athame to hover above the altar touched only by her magick. Her concentration sharpened, enabling her to twirl the knife slowly as it hung above the altar. The thud resounded as the knife, driven by her energy, slammed straight down into the target fixed to the top of the altar.

She stared at her accomplishment, letting her muscles relax. *I did it!* Her mom's face said it all. She beamed with pride and joy. Russ nodded his head and gave her a thumbs up. She had a long way to go but being able to levitate and direct her athame assured her of her potential as an accomplished witch.

One sway and her mom, dad, and Edward supported her, trading off to dismiss the God, Goddess, and elements. When Edward opened the circle, she took a step towards the dining room, where a feast waited for them.

Before she could take another step, her parents wrapped their arms around her, speaking at the same time, "We are so proud of you!" A kiss landed on each cheek as they escorted her to the food.

Once there, Bryce handed her a plate of food and a glass of wine. He planted a kiss on her forehead. "Congratulations, I'm impressed."

"Thanks." Shyness overtook her for the moment. She had just shifted into a werewolf and levitated her athame into a target, and yet, she had no clue what to say to the man who believed in her. Loved her. Before she could say more, Jonathan grabbed her in a full body hug, lifting her off the floor.

"You were fabulous!" He sat her down in time for Edward to grab her up.

By the time Edward finished, she spotted her mentor.

Night Sky's concern for her, led him not to admit he was a werewolf in the past, but Mom had explained the need for him to help her shift. Her mom had been right. The understanding and skill he brought helped her to taper off her werewort except for rare occasions.

She wrapped her arms around Night Sky causing him to grunt a little. "You don't know your own strength." The wide smile on his face pleased her.

"I can't thank you enough for your help these last few days, and well, for this past year. I feared I would never be able to shift without horrible blackouts."

He nodded. "You're welcome. Remember, anytime you need help, call me, okay?"

"Okay." She managed to eat most of her food and drink her wine, before she found herself ready to drop. Bryce rescued her plate and glass and offered his arm.

"I think everyone is heading out. Shall we say goodnight?"

She took his arm. "Great idea. I'm tired."

As the last guest closed the door, her mom grabbed her other arm.

"Let me run you a cleansing bath and then tuck you in bed."

The resigned expression on Bryce's face left her torn between the two. She needed her mom's attention but craved her lover's touch. At the thought, she cringed. Most of her scars had faded, but her left breast still carried a deep mark. He would have seen it tonight. Did bother him? What if he never wanted to make love with her again? Maybe that's why he let her mom take over. Oh Goddess, he pities me because I'm a scarred monster.

Oblivious to her panic, her mom helped her into a warm bath and then into her bed. Exhaustion overtook her fears, dropping her into a deep sleep.

The wolf sat on her haunches, soaking up the peace and quiet of her surroundings. Her body was healed. She had plenty of food and rest. Uncertainty still lived in her when she thought of the vampire. Not her kind. She spotted him walking down the path towards her and froze. Run away. But

she made herself stay. He stopped a few feet from her and squatted down to her level. They eyed each other for a moment.

"Wolfie, I miss you, but I understand you've needed time. I'll wait for you to give me a sign that you want me back as your lover. If you don't... I'll let you go." He rose and she watched him walk away from her.

Daylight poured into her bedroom, waking her. The last vestiges of her dream still floating in her mind. Last night's ritual had left her with a confusion of thoughts. The dream reflected the one that frightened her the most: reconnecting with her lover. Two weeks had passed, leaving her physically healed and with help from magick and medicine, her scars were fading. Her nightmares calmed into dreams. She and her wolf negotiated safe boundaries, and she worked daily with her grandma's grimoire. However, she couldn't bring herself to make love to Bryce.

The aroma of fresh flowers drew her attention to a bouquet of lavender orchids and roses on her dresser. The florists in town must love the business she had stimulated for them in the last couple of weeks, along with the jewelers, and lingerie shops. The man had showered her with gifts and attention but had not touched her. Well, okay, he had patted her hand and kissed her cheek, but nothing sexually. Now, he tells her she has to give him a sign.

She shook her head as she laughed at herself. The mixed messages she had sent him probably messed with his mind. Okay, she was being a coward. Sometime this last week, her passion for him had returned in force. Her wolf was still leery, but she wanted him. The ivory and blue envelope by the flowers released a sweet lavender odor when she opened it. The lacy card held a poem dedicating his love to her. She sighed. Why couldn't it have said something along the line of, "I can't take another day without fucking you. Meet me in my bedroom this morning and be naked." At least she would know he wasn't turned off because of her scars.

She wasn't vain, but the deeper scars on her left breast were going to take more time to fade, if they faded at all. When she looked at them, the disgust of how she let Stephan fool her came over her. How would Bryce react to the outline of his worst enemy's fangs on her breast? On the way to her bathroom, she paused at the open door to his bedroom. In the darkness, her sensitive eyes could see him sleeping. The vulnerability on his face struck a deep chord within her. Her big, bad vampire was scared. Somehow, in all of her trauma, she had forgotten how much he must have suffered. Stephan went after his last wife and killed her. When he went after her, what had it done to Bryce? Time to put on her big girl lingerie and give him a sign that would leave no doubt in his mind.

After a phone call to check on the clinic and saying goodbye to her parents, she met Donna in the kitchen.

"I need your help in getting Bryce in the mood."

Donna raised her eyebrows. "Do you now? From what I see, you're pretty good at it."

Her face flushed with heat. "Not recently. I need your expert advice on his midnight dinner. What do you suggest?"

Her hand patted Rosemary's. "I didn't mean to embarrass you. I will fix one of his favorites." She opened a book that contained recipes her family had collected over the years. "Here we go. Czernina Przepis. Not only does he love the taste, it will make him very receptive to your plans."

She read the ingredients. "Perfect. Do I need to run to the grocery to get you supplies?"

"You're sweet to offer, since the delivery has been made for the day, but no. The frozen duck and blood in the freezer will work."

"I'm going anyway to buy a couple of bottles of that new champagne blend called: Bubbly Blood. If you think of something, let me know."

Can you die from not having sex? Oh, uh guess not. His face wrinkled into a grimace. *Vampire.* The tent in his slacks looked like it could sleep four people. *Good thing I'm in my car.* Rosemary's scent from the passenger side seatbelt surrounded him in a cloud of floral spices producing the uncomfortable rise in his pants. During the last two weeks, he gave her the space she needed for the physical healing, but now, no amount of long, hot showers filled with fantasies about her helped.

Sadie and Russ left this morning, leading him to high hopes she would be in the mood. If not, he and his constant tent pole would seek relief in his large, lonely shower. With a long sigh, he started his car, pulled out of the Community Blood Bank parking lot, and headed home. Normally, his Sundays were free. However, he had come in for a few hours to catch up. Rosemary's parents didn't prevent them from having sex, in fact, Sadie made several hints, but his lover had reverted to a very childlike dependency on them. Did he do that to her? If he'd kept the relationship causal, never fallen for her, then she would have never been attacked. Maybe she'd never get over her fears of vampires or him, now. He had courted her for the last two weeks as much as he dared. Perhaps it was time to accept she wanted to go her separate way.

The security gate opened, allowing him to drive his SUV down the driveway. The lights burning in the family room made his heart jump with hope that Rosemary was still up. After balancing his briefcase in one hand, he managed to pick up the miniature red orchid he brought for Rosemary late this afternoon. Full of fragrant blossoms, he hoped it would remind her of when they first met. The garage door shut and locked, he made his way into the house. An enticing odor caught his attention. A sweet and sour duck blood soup, if his nose was right. A bit of his hope faded. Donna must think he needed cheering if she made Czernina Przepis for him. He sat the orchid down and hung up his coat.

"I expected you around ten, not midnight." Donna came around the corner with place settings.

"I had more fires to put out than I expected. Do I smell your Czernina Przepis?" His fangs dropped.

"Impressive nose. Your food and drink are all set up in the family room."

"Let me wash up and I'll be right there." He hesitated. "Is Rosemary asleep?"

A sly grin played at her lips. "I don't think so, but she's planning on being in bed soon." Donna disappeared into the family room.

Acceptance settled over him. He'd clean up and tuck her in before he ate. A few minutes later, he came out of his room and headed for hers but found it empty. Confused, he made his way to the family room. The first thing he saw when entering the room was Rosemary's back. Dressed in a tight turquoise dress that left her back bare to the waist, she turned to face him. For a moment, his breath just stopped. The front of the dress plunged almost as far as the back. No one needed to bring a stake to still him, the wood in his pants did the trick.

With a shy smile, she handed him a glass flashing her engagement ring on her finger. "Have some Bubbly Blood."

"Thanks. Have a red orchid." All of his blood had gone south. Eyes on her ring, he took a gulp. The champagne and blood blend loosened his muscles and tongue. "Oh, my gods, you are gorgeous."

The blush that spread from her face downward made him jerk back. "I'm sorry. I didn't mean…"

"I hope you meant it. I like your compliments and the orchid." Her dress shifted with each step, revealing the curve of her perfectly rounded breasts, as she set the exotic flower on the table.

He stood like a deer caught in headlights as she stopped in front of him. Taking his arm in hers, she steered him to the table. "Shall we eat?"

His manners returned long enough for him to pull out her chair. After pushing her up to the table, he stood over her smelling her hair. Cinnamon and honeysuckle.

"Are you smelling my hair?" She turned his way.

The last clamp he had on his will snapped. "And your neck and your lips…" His mouth possessed hers. She didn't respond for a second, filling him with fear he'd misread her. When he started to back away, she moaned and stood, wrapping herself around him. Gratitude for her reaction urged him to run his tongue along the seam of her lips. Her opening to him drove his excitement higher as he explored her mouth. Her soft body plastered against his hardness took him close to a place where he couldn't stop. He drew back, eliciting a groan from her.

Barely able to pant out the words, he asked, "Can I assume you would like to have sex?" Her blue eyes blinked in confusion. *Crap! Did he miss something?*

She dropped her eyes as her shoulders slumped forward. "Only if you want to."

Panic shook him as he tried to understand what had happened. "I want to make love to you. Look at me." He raised her chin, only to feel his heart sink at the beginning of tears in her sad eyes. "Oh, Wolfie, what's wrong? What did I do?"

"I want you, but my scars are ugly." Like a shield, her hand covered her left breast.

"Not to me." Bryce lifted her hand and kissed the palm. She shuddered, as he stroked her face with one finger. Her feminine scent called to him. "Can I help by giving you a bit of courage?"

"You mean mind control?" Her eyes widened as she drew back.

Her hand still in his, he maintained his hold. "Not mind control, just a suggestion to be comfortable with me."

She studied him for a moment then nodded. "Okay, how does it work?"

He returned her gaze. "I find the connection we previously created and allow my mind to flow into yours. If at any time you want me to stop, you can tell me or imagine blocking me from your mind."

The question on her face dropped away. "Let's do it. Oh! Ohhhhh! You're there."

His thoughts slipped a little bit at a time into her head shoring up her self-esteem and confidence in his attraction to her.

Rosemary's eyes glazed over with a relaxed aura that had her limp in his arms. "Why didn't you tell me how fantastic it feels?"

"Would you have believed me?" He held her gently in his arms, rocking her back and forth.

She closed her eyes and swayed with him. "Probably not." A chuckle slipped from her lips.

The connection with her calmed him and filled him with the

knowledge she still loved him. He wanted to give her time to adjust to the intensity of their minds linking. "Would you like to fool around for a while, until you get comfortable?"

She buried her face against his throat, kissing and licking in tiny flicks.

His desire for her rocketed. "Ca...Can I take that as a yes?"

She lifted her head to meet his eyes. "I trust you. Come share my body, scars and all."

Bryce gingerly withdrew his mind from hers. "My mind is out of yours just to make sure you are doing this of your own free will."

The determination on her face, told him she was in back in control. "I do trust you. I'm sorry to have taken so long to reconnect with you."

"Like I've said in the past, you're worth the wait, and honestly, two weeks isn't a long time. It just seemed like it to me." He ran his hands down her arms dragging the top of her dress off. He cupped her breasts, enjoying the warm fullness that filled his hands. A potent aphrodisiac, her scent urged him to bend and kiss one breast and then the other. Rage boiled up in him as he caressed the fang mark on her nipple. His eyes shot up to lock on hers. Stephan had hurt and tried to claim his Wolfie.

The gentle squeeze she gave his hands brought him back to the present.

"We can't live in the past, so let's love in the future." Her warmth and courage washed over him.

"You're right." The quick tap on her nipple made it pearl. "This tiny little scar will remind me how much you love and trust me." He embraced her as the blaze of passion and yearnings of love flashed between them.

Her voice was a soft whimper. "Need you..."

His lips claimed her mouth in a celebration of her return. The energy around them crackled with an electric desire. Her soft body cradled in his arms, he used vampire speed to carry her to his bedroom before the kiss ended.

"How did you manage that with your..." She dipped her head to glance at the front of his slacks sticking out.

"Are you kidding? He was leading the way." The humor relaxed the energy for a moment.

The kiss she landed at the base of his neck while slowly putting her hands over his shoulders ignited the bond between them again. A big step for her, he stood still until she slipped her hands under his shirt. The soft touch of her hands on his nipples triggered his body to lean towards her, but her pinch shot lust straight to his groin.

The pleased look on her face motivated his slipping her dress to the floor. Creamy shoulders flowed into luscious breasts. Rosy nipples tightened to points made his mouth water. But her strong hips framing her strip of red curls that protected her sacred center seized his attention. "No underwear?"

With a quirk of an eyebrow, she slipped her hands down his pants. "Didn't think I'd need it since I'm sending you a sign."

"And, what a beautiful sign it is."

Her strong hand grasped his already engorged member to the point he had to stop her or embarrass himself. Apparently, pleasuring himself in the shower, among other places several times a day for the last two weeks hadn't made a dent in his need for her.

"Let me..." Taking her hand out of his pants, he ripped off his clothes.

Before she could return to his cock, he laid her on the bed. He started at her feet, kissing the top of each one. "You have beautiful feet." His lips trailed up one leg and the other, stopping to meet her eyes. "You are my goddess. My light." He kissed her right breast and paused above the left. "You will always be my vision of perfection." With a kiss that displayed his love for her, his lips caressed her left breast. "Your soul shines through you in every aspect of life."

Tears streamed from her eyes. "I missed you." Arms reaching out to him, her embrace surrounded him with her essence.

His lips met hers, capturing the love pouring from her.

Physical need for her building, he cupped her mound, slipping a finger between her folds delighted to discover her ready for him. The insertion of a second finger caused her to buck her hips, pushing him deep within her wetness. He pulled back from her without warning, smiling at her gasp. A quick flip and she stood in her favorite position on all fours.

A nod of approval from her assured him she understood. When her delectable ass rose in the air, his reason flew out the window. The temptation too great, he licked her from her clit to bury his tongue deep within her to lap at her juices. The little spasms of pleasure from her added to his increasing ache.

"Please!" Her breath came out in quick pants.

In position behind her, he circled her nub with his cock. "Is this what you want?"

"Oh yes!" She arched her back trying to take him inside.

"Well, since you said please." He sank every long hard inch of his member in her core, pausing to let her adjust and to keep from coming immediately.

A string of curse words, some unknown to him, came out of her mouth as she tried to swivel her hips.

His iron grasp held her still. "Let me feel you around me for just a moment more."

The golden eyes of a wolf met his vampire gaze in the mirror. She had never let him see her this close to shifting during sex. The searing electricity between them sparked his craving for her. Unable to hold back, he plunged into her again and again. The strokes building like the dance of a raging fire. His fangs dropped. Still pushing deep within, he leaned over her. Her aroma filled his lungs bringing on his need to mark her, taste her. He growled when his mouth found the vein on her neck.

Her head tilted. "Do it!"

The necessity to drink her blood was only thing he understood as he sunk his fangs into the sweet spot. Warm red liquid coated his tongue, sending him into a world of sensation. He floated on the connection between them as her blood fed the lonely places in his soul.

The release of hormones from his fangs, brought about a howl of pleasure from her as an orgasm hit with a fierce wave. The tightness of her flesh around his member milked him to an explosion. Each throb of his cock pressed him deeper into her body renewing the connection between them.

When Rosemary collapsed beneath him, he rolled to his side positioning her in front of him. "You've come home to me."

She responded by snuggling up to him. "And you have welcomed me with open arms."

Bryce wrapped his arms around her until he heard soft breaths of sleep from her. Even though it was early for him to sleep, he relished the closeness. Eyes closing, he drifted into the best slumber he'd experienced in months.

~

A tilt of her head allowed the wolf to tune in to the night creatures in the forest. She could smell their fear when they got close to her. They were safe. No hunt for her tonight. She was satiated in many ways. The return of her mate settled her angst. Her need for his strength and protection was how it worked with her kind. Her witch side wanted to overthink the relationship. Not necessary. The time had come for her and the witch to work together. For that matter, time for her and the vampire to team up. Her head nodded and her eyes glowed.

Rosemary raised sleep-laden eyes to glimpse in Bryce's direction. The odd feeling of not being all there hung on. When his eyes opened, they grew wide.

"Wolfie, glad to see you're comfortable in your fur." He ruffled her ears.

Still in wolf form. That explains the odd sensations. With a grin, she licked his face from chin to forehead and curled up to rest just a bit longer.

He wiped his face. "Thanks for the kiss." Pulling her close, he nestled next to her.

The self-satisfied smile broke across her wolf's face. *He loves me, wolf and all.*

ACKNOWLEDGMENTS

To my husband, Gregory, for all you do, thank you.

Thanks to my critique group, Romance and More. Abby Letner, Deb Sutton, Amy Ewing, Amy Denninghoff, and Robin Byars, you ladies are the best.

Thanks to the women who encouraged me to first write. Fran Reynolds, Karen Dabson, and Jeanne Stewart, you will always be with me.

Thanks to the Columbia Chapter of Missouri Writers' Guild, especially Frank Montagnino, and your delightful werewolf Christmas card.

Thanks to my beta readers and my writing buddies that have answered so many questions. Especially Amanda Booloodian.

Thanks to my editor, Frankie Sutton for her great insights, to my cover designer, Angela Fristoe of Covered Creatively for bringing Rosemary and Bryce to life, and Holly Atkinson of Evil Eye Editing for formatting this book when I was losing my mind.

ABOUT THE AUTHOR

Author of paranormal romance, Rexanna's debut novel, Rosemary Wolfe, M.D., (Monster Doctor) launched in 2018. She has a background in writing and reading in fiction and nonfiction. She communes with other authors as a member of the Romance Writers of America and the Columbia Chapter of Missouri Writers' Guild.

The psychic natures of Rexanna's characters are drawn from her work as a psychic consultant. She has assisted police departments, call-in guests on radio, and headlined on local and national television.

Her true passion is helping individuals understand and resolve those previously unanswerable questions that everyone has in their lives.

She married her college sweetheart, who loves reading, too. They eat lunch out and go to a library or bookstore on most of their Saturdays. Her favorite hobbies include walking her rescue dog, collecting crystals, and reading romance novels.

If you would like to be notified of new releases, special sales, and receive free eBooks, subscribe here: www.rexannaswritings.com

You can also find Rexanna at
Rexannaswritings@gmail.com

www.ingramcontent.com/pod-product-compliance
Lightning Source LLC
Chambersburg PA
CBHW070646180626
46817CB00006B/2259